Her Latin Revenge

When only seduction will settle the score!

Her Latin Lover's Revenge

DON JOAQUIN'S PRIDE
by
Lynne Graham

A SICILIAN SEDUCTION
by
Michelle Reid

LAZARO'S REVENGE
by
Jane Porter

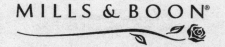

MILLS & BOON®

*MILLS & BOON and MILLS & BOON with the Rose Device
are registered trademarks of the publisher.
Harlequin Mills & Boon Limited,
Eton House, 18-24 Paradise Road, Richmond, Surrey, TW9 1SR*

HER LATIN LOVER'S REVENGE
© by Harlequin Enterprises II B.V., 2005

*Don Joaquin's Pride, A Sicilian Seduction and Lazaro's Revenge
were first published in Great Britain by Harlequin Mills & Boon
Limited in separate, single volumes.*

Don Joaquin's Pride © Lynne Graham 2000
A Sicilian Seduction © Michelle Reid 2001
Lazaro's Revenge © Jane Porter-Gaskins 2002

ISBN 0 263 84481 1

05-1105

*Printed and bound in Spain
by Litografia Rosés S.A., Barcelona*

Lynne Graham was born in Northern Ireland and has been a keen Mills & Boon reader since her teens. She is very happily married with an understanding husband, who has learned to cook since she started to write! Her five children keep her on her toes. She has a very large dog, which knocks everything over, a very small terrier which barks a lot, and two cats. When time allows, Lynne is a keen gardener.

DON JOAQUIN'S PRIDE

by

Lynne Graham

CHAPTER ONE

'I COULDN'T possibly pretend to be you...' Lucy's shaken voice trailed away, her incredulity unhidden.

'Why not?' Cindy demanded sharply. 'Guatemala is half a world away and Fidelio Paez has never met me. He doesn't even know I *have* a sister, never mind an identical twin!'

'But why can't you just write back and explain that you're not in a position to visit right now?' Lucy asked uneasily, struggling to understand why her sister should have suggested such an outrageous masquerade in response to a mere invitation, and why on earth she was getting so worked up about the matter.

'I wish it was that simple!'

'You're getting married in a month,' Lucy reminded her soothingly. 'As I see it, that makes a tactful refusal *very* simple.'

'You don't understand. It wasn't even Fidelio who wrote to me. It was some neighbour of his, some wretched interfering man called Del Castillo!' Cindy's beautifully manicured hands knotted together in a strained gesture, her full mouth tightening. 'He's demanding that I come over and stay for a while—'

'What business is it of his to demand anything?'

Cindy gave her an almost hunted look. 'He thinks that as Fidelio's daughter-in-law, his only surviving relative... well, that I owe the old boy a visit.'

'Why?' In other circumstances Lucy would have understood the demand, but it seemed rather excessive when seen in the light of her twin's short-lived first marriage five years earlier.

While working in Los Angeles, Cindy had enjoyed a whirlwind romance with the son of a wealthy Guatemalan rancher. However, her sister had been widowed within days of becoming a bride. Although a young and apparently healthy man, Mario Paez had died of a sudden heart attack. At the time, Guatemala had been suffering severe floods. The whole country had been in uproar, with the communications system seriously disrupted. With what little she had known about her late husband's background, Cindy had found it impossible to get in touch with Mario's father in time for the funeral, so it had gone ahead without the older man and afterwards Cindy had flown straight back home to London.

'You know, you never even mentioned that you still kept in touch with Mario's father,' Lucy admitted, her violet-blue eyes warm with approval.

High spots of colour lit Cindy's taut cheekbones. 'I thought keeping in touch was the least I could do, and now that Fidelio's sick—'

'The old man's ill?' Lucy interrupted in dismay. 'Is it serious?'

'Yes. So how can I write back and say that I can't visit a dying man because I'm getting married again?'

Lucy winced. That would indeed be a most unfeeling response. In fact, from Fidelio's point of view it would only serve as a horribly cruel reminder of the tragically premature death of his only son.

'That man, that neighbour of his, has actually sent me plane tickets! But even if I wasn't getting married to Roger I wouldn't want to go,' Cindy confessed in a sudden raw rush of resentment. 'I *hate* sick people! I can't bear to be around them. I would be totally useless at being sympathetic and all that sort of stuff!'

Lowering her gaze, Lucy suppressed a sigh, unhappily aware that her twin was telling the truth. When their mother had become an invalid, Cindy had been hopeless. On the other hand, her sister's financial help had eased the more practical problems of those long difficult months when she herself had been forced to give up work to nurse their mother. Cindy had bought them a small apartment close to the hospital where their parent had been receiving treatment. Right now that apartment was back on the market; Lucy was keen to repay her sister's generosity.

'But you could easily cope with Fidelio,' Cindy pointed out, her eagerness to persuade her twin to take her place unhidden. 'You were absolutely marvellous with Mum. Florence Nightingale to the life!'

'But it wouldn't be right to deceive Fidelio Paez like that,' Lucy interposed uncomfortably. 'I think you should discuss this with Roger—'

'Roger?' Cindy froze at that reference to the man she adored and was soon to marry. 'He's the very last person I want to know about this!' Crossing the room, she reached for her sister's hands, a pleading look in her eyes. 'If Roger knew how much I owe Fidelio he would probably think that we should cancel the wedding so that I could go over there…and I couldn't *bear* that!'

Lucy stared back at her twin in bewilderment. 'What do you *owe* Fidelio Paez?'

'Over the years, he's…well, he's sent me a lot of money,' Cindy admitted with visible discomfiture.

Lucy's brows pleated, for her sister lived in some comfort and had never to her knowledge been short of cash in recent years. 'Why would Mario's father have sent you money?'

'Well, why shouldn't he have?' Cindy demanded almost aggressively. 'He's loaded, and he's got nobody else to spend it on. I got nothing when Mario died!'

Lucy flushed at her twin's frank annoyance over that reality.

Cindy's taut shoulders bowed then, and she breathed in deep. 'Yet in spite of all Fidelio's invitations I never visited him, and when he tried to arrange a date to come over here to meet me a couple of years back, I made excuses.'

Lucy was shocked by that confession. 'For goodness' sake, why?'

Cindy grimaced and shrugged. 'I haven't always been the world's nicest person, like *you* are, Lucy!' she muttered irritably, wiping away the tears in her eyes with an infuriated hand. 'Why would I want to go and stay on some ranch in the back of beyond with an old man? And why would I have wanted to be landed with entertaining him here in London? I always had something better to do, but I did *intend* to meet him sooner or later...only right *now* happens to be lousy timing!'

'Yes.' Lucy could see that, and no longer wondered why her sister's conscience was troubling her so much.

'Roger knows nothing about Fidelio, and I wouldn't like him to know about the money because he wouldn't think very much of me for just taking and taking and never giving anything back,' Cindy confided grudgingly, biting at her lip, her eyes filling with tears again. 'There's a lot that Roger doesn't know about my past, Lucy. I've put it behind me. I've changed. I made a new start when I got back in touch with you and Mum last year, and I haven't taken a penny from Fidelio since then—'

'It's all right,' Lucy muttered, her own eyes smarting at her twin's desperation and her uncharacteristic honesty.

'It *will* be if you go to Guatemala for me. I know I'm asking a lot, especially when I haven't exactly been honest about some things,' Cindy continued tautly. 'But I really do need your help with this, Lucy...and if you can do this *one* thing for me, I swear I'll be your best friend for ever!'

'Cindy, I—' Enveloped in a huge, grateful hug, Lucy was touched to the heart, because her sister was rarely demonstrative.

The twins had been separated by their divorcing parents at the age of seven and had spent the following fifteen years apart. Only recently had Lucy had the chance to get to know her sister again, and that had not been an easy task. Until now Cindy had hidden behind a reserve foreign to Lucy's more open nature, and their lifestyles and interests were so different that it had been a challenge to find shared ground on which to bridge those years of estrangement.

But now, for the first time since they were children, Cindy had confided in Lucy again and asked for her help. The idea that she could be needed by her infinitely more glamorous and successful sister astonished Lucy, but it made her feel proud as well. Once the quieter, more dependent twin, Lucy had been devastated when her bossier, livelier sister had disappeared from her life. She had never lost that inner ache of loneliness and loss, and Cindy's appeal for her help, Cindy's *need* for her, touched a deep chord of sympathy within her. Blocking out the more practical misgivings threatening at the back of her mind, Lucy smiled with determined eagerness to offer all the assistance within her power.

Cindy drew back and surveyed her twin with the critical eye of a woman who had worked as both a make-up artist and a fashion buyer and who took a great deal of interest in her own appearance.

Ironically, few identical twins could have looked more different. Lucy never used make-up and tied her defiantly curly caramel-blonde hair back at the nape of her neck. Her blue denim skirt was calf-length, her check shirt sensible and her shoes flat and comfortable.

'I sent Fidelio a photo of me last year and I was dressed

to kill. I'm going to have my work cut out turning *you* into
me!' Cindy confessed with a rueful groan.

Lucy just stood there, slightly dazed, suddenly not quite
sure she could have agreed to do such an outrageous thing
as pretend to be her sister instead of herself. Her *homely*
self. Now that they were both adults, she simply couldn't
imagine looking like her twin. Cindy had the perfect
grooming of a model and confidently revealed far more
than she concealed of her slim, toned figure. Her blonde
mane of hair hung in a smooth fall down her back, both
straightened and lightened. Not one inch of Cindy was less
than perfect, Lucy conceded, hurriedly curving her bitten
nails into the centre of her palms and sucking in her stomach.

Outside the shabby bar, which was little more than a shack
with a tin roof, a wizened little man in a poncho tied up
his horse to the roadside post available and stomped in out
of the sweltering heat. He joined the tough-looking cowboys standing by the bar and within ten seconds he was
gaping at Lucy with the rest of them. In a badly creased
pale pink designer suit and precarious high heels, she was
a sight such as was rarely seen at this remote outpost in
the Guatemalan Petén.

The humidity was horrendous. Pressing a crumpled tissue to her perspiring brow, Lucy studied the scarred table
in mute physical misery. Cindy had insisted that she would
need to dress to impress throughout her stay. But Lucy felt
horribly uncomfortable and conspicuous in her borrowed
finery. Furthermore the wretched shoes pinched her toes
and nipped her heels like instruments of torture.

Yesterday she had flown into Guatemala City and connected with a domestic flight to Flores, where she had spent
the night at a small hotel. She had expected to be taken
from there to the Paez ranch, but instead she had been

greeted with the message that she would be picked up at the crossroads at San Angelita. Once her ancient rattling cab had turned off the main highway the landscape had become steadily more arid, and the road had swiftly declined into a rutted dirt track. That incredibly long and dusty journey had finally brought her to a ramshackle little cluster of almost entirely abandoned buildings in the middle of a dustbowl overshadowed by what looked very much like a volcano and, according to her guidebook, probably was. Exhaustion and a deep, desperate desire for a bath now gripped Lucy, not to mention an increasingly strong attack of cold feet.

Suppose Fidelio realised that she *wasn't* Cindy? Suppose she said or did something that exposed their deception? It would be simply appalling if her masquerade was uncovered. A sick old man certainly didn't require any further distress. But what would have been the alternative? Lucy asked herself unhappily. Cindy wouldn't have come, and the thought of Fidelio Paez passing away without a single relative to comfort him filled Lucy with helpless compassion.

Belatedly registering that the noisy clump of men at the bar had fallen silent, Lucy looked up. A very tall male, who looked as if he had walked straight out of a spaghetti western in the role of cold-blooded *killer*, now stood just inside the doorway, spurred and booted feet set slightly astride. Intimidated by one glittering glance from beneath the dusty brim of the black hat that shadowed his lean, hard-boned features, Lucy gulped and hurriedly endeavoured to curl her five foot tall body into an even less noticeable hunch behind the table.

The barman surged out from behind the counter and extended a moisture-beaded glass to the new arrival. A doffing of hats and a low murmur of respectful greeting broke the silence. Emptying it in a long, thirsty gulp, the man handed the glass back and sauntered with disturbing cat-like fluidity and jingling spurs across to the far corner where Lucy sat.

'Lucinda Paez?' he drawled.

Lucy focused wide-eyed on the leather belt with gleaming silver inserts that encircled his lean hips. Then, not liking the menacing manner in which he was towering over her, she thrust her chair back and hurriedly scrambled upright. Even in her four-inch heels, it didn't help much. He had dwarfed the other men at the bar. He had to be six foot three, and the crown of her head barely reached his shoulder. Wondering if she was going to need her Spanish phrase book to make herself understood, she gazed up at his aggressive jawline and swallowed hard. 'You're here to collect me?' she queried weakly. 'I didn't hear a car.'

'That could be because I arrived on a horse.'

For a split second his smooth grasp of colloquial English took her by surprise, and then an uneasy laugh escaped her. He could only be cracking a joke. You didn't turn up on horseback to collect a person with luggage. Tilting her golden head back, and fighting her natural shyness with all her might, Lucy said apologetically, 'Could you show me some identification, please?'

'I'm afraid I have none to offer. I am Joaquin Francisco Del Castillo, and I am not accustomed to doubt on that point.'

Lucy tried and failed to swallow on that staggeringly arrogant assurance. He had thrown his head high as if she had insulted him, his strong jawline rigid. 'Well, Señor...er...Del Castillo, I am not accustomed to going off with strange men—'

'*Es verdad?* You picked up Mario in a Los Angeles bar and shared his bed the same night. That knowledge does not lead me to believe that you are a particularly cautious woman,' he drawled, his growling accent roughening the vowel sounds.

Lucy was nailed to the spot, still focusing on that firm male beautifully modelled mouth. She blinked, her soft lips opening and closing again in shock. She just could not *believe* that he had said something so offensive right to her face. Burning colour slowly crawled up her throat. 'How dare you?' she whispered in a shaken undertone. 'That is a complete untruth!'

'Mario and I grew up together. You are wasting your time putting on an act for my benefit. Save it for Fidelio. Are you coming...or are you staying here?'

'I'm not going any place with you! They can send someone else out from the ranch,' Lucy informed him with restraint, from between clenched teeth.

'There *is* no one else, *señora*.' And, with that clipped retort, Joaquin Del Castillo simply turned on his heel and strode back outside, command and cool writ large in his straight back, wide shoulders and fluid measured carriage.

Still awash with sheer paralysed shock at being treated with so shattering a lack of respect, Lucy stayed where she was. The men at the bar were talking between themselves. She stole a cringing glance at the growing male huddle, appalled by the suspicion that one of them might have understood enough English to follow what Joaquin Del Castillo had slung at her. Her cheeks aflame with colour, she grabbed up her heavy suitcase and struggled back outside with it.

Joaquin Del Castillo was waiting for her.

'You are the most rude, foul-mouthed man I have ever met,' Lucy announced, giving him only the most minimal sidewise glance of acknowledgement. 'Please do not speak to me again unless it is absolutely necessary.'

'You can't bring that case.' Before she could even guess

his intention he had swept it up in one lean brown hand, planted it down in the dust and sprung it open.

'What are you doing?' Lucy gasped, her frigid air of desperate dignity fracturing fast.

'It's a long ride and I want to make good time. You will have no need for all these fripperies on the ranch,' Joaquin Del Castillo asserted grimly. 'Pick out a few necessities and I'll put them in the saddlebags. The bar owner will look after your case until you return.'

'A long ride…?' Lucy repeated weakly. 'Are you seriously expecting me…to get on a horse?'

'Fidelio sold his pick-up.'

'A h-horse?' Lucy said again, even more shakily.

'In a few hours it will be getting dark. I suggest you go behind the bar and change into a more appropriate outfit for the journey.'

Fidelio had sold his pick-up? Certainly a seriously ill old man would have little need of personal transport. But Fidelio Paez was also a wealthy man, and Lucy would have thought that any big ranch needed at least one vehicle. But what did she know about ranching? she asked herself, ruefully conceding her abysmal ignorance on the subject. Evidently Joaquin Del Castillo didn't have motorised transport either, and she had seen for herself how poor and few were the roads in the Petén.

Lucy snatched in a deep shuddering breath. She had never been on a horse's back in her life. 'I can't ride…'

A broad muscular shoulder sheathed in fine black cotton shrugged. It was fluid, it was dismissive, it was impatient. In fact Joaquin Del Castillo had the kind of highly expressive body language that made speech quite unnecessary. With the heel of one lean brown hand he pushed back the brim of his hat and surveyed her without pity. Sunlight illuminated his lean dark features for the first time.

Lucy's breath tripped in her throat. He was so incredibly

handsome she just stared and kept on staring, involuntary fascination gripping her.

His eyes were a clear startling green, framed by spiky ebony lashes and shockingly unexpected in that bold sunbronzed face. His high, proud cheekbones were dissected by a lean, arrogant blade of a nose, the brilliant eyes crowned by flaring black brows, the whole brought to vibrant life by a mouth as passionate and as wicked as sin. He was just so gorgeous she was transfixed to the spot.

Their eyes met. An infinitesimal little tremor ran through Lucy. Her heart skipped a beat, began thundering in her ears instead. Green like emeralds, green like fire. A thought which didn't make any sense at all, but then nothing that Lucy experienced in that moment had anything to do with normal thought. She watched the colour score his fabulous cheekbones with a level of wonderment that was undeniably mindless. Insidious heat curled up in the pit of her stomach, making her suck in her breath and blink, and at the same moment she blinked *he* turned away.

Sudden appalled embarrassment engulfed Lucy as she realised how she had been behaving. She was supposed to be choosing clothes from her case. What on earth had she been doing, gaping at him like some starstruck schoolgirl? Mortified by her own adolescent behaviour, Lucy crouched down beside her case and struggled to concentrate. 'I can't ride,' she muttered afresh.

'The mare is quiet.' His rich, dark drawl had a disturbingly rough edge.

Her hands were trembling as she rooted clumsily through all the designer clothing which her twin had given her on loan. *He* was standing there watching her, and every time she turned up a piece of lingerie she blushed furiously and thrust it hurriedly back out of sight. He looked like a film star but he had the manners of a pig. But then he probably didn't know any better, born and bred in the back of be-

yond, surrounded by a lot of cattle and grass, she told herself bracingly. She pulled out a pair of pale blue stretch
cotton pedal pushers and an embroidered gypsy top, neither
of which she fancied wearing—but unfortunately they were
the only remotely casual garments which Cindy had been
prepared to include.

'I can't get changed without privacy,' she told Joaquin
tautly.

'You're not modest…why pretend? Not two months after
Mario died you were flashing everything you've got in a
men's magazine centrefold!'

Lucy closed stricken eyes in horror and chagrin. She
knew so little about her twin's life during the years they
had been apart. And this hateful, dreadful man seemed to
be revelling in making offensive allegations. How did he
know so much about Cindy? *Had* her sister met Mario in
a bar and slept with him the very same night? Lucy cringed,
knowing she was a real prude but unable to stifle her shame
on her sister's behalf. *Had* Cindy engaged in nude model-
ling before she'd decided to train as a make-up artist?

But then stripping off for the camera was not the shocking choice it had once been, Lucy reminded herself bracingly. Famous actresses did it now, proud and unashamed
of their beautiful bodies. Adam and Eve had been unclothed
and unashamed too, until the serpent got at them. How
dared this crude backwoods rancher sneer at her twin?

'I believe I asked you only to address me again if it was
unavoidable,' Lucy reminded him in the same icy tone she
would have used to quell a very badly behaved child in the
library where she had once worked.

Behind the bar, which rejoiced in nothing as sophisticated as a window on the back wall, she kicked off her
shoes and peeled off her tights at frantic speed, and then
hauled up the clinging pedal-pushers beneath her skirt. By
the time she reappeared her elaborately teased mane of

carefully coiffed hair, which she had refused to have straightened or tinted, was flopping into a wild torrent of damp ringlets, and the nape of her neck, the slope of her breasts and her face were wet with perspiration.

Joaquin Del Castillo then subjected Lucy to the kind of long, slow scrutiny she was wholly unused to receiving from his sex. But Cindy enjoyed attracting male attention and chose her wardrobe accordingly. So the pedal-pushers were a tight fit, chosen to accentuate the lush female curve of hip and thigh, and the cropped gypsy top was thin and low-cut. Lacking her sister's confidence, however, Lucy was plunged by that insolent male appraisal into instant red-hot discomfiture.

The silence seemed to go on and on and on. Her cheeks burned. She was conscious of her body in a way she had never been conscious of it before. Her breasts felt oddly full and heavy, stirring with the increased rapidity of her breathing. He looked, and she...*and she*? She couldn't think straight.

Joaquin Del Castillo veiled his gaze.

In bewilderment, Lucy lowered her own gaze, dismayed by the accelerated thump of her own heartbeat, the short-ness of her breath, that lingering sense of being dislocated from time. She frowned at the space where she had left her case earlier and muttered unevenly, 'Where's my case?'

Without the slightest warning, Joaquin strode forward and dropped a rough wool poncho over her shoulders, en-gulfing her in yards of scratchy malodorous fabric. 'What on earth are you doing?' she cried, pulling at the garment with distaste.

Impervious to her reaction, Joaquin Del Castillo planted a battered straw hat on her head. 'Treat the sun with respect or you will burn your skin to a withered crisp!'

'Where's my case?' Lucy demanded afresh.

'I packed for you. Come on. We have no more time to waste.'

'You went through my personal things?' Lucy was aghast at the idea of a man rustling through her panties and her bras.

'Let's go,' he grated impatiently.

For some reason there was a general exodus from the bar at the same moment. The cowboy horde poured out through the door to watch Joaquin prod a deeply reluctant Lucy round to the side of the sleek brown mare tethered to the rail.

'You grasp the rein, place your left foot in the stirrup and then you swing yourself up into the saddle,' he instructed smoothly.

Lucy's teeth gritted. She could hear suppressed male laughter behind her. Planting a canvas-shod foot into the stirrup cup, she hauled herself up by dint of sheer determination, but she didn't raise her other leg quite high enough and simultaneously the mare changed position. Unbalanced, Lucy fell back hard on her bottom and snaked her flailing legs back in fright as the mare's hooves skittered too close for comfort.

A powerful hand closed over hers and hauled her upright again with stunning ease. 'Would you like some help, *señora*?'

Sardonic amusement was audible in that honeyed dark drawl. A tide of unfamiliar rage drew Lucy's every muscle taut. She snatched her fingers free of his patronising hold. 'I'd have managed if the blasted horse hadn't moved!' she told him with furious resentment. 'And I'll do it without your help if it kills me...so stand back and snigger with your friends, because it's obvious that that's all that you're good for!'

A line of dark colour highlighted his amazing cheekbones. Then that expressive mouth set like moulded steel. 'As you wish…but I would not like to see you injured.'

'Get out of my way!' Lucy snarled, a tiny proportion of her brain standing back in disbelief at her own fiery behaviour.

Grasping the rein afresh, Lucy was now powered by so much temper she could have swung up high enough to touch the sun. Seconds later, she found herself surveying the ground from an elevated position. Squaring her slight shoulders, she tried to ease her right foot into the other stirrup. But it was done for her. Long cool fingers clasped her ankle and provided guidance. Lucy was in no way mollified by that belated piece of assistance, but she said thank you in a cold little voice just to show that she had been better brought up than he had been.

'I will attach a leading rein to the mare. You will not be in any danger,' Joaquin Del Castillo asserted with a chilling lack of expression.

Briefly her forehead indented. He sounded for all the world like a drawling, icily self-contained aristocrat depressing the rude pretensions of a member of the lower orders. She shook her head at that foolish false impression.

Obviously her outburst had offended him. Good, she told herself. He had been asking for it. Boy, had he been asking for a metaphoric slap in the face in front of their now silent audience! Nobody was smirking or sniggering now; she might feel somewhat shaken by the experience of having shouted at someone for the first time in her life, but in the aftermath she was *proud* of herself. And then the living, breathing animal beneath her rigid hips shifted with alarming effect.

'*Joaquin…?*' Lucy whispered with sick but definite emphasis. 'The horse is m-moving again.'

'Try not to stiffen up. It will make Chica nervous,' he

responded in a curiously constrained tone as he bent his head.

'Do you think I'm not nervous, stuck up here ten feet off the ground?' Lucy gasped before she could snatch the words back.

He spread fluid hands very slowly and stepped back. 'I assure you that you will come to no harm.'

In strained silence, she watched him attach what he had called a leading rein to the huge black stallion twitching its hooves like a threatening volcano several feet away. 'I hope you can control that monster...I hope it's not going to run away with you—'

'No horse has ever run away with me, *señora*,' Joaquin Del Castillo gritted, half under his breath.

And if any had he certainly wouldn't admit it, Lucy decided. Joaquin Del Castillo was of a breed of male utterly unknown to her. All sizzling, musclebound temperament and just bursting with pride over the fact. Any form of weakness, she sensed, would be anathema to him. And he despised her...well, he despised Cindy, and, as she was pretending to *be* Cindy, she was stuck with being despised.

But why was Joaquin Del Castillo being so hostile and rude? After all, she had dutifully come to visit Fidelio, as he had demanded. And, whether he knew it or not, he could thank his lucky stars that she *wasn't* Cindy. Her twin would have been halfway back to the airport by now! Cindy had a very quick temper, not to mention a love and expectation of comfort. Furthermore, accustomed as she was to male admiration, Cindy would never have withstood the attacks and indignities meted out to the sister eleven minutes her junior.

Ironically, Cindy had forecast that Lucy would be treated like a princess from the moment she arrived in Guatemala. Apparently Fidelio Paez's letters had shown him to be an old-fashioned gentleman with an instinctive need to be protective towards any member of the female sex. But Fidelio was generations older than his neighbour, Joaquin Del Castillo, Lucy conceded wryly. There was no intrinsic old-world Latin gallantry to be had from her companion. Why? Evidently he saw Cindy as a scarlet woman just because she had slept with Mario on their first date. What did he think a whirlwind romance entailed? So Cindy had got carried away by love and passion. How dared he sneer?

'How is Fidelio?' Lucy suddenly asked.

Joaquin shot her a grim glance. 'You finally remembered him?'

Lucy flushed.

'He is as well as can be expected in the circumstances.' With that scathing and uninformative assurance, he leapt up into the saddle and made further enquiry impossible.

As the horses plodded at a snail's pace out of the tiny settlement, Lucy focused on his wide-shouldered back view. Joaquin Del Castillo moved as if he was part of the stallion. Lucy endeavoured to unknot her own tense muscles, but she was so terrified of falling off that no sooner did she contrive to loosen one muscle than two others tightened in compensation.

'Slow down!' she called frantically within minutes, when the pace speeded up and her hips started to rise and fall bruisingly on the hard saddle beneath her.

He reined in and swung round. 'What's wrong?'

'If I fall off and break a leg, I won't be much use to Fidelio!' Lucy warned, with a strained attempt at an apologetic smile.

'Soon it will be dark—'

'So you keep on promising,' Lucy muttered limply, convinced she was boiling alive beneath her poncho. 'I can hardly wait for that sun to sink.'

'I am so sorry that this means of travel is not to your taste, *señora*.'

'Oh, call me Lucy, for goodness' sake. That formal address is a nonsense when you match it with your appalling manners!'

Before her eyes Joaquin Del Castillo froze, hard jawline squaring, nostrils flaring.

'I do realise that you neither like nor approve of me, and I can't stand hypocrisy,' Lucy admitted uncomfortably, her voice dying away in the stillness of his complete silence.

'Your name is Cindy. Why would I call you Lucy?'

In horror at her accidental slip, Lucy bent her head, suddenly belatedly grateful that her late parents had seen fit to name their twin daughters Lucinda and Lucille. 'Most people call me Lucy now. Cindy was for the teen years,' she lied breathlessly.

'Lucinda,' he sounded out with syllabic thoroughness, and pressed his knees into the stallion's flanks.

Lucy struggled to stay on board the mare as they wended their way out across the bleached grass plain. The emptiness was eerie. Sky and grass, and all around the heat, like a hard physical entity beating down on her without remorse. There were no buildings, no people, not even the cattle she had dimly expected to see. The eventual sight of a gnarled set of palm trees on a very slight incline should have been enough for her to throw her hat high in celebration. But she didn't have enough energy left. Indeed, by that stage she had already lost all track of time. Even to shrug back the poncho, lift one wrist and glance at her watch felt like too much effort.

'I need a drink,' she finally croaked, her mouth dry as a bone.

'There is a water bottle attached to your saddle,' Joaquin informed her drily over his shoulder. 'But don't drink too much. You'll make yourself sick.'

'You'll have to get the bottle,' Lucy told him in a small voice, because really she was beginning to feel like the biggest whiniest drag in the whole of Guatemala. 'I don't like looking down. It makes me feel dizzy.'

Joaquin Del Castillo rode the stallion round in a circle, leant out across the divide between their respective mounts with acrobatic confidence and detached the water bottle, the fluid movement simplistic in its highly deceptive air of effortless ease. Indeed, the whole operation took Lucy's breath away.

'I saw a Cossack rider do something like that at a circus once,' Lucy confided shyly.

'I did not learn to ride in a circus, *señora*,' Joaquin Del Castillo responded with icy hauteur.

'It was meant to be a compliment, actually.' Turning her discomfited face away, Lucy let the water drift down into her parched mouth.

'That's enough,' Joaquin Del Castillo told her within seconds.

Lucy handed the bottle back, wiped her mouth with an unsteady hand and drooped like a dying swan over Chica's silky mane. With a groaned imprecation in Spanish, Joaquin Del Castillo sprang out of the saddle and planted his hands on her waist. 'Let go of the reins.'

In surprise, Lucy unclenched her stiff fingers and found herself swept down from the mare into a pair of frighteningly powerful arms. 'What on earth—?'

'You will ride with me on El Lobo,' Joaquin announced as he swung her up on to the huge stallion's back, following her up so fast into the saddle she didn't even have the chance to argue.

As Lucy curved uneasily away from the hard heat of his lean, muscular thighs, a strong arm settled round her abdomen and forced her inexorably back. 'Stay still...I will not allow you to fall,' he said impatiently.

Shaken by the sudden intimate contact of their bodies, Lucy dragged in a deep, shivering breath. The disturbingly

insidious scent of warm male assailed her. Her dry mouth
ran even dryer. He smelt of hot skin and horse. Something
twisted low in her tummy, increasing her nervous unease,
but at least she felt safe in his hold. As her tension ebbed,
slow, pervasive warmth blossomed in its stead, making her
feel strangely limp and yielding. The soft peaks of her
breasts tightened into hard little points, filling her with a
heat that had nothing to do with the relentless sun above.
She jerked taut on the shattering acknowledgement that her
body was responding without her volition to the sexually
charged sizzle of Joaquin Del Castillo's raw masculinity.

'Relax,' he murmured softly, long brown fingers splaying
across her midriff to ease her back into position again.

When he talked, soft and low, he had the most beautiful
dark honeyed accent, she thought abstractedly, and never
had she been as outrageously aware of anything as she was
of that lean hand pressing just below her breasts. Her heart
was pounding like a hammer inside her ribcage.

'You're holding me too tightly,' she complained uneasily, horrified and embarrassed by the effect he was having
on her.

'You are not in any danger,' Joaquin Del Castillo
drawled silkily above her head. 'I am not attracted by
stunted women with bleached hair and streaky fake tans.'

A lump ballooned in Lucy's convulsed throat. Mortified
pink chased away her strained pallor. 'You really are the
most loathsome man,' she gasped. 'And I can't wait to see
the back of you! When will we reach Fidelio's ranch?'

'Tomorrow—'

'Tomorrow?' Lucy croaked in stunned disbelief.

'In an hour, we will make camp for the night.'

Camp…camp? Aghast at the prospect of spending the
night outdoors, Lucy swallowed back a self-pitying moan
with the greatest of difficulty. 'I thought we would be arriving soon—'

'We have not made good time, *señora*.'

'I had no idea that the ranch was so far away,' she confided miserably.

They rode on in silence, and slowly the sun became a fiery orb in its sliding path towards the horizon. Lucy was by then dazed with exhaustion and half asleep. She was plucked from the stallion's back and set down on solid earth again, but her legs had all the strength of bending twigs. She staggered, aching in bone and muscle from neck to toe. Dimly she focused on a trio of gnarled palm trees silhouetted against the darkening night sky and experienced a vague sense of *déjà vu*. But they couldn't possibly be the same trees she had noticed hours back! No doubt one set of palm trees looked much like another, Lucy conceded wearily, and she definitely couldn't recall the slender ribbon of river she could now see running nearby.

With every step she cursed her own bodily weakness. She had lost a lot of weight while her mother had been ill, and only the previous month had come down with a nasty bout of flu. After two solid days of travelling she had no energy left, and was indeed feeling far from well. It had not occurred to either her or Cindy that Fidelio's ranch might lie in such a remote and inaccessible location.

The Guatemalan lowlands had looked infinitely less vast and daunting on the map than they were in reality, and, torn from the familiarity of city life and her own careful routine, Lucy felt horrendously vulnerable. Her twin might have travelled the globe but this was Lucy's first trip abroad. Freedom had been the one thing her adoring but possessive mother had refused to give her.

Joaquin was seeing to the horses by the river when Lucy returned. She saw him through a haze of utter exhaustion. Her legs were trembling beneath her. She sank down on the grass. He dropped a blanket beside her.

'You must be hungry,' he murmured.

Lucy shook her head, too sick with fatigue to feel hunger. Slowly, like a toy running out of battery power, she slumped down full length. 'Sleepy,' she mumbled thickly.

Surprising her once again, he spread the blanket for her. Then, bending down, he shook her even more by sweeping her up in one easy motion and laying her down on the blanket. 'Rest, then,' he drawled flatly.

Joaquin Del Castillo was a male of innate and fascinating contradictions, Lucy acknowledged sleepily. Fiercely proud and icily self-contained in his hostility towards her, yet too honourable, it seemed, to make her suffer unnecessary discomfort.

Against the backdrop of the flaming sunset, he stood over her like a huge black intimidating shadow. 'You look like the devil,' she whispered, with a drowsy attempt at humour.

'I will not take your soul, *señora*…but I have every intention of stripping you of everything else you possess.'

Stray words fluttered in the blankness of Lucy's brain. They did not connect. They did not make sense. With a soundless sigh of relief, Lucy sank into the deep, dreamless sleep of exhaustion.

CHAPTER TWO

LUCY opened her eyes slowly.

A small fire was crackling, sending out shooting sparks. No wonder she had awakened, she thought in astonishment. The night was warm and humid, yet Joaquin Del Castillo was subjecting her to the heat of a fire. She scrambled back from it, her eyes adjusting only gradually to his big dark silhouette on the other side of the leaping flames.

Pushing a self-conscious hand through her tangled curls, Lucy sat up just as a hair-raising cry sounded from somewhere out in the darkness. Lucy flinched, her head jerking as she glanced fearfully over her shoulder.

'What was that?'

'Jaguar...they hunt at night.'

Lucy inched back closer to the fire and her companion and shivered. He extended a tin cup of coffee and she curved her unsteady hands round the cup and sipped gratefully, even though the pungent bitter brew contained neither sugar nor milk. 'How soon tomorrow will we get to Fidelio's ranch?' she pressed.

In the flickering light his strikingly handsome features clenched, the lush crescent of his ebony lashes casting fan-like shadows on his hard cheekbones. 'Early.'

'I suppose we would have got there tonight if I'd been able to ride,' Lucy conceded, striving to proffer an olive branch for the sake of peace. He might despise her, but she was remembering the plane tickets he had sent at his own expense. He didn't look as if he was terribly well off, yet he had made a very generous gesture. Without doubt Fidelio had a caring and concerned neighbour, willing to

27

go to a lot of trouble on his behalf. She might loathe Joaquin Del Castillo, and every bone in her body might feel battered by that almost unendurable ride, but she could still respect the motives which had prompted him to demand that Cindy visit her father-in-law.

Joaquin shrugged a sleek, muscular broad shoulder and passed her a plate.

Lucy surveyed the roughly sliced bread and cheese, and a fruit she didn't even recognise, and then tucked in with an appetite that surprised her.

Having cleared the plate, and drained the coffee in a final appreciative gulp, she felt the continuing silence weigh heavily on her. 'Perhaps you'll tell me now how Fidelio really is,' she prompted, with a small uncertain smile of encouragement.

'You will see the situation soon enough.'

His cool steady gaze and his sonorous accented drawl had a curiously chilling quality. A faint spasm of alarm crawled up Lucy's spine and raised gooseflesh on her arms. But as quickly as she found herself reacting in fear, she told herself off. Being brought up by a mother who hated and distrusted all men had made her over-sensitive.

Lucy had been seven when her father met another woman and demanded a divorce. Cindy, always his favourite, had become a real handful after he'd moved out. Infuriated by her daughter's increasingly difficult behaviour, their mother had complained that it wasn't fair that she should be left to raise both children alone. In the end Peter and Jean Fabian had divided their twin daughters between them in much the same way that they had divided their possessions.

Her father and Cindy had moved to Scotland, where her father had set up a new business. He had promised that his daughters would be able to exchange visits but it had never happened. And, embittered by her husband's desertion for the younger, prettier woman he had replaced her with, Jean Fabian had clung to the daughter who remained with feverish protectiveness. A rebound romance in which she had once again been betrayed and humiliated had set the seal on her mother's prejudices. Lucy's teenage years had been poisoned by her mother's hatred for the male sex. The endless restrictions she had endured had made it impossible for her to hang on to her friends.

By the time she had been ready to make a stand and demand a social life of her own Jean Fabian's health had been failing, and Lucy's imprisonment outside working hours had become complete. When she had tried to go out even occasionally she had been treated to sobbing hysterical accusations of selfish neglect and threats of suicide.

However, her poor sister had suffered infinitely more in their father's care, Lucy reminded herself, ashamed of her momentary pang of self-pity. Her mother *had* loved and looked after her. But when her father's new business had failed and his girlfriend had walked out on him, Peter Fabian had apparently degenerated into a surly drunk, forever in debt and unable to hold down a job. Cindy had been frank on the subject of her childhood experiences at least. Her sister had had a rough time. Indeed, listening to her talk, Lucy had felt horribly guilty about the security which she herself had taken for granted.

Tugging the blanket back round her again, Lucy lay down and stared up into a night sky studded with stars. She could cope with Joaquin Del Castillo's icy antagonism for another few hours. He didn't matter, she told herself. She was here for Fidelio's sake, and instead of feeling threatened by what was strange and different in Guatemala she should be seizing the opportunity to enjoy what she could of the experience.

Lucy was in agony when she tried to move the next morning. Her mistreated muscles had seized up and a night on the hard ground hadn't helped to ease her aching limbs. Sore all over, she accepted the small amount of water and the toilet bag which Joaquin silently offered her and removed herself to the comparative shelter of the palms to freshen up as best she could.

She could hardly walk. If anything, she felt worse than she had the night before, and the air was surprisingly cool. Shivering violently, she returned to the low-burning fire and donned the old poncho without being asked, grateful for its shielding warmth.

Joaquin passed her a cup of black coffee and more bread and cheese. He ate standing up, with the quick economical movements of an energetic male in a hurry.

As he helped her mount Chica Lucy gritted her teeth when her every muscle screeched in complaint. Another couple of hours at most, she told herself bracingly, but in no time at all the ride became yet another endurance test.

When the mare finally drifted to an unannounced halt, Lucy muttered, 'Why have we stopped?' sooner than go to the trouble of raising her aching head.

Joaquin lifted her down from the mare. For a split second she was in close contact with his lithe, superbly masculine body. The sun-warmed virile scent of him engulfed her. As he lowered her to the ground her breasts rubbed against the muscular wall of his chest. Her nipples pinched taut and throbbed and Lucy sucked in a dismayed breath, her face colouring with embarrassment.

A pair of lean hands curved over her stiff shoulders and carefully turned her round. Her already shaken eyes opened even wider in surprise. A dingy little house with stucco walls lay only a few yards away. Tumbledown out-housing and a broken line of ancient fencing accentuated its forlorn air of desertion and neglect.

'Where are we?' she whispered in bewilderment.

'This is Fidelio's ranch, *señora*.' Joaquin Del Castillo raked her stunned face with hard, glittering eyes. 'I do hope that you will enjoy your stay here.'

'This...*this* is Fidelio's ranch?' Lucy queried unevenly, staring with glazed fixity at the hovel before her.

'No doubt you were expecting a more luxurious dwelling...'

Inwardly, Lucy winced at his perception. Swift shame engulfed her. The old man was ill and alone and he had evidently come down in the world over the past five years. He had fallen on hard times, *very* hard times. Her compassionate heart bled for Fidelio, and now she understood exactly why Joaquin Del Castillo had thought it necessary to send those plane tickets. Clearly Cindy's father-in-law couldn't possibly have afforded such a gesture on his own behalf.

'I would suggest that this humble abode is a most unpleasant surprise to you, *señora*. We both know that you would not have troubled to make this journey had you not believed that it would be well worth your while to attend a dying man's bedside,' Joaquin Del Castillo drawled with freezing bite.

With a frown of confusion, her concentration running at a tenth of its usual efficiency, Lucy gazed blankly back at her dark brooding companion with his unnerving air of command and authority. He was towering over her like an executioner, and involuntarily she took a nervous step back from him. 'What are you talking about? Why aren't we going inside? I want to see Fidelio—'

Joaquin vented a harsh laugh of disbelief. 'Fortunately for him, he is not here.'

'Not here?' Lucy frowned. 'You mean he's been taken into hospital?'

'No. Only the sick go to hospital, and Fidelio is *not* sick.'

A wiry little man of Central American Indian ancestry

suddenly appeared out of the deep shade cast by the out-housing and cast Lucy into even greater confusion. 'Who's that, then?'

'Mateo works for me.'

With that assurance, Joaquin strode forward to greet his employee. A brief exchange of a language she didn't even recognise took place. Then the older man retreated back into the shadows again. Not once had he angled so much as a curious glance in Lucy's direction.

Returning to her side, Joaquin threw wide the battered door on the little stucco house. 'Fidelio is not on his death-bed,' he then informed her with grim satisfaction. 'He is currently working many miles from here and he has no idea that you are even *in* Guatemala.'

'I don't understand—'

'I imagine you're in shock.' Joaquin closed a domineering hand over her shoulder and urged her into the dim depths of the interior, which contained only a few pieces of dusty decrepit furniture. It was obvious that the little house had stood empty for some time. 'You thought you had got away scot-free with your confidence tricks. In fact you believed you were about to enrich yourself yet again at Fidelio's expense—'

'I don't know what you're talking about!' Lucy protested.

'Then listen and you will find out,' Joaquin advised very softly. 'I took it upon myself to bring you here, and here you will stay for as long as I choose to keep you.'

Pale with apprehension, her head reeling, Lucy felt her way clumsily down into a rough wooden chair before her legs gave way beneath her. 'Fidelio isn't here,' she recited in shaky repetition. 'And he's *not* ill…and you are saying that you plan to *keep* me here…what on earth are you try-ing to say?' She pressed a weak hand to her pounding tem-ples. 'I must have misunderstood you—'

'You have misunderstood nothing. But you are naturally reluctant to face the reality that the golden goose will lay no more eggs,' Joaquin intoned grimly. 'And that while your pathetic begging letters were sufficient to impress Fidelio, they left a very different impression on me!'

'Begging letters?' Lucy questioned, her brow indenting.

With a scorching glance of savage contempt, Joaquin Del Castillo swept up the small wooden box resting on the hearth. Opening it, he planted it down on the rickety table beside her. 'Your own letters, *señora*. In every single one of them you talk of your poverty, your terrible struggle to survive…your desperate need for financial help!'

Like a woman caught up in a bad dream, Lucy reached out an unsteady hand and lifted an envelope, instantly recognising her sister's distinctive handwriting. As she dropped the envelope again her stomach performed a sick somersault. Poverty…struggle to survive…*Cindy*? Cindy, who had inherited a large amount of money from their father in an insurance pay-out at nineteen? Cindy, who spent like there was no tomorrow and who only ever bought the very best?

'And yet throughout that entire period you were living in style and security,' Joaquin Del Castillo delivered with fierce condemnation.

'How do you know that?' Fathoms deep in shock at what she was being told, Lucy nonetheless struggled to concentrate.

'I had enquiries made in London. You own an expensive Docklands apartment and take regular trips abroad,' Joaquin derided with a curled lip. 'You have enjoyed a most lavish lifestyle at Fidelio's expense. You played on the chivalry and compassion of a trusting, unworldly old man and it has taken you only five years to fleece him of all his savings!'

'Oh, dear heaven…' Lucy mumbled in sick comprehension.

'Your constant demands for money ruined him. This *was* to have been Fidelio's retirement home,' Joaquin Del Castillo shot at her with harsh condemnation. 'Before you began dipping your hand deep into his pocket Fidelio had the means to transform this place and look forward to a comfortable retirement after a lifetime of hard work. But now, when he should be taking his ease in his old age, he has been forced to take another job just to support himself!'

'I thought that Fidelio was a wealthy man—'

'How could you think that a ranch foreman was wealthy, *señora*?' Joaquin demanded with crushing derision.

'A ranch *foreman*? I think there's been a t-terrible misunderstanding,' Lucy stammered, a look of growing horror in her strained eyes.

The Central American rancher dropped down into an athletic crouch and gripped the arms of her chair, making her feel cornered and trapped. Blistering green eyes glittered threat at her. 'Don't play stupid with me…I'm not a patient man. There has been no misunderstanding. Accept now that there will be no easy escape from your imprisonment—'

'Imprisonment?' Lucy yelped, already recoiling from his menacing proximity. 'For goodness' sake…are you threatening me?'

'Until such time as you choose to sign a legally binding agreement to repay the money you virtually stole from Fidelio you will remain here,' Joaquin Del Castillo decreed. 'But you are in no danger of suffering any form of violence. I would not soil my hands with you!'

'Is that supposed to be reassuring?' Lucy asked in a very wobbly voice, while she wondered what was wrong with her malfunctioning brain. For on one level she was jerking back from him like some prudish Victorian maiden, and on another level she was staring into those extraordinary green eyes of his and marvelling at their beauty.

'Do you dare to suggest that I would use physical force on a woman?' Joaquin demanded in outrage. 'I...a Del Castillo, stoop to so shameful an act?'

Dry-mouthed, Lucy simply gaped at him. Sizzling eyes the colour of jade were focused on her. All that passion, all that fire, concealed from her and rigorously suppressed throughout their journey. No wonder Joaquin Del Castillo hadn't been able to manage much in the way of casual conversation! His efforts to conceal that incredibly volatile temperament from her must have been as constraining as a gag.

He sprang fluidly upright again. His bold sun-bronzed features were hard as iron. 'Mateo remains outside, purely to ensure your safety. There is nothing around you here but mile after empty mile of cattle country. This is a most dangerous and inhospitable terrain for the inexperienced.'

'You can't *make* me stay here,' Lucy told him dazedly.

He swept up a folded document from the table and extended it. 'If you sign this, you may leave immediately. Without a signature, you remain.'

Lucy snatched the document from him. Mercifully it was written in English, but it was couched in long-winded legalese. Slowly and with a straining frown of effort she worked down the page, and then came to a sum of money that was so large it jolted her into even deeper shock. According to what she was reading, Cindy had received the most enormous sum of money from Fidelio Paez over the past five years. And the document was an agreement to repay the entire sum immediately.

Beads of perspiration formed on Lucy's furrowed brow. Whether this monstrous man accepted it or not, there *had* been a ghastly misunderstanding. Cindy genuinely believed that her father-in-law was rich, and if she had written asking for money it had definitely been done in the mistaken conviction that Fidelio Paez could well afford to be generous.

Fidelio was almost seventy years old. On a foreman's wages it must have taken him a lifetime to build up so healthy a savings account. Two lifetimes, Lucy adjusted, marvelling that a ranch foreman could ever have amassed such a sum. But now all that money was gone, and with it the old man's security. How on earth was such a huge amount to be repaid?

The small flat which Cindy had bought for Lucy and their late mother was already up for sale, Lucy reminded herself in a rush of relief. But even if the property fetched its full asking price it would still only cover about half of the outstanding debt. Did Cindy *own* her expensive Docklands apartment? And how much of Cindy's original inheritance at nineteen still remained intact? Any of it?

Her twin had joked that buying the flat for her sister and her mother had been a good way of preventing her from spending all her money. 'I'm too extravagant…I *know* I am, but why shouldn't I treat myself?' Cindy had asked her twin defensively. 'I just can't resist nice things. Roger gets really angry with me, but he's always had it easy. How could he understand what I went through living with Dad? Roger never had to go without food or decent clothes because his father had taken every last penny and blown it on booze!'

The memory of that revealing conversation still pierced Lucy like an accusing knife. When her twin had castigated Roger for his lack of understanding of what made her a spendthrift, she might as well have thrown in Lucy's name too. Lucy had been protected when she was a vulnerable child. Cindy had been betrayed by an adult in the grip of an addiction out of his control. And without doubt her sister still bore those scars.

'Will you sign, *señora*?' Joaquin Del Castillo challenged softly.

Lucy trembled on the brink of speech. She stifled a craven desire to tell him that he had entrapped the wrong sister. Not yet, an inner voice screeched. Impulsive speech or action would be an act of insanity with a male who had gone to such frightening lengths to corner a woman he believed to be a heartless confidence trickster. Furthermore a confession of her true identity would at this moment make him even angrier. And Lucy was no longer labouring under the naive conviction that she was dealing with some straightforward rancher from the backwoods.

The repayment agreement still tightly gripped in her hands had been drawn up by a top-flight and no doubt very expensive legal firm in the City of London. Joaquin Del Castillo had also admitted to having had enquiries made about her sister in London. All that sort of thing cost a great deal of money. Joaquin Del Castillo was also wearing what looked very much like a Rolex watch. She had noticed it the night before but had assumed that it was a cheap fake. Now she was no longer so sure. The cowboys in that ramshackle bar the day before had been doing an extraordinary amount of respectful bowing and scraping around Joaquin Del Castillo.

'Who *are* you?' Lucy questioned tautly.

'You know who I am, *señora*.'

'I know nothing about you but your name,' Lucy argued feverishly.

'It is not necessary that you should know more,' Joaquin fielded with supreme disdain. 'Now...will you sign that document?'

Lucy tilted her chin and said shakily. 'I'm not prepared to sign anything under duress.'

Shimmering green eyes raked over her pale frightened face. 'So I will call with you next week and see how you feel then,' Joaquin drawled silkily, and in one long fluid stride he turned on his heel.

'Next *week*…?' Lucy gasped incredulously, her head thumping so hard that she was beginning to feel slightly sick. 'I assume that's your idea of a joke—'

He swung back with innate grace. 'Why would I be joking?'

'You can't possibly mean that you intend to leave me here until next week!'

'Why not?'

'*Why not?* Because I don't want to be here and you've got no right to keep me here against my will…I could put the police on you for this!' Lucy sliced back frantically as she forced herself upright again on wobbling knees.

'And what crime would you then accuse me of committing, *señora*?' Joaquin Del Castillo prompted with sardonic amusement. 'You are not even on my land. You came here of your own volition and now you are taking up residence in your father-in-law's home. What do either of those actions have to do with me?'

Aghast at that subtle and devious response, and the clear forethought and planning which must have preceded it, Lucy stared at him with increasing desperation. 'I could never find my way back to San Angelita without your help!'

Joaquin shrugged without remorse. 'And you won't get it unless you sign that agreement. By the way,' he murmured in casual aside as he paused in the open doorway, 'don't waste your time trying to suborn Mateo. He speaks no English, and in common with all Fidelio's friends and well-wishers he is disgusted by what you have done!'

A cold sweat of panic breaking out on her skin, Lucy got up and hurtled dizzily through the door in his wake. 'I can't sign that agreement…I don't have that kind of money.' She stumbled clumsily over that driven admission as she gazed pleadingly up at him. 'We need to talk about this. Surely there's some other way of sorting this awful business out…'

Joaquin Del Castillo stared down at her, stunning eyes narrowed to a sliver of glinting light in his darkly handsome features. Her breath locked in her dry throat. Those spectacular eyes, scorching as the sun's heat, beat down on her. All of a sudden she felt as if a hundred trapped butterflies were going crazy inside her. Her heart crashed against her breastbone, shock shrilling through her as she trembled, paralysed to the spot by the most extraordinary rising sense of excitement.

'Some *other* way would naturally be the only way you know,' Joaquin breathed huskily, a derisive slant to his hard, compelling mouth. 'Sex is your currency and I can see that you would not find lying back under me a punishment.'

Lucy gave him an incredulous look, reeling under the onslaught of that insult.

He lowered his imperious dark head, sunlight gleaming over the glossy luxuriance of his blue-black hair. 'That air of gauche uncertainty and fragile femininity is remarkably convincing…or at least it would be if I wasn't aware that you have been the mistress of at least two wealthy married men!'

'How…*dare*…you?' Lucy gasped, cheeks aflame and incensed.

'How very easy it must have been for you to fool Mario into believing that he had found the love of his life!'

Cindy had adored Mario Paez, and had been totally gutted by his death. Sheer outrage ripped through Lucy and she flew forward, swung her arm back like a champion golfer to gain momentum, and took a violent swing at another human being for the first time ever. Joaquin sidestepped her with such speed and dexterity that she almost

lost her balance and fell flat on her face. A pair of large
and very powerful hands snapped around her waist and the
next minute she was airborne.

Out of her head with frustrated fury as Joaquin held her
at extended arm's length, with her feet dangling out of contact with solid ground, Lucy flailed her clenched fists about
uselessly, because she couldn't get close enough to hit him.
'Put me down...put me down, you pig!' she screeched at
him full blast.

Savagely amused green eyes raked over her hectically
flushed and outraged face. 'There's also a certain piquancy
to your extreme lack of size. You look like a dainty doll
but you have the temper of a shrew—'

'Let go of me, you great hulking bully!' Lucy spat at
him.

'*Claro!* I am seeing the *real* woman now,' Joaquin Del
Castillo purred as he surveyed her, lush inky black lashes
low on smouldering eyes. Raw sexuality emanated from
him in unashamed waves. 'And what a tigress you must be
between the sheets...all teeth and claws and hunger.'

About to launch another seething outburst at him, Lucy
blinked in sheer bemusement, her soft full mouth falling
open. Never before had any man addressed her in such
terms. He wiped out her anger. She was more fascinated
by that tantalising and false image of herself than insulted.
Unwarily she clashed with those amazingly intense eyes of
his and gulped. He looked like a mountain lion about to
leap on a little fluffy lamb. 'No...'

'The word you use with me is *sí*...it means yes, and I
like to hear it,' Joaquin Del Castillo confided in a deep dark
drawl that rasped down her spine like sandpaper on silk,
and he drew her in to him and banded his arms round her
narrow ribcage instead. 'Say it for me...'

A strange all-pervasive ache stirred deep in Lucy's pelvis, wiping out her ability to concentrate. 'No—'

'Sí…' Joaquin instructed, slowly crushing her swelling breasts into the hard wall of his chest, one strong arm sliding down her back to curve round her hips and hold her fast as he studied her with flaming mesmeric intensity. 'Dios…you will say it to please me.'

'Please you…' Lucy echoed, her entire body plastered to every vibrant masculine angle of his and assailed by a quivering seductive pliancy. Her heart was racing so fast it threatened cardiac arrest. Driven by a temptation stronger than she could resist, she raised her hand and traced the sculpted line of one slanting male cheekbone, smooth golden skin overlying a truly spectacular arrangement of bone.

His dark head lowered to capture her exploring forefinger between his lips. Lucy watched him in shaken fascination. A soft gasp was dragged from low in her convulsing throat. Every pulse in her treacherous body went crazy as he gently sucked, silken black lashes almost hitting his cheekbones. Like ice cream on a hot stove she could feel her flesh melting over her bones in a sweet, strong agony of need so new to her experience it overwhelmed her defences.

'Sí…' Joaquin prompted thickly as he lifted his arrogant dark head.

'Sí…' Lucy framed without even knowing what she was saying, utterly enthralled by the wash of agonising sensation pulsing up inside her.

He caught her parted lips with his and tasted her. Raw, burning excitement blazed up in a head-spinning tide that swept her away. Just one kiss… She had never dreamt but had often fantasised, never once expecting to experience such a response in reality. But the hard hot heat of Joaquin Del Castillo's hungry mouth on hers was a passionate revelation to Lucy. The passion he summoned up inside her controlled her utterly. She couldn't get enough of him even when the need to breathe sobbed in her deflated lungs.

'The face of a sweet Botticelli angel, the brain of a calculator and the sexual appetite of a natural whore,' Joaquin spelt out silkily, lifting his head and holding her back from him. 'It would please me to throw you down and take you here...to use you as you once used poor Mario. But I believe I can withstand the temptation.'

Lucy was shell-shocked, gasping for air. Her every nerve jangled with a sense of deprivation so strong she almost cried out in protest and grabbed him back to her again. Stunned by a complete inability to work out how she had turned into a wanton stranger in Joaquin Del Castillo's arms, and finally forced to support her own weight again, Lucy reeled dizzily. The sick pounding behind her temples made her weary mouth curl in a little moue of pain.

'Looking pathetic doesn't work with me either,' Joaquin slung down at her with grim emphasis.

Lucy focused on him hazily and noticed, really could not have helped noticing when he wore such close-fitting pants, that he was in a very masculine state of arousal. And so shaken was she by the sight of a male in that condition she stared and abstractedly recalled that he had begun the assault on her senses by doing wildly indecent things to her finger. Suddenly she was undyingly grateful that matters hadn't proceeded any further than that one breathtaking kiss, for she had no idea, absolutely no idea, just *how*... Her mother had warned her that what a woman often thought she wanted wasn't much fun once she actually got it. She was now more than ready to be convinced.

'I feel ill...' Lucy confided helplessly, swaying without even realising it and wondering why her skin still felt as if it was on fire when he was no longer touching her.

'You cannot fool me into removing you from here,' Joaquin drawled with derisive cool, his lean dark face unimpressed. 'I fully intend that you should endure the privations of what you would sentence Fidelio to endure when he is no longer fit to work.'

She wasn't well; that was what the matter was with her. In fact, she felt just as she had felt when she had had the flu a month back, only *worse*, she conceded absently. Had she imagined Joaquin Del Castillo kissing her? Why would he have kissed her? What sense did that make?

'Men don't make sense...men are animals,' Lucy announced with semi-delirious conviction, without even realising that she was talking out loud. 'You are the prime example...you are the definitive proof. I should never have argued with Mum—'

'*Madre de Dios*...' He interrupted her rambling spiel with incredulity. 'What—?'

Lucy groaned, pushing a shaking hand over her wet brow, no longer able to focus properly, just as her knees began to shake and crumple beneath her. 'Awful...feel awful—'

Joaquin Del Castillo's dusty black riding boots appeared in her vision. 'I will not be taken in by this outrageous theatrical display, *señora*.'

Lucy slumped down on one elbow. And then with a faint moan, as the world swung tipsily and blackness folded in entirely, she passed out altogether.

CHAPTER THREE

LUCY stirred and shifted. An experimental movement of her head confirmed that the awful pounding there had mercifully subsided. But even before she opened her eyes, she was assailed by a bewildering surge of powerful images.

Joaquin looking down at her, fabulous eyes green as jade, his concern palpable. Joaquin murmuring in soothing Spanish as she tossed and turned in a fever. Joaquin laughing. *Laughing?* But only for a split second. His lean dark face had swiftly shuttered again, leaving her with a sharp sense of loss. So confusing were those pictures flashing through her reawakening brain she blanked them out.

Opening her eyes, she discovered that she had not dreamt up the incredible bedroom in which she had lain since she had succumbed to her second attack of flu. Afternoon sunlight illuminated the exquisite antique furniture and the wonderful watercolours on the walls. It was a huge room. Elegant and unbelievably luxurious, right down to the solid six inches of superb lace edging the sheet beneath her hand. Her fingers stroked the lace and then stilled uncertainly again as Joaquin came back into her thoughts at the speed of a shooting star. Was this *his* house? If it was, he was a seriously wealthy male. Who was he?

Twenty-two. In spite of all her efforts to the contrary, she had got to twenty-two years of age without meeting one moment of serious temptation, Lucy conceded ruefully. And then the biggest, bossiest creep in Guatemala, who unfortunately happened to enjoy devastatingly spectacular good looks and the kind of sensual technique she had doubted even existed, had made a sexual advance on her

44

finger. She quivered just thinking about that moment and felt her foolish tummy churn and leap at the memory of the kiss which had followed.

A bemused indent forming on her brow as she realised that she was thinking about Joaquin Del Castillo yet *again*, Lucy sat up and sent her gaze winging round the room. She needed to phone Cindy, but there was no telephone. Sliding out of bed on wobbly legs, she went into the *en suite* bathroom. Weak though she was, she headed straight for the shower cubicle.

Afterwards, she studied her reflection in the vanity mirror and heaved a sigh over her pale face and the childishly curly torrent of caramel-blonde ringlets forming as her hair dried. She smoothed a hand over the mint-green nightdress she wore. It was beautiful, and, like everything else she had brought to Guatemala, it belonged to her sister. Light as silk and whisper-thin, the fabric moulded every female curve and was a far cry from the cotton jersey nightwear which Lucy usually favoured.

Freshening up had tired her out again. She walked slowly over to the bedroom windows. There she froze in her tracks, for the view beyond those windows made her head swim afresh. She clutched at the tassel-edged curtain to steady herself, shut her eyes and opened them again, but still that breathtaking vision of steep, lush forested green slopes and wildly colourful tropical vegetation confronted her stunned gaze. She could hear but only now recognise the cries of exotic birds which had become eerily familiar during her illness. Surely such a fantastic and exotic landscape could not exist close to Fidelio Paez's little stucco retirement home? Where on earth was she?

'Welcome to the most *boring* place on earth…' A female voice murmured drily from behind her.

Startled, Lucy spun round so fast she staggered slightly. A tall stunning brunette with smooth black hair and a perfect oval face was studying her from the far side of the room. Her short strappy silver dress and her jewelled choker exuded designer chic and sophistication.

'Hacienda de Oro...literally the House of Gold. The conservationist's paradise, the archaeologist's dream destination...but the It Girl's living death,' the self-possessed brunette completed, with a dissatisfied twist of her sultry mouth.

'The It Girl's living death...?' Lucy repeated weakly, not quite sure she had heard her correctly.

'I'm Yolanda Del Castillo, Joaquin's sister. Surely you know what an It Girl is?'

Lucy nodded, but only slowly. She had read about the cult of the new It Girls in newspapers. Young, rich, high society British women, who were wildly popular with the media. They partied from dawn to dusk, wore fabulous clothes and dated only the most newsworthy men. Such an existence was so far removed from Lucy's own that she just stared at Yolanda Del Castillo, who undeniably seemed to possess all the attributes it took to be an It Girl, continually photographed, pursued and envied. Even in daylight, it seemed, Yolanda dressed as if she was about to go to a party.

'You speak wonderful English,' Lucy remarked, awkward in the presence of such exoticism.

Yolanda uttered a rueful groan. 'Where do you think I was educated?'

Most probably in a British school, Lucy gathered, feeling foolish.

'Where is this house?' Lucy pressed.

'You're still in the Petén, just a different part of it.'

'So how did I get here?' Lucy asked.

'Joaquin had you airlifted in.'

'Airlifted?' Lucy interrupted helplessly. 'Who are you people?'

'You really *don't* know, do you?' Yolanda rolled her dark eyes in dramatic disbelief, momentarily looking much younger than the twenty-two or twenty-three which Lucy had estimated her to be. She threw the bedroom door wide again. 'Hang on a minute—'

'Yolanda...is there a phone I could use?' Lucy hastened to ask, before Joaquin's sister could disappear again.

Yolanda's attention shifted to the vacant spot by the bed. She frowned in surprise. 'Well, I don't see *why* you shouldn't have a phone!' she remarked with instant sympathy. 'You may be a con-artist, but for Joaquin to have the phone removed is total sensory deprivation! I couldn't exist for five minutes without a phone!'

Lucy turned white as milk. 'You *know*...I mean—?'

'You thought I didn't just 'cos I came in to chat?' Yolanda shrugged a languid shoulder. 'I'm bored out of my mind here without company. But I know what you did... Of course I know, and it was disgusting! Fidelio is the sweetest old man.'

Cut to the bone by that blunt condemnation from yet another source, and feeling as limp as a wrung-out dishrag, Lucy sank down on the edge of the bed. Within minutes Yolanda reappeared, to toss a glossy magazine down beside her.

'Fidelio Paez started working for my family when he was fifteen, *señora*,' Yolanda informed her with cool dignity. 'We threw a big retirement party for him. Imagine how we felt when we later found out that Fidelio had gone to work for a neighbour because he was too embarrassed to ask Joaquin if he could continue working for us!'

'And then Fidelio told your brother what had happened to his savings,' Lucy assumed uncomfortably.

'No! Fidelio has no idea that you cheated him out of his money,' Yolanda contradicted instantly. 'Joaquin had to do his own detective work.'

In considerable discomfiture, Lucy dropped her head.

'And while we're on the subject of my brother, stop embarrassing me by making a total ass of yourself around him!'

Her lips parting company in sheer shock, Lucy looked up.

'The way you were carrying on when you were ill, I initially thought that Joaquin had brought his mistress home!' Yolanda admitted in exasperation.

'His...m-mistress?' Lucy stammered with incredulity.

'All Joaquin's mistresses have been foreigners like you. Guatemalan women don't sleep around. We know better,' the brunette told her with unapologetic superiority.

'What way was I...''carrying on''?' Lucy tilted her chin, denying the charge.

'OK, so you had a fever, but you were continually moaning on about how beautiful Joaquin's eyes were and asking him to kiss you...talk about deeply uncool! Listening outside that door, I was just *cringing* for you!'

A tide of truly painful colour illuminating her face, Lucy turned her shaken gaze away from her visitor in self-protection. Suddenly her eyes were stinging with stupid tears.

Yolanda walked round the bed to get a better look at her victim and frowned in frank bewilderment. 'You know, you just don't add up...you are acting *so* wet!'

Lucy chewed at her wobbly lower lip. 'I'm only feeling weepy because I've been ill—'

'No...you fancy my brother something rotten,' the brunette countered, unimpressed, and she shook her head in wondering pity. 'I have problems, but you have got an even *bigger* problem, Lucy!'

The door snapped shut on Yolanda's departure. Drawing in a deep shuddering breath, Lucy lifted the magazine she had left behind. Her hands were trembling and she felt as weak as a kitten. But, worst of all, she felt utterly humiliated. A con-artist who had made an ass of herself? Evidently while her temperature had been high she had rambled on like some dizzy teenager suffering from a severe crush.

The cover of the magazine bore a picture of Joaquin emerging from a limousine with a very beautiful blonde. Lucy leafed through and found the relevant page. It was a North American magazine dedicated to depicting the lives of the rich and famous. Correction, Lucy adjusted as she slowly scanned the pages of photos, the lives of the *super-rich*…

For Joaquin Del Castillo appeared to own a whole selection of homes around the globe. There were several shots of various enormous properties, sheltering behind high walls and huge gates. Her heart beating very fast, Lucy skimmed through the brief blurb for actual facts. Joaquin was variously described as a 'billionaire industrialist' and a 'reformed playboy', who now spent much of his time advising governments on conservation. He was thirty years old, single, and he changed women like he changed his shirts. His late father hadn't married for the first time until he was sixty, and there was strong speculation that Joaquin was planning to do the same.

Lucy snapped shut the magazine again. So, a gorgeous billionaire had kissed her! Where had that naff thought come from? Mortified by her rebellious mind, which refused to focus on what was truly important, Lucy instead pondered the likely power at Joaquin's fingertips. Her blood duly chilled. Cindy had made a very dangerous enemy who had the resources to cause a great deal of trouble.

Since she was now totally exhausted, and in no state to leave her room in search of a phone, Lucy crawled back into bed, sinking beneath the cool sheets to close her eyes in weary relief.

* * *

'Lucy…?'

Even as Lucy surfaced from sleep again every fibre in her body knew that the speaker was Joaquin, for nobody else had ever managed to make her name sound that exciting. That wonderful sexy drawl, rich as honey with smoky overtones, haunted her dreams, so she kept her eyes shut, warding off temptation as best she could.

'Go 'way,' she mumbled in sleepy self-defence.

'Wake up, Lucy…'

With drowsy reluctance, Lucy focused on the male poised at the foot of her bed. It was dusk. But, even in that duller light, his dark-as-midnight hair gleamed with vitality and his fabulous eyes glittered like jewels. That Joaquin should always look spectacular was no longer any surprise to Lucy, for other memories were stirring to endow him with a familiarity she accepted without question. Joaquin had been with her when the fever had been at its worst. Whenever she had become momentarily conscious of her surroundings again Joaquin had been there.

With a sigh, Lucy stretched to loosen her muscles. Belatedly conscious of the tension zapping through the air, she glanced up and connected with the direction of Joaquin's intent gaze. As she dropped her own attention to the straining mounds of her breasts, now so clearly delineated beneath her nightdress, she froze in dismay. Mortified by the provocative display she had unintentionally made of herself, Lucy flushed a rosy red and grabbed at the sheet to tug it up over her scantily clad frame.

Joaquin tilted back his proud dark head and continued to look at her levelly. However, his handsome mouth had now taken on a distinctly cynical twist. 'You're obviously feeling much better.'

'Would you mind telling me exactly where I am?' Lucy was breathless and hugely self-conscious, and desperate just to fill the silence.

'In one of my guestrooms,' Joaquin imparted with formidable cool. 'It is three days since you fell ill.'

'You're wearing a suit…' Lucy noted inconsequentially, taking in the beautifully tailored cream linen sheathing his lithe powerful physique. The shade merely enhanced his dark and vibrant animal magnetism. Her brain refused to dwell on one thought for longer than two seconds. She watched his sleek and aggressive jawline clench. 'And you seem so…so constrained…' She noted this to herself in instinctive confusion, for she could not help but contrast his concern when she had been ill to his current frozen demeanour.

Volatile green eyes flashed down at her in flaring anger. 'Let me tell you what I am repressing, *señora*,' Joaquin Del Castillo spelt out, the deep-freeze act fracturing fast. 'A near overpowering desire to drag your scrawny little body out of that comfortable bed and make you dig ditches and sweat in honest labour as you deserve!'

Sprung finally from all introspection, Lucy flinched and paled.

'Indeed it is a great challenge for me to treat you with the consideration due to an invalid,' Joaquin Del Castillo admitted in a driven undertone. 'But I wish to impress on you that I never at any stage intended you to suffer harm or injury. The doctor believes that you were not very fit to begin with. Had I been aware that you were genuinely as physically frail and weak as you appeared, I would have ensured that the journey you underwent to Fidelio's home was less taxing.'

He could use an awful lot of words without actually grasping the nettle and apologising, Lucy registered. For of course, she conceded with the sense of hindsight, that long arduous ride must have been completely unnecessary to a male with Joaquin Del Castillo's financial resources. Even she knew that a four-wheel drive could have traversed so flat a terrain with ease.

'Is it your wish that I contact your fiancé to inform him that you have been ill?' Joaquin enquired icily.

A blank look flowered in Lucy's eyes. 'But I don't have a fiancé…'

Joaquin stiffened, and then surveyed her with sudden intense derision. 'So you have jilted Roger Harkness! I noticed that you wore no ring and I should have guessed. He was the one aspect of your lifestyle which failed to make sense. Why would a woman with your expensive tastes choose to marry a newly qualified accountant?'

Recalling too late that she was supposed to be pretending to *be* Cindy, and deeply shaken that he should be aware not only that her sister was engaged but also of the identity and occupation of her fiancé, Lucy gasped. 'I…I—'

'*Dios*…so you were only playing with Harkness? Amusing yourself while you waited for your next rich protector to come along?' Joaquin Del Castillo assumed with contemptuous distaste. 'You have deprived me of the pleasure of telling him exactly what you are, for no man should take such a bride without forewarning!'

An anxious burst of low-pitched Spanish interrupted him. A stout little woman with grey hair had come into the room. She wasted no time in sliding a thermometer between Lucy's lips. Studying the younger woman's drawn face and anxious eyes, she glanced at her employer in speaking reproach.

Lucy watched Joaquin's powerful chest swell with the effort it took to bite back his temper. His expressive mouth compressed into a bloodless line of rock-steady restraint, but slight colour now delineated the hard jut of his high cheekbones. With an inclination of his imperious dark head, he squared his broad shoulders. 'We will discuss this matter again when you are stronger,' he informed her glacially.

Like a fish let off the hook at the very last moment, Lucy felt her tension evaporate, and she slumped back against the comfortable pillows. An hour later, as she dined from a tray set with exquisite porcelain, fine crystal and solid silver salt and pepper shakers, she perfectly understood Joaquin Del Castillo's outrage at the situation in which he now found himself.

He had brought her to Guatemala to confront and punish her. He had intended to corner her into signing that repayment agreement by marooning her in Fidelio's isolated home and making her rough it. Yet here she was, lying back against freshly laundered pillows being waited on hand and foot. Only the very rich could afford such a level of service. And the more Lucy pictured Joaquin's lean dark aristocratic face, the more she marvelled that she had not instantly recognised that blazing aura of power and expectation for what it was.

She really had to get hold of a phone and warn Cindy. That had now become a matter of even greater urgency. 'No man should take such a bride without forewarning'. The memory of that devastating assurance from Joaquin filled Lucy with fear on her sister's behalf. Cindy's wedding was only a few weeks away. Very probably Joaquin knew that date as well. His continuing belief that *she* was Cindy, but no longer a bride-to-be, was currently her sister's only protection from such a vengeful act.

With decision, Lucy got out of bed. It was after ten in the evening. Hopefully most of the occupants of the house would be downstairs. The wrap that matched her nightdress lay across a chair. Donning it, she crept out of her room into a long well-lit corridor with a highly polished wooden floor adorned at intervals with superb woven rugs. She passed by closed doors with her nerves humming a tattoo that made the hair on her nape prickle with forboding.

It was an enormous house. From the mouth of the corridor she peered out on to an impressive gallery with a ceiling that soared high above, hearing first the distant echo of voices and then quick steps traversing the hall which she assumed lay below. Several feet from her, she noticed a door lying ajar. On tiptoe, she approached, listened, and, hearing nothing, gently pushed the door wider.

Seeing that the bedroom, which was even more grand than her own, was empty, she hurriedly checked that there *was* a telephone before quietly closing the door behind her again to ensure that she would not be overheard. Since sneaking about like a cat burglar did not come naturally to Lucy, her heart was now beating so fast that it was threatening to choke her. She switched on the massive lamp behind the phone.

At speed she punched out the number of her sister's apartment, praying that her twin was at home. The instant Cindy heard her voice, she laughed, and said brightly, 'I suppose you've been having too good a time to call before this!'

'Don't I *wish*!' Lucy groaned, and sucked in a deep calming breath before she continued, 'I've landed into a really serious situation here, Cindy.'

In as few words as possible, she then hurried to tell her twin what she had to be told about her father-in-law Fidelio Paez's predicament.

However, it was a very difficult dialogue. Cindy kept on interrupting, first with ringing cries of disbelief and argument and finally with growing anger and resentment.

'Mario showed me a photo of the most incredible big ranch house...and he was staying in a five-star hotel suite when we met. Was he lying to me...*deliberately* lying about his background? Explain that to me!'

'Look, I know nothing about that end of it,' Lucy admitted unhappily, and as once again she repeated the cold facts which Joaquin had laid before her, a thunderous silence began to build at the other end of the line in London.

'If Fidelio couldn't afford to give me all that cash, he shouldn't have sent it,' Cindy finally framed in a cool, brittle voice which sounded alien to her anxiously waiting twin.

'Cindy...Joaquin Del Castillo wants that money repaid. At least there'll be the proceeds of the flat you bought for Mum and me...hopefully it will sell soon,' Lucy pointed out awkwardly in the seething quiet. 'Is there anything more left of that insurance pay-out you got when you were nineteen?'

'Do you seriously expect me to leave myself as poor as a church mouse over this nonsense?' Cindy demanded shrilly.

'As much as possible of Fidelio's money has to be returned to him—'

'I didn't *steal* that rotten money, nor did I *borrow* it! I asked and Fidelio gave, and I'm very sorry if he's broke now, but that's not my fault and it's not my responsibility either!' Cindy practically shouted, her increasing panic at what she was being told audible.

'Cindy—'

'This guy Del Castillo has really got to you, hasn't he? Well, you can stop talking about handing over what the sale of the flat brings in because Roger's expecting to put that money towards a house, and I can't tell him about all this nonsense...I *can't*!'

'It's not nonsense, Cindy. Joaquin Del Castillo is a very rich and powerful man and I don't think he'll let this matter drop—'

'If he's so darned rich, let *him* repay the money! No wonder rich people are rich,' Cindy cried wildly. 'They hang onto what they've got!'

There was a jarring noise, as if the phone handset at the

other end had been thrown down, but the line had not been disconnected. In the background, Lucy could hear her unfortunate twin giving way to angry sobs. Lucy hung on to her receiver, hoping that her sister would return to the call she had abandoned and start speaking to her again. Maybe crying would help Cindy to calm down, Lucy told herself, but there was no denying that her twin's outraged and defiant response had been an unpleasant surprise.

But possibly she had been hugely naive to expect any other reaction, Lucy reflected guiltily, belatedly struggling to put herself in her twin's place. Cindy had just received an awful shock. The news of Fidelio Paez's true station in life had shattered her sister. Cindy had sincerely believed that her father-in-law was a wealthy man. And if Cindy now had to replace Fidelio's savings, she would be surrendering the financial security she had learnt to take for granted in recent years. Nor had her sister any hope of concealing her changed circumstances from the man she was soon to marry.

Roger, stolid and conservative, Roger, who was prone to giving her sister lectures on money management. Roger, whom Cindy had already admitted was in the dark as to certain aspects of her past. Oh, dear heaven, what a dreadful, dreadful mess, Lucy conceded, her heart twisting over the situation her twin was now in. No wonder Cindy was panicking! How was Roger likely to handle this ghastly business breaking just before their wedding took place?

As Lucy hovered, literally frozen to the spot as she grasped what must now be her twin's deepest fear, it was a great relief when her sister returned to the phone again.

'*Lucy…?*' Cindy wailed chokily. 'What am I going to do?'

Lucy murmured as soothingly as she could, 'We'll work this out somehow. I'll get a job and help—'

'*After* the wedding!' Cindy broke in to stress tremulously. 'Promise me that you'll keep this Del Castillo guy in the dark and occupied until my wedding is safely over.'

Lucy paled at that demand. 'But...but, Cindy—'

'Roger will dump me if I tell him about this now...any man would! I've gone from being a good catch to a liability, and if I was Roger I know I'd run, because I'm going to be living off him now and I'm no good at budgeting!' Cindy sobbed out, becoming more hysterical with every passing second. 'Promise me, Lucy...*promise me!*'

An instant later, although she could see many potential pitfalls in continuing such a deceptive course of action, Lucy heard herself uttering reluctant agreement. How could she urge Cindy to tell her future husband the truth in advance of their wedding? Suppose Roger *did* break off their engagement? Lucy didn't want to carry the blame for that development.

'Whatever happens, don't call me again,' Cindy urged in a frantically nervous surge. 'Oh, yes, and whatever you do, *don't* sign that repayment agreement in my name!'

'Sign in your name...?' Lucy repeated in a strangled tone, because she would never have dreamt of forging her twin's signature on any document.

'I must say he has a nerve, expecting me to come up with the whole sum. The best I can offer is a ten-year instalment plan!' Cindy asserted bitterly.

'I'll try to sort something out—'

'But don't you run the smallest risk of Del Castillo finding out that there are *two* of us,' Cindy warned fearfully. 'And if you can't make it back in time for the wedding, don't worry about it...as long as my bridegroom turns up, I'll be OK!'

A split second later, the connection was cut.

Having replaced the phone, Lucy was just drawing in slow, sustaining oxygen when the bedroom door opened. She almost died of fright on the spot. Dropping down on her knees, she grabbed at the fancy fringed valance which swept down to the carpet, intending to conceal herself under the bed. Unfortunately, the mahogany bedframe she exposed went to within a couple of inches of the floor.

As she heard Joaquin's awesomely familiar drawl respond to whoever he was speaking to, either in the corridor or just inside the bedroom—for she couldn't see where he was now that she had dropped down below the level of the bed—absolute panic took hold of her. Feverishly scanning the nearest furniture for a potential hiding place and seeing nowhere, she listened, horrorstruck, to his conversation coming to an end. The door thudded shut. Lucy flattened herself to the carpet and stopped breathing altogether.

A phone buzzed; not the phone by the bed. Possibly a portable. Joaquin answered it. He didn't speak long and concluded the call in a rather impatient tone. It finally dawned on Lucy that she was in Joaquin's bedroom. But it was early yet, she reasoned, maybe he would just go back downstairs again. Surely he didn't go to bed before eleven in the evening? Going by the pictorial evidence of his social life in that magazine, Joaquin Del Castillo was the It Girl's male equivalent, ungiven to the sobriety of early nights.

She listened to the soft slither of cloth against cloth and then just cringed. He was getting undressed. But as long as there remained the smallest chance of her creeping out again unseen, Lucy preferred to stay where she was. How could she possibly emerge from hiding now and make any credible excuse for her behaviour? Another door opened. Another light went on. Her hope of escaping undetected rose high. He was in the *en suite* bathroom! Just as Lucy was about to crawl to the corner of the bed and make a break for freedom, a pair of bare brown male feet appeared in the path of her vision.

'Are you planning to join me in the shower?' Joaquin drawled the enquiry, his intonation smooth as black velvet.

CHAPTER FOUR

IN SHATTERED receipt of that slumbrous invitation, and the obvious fact that Joaquin Del Castillo had been aware all along that she was cowering on the floor on the far side of his bed, Lucy's tongue just glued fast to the roof of her dry mouth. 'I...I...'

Slowly, she lifted her head, so engulfed by embarrassment that she didn't know where to put herself, wildly wishing herself anywhere but the place she now was. At his feet in her nightie in *his* bedroom late at night! His fine white linen shirt hung unbuttoned and loose over his well-cut beige trousers, revealing a powerful torso, and his pectoral muscles were lightly defined by rough dark curls of hair. His skin was the colour of rich honey. Presented with that impressive expanse of male chest, she tried and failed to swallow.

'Even from the door, I can see over the bed, *querida*. I'm a lot taller than you are,' Joaquin said drily.

Maybe that crack about sharing his shower was some sort of Central American joke, Lucy decided, it not occurring to her for one moment that he could possibly have been serious. As he reached down a lean brown hand to close it over hers and pull her upright, she looked up and collided with those extraordinary black-fringed green eyes head-on. Whoosh...it was like falling on an electric current! Whatever desperate excuse might have been struggling for utterance on her tongue evaporated from her brain like Scotch mist.

'Lucy...Lucy,' Joaquin chided silkily in that dark, deep

sensual accent of his, curving long brown fingers over her sensitive jawbone.

Her head felt light. The butterflies in her tummy were back. She could feel every tiny muscle she possessed tauten, even her skin tightening over her bones. But this time she recognised what was happening to her. She saw into the dark secret heart of that surge of excitement rising and her breath snarled up in her throat in shock.

'Don't tell me you've lost your nerve,' Joaquin prompted lazily, his intent gaze scanning her upturned face.

In turn, Lucy was helplessly studying him. The high cheekbones which gave his lean features such proud definition, the cool, straight dark brows, the strong nose, hard jawline and wonderfully shaped mouth. 'You fancy my brother something rotten,' Yolanda had said, and Lucy finally acknowledged just how right his sister had been. A wash of colour burned her cheeks, for she felt the full weight of her own foolishness.

'No, I—'

Joaquin elevated a satiric dark brow. 'You weren't expecting me this soon, *es verdad*?'

Desperately trying to wrench herself free of the effect he was having on her, Lucy made a huge effort to concentrate. But she couldn't work out what he was talking about, which scarcely helped. 'I don't—'

'No importa…' His brilliant green gaze shimmered.

As she collided afresh with that searching scrutiny, her heart started to race. Sense told her to move, but the whirring tension in the air was the most deliciously seductive sensation. Paralysed to the spot in mesmerised stillness, she could feel her pulses racing, the very blood coursing through her veins. He was so close to her she could smell the hot vibrant scent of him, and it made her head spin and her body quiver with the kind of longing that left her weak.

The silence thickened to an almost unbearable level.

His bright gaze narrowed. Lifting his hand, he tugged loose the ribbon tie of the wrap she wore. It was done in such an entirely natural way that she simply stood there as he tipped the silky wrap from her shoulders and let it slide down into a pool at her feet. 'Joaquin…what on earth?' she whispered, just a split second too late.

In answer, Joaquin gave her a wolfish smile. Settling his hands on her taut shoulders, he lowered his proud dark head. She knew he was going to kiss her. Sheer anticipation wiped her mind clear of all else. She just wanted him to *do* it! In fact she could hardly wait: it was like a tremendously important test. The last time he had kissed her, she had had a fever. And ever since then she had wondered and wondered whether she had truly felt what she remembered.

With a smoky laugh that acknowledged the height differential between them, Joaquin sank down on the side of the bed and tugged her towards him. Then he slid his hands to her hips and lifted her on to his lap. What are you *doing*? a little voice screamed in the back of her bemused brain.

'No, this isn't… Well, it isn't…' Lucy began tremulously as self-consciousness and a sense of events moving too rapidly out of her control almost freed her of the spell he cast.

Unconcerned by such minor mutterings, Joaquin settled her down on him. He spread long graceful fingers to cup her cheekbones and she was lost again. Meeting those beautiful crystal-clear eyes of his, she just wanted to fling herself at him. Her whole quivering body was poised on a wild high. Her breasts were full, their straining peaks almost painfully sensitive. At the heart of her there was the most intense ache.

'You understand…*this* has nothing to do with Fidelio,' Joaquin warned her in a roughened undertone.

'Kiss me…' Lucy urged, all shyness put to flight by the agony of eagerness clawing up inside her.

And he did. Slowly and thoroughly and with the sort of smooth sensual expertise that she was defenceless against. Yet she sought no defence. He pried apart her lips and used the tip of his tongue in a teasing darting foray into the tender interior of her mouth. She almost passed out from the fierce surge of excitement he generated. Her hands broke the hold of his so that she could wrap her arms round him.

'Witch…' Joaquin husked with sensual fervour, before he took that invitation and possessed her mouth again with wild hot hunger.

Like oil thrown on embers, that hunger set Lucy alight. As he drew her down on to the bed she let her fingers sink into the thick dark strands of his hair. With a growling sound deep in his throat, he rolled over and came down on her. The heat and weight of his long powerful body on hers added a whole new dimension to the experience. With every seeking intimate thrust of his tongue which imitated a far more intimate possession Lucy burned. She was so hooked on that raw, drugging charge of ever-rising excitement she could barely breathe. His hands stroked her breasts, expert fingers teasing at a tender tip, making her moan her response under the onslaught on his mouth, all control abandoned.

A knock sounded on the bedroom door. Lucy didn't hear it, but Joaquin wrenched himself free of her with shocking abruptness. She felt that, and could hardly have remained unaware of the change in mood when she found herself being unceremoniously dumped back on to the carpet and told to stay there.

She was even more startled then to hear Yolanda, speaking in her own language several feet away. Only then did she lower her spinning head in shaken dismay at her own behaviour. Even as the unmistakable sound of an argument between brother and sister took place at the door, with the brunette's voice growing ever more shrill and angry while Joaquin's grew ever colder and steadier, Lucy just sat where she was, staring into space with shocked eyes.

She was still trembling, and deeply conscious of the after-pains of such unbridled passion. That hot greedy craving was still inside her, taking no account of place or person or indeed anything but its own existence. Her body wanted Joaquin Del Castillo. *She* wanted Joaquin, she adjusted in raw mortification. Until that moment she had never understood just how frighteningly powerful such physical need could be. And how could she blame him for taking advantage of her scantily clad presence in his bedroom? She had just let him…indeed had actively encouraged him to make love to her.

The noisy tap-tap of high heels stalking away penetrated Lucy's reverie.

'One down, one to go,' Joaquin spelt out, bending down to scoop her off the carpet with grim determination.

'One down…one *what*?' Lucy gasped.

'You're going back to your own bed!' His high proud cheekbones scored with dark colour, and his eyes bright and hard as emeralds, Joaquin raked her pink face with angry derision.

'Of course I am,' Lucy mumbled, every vowel sound strangulated by an inability to come up with any other response. Even she was prepared to concede that but for his sister's interruption where she herself was to spend the night might reasonably have been in doubt.

'*Of course?*' Joaquin stressed with stinging scorn as he strode to the door. 'I can't believe that I almost fell for that cheap seduction routine!'

'I…I b-beg your pardon?' Lucy stammered.

'*Por Dios*…you know what you are about with a man…you brought me close enough to the edge!'

'Don't you dare talk to me like that!'

Having made the return trip to her bedroom in record time, Joaquin dumped her back down on her comfortable bed. She fell back against the tumbled pillows, her caramel-blonde hair spilling round her hectically flushed heart-shaped face, her violet eyes bright with chagrin.

'There *was* no seduction routine!' Lucy spluttered.

'You were waiting for me.' With brooding intensity, Joaquin stared down at her, eyes a glimmering crystalline flash below lush black lashes. 'With my kid sister under the same roof…have you no decency?'

In receipt of that continuing appraisal, Lucy was startled to feel her entire skin surface burn with a sensation that was far from being the shame it should have been. Excitement still shimmered in the air between them like a barrier begging to be broken. It was impossible for her to defend herself against his accusation without revealing that she had been using his phone. If she admitted that, he might check out the number and discover that she had called what should have been her own empty London apartment.

'Obviously not,' she heard herself confirm, thrilling in the strangest way to that image of herself as a sexually confident and immorally manipulative female.

Goaded by that response, Joaquin came down on the side of the bed and leant over her. 'So you admit that?'

His brilliant eyes clashed with hers. Invisible sparks seemed to fly up. Her breath caught in her throat. 'I admit nothing,' she muttered unevenly, every sense quickening to his proximity.

Joaquin reached out a hand and slowly wound his fingers into a whole handful of her glossy ringlets. His astonishing eyes never left hers for a second. 'I swear you will not profit by my desire for you, *querida*,' he asserted in a dangerous growl.

But even the danger excited Lucy. To be desired was to feel like a seductive stranger inside her own homely skin. Her tongue snaked out to moisten her dry lips. She watched his attention drop to the moist fullness of her pink mouth and she trembled. A pin would have sounded like a rock falling in the charged silence which now stretched between them.

'Oh, dear...I didn't realise you still needed to be tucked in at night, Lucy,' Yolanda remarked in dulcet surprise from the doorway.

Joaquin drew back from Lucy and slowly sprang upright. His beautiful mouth quirking with what could have been suppressed amusement, he veiled his gaze and walked out of the room with a cool aside in soft Spanish to his sibling.

'*Buenas noches*, Lucy,' his sister sighed, looking nothing at all like the kid he had styled her as, she cast a martial glance of reproof in Lucy's direction.

Embarrassed to have been surprised that close to Joaquin, and enveloped in a burning blush, Lucy scrambled under the sheets with a muttered goodnight of her own. But she lay back unable to sleep. In twenty-two years she had never felt so *alive* as she had felt in Joaquin Del Castillo's arms. That was a pretty pathetic admission, she decided, reluctantly forced to admit to her own slender experience of men.

At school she had always been too quiet to interest any of the boys she'd liked. She had been nineteen when she met Steve. She had fallen head over heels for him when he came to work at the library. They had often lunched together and he had seemed to really enjoy being with her. But she had totally misunderstood the precise tenor of his interest and she had been devastated when it had finally dawned on her that Steve was gay. He had thought of her as a friend, no more, and had assumed that she knew that his flatmate was rather *more* than a friend.

The following year she had met Larry, an engineering student, who had been keen enough to ignore her excuses about not being able to go out in the evening and who had eventually just turned up on the doorstep. Sadly, his interest in Lucy had not been strong enough to prevent him from taking furious offence at her mother's extremely rude and contemptuous reception. And that had been the end of that.

Little wonder that in Joaquin Del Castillo's radius Lucy was now becoming painfully conscious of her own naivety. For too long she had been denied the independence to make her own choices in life. Naturally that lack of experience had left its mark. As her mother's carer she had had to be mature beyond her years, but in so many other fields, she was now discovering, she was still as unsure of herself as an adolescent.

So it was hardly surprising, she reasoned feverishly, that she didn't recognise the wanton female she turned into around Joaquin. When had she ever had the chance to express that side of her nature? She was a normal flesh and blood woman and it was natural that she should want to…should want to flatten him to the bed and *rip* his clothes off? She cringed, but that was how she had felt.

But was it also natural that when Joaquin entered the same room her brain went into freefall? Natural that she should totally forget that she was supposed to be pretending to be her sister every time he looked at her or touched her? Was sexual attraction that intense and all-consuming? Or was it just that she had been living like a nun for too long so that she was now, as Yolanda had so succinctly put it, making a total ass of herself around Joaquin Del Castillo?

Where were her wits? Lucy asked herself fiercely. What had she so far done to try and sort out this gruesome situation concerning Fidelio's money? One big fat nothing, she conceded, shame and guilt engulfing her. This very day she had seen Joaquin on two separate occasions and she hadn't even raised the subject, never mind tried to talk him round into agreeing to a workable solution. Tomorrow, she promised herself, she would do what she *should* have been doing from the start...

As soon as Lucy had had breakfast the following morning, she got dressed. The contents of the suitcase that had been left behind at the bar at San Angelita now hung in the wardrobe, freshly pressed and pristine.

Lucy chose a pale blue suit. The skirt was short, the jacket very fitted, but it was a smart combination and infinitely better than wafting around in skimpy nightwear, she told herself censoriously. No wonder Joaquin had picked up the wrong signals from her! She could scarcely condemn him for assuming that she was the sort of woman who was willing to employ sex as a persuader. Now that she was properly garbed, he would naturally take her far more seriously.

Her strappy shoes were so perilously high that it was a challenge to descend the stairs with grace. Yolanda was crossing the magnificent big hall below, looking stunning but also a little startling in an incredibly tight scarlet skirt and a beaded crop top adorned with strategic cut-outs.

'Good morning,' Lucy said awkwardly to attract the brunette's attention. 'Could you tell me where I could find your brother?'

Yolanda whirled round with a frown. 'In his office, down there...' She stabbed the air with an imperious hand to indicate the branch corridor at the rear of the hall. 'But I don't think it would be a good idea to bother him right now!'

'Why?'

The volatile brunette focused smouldering dark eyes on

her and ignored the question to ask another. 'Do you have a father, Lucy?'

'He's dead—'

'A brother?'

Lucy shook her head in denial.

Yolanda's sultry mouth compressed. 'Then how could you *ever* understand our macho-dominated culture?' she demanded with unconcealed bitterness. 'A Guatemalan woman must obey first her father, then her brother, and finally her husband. All male relatives take precedence over her. What I want doesn't come into it. No, I must *still* do as I am told, like a little child! Have you any idea how that feels?'

Involuntarily, Lucy heard the echo of her late mother's constant controlling criticisms which had marked out very effective boundaries in every area of her own life.

'Lucy, you're not a teenager any more and you look ridiculous in that dress...'

'Lucy, only street-walkers wear make-up like that...'

'Lucy, you're not bright enough to go to university...'

'Lucy, how can you expect me to sit here on my own while you go to some silly evening class...how can you be so selfish?'

'I know *exactly* how it feels,' Lucy heard herself whisper.

In the act of already moving away, Yolanda turned back in surprise at that confirmation.

'My mother was rather...er...domineering,' Lucy confided in a rush.

Their eyes met in a moment of shared understanding. This time Lucy turned away first, feeling horribly disloyal for having expressed that opinion.

'My mother remarried soon after my father died and had a new family,' Yolanda framed curtly. 'I was in the way, so I was sent off to school.'

Lucy stilled, and would have responded, but Yolanda grimaced. 'Poor little me!' she completed with cool self-mockery, and started up the grand staircase.

As Lucy headed in the direction which Yolanda had indicated, she recalled that brother and sister had been arguing the previous night as well. At least, the brunette had been arguing, she adjusted, for Joaquin had stayed cool as ice. But Lucy's sympathy quite naturally lay with Yolanda. Since she herself found standing up to powerful personalities an enormous challenge, she assumed Joaquin's sister had a similar problem, worsened by a cultural bias which suggested that women were not the equal of their male counterparts. And there was no denying that Joaquin Del Castillo laid down the law like a born autocrat.

She knocked on the door and then, after waiting a moment, opened it. The room was large and imposing, more of a library than an office, with the bookshelves and the darker decor imposing a pervasively male ambience.

Joaquin had already risen from behind an immaculately tidy desk. Across the room, French doors stood wide on the lush grounds. Sunshine flooded in, gleaming over his black hair, luxuriant as polished silk. Even in the more casual garb of a short-sleeved white shirt and cream chinos, Joaquin contrived to look incredibly exclusive. The beautiful cut of his clothing exuded faultless designer tailoring and elegance. His deep-set bright eyes arrowed in on her and narrowed, his lean, dark forceful face settling into impassivity.

Lucy's heart sank in the forbidding silence which he allowed to continue. Her nervous tension increased. She dragged in a foreshortened breath. 'We need to talk about Fidelio's money,' she pointed out tautly, hating the note of apology she could hear in her own uncertain voice.

'I have already said all that I have to say on that subject,' Joaquin countered with intimidating authority and finality.

'When you sign that document, you may go home. You have no other options.'

'But there's *got* to be another option…it would be impossible to come up with that much money all at once!' Lucy protested in a burst of desperation.

Joaquin looked hugely unimpressed by that plea of poverty.

Lucy bit at her lower lip. 'Surely the offer of a substantial first payment followed by instalments would be sufficient proof of good intentions?'

'Without a legal agreement, you would back out on the promise as soon as you got back to London,' Joaquin responded very drily.

'No, I wouldn't. There's actually a property of…er… mine up for sale at the moment—'

'The only property you own is the one you live in, and it's not on the market.'

So he *didn't* know about the flat which Cindy had bought for her mother and her sister. No, of course he didn't know! Had that connection been made, he might well have discovered that Cindy had an identical twin. So persisting on the subject of that property could be downright dangerous. Lucy closed her restive hands together in front of her, for the first time admitting how much she hated the necessity of pretending to be her sister. But Joaquin had personally ensured that telling the truth was out of the question when he had all but threatened to tell Cindy's bridegroom what she was really like. At least what *he* thought her sister was really like, which would be a very biased and cruelly unjust report!

'The remainder could be repaid in instalments,' Lucy proffered a second time, standing her ground and squaring her slight shoulders.

'At Fidelio's age, such an arrangement would not be viable.'

'But I can *prove* that it was all a horrible misunderstanding and that there was no intent to cheat anyone out of anything!' Lucy exclaimed, thrusting up her chin. 'If I had known that Fidelio was working as a ranch foreman, why would I have been under the impression that he was wealthy enough to give away large amounts of cash?'

'Specious,' Joaquin styled that argument, a sardonic ebony brow elevating at her persistence. 'Naturally Mario must have told you that my father had left Fidelio a legacy in his will.'

Lucy paled as she finally understood *how* Fidelio Paez had amassed such a healthy sum for his retirement years. He had inherited the greater part of it from Joaquin's late father, which no doubt gave Joaquin an even more personal stake in the affair. His family resources had ensured the comfort of the older man's retirement, only for Cindy to take it away. But her sister had been guilty of selfish and opportunistic greed, *not* of fraud! There was a distinction and he had to be made to see it. Cindy would not having knowingly injured Mario's father.

'But Mario never mentioned that legacy!' Lucy argued, curling her taut fingers into fists. 'You seem to forget that Mario and...' She stumbled, as she had almost slipped and said her sister's name. 'Mario and *I*,' she stressed, 'were only together for a very short time.'

'Not even long enough for you to play the grieving widow,' Joaquin agreed, studying her with immovable calm.

'If that's another one of those nasty cryptic remarks angled at making me uncomfortable, I'm not listening!' Lucy shot at him in shaken reproach.

'Start facing the fact that I know you for the con-artist you are,' Joaquin countered with unblemished cool, letting his brilliant green eyes roam with insolent thoroughness over her small stiff figure.

Beneath that appraisal Lucy squirmed, with an awareness of his raw masculinity that filled her with furious self-loathing. She could feel the heat rising in her cheeks and the sudden dryness of her mouth but she couldn't afford to stop focusing on the subject at hand. 'You don't know what you're talking about—'

'Don't I? The pre-Raphaelite hairstyle, the big dark blue eyes and the schoolgirl blushes must go down well with men who only see what they want to see...a cute little porcelain doll, the very image of fragile femininity!' Joaquin specified with silken derision. 'But I'm in a rather different league, *querida*.'

'How *dare* you compare me to a doll?' Lucy launched at him with angry incredulity at such a scornful image. 'I came in here to have a perfectly sensible and serious conversation with you—'

Joaquin lounged back against his desk with fluid grace and continued to survey her. 'Did you *really*? Is that why you're all dressed up in that short skirt, those towering heels, and wearing only a jacket next to your beautiful bare skin?'

Lucy ran out of breath and speech simultaneously. She stared at him, totally thrown by that sudden attack of her appearance.

'I'm enjoying the view. I'm a man...' Joaquin trailed out the last word with sardonic cool. 'Yet I've already warned you that I'll accept the invitation but that I won't *pay* for the privilege. I will not settle your debt to Fidelio Paez for you.'

Lucy was engaged in frantically unbuttoning her jacket to display the fine camisole she wore beneath, but then she remembered that she wasn't wearing a bra and just as hurriedly began to button herself up again.

'Oh, not *another* one of those sudden attacks of unconvincing modesty when you blush and lower your eyes and lock your knees together?' the Guatemalan tycoon delivered with withering scorn. 'You're dealing with a true cynic, and let's face it, there was nothing subtle about your visit to my bedroom last night. That was a pretty crude, up-front offer—'

'If you don't shut up, I'll swing for you!' Lucy suddenly exploded back at him, goaded beyond bearing into finally losing her temper. 'You just don't listen to one word that I say. You just won't stop making inappropriate personal comments—'

'On a scale of one to ten, lying on my bed under me is at least a *nine* in the personal stakes. Leaving me aching for the rest of the night made the chances of you attaining a sympathetic hearing this morning doubtful to say the least.'

Oh, how could he say that right to her face? How could he be so *graphic*? Lucy was startled to find herself actually looking wildly around herself for something to hit him with! Freezing to the spot then, she crammed shaking hands to her mouth, appalled by the promptings he roused in her. 'You make me feel violent!' she gasped accusingly.

'I'm not a patient man. Your pathetic attempts to portray yourself as being as pure as driven snow are beginning to irritate me,' Joaquin responded without remorse.

'I-Irritate you?' Lucy stammered, at what struck her as a grotesque understatement for his feelings when it was obvious to her that he utterly despised her. Her looks, her clothing, her character. And somehow accepting that reality emptied her of anger and fight and only pride kept her backbone straight.

'So far I have been very reasonable—'

'Reasonable?' Lucy spluttered. She felt like someone who had been ground into the dust by a large unstoppable truck and then asked to apologise for getting in the way. 'You won't agree to any sort of compromise, even though

I'm willing to repay the money in instalments and do whatever it takes to reassure you as to my reliability—'

'Reliability?' Crystalline green eyes widened and shimmered over her in rampant disbelief at her use of that particular word to describe herself. *'Infierno!* What sort of a fool do you think I am? At this moment you don't even have employment on which to base such promises!'

Once again Lucy cursed her lack of foresight in appreciating just how much Joaquin knew about her sister. Cindy's well paid but temporary contract to work as a television make-up artist had indeed ended, just a few weeks back. But her sister had been promised permanent employment as soon as a vacancy arose.

'In fact over the past five years you have spent only *eight* months actually working for a salary,' Joaquin Del Castillo informed her with considerable contempt. 'I cherish serious doubts that you have *any* ambition to subject yourself to the rigours of daily employment. You're lazy and you're frivolous. If you can find a man to keep you, you don't bother to work—'

Listening to that assessment, Lucy was outraged. 'That's rubbish. I'm a really hard worker, and if I *had* a job, I could make you eat every prejudiced word!'

A charged silence fell.

Her spine rigid with offended pride, Lucy tilted her chin.

Joaquin cast her a glittering glance from below lush black lashes. 'When would you like to start?'

CHAPTER FIVE

'START?' Lucy questioned blankly. 'Start what?'

'Working for me,' Joaquin Del Castillo drawled in challenge. 'What talents do you have beyond the bedroom door?'

Lucy's soft mouth opened and shut again.

'I seem to vaguely recall that you once spent a few weeks toiling as a typist,' Joaquin murmured reflectively, studying her transfixed expression with cynical amusement.

But he had misunderstood the reason for Lucy's absolute paralysis. A typist? He knew more than she did about her twin! No such skill featured in Lucy's repertoire. Nor could she get her mind round the enormous shock of him suggesting that she work for him in any capacity. 'You're…you're offering me a job?' she virtually whispered.

'So that you can make me eat my prejudiced words and prove how reliable you can be,' Joaquin supplied softly. 'Although I'm afraid I couldn't offer you the meteoric rise to promotion which you enjoyed the last time you worked in an office…'

Lucy frowned. 'I don't follow.'

'What a selective memory you have, *querida*. After mere days in the typing pool, the managing director made you his secretary. By the following week you were out of the office and a married man's mistress once more.'

In angry mortification Lucy parted her lips, thought about arguing, clashed with Joaquin's shimmering jade-green gaze and thought better of it. What was the point of getting into another dispute? Right now, although it galled her to admit it, *he* had the whiphand. So she gave a jerky shrug, striving to look untouched and indifferent, just as she knew Cindy would have done under such fire.

Joaquin straightened slowly. 'This is the moment where you tell me that you're still feeling far too fragile to work.'

Meeting his expectant gaze and reacting to it, Lucy flung back her head and snapped defiantly, 'I'm feeling terrific!'

Striding past her, Joaquin flung wide the door with an air of strong satisfaction. 'Then I have the perfect position for you—'

'Here?' Lucy stressed with a frown of incomprehension.

Planting a lean hand on her shoulder, Joaquin Del Castillo guided her out into the corridor. Before she could even think, he had shown her through the door at the foot of the passage into a spacious office furnished with what looked to her like the latest in high-tech work stations. 'I maintain only a small staff at here. These ladies handle my personal correspondence and co-ordinate various projects in which I am involved.'

Three female heads lifted. Lucy froze.

Joaquin spoke in Spanish to the older woman who had come forward to greet him. 'This is my secretary, Dominga...Dominga, this is Lucy Paez.'

Lucy received a frigid nod of acknowledgement from the stern Dominga. Like a schoolgirl dragged up in front of the headmistress for some wrongdoing, she quailed inside herself. One glance was sufficient to warn her that Joaquin's secretary knew all about her supposed career as a heartless fraudster. Oh, dear heaven, what had her foolish attempt to defend herself plunged her into now? Joaquin was calling her bluff by offering her the chance to work for him.

'Dominga will keep you occupied,' Joaquin informed her with a slow smile that told her that he had already picked up on the level of her discomfiture.

What followed over the next few hours was one of the most mortifying experiences of Lucy's life.

Cold the older woman might be, but Lucy could not have faulted her fairness. However, finding work to occupy Lucy was not easy. She could not answer the phone or organise documents because she could neither speak nor read Spanish. She had never had access to a computer before either. Asked to fill up the printers with paper, Lucy put the wrong paper in one and provoked a paper jam in the other. Not a woman to give up easily on a challenge, Dominga then went to the trouble of having a typewriter brought in and installed while Lucy hovered, pale as death, unable to muster sufficient courage to admit that she couldn't type.

But the moment of awful revelation was not long in coming. Joaquin's secretary stood like a stone image watching Lucy's desperate two-fingered attempts to pass herself off as a rotten typist but nevertheless a typist. Then the older woman just left her to her foolish charade while the other two women laughed and whispered to each other until Lucy was the colour of a beetroot.

The lunchtime break could not come soon enough for Lucy. Her back aching, she rose from the now hated typewriter and approached the older woman. 'I'm sorry for wasting so much of your time,' Lucy murmured guiltily.

Informed that she might as well take the afternoon off, Lucy turned away, assuming that that was a polite way of telling her not to bother coming back. Her relief was intense. But Dominga then went on to tell her that she would receive basic instruction on how to use a computer the following morning.

Lucy departed, feeling anything but grateful for that offer. Her pride had been hurt by the poor showing she had already made and she was afraid that further embarrassment now awaited her. But then what had she expected? she asked herself ruefully. Her job at the library had been un-skilled. She had stamped books, packed shelves and occasionally assisted people to find a particular volume. More demanding responsibilities had been the province of staff with degree qualifications. Offered the chance to do evening study, which would have enabled her to apply for a better position, she had had to refuse because she couldn't attend the classes.

As she crossed the magnificent hall towards the staircase, Joaquin strode in through the front doors. He had obviously been out riding. Sheathed in a crisp white polo shirt, beige jodhpurs and gleaming dark brown leather boots, he took Lucy's breath away. 'Drop-dead gorgeous' might have been a phrase specially coined just for Joaquin Del Castillo's benefit. The shirt outlined his wide shoulders, muscular chest and taut flat stomach. The jodhpurs accentuated every sleek line of his long powerful thighs and narrow hips. His black hair was ruffled, his jade-green eyes brilliant as jewels beneath his level brows.

Her heartbeat went crazy. He was just so beautiful, so vibrant. He moved with the prowling grace of a jungle cat. He also emanated a level of high-octane energy which fascinated her. And when he looked at her she felt dizzy, excited, weak at the knees with a wild pent-up anticipation she couldn't control. He signalled her with a fluid movement of one imperious hand.

It was a moment of revelation for Lucy. It was the moment she admitted that in all her life no man had ever made her feel the way he did, and that very probably no other man ever would. She had started falling for him when she was ill, had learned to look for him then, had felt more secure when he was around. Trust...was that when she had given her trust? For, most ironically, she *did* trust Joaquin Del Castillo.

He might be a serious threat to the happiness of the sister

she adored, but she respected the strong sense of ethics which drove him. How many wealthy powerful men would have taken the time and the trouble to establish why a former employee had decided to keep on working beyond retirement? And how many would have then attempted to right the wrong which had been done?

'Lucy…' Joaquin breathed, his accent very thick.

His crystalline gaze dazzled her. She stilled, and a split second later, his mouth claimed hers in hungry possession. She did not know who moved first. It didn't matter. Nothing mattered but that the awesomely necessary physical connection was made. Her heart thumping like a pounding drum, she clung to his shoulders as he crushed her closer. With the hard heat of his lean, powerful physique welded to her smaller, softer frame, she trembled violently, excitement surging through her like a dangerous drug.

Joaquin freed her mouth and dragged in a jagged breath. He stared down at her with brilliant eyes. 'The *next* time I won't let you go, *querida*.'

Only slowly returning to an awareness of her surroundings, and literally reeling on her feet in the aftermath of that embrace, Lucy drew back from him, stiff as the doll he had labelled her in her efforts to reclaim some composure. 'We—'

His nostrils flared 'There is no "we",' he cut in with ruthless cool.

The heady colour in her cheeks ebbed. 'Of course not…I know that.' But her voice rose in pitch on that admission, a slight quiver betraying her flagging control. She turned away in a rather uncoordinated circle, struggling to get a grip on both her flailing emotions and her treacherous body, which had let her down in the most revealing way of all.

'Have you finished playing at being a typist?' Joaquin enquired smoothly.

'Yes…' Lucy mumbled as she headed for the stairs as if her life depended on getting there.

'I thought you were going to make me eat my words…'

A humourless laugh escaped Lucy. 'Why bother?'

'Sign that agreement. We both *know* that you can afford to reimburse Fidelio,' Joaquin drawled in a tone of derision. 'I'll have you back at the airport within the hour…'

Lucy shut her eyes so tight that they ached. Rigid-backed, she mounted the stairs. Afraid that she was being watched, she didn't dare quicken her steps until she knew herself to be out of sight. Then she hurtled down the corridor and into her bedroom to fling herself in a heap on the bed.

Was it true? Was it true that Cindy had sufficient funds to immediately reimburse Fidelio Paez? Lucy didn't think so. Lucy couldn't credit that her twin could have that much money stashed away. Then the tears she had hoped to hold back by concentrating on that more practical question simply overflowed. Furious at her own weakness, she stuffed her face into the pillows and cried.

She was all worked up, and over what? So she was powerfully attracted to Joaquin Del Castillo, and was savaged by the nasty reality that *he* couldn't wait to get rid of her! Was it her reaction to him which was creating the problem? Or was he just one of those guys who was over-sexed and would make a pass at any reasonable-looking female? Face it, Lucy, a little voice said drily, he's out of your league anyway, and he wouldn't be looking at you twice if there was any competition.

She was already so sick and tired of pretending to be Cindy. Every natural sense prompted her to tell the truth, but intelligence warned her that Joaquin would be even more outraged by the deliberate deception she and her sister had practised. There was no easy way out—no way she could turn something bad into something even acceptable.

The minute Joaquin found that the real Cindy Paez was still in London, he would swing into vengeful action. What might he do in the heat of the moment? She shivered. Cindy did not deserve to have her life wrecked a second time. Lucy would protect her sister for as long as she could while Cindy decided how she was going to handle the situation with Roger.

The arrival of a maid with a lunch tray wakened Lucy up out of the doze she had slid into so easily. She ate with appetite and then decided to go out for a walk. Discarding her twin's now crumpled suit, she donned a floral chiffon skirt. She ignored the long fancy jacket the skirt was supposed to be worn with and teamed it instead with the gypsy top and canvas shoes which she had worn on her arrival at Hacienda de Oro.

Walking out through the front doors minutes later, Lucy breathed in deep in the golden sunshine, delighted to be back in the fresh air. She soon discovered that the lush, informal gardens which contained some incredibly beautiful flowering trees were as spectacular as the views across the deep valley. In the distance she could see the top of an old building showing above the tree canopy, and she began to move in the direction of the forest that ringed the grounds of the house.

A ancient-looking paved lane wound through the trees and Lucy followed it. It was late afternoon by then, and very, very hot, but the further she explored, the more entranced she became. Wildly colourful birds wheeled and dipped overhead, uttering shrill and strange cries. A monkey swung across an overhanging branch, startling her. She laughed as she watched the bright-eyed little creature perch on a tree nearby to study her with patent curiosity. It was like no other world she had ever seen.

Calmer now that she had had the chance to reflect, she saw that she had taken entirely the wrong attitude towards the office job which Joaquin had so facetiously offered her. Naturally he didn't expect her to stay the course! And it was for that very reason that she should stick it out until he got tired of having her around. If she couldn't prove that she was reliable, how could she expect him to believe any promise she might make about repaying Fidelio's money? A half-hearted approach allied to ineptitude was scarcely the way to impress a male who already thought she was lazy and frivolous! So tomorrow she would make a real effort with the computer training.

That decision made, Lucy rounded another bend on the worn path she was following. There she faltered to a startled halt, violet eyes opening very wide. Only now did she recall Yolanda's comment about the Hacienda de Oro being an archaeologist's dream destination. Before her in a vast clearing stretched a seemingly endless expanse of Mayan ruins. The roofcomb of a temple was what she had glimpsed above the trees from the grounds of the house.

Lucy had always had been interested in the ancient world. Had she gone to university, she would have studied archaeology. Then, five years earlier, Cindy had sent her mother and her sister a casual postcard announcing her marriage to a Guatemalan citizen. Deafening silence had followed until her twin had contacted them again just eleven months ago. For years Lucy had fondly imagined that her long-lost sister was living in Guatemala with her husband. So she had had a special interest in reading about the astounding ruined cities of the Maya which were sprinkled across Central America.

She was thrilled to see the extensive and well-maintained site stretching before her. Before she left London, she had rather guiltily wondered if she would get an opportunity to visit one of the famous sites in the Petén, but had deemed it unlikely when she had believed she was travelling out to spend her time comforting a dying man. And yet now, here on the very doorstep as it were, lay the ultimate experience for a keen amateur archaeologist…

Some timeless period later, wholly absorbed in examining in stone what she had previously only studied on a printed page, Lucy's wandering exploration was finally disturbed.

'What the hell have you been doing all this time?' A familiar accented drawl shot at her from a good twenty feet away.

Not having heard Joaquin's approach, Lucy jumped and whirled round in shock. Joaquin was poised by a giant stone stela, surveying her with apparent outrage.

'Sorry…?' As always, he looked staggeringly handsome, and with a feeling of embarrassed self-loathing Lucy tore her gaze from him again. She didn't want to see him. She didn't want to think about him either. Uppermost in her memory was a recollection of her own distress earlier. 'There is no "we",' Joaquin had said drily. He should not have needed to state the obvious. He might not be averse to the inviting signals she could not help putting out in his direction, but essentially Joaquin Del Castillo despised her!

'Armed guards patrol these ruins twenty-four hours a day to protect them. Suppose you had been mistaken for a looter? Where are your wits? You can't just wander off into the jungle as if you're strolling down an English country lane!' Joaquin thundered at her, jade-green eyes glittering with dark fury.

'I'm not in the jungle—'

'You're in the rainforest, you stupid fool!' Joaquin launched at her on full throttle, making her flinch where she stood. 'Have you any idea how long it has taken me to find you?'

'But I wasn't lost…I just followed the path!' Lucy wondered why he looked as if he was just getting more furious with every word she spoke, and then, realising that she was staring at him again, she flushed miserably.

Joaquin snatched in an obvious breath of restraint, a feverish line of colour demarcating his fabulous cheekbones. He punched out a number on the mobile phone gripped in one lean hand and spoke into it in urgent Spanish. Then he studied her afresh. 'We've been worried about you! You left the *hacienda* over three hours ago.'

Three hours ago? People worrying? In dismay, Lucy checked her watch. 'Oh, my goodness, I'm so sorry...I had no idea I'd been out here so long!'

'Stop playing it cool. I'm not fooled,' Joaquin delivered with withering derision. 'You were *lost*.'

'No...' But Lucy looked back in the direction she had come, only to find that she was no longer so sure of that direction. She might well have had some difficulty finding her way back to the path, she conceded grudgingly.

'And since I cannot believe that Mayan civilisation is an overwhelming passion of yours—'

'I'd just like to see the temple before I leave...' Screening him out with obstinate determination, Lucy focused on the massive elaborate building which she had been steadily working towards but continually tempted away from. 'Please, just give me five minutes.'

'Lucy...'

Since it seemed pretty obvious that she was unlikely to get the chance of a return visit, Lucy closed her ears and hurried off.

'Just who are you trying to impress here? Have you even the slightest conception of what you're looking at?' Joaquin demanded crushingly.

From the steps, Lucy was engaged in studying the vast weathered masks of deities adorning the huge ornate entrance.

'Well, that's Hun Hunapu, the maize god...and that one

is—I think—Chac, the god of rain…and this one's Kinich Ahau, the sun god,' she replied self-consciously, and then passed on into the dim interior. 'And I bet I'm mispronouncing those names, because I've only read them and never heard anyone say them out loud. Does this temple have a *pib na*?'

In the incredibly charged silence which followed, Lucy chewed her lower lip and glanced at Joaquin. A deep frownline between his level dark brows, he was studying her with fixed intensity.

'Is there something wrong?' she asked.

Joaquin breathed in deep. '*Sí*…the temple has an underground room.'

'With murals?' Lucy prompted, and then she sighed. 'I suppose the humidity has wrecked them?'

'Not quite…' Joaquin continued to scrutinise her with brilliant green eyes while giving out the impression of a male having a rare struggle to concentrate. 'But while the conservation project is underway to preserve them they are not available for viewing.'

The silence lay heavy between them. Joaquin was very still. Lucy stole a questioning glance up at his lean strong face.

His aggressive jawline squaring, he met her eyes levelly. 'On one count I have wronged you, and for that I owe you a sincere apology. Only out of respect for your late husband's memory could you have taken such an interest in the Maya.'

His sincerity was patent. But that apology hit Lucy like a slap. The colour drained from her cheeks. Joaquin believed he was addressing Mario's widow and he was finally showing some respect. Only he had naturally misinterpreted the connection which had first fired her fascination with the Maya. Suddenly she felt desperately ashamed of the deception she was engaged in.

'It's getting late,' she said stiffly.

But Joaquin rested a light staying hand on her arm. 'You must have loved Mario very much—'

Her discomfiture increasing, Lucy tugged free and started down the steps again. 'It's not something I want to talk about.'

'Perhaps not, but when we were children Mario and I were close friends.'

'I'm sure that didn't last long,' she heard herself snipe, because she was so keen for him to change the subject. 'The heir to the Del Castillo fortune and the ranch foreman's son?'

'It was never like that between us,' Joaquin responded in a quiet tone of rebuke. 'Mario still thought enough of that bond to call me on your wedding day and confess that he was happier than he had ever hoped to be in this life.'

That was an admission which Lucy knew she would pass on to her twin when the timing was right. Only at that particular moment she did not want to be drawn into Joaquin's recollections of his childhood playmate. With every honest word he spoke her own subterfuge made her feel like the lowest of the low.

Joaquin caught her hand in his. 'Look at me…' he urged. 'I pride myself on my judgement, but perhaps I was too quick to judge you for failing my standards after Mario's death.'

'It was a long time ago,' Lucy cut in dismissively.

'*Por Dios!* At least give me credit for finally trying to comprehend what might have made you behave in such an unseemly fashion within weeks of the funeral!'

Lucy yanked her fingers free of his. At that demand, her discomfiture blazed up into angry resentment, 'You patronising bastard…' she whispered in furious reproach.

'*Que pasa?*' Joaquin demanded, his lean darkly handsome features clenching hard on that unexpected attack.

'You…you're wrong about everything!' Lucy flung at him in impassioned defence of the sister she loved. 'And you're far too spoilt to be capable of understanding.'

'Spoilt?' Joaquin repeated in ringing disbelief.

'How many houses does one man need to live in? How could you ever know what it's like to be poor and depressed and not care about anything any more?' she asked in blunt condemnation. 'What would *you* know about the kind of terrible grief that sends people off the rails?'

After that outburst, which had truly come from the heart, Lucy flung him a final look of disgust and took off. He shouted in her wake. Lucy ignored him, which wasn't difficult when he was calling after her in Spanish. In any case she could see the path now and could see no reason to put up with his company when she could find her own way back to the house.

As she sped down the path, she was recalling the evening that her twin had talked about Mario's sudden heart attack. Cindy had confided that she had felt so devastated and wretched after Mario died that she had done some things she had since regretted. Lucy hadn't pried but she guessed she knew what those things had been now. Stripping off for the camera, getting involved with married men. Men who ought to have had more decency, for Cindy could only have been seventeen at the time!

Emerging from her troubled thoughts, Lucy noticed that the vegetation surrounding her seemed much more dense than she had noticed earlier. Exotic plants flourished in a fantastic lush carpet below the trees. Huge ferns, spiky bromeliads and pale orchids shone in the dim, misty light. Yes, the light was fading, or possibly the tree canopy was heavier at this point, she reasoned, and then she heard the sound of rushing water.

She stilled in astonishment at the sight of the waterfall tumbling down over a jutting outcrop of limestone rock into a wide glistening tranquil pool below. The water was so clear she could see each individual pebble below the surface. It was very beautiful. But she was obviously *not* on the same path she had used before.

Joaquin was going to kill her, she conceded ruefully. Bending down, she dipped a finger into the water. It was deliciously cool. Slowly, she raised herself again. She listened to the silence. Even the birds had gone quiet. She was so hot that her damp clothes were sticking to her skin, and getting mad at Joaquin hadn't helped. Just a quick two-minute dip, she decided, succumbing to temptation. Then she would retrace her steps, for goodness knows where she would end up if she stayed on the path she was on!

Peeling off her skirt and top with a sigh of relief, she stepped into the pool. *Heavenly.* She scooped up water and splashed herself all over, revelling in every sparkling water droplet that cooled her overheated flesh.

'Freeze, Lucy…'

Joaquin's drawl was so much quieter than its wont, and such an unwelcome shock, that for a split second she *did* freeze with appalled chagrin, her lack of clothing her most overriding concern. Automatically her head then jerked up and she began to whip her hands over her bare breasts, and then what she saw in that one mortified upward glance filled her with absolute terror…

CHAPTER SIX

IN THE deep shadow below the trees, no longer screened by the thick vegetation, stood the most huge and terrifying beast Lucy had ever seen outside a zoo.

The jaguar was barely fifteen feet away on the other side of the pool. His big golden eyes were drilling holes into her and her mouth fell open. So intense was her fear that she could neither draw breath nor remove her shattered gaze from the animal. And then, with a sudden movement that scared the living daylights out of her and provoked a startled gasp from her straining lungs, the great muscular cat sprang through the trees and was gone.

'Oh, my heaven…oh, my…oh, *my*!' Lucy spluttered through chattering teeth, her near nudity now the very last thing on her mind.

A pair of powerful arms lifted her out of the water and brought her back on to dry land. Trembling violently with fear, she couldn't have spoken to save her life.

'You know the Maya believed that when night fell the sun turned into a jaguar that prowled the underworld,' Joaquin murmured as he peeled off his shirt and dropped it round her shaking shoulders.

'They also called it "the beast that kills its prey with one b-bound"!' Lucy stammered sickly.

'They are rarely aggressive towards humans.'

'Thank the good Lord that he didn't fancy getting those big paws wet!' she gabbled, clutching at a bare broad male shoulder to keep herself upright.

'He is an excellent swimmer, *querida*. This is the pool where he catches fish. You were trespassing.'

'Get clothes on,' Lucy mumbled, not keen to hear any further revelations of the big cat's habits.

Joaquin crouched down to gather up her discarded garments. She crouched down with him, pale as death and still shaking like a leaf. 'I was scared—'

'That's good, *querida*. That's more sensible than skinny-dipping in a rainforest when twilight falls.'

'Never again,' Lucy promised in a wobbly voice.

In a deft movement, Joaquin dropped the gypsy top over her head and freed her from his shirt. 'But in all my vast experience I do not think that I ever saw anything as lovely as you were in that brief instant before I saw that you had attracted another admirer.'

With complete calm, he then began inserting her arms into the sleeves of her top while she knelt on the ground in front of him, still virtually paralysed by shock. 'Lovely?' she queried unevenly.

'You...exquisite...your breasts, your hair, the way the light fell on your skin...'

'Oh...' Lucy collided unwarily with shimmering green eyes, conscious of a soaring wicked response she could no more have prevented than she could have denied herself air to breathe. She moistened her dry lips.

'No...' Joaquin decreed in a low-pitched undertone, as if she had spoken.

Only she didn't need to speak to know what he was talking about, and it gave her the most extraordinary sense of power to note the slight tremor in his lean brown hands as he extended them to help her back to her feet. He proceeded to feed her shaky lower limbs into her skirt. She recognised his dexterity without surprise and was amazed by her own lack of concern at being dressed by him. She tried to picture how she must have looked to him in the pool. Clad in nothing but a pair of panties that were wet and probably transparent.

'Did I look sexy?' she heard herself whisper with help-less curiosity.

Joaquin closed big hands over her shoulders and flexed his fingers. 'Like a water nymph in an old painting.'

A water nymph was next door to a wholesome cherub in Lucy's mind. He urged her back the way she had come. Her legs felt ridiculously wobbly. Time itself felt dislo-cated. Traversing the periphery of the ruins, Joaquin turned into the original path where a big four-wheel drive now sat parked. He lifted her into the front seat, hands steady now, and impersonal. As he reversed the vehicle she studied his bold bronzed profile in the dusk light, her heartbeat ham-mering out a dangerous tattoo. In all her life she had never wanted so badly to touch anyone as she wanted to touch him.

When had they stopped talking? When had the silence fallen and the tension begun to build? She didn't know, only that she was awesomely aware of that crackling ten-sion and of *him*. He flipped on the air-conditioning, the click sounding preternaturally loud. He turned towards her, dense spiky lashes screening his gaze to a glimmer of the purest jade. Her fingertips curled in on themselves as she fought the crazy, shameless need to reach out to him.

In the rushing silence she noted everything about him. The faint sheen on his high proud cheekbones, the powerful lure of those bright eyes, the roughened darkness of his uncompromisingly male jawline in contrast to his beauti-fully modelled mouth. A tiny pulse was flickering like mad at the base of her throat as she let her head fall back and just looked at him.

'You like to flirt with danger, *querida*,' Joaquin com-mented, his accent rough as sandpaper gliding over silk.

Never before, probably never again, her rational mind responded. She was dizzy with the tension that held her wire-taut, outrageously aware of the heavy fullness of her breasts and the tiny little twisting sensation curling in the pit of her stomach. He looked and she burned and she melted. It was that simple, that basic, and way too potent a force for her to control. It both thrilled and terrified her to feel the magnetic pull of that power he had over her.

'It's not fair to blame me…' she muttered, dry-mouthed.

Joaquin lifted a lean hand and rested a fingertip against the pulse fluttering wildly at her collarbone. 'No…' he conceded, drawing out the word huskily. 'Desire is rarely so immediate as it is between us. That intrigues me, but it won't hold me. Don't fantasise about a future beyond tomorrow…'

Lucy heard what he was saying and she understood, but she couldn't think about it. She let the words sink unmourned into her subconscious, her whole being concentrated on the mesmeric brilliance of his eyes, the delicious, utterly electrifying sensuality of that light and confident finger now tracing the full curve of her lower lip.

'I've never felt like this before,' she whispered breathlessly.

He cupped her cheekbone, watched her curve her face instinctively into his palm. 'Only teenagers talk like that, Lucy,' he censured with lazy mockery.

'Maybe…' she framed, sealing up the pain of that putdown as soon as she felt it, stowing it away with his words earlier, banishing all that she could not deal with.

'You want me…I want you,' he countered. 'Sexual hunger needs no other label.'

Releasing her then, he turned back to the steering wheel and drove off. She was all of a quiver, intoxicated with longing. She closed her eyes but she couldn't bear it. She had to look at him again. *Sexual hunger?* Not a label she liked. She pushed that knowledge away hurriedly, afraid to face it.

Darkness had fallen at bewildering speed. In the path of

the headlights, Lucy watched him shoot the car to a halt in a courtyard which she assumed lay to the rear of the house. He sprang out and strode round the bonnet. Opening the passenger door, he just scooped her out into his arms.

A shaken laugh escaped Lucy as Joaquin lifted her high in a wholly unexpected manoeuvre that reminded her just how volatile he could be and also deprived her of her shoes, for they fell off. Simultaneously, she noticed that the lights burning in a couple of the ground-floor windows had mysteriously dimmed since their arrival, possibly to allow any staff looking out a better view of what was happening outside.

'My shoes…Joaquin, put me down, *please*,' she urged, hot-cheeked.

'Not until we hit the bedroom.'

'But what about Yolanda?' she gasped, distinctly taken aback by that open avowal of intent.

'My sister has gone to Guatemala city to stay the night with her cousins,' Joaquin imparted. 'Retail therapy will hopefully improve her temper.'

'Retail therapy?'

'Shopping,' Joaquin rephrased, in some surprise that the explanation was necessary.

He swept through a door off the courtyard to mount a back staircase while still holding her as if she weighed no more than a child. He paused on the lofty landing above to claim her lips in a slow, sensual kiss that she found totally electrifying.

Hot and breathless in the aftermath, Lucy opened eyes she didn't remember closing and found herself spread across Joaquin's imposing bed. Her critical faculties were not working at speed and her entire attention was absorbed by the fact that Joaquin had just finished extracting her from her skirt. As she sat up in some confusion, for matters were moving faster than she had naively expected, Joaquin settled crystalline green eyes full of intent on her and peeled off his shirt.

'Oh…' Lucy gasped.

'Oh…what?' The most glorious smile she had ever seen curved Joaquin's mouth.

She was just dazzled by that smile. Heart going nineteen to the dozen, she rested back on her elbows and just stared at him. Shorn of his shirt, he was magnificent. Bronzed skin, black hair, whipcord muscles. As he embarked on his chino trousers she could feel her face hotting up, but she could not resist her own curiosity when that lithe powerful physique was being revealed inch by tantalising inch.

She focused on his washboard-flat stomach and the tantalising silky furrow of hair arrowing down to disappear below his waistband. Then her scrutiny strayed lower and she blinked, jolted out of her voyeuristic reverie. The potent thrust of his arousal was patent. Enervated by the sight, and suddenly desperately self-conscious, she jerked her head away and stared a hole in the door instead.

Nervous as a kitten now, she sat forward, hands linking together. Curiosity had certainly been satisfied. Long past time too, she told herself urgently. Here she was, pushing twenty-three and a virgin. She loved him. He might not love her, but if she chose to overlook the fact that was her business, wasn't it? But if being in a bedroom just watching Joaquin remove his clothes struck her as being the ultimate in intimacy, how was she going to handle what followed? Oh *no*, she thought, gripped by sudden panic, suppose he realised that she wasn't the experienced lover he thought she was?

'Joaquin…?' she began tautly.

'Getting impatient?' Joaquin teased in his dark deep drawl.

'Well…er, no—'

He came down on the bed beside her and separated her

hands so that he could divest her of her top. The operation was so slick she started talking again, only to discover that what she was saying was being muffled by the fabric.

'*Cómo?*' Joaquin prompted with a frown.

Lucy tugged the gypsy top from him before he could dispose of it and ventured, 'Maybe we shouldn't be rushing into this—'

'Do you feel rushed?' Joaquin rested his hands lightly on her slight shoulders and very gently eased her back against the pillows. 'You are very tense, *querida.*'

'Yes, but…b-but…'

'I love your mouth,' Joaquin confessed as he leant over her, his breath fanning her cheek, his proximity sentencing her to stillness.

She stared up into his burnished eyes. He lowered his arrogant dark head and very gently brushed her lips with his. 'Oh…'

'You were saying?'

'Nothing…' Engaged on stroking her fingers through his hair, Lucy blinked and turned her mouth up under his in a move so instinctive she didn't even have to think about it.

With a sexy sound, low in his throat, Joaquin pulled her under him and tasted her parted lips hungrily with his own. The concept of escape had evaporated from her mind. As he crushed her into contact with every angle of his over-poweringly male body, she was in more danger of expiring from over-excitement. Her pulses were racing. With the achingly familiar scent of him in her nostrils, every sense she possessed went into overdrive.

He lifted his head and whisked away the crumpled top which still lay between them. His hand curved over the small pouting mounds of her breasts and she quivered, heat curling in her pelvis, making her restive.

'I love your breasts too,' Joaquin muttered unevenly as he disposed of her last garment.

He ran an exploring fingertip over a swollen pale pink nipple and then he dropped his head and let his mouth close round that straining peak instead. The hot rush of physical pleasure took her by storm. She jerked, her whole body trembling. Her skin felt super-sensitive, the force of her own response shocking her, but there wasn't time to dwell on that discovery. His erotic appreciation of her tender flesh was utterly absorbing—until her rising need demanded more.

'Please...' she moaned then.

Eyes glittering, Joaquin surveyed her and let a relaxed hand skim down a taut thigh. Her muscles contracted. She reached up to him, possessed of a fever she barely understood but which nonetheless controlled her. The forceful kiss he claimed only partially eased her nagging tension.

'So you really *do* want me...' Joaquin husked, hauling her even closer with glittering eyes full of conquest.

'Don't you know that?' She gave him a bemused look.

'Women are better liars than men.' He studied her with slumbrous satisfaction. 'But if you had tried to fake your response I would have known it, *gatita*.'

He smoothed a possessive hand over her quivering length. He let his tongue delve between her reddened lips, stoked the hunger she couldn't hide with a carnal level of expertise that she could not resist. As he traced the hot thrumming centre of her body, she arched her spine, a sob of response escaping her convulsed throat. The pleasure became so intense she writhed, driven mindless by her own lack of control.

And then, when she was at the stage when she might have pleaded could she have found her voice, Joaquin came over her, settling between her thighs. 'You're so small, I'm afraid I'll hurt you, *querida*,' he complained raggedly.

Duly forewarned, she still retained enough brain power to react and tense. 'Joaquin?' she gasped.

'*Cristo*…I *know*,' he groaned feelingly, scanning her with glittering eyes filled with need. 'I can't wait any longer either. Never have I been so hot for a woman as I am for you!'

In an instant, the incipient panic she was fighting vanished. Lucy had a vision of herself as the kind of woman who drove a man crazy with desire. She loved that vision. He moved against her. She closed her eyes, and then he was there and it was the most extraordinarily intense moment. Her whole being was centred on that alien intrusion, the sharp stab of momentary pain which made her grit her teeth, but then, caught up in returning excitement, she stopped thinking and started just feeling again.

'You feel incredible, *gatita*,' Joaquin groaned, driving deeper inside her, provoking the most awesomely pleasurable sensations.

From that point on she was lost in her own stormy response. Heart thumping, breath catching, she was caught up in the wild passion he generated. With every smooth rhythmic thrust, he drove her hunger for him higher. She was burning, reaching for the mindless peak of ultimate fulfilment. And then she was there, plunged into ecstasy, crying out in surprise at the height of that pleasure before slowly sinking down to planet earth again.

In the aftermath, she studied Joaquin with wondering eyes. She remembered him shuddering with a driven growl of raw release and she quivered, cocooned in a feeling of decided smugness as she curved up against his big damp body and kissed his shoulder. She was awash with sunny feelings and satisfaction and appreciation.

'You're wonderful,' she whispered dreamily.

'It was good…' Joaquin purred like an indolent jungle cat above her head, accepting the compliment as his due with complete cool. 'In fact, it was spectacular, *gatita*.'

He rolled over, carrying her with him. Then he rearranged her on top of him. He looked down at her, smoothed her tumbled curls back from her brow and slowly eased her back up level with him again to study her with almost frowning fascination. 'I want you all over again.'

'Sí...' Lucy said, suddenly feeling confident enough to tease him.

A heartbreaking smile curved Joaquin's beautiful mouth and he relaxed even more. 'And again,' he confided with a husky laugh. 'And again. How many repeat encounters am I allowed?'

She blushed, and pushed her happy face into a broad brown shoulder. 'Who's counting?' she whispered shyly.

He kicked back the sheet. Then he frowned and sat up. She followed the path of his gaze and froze in dismay and chagrin, for there was a small bloodstain on the sheet.

'Por Dios...' Joaquin exclaimed.

Thinking faster than she had ever thought in her life, Lucy muttered, 'My knee...I fell when I was scrambling round the ruins this afternoon—'

'And you said nothing?' Joaquin broke in censoriously. 'In this climate, any injury needs attention!'

Her scraped knee was duly inspected. Joaquin sprang out of bed, insisting that the cut ought to be bathed and treated with antiseptic. While he occupied himself at that praiseworthy endeavour, Lucy began breathing more normally again.

'You're so careless of your own well-being!' Joaquin's concern was liberally laced with exasperation. 'Even a small wound can lead to a serious infection, and if it's bled again, it hasn't yet begun to heal.'

Lucy withstood the lecture, giddy relief seeping through her as she realised just how close she had come to having her fake identity exposed. Had Joaquin realised that he had been her first lover, he would have known that she could not be Cindy Paez. Joaquin affixed a plaster to the offending limb and surveyed her where she sat, head humbly bowed.

'Under no circumstances will you enter the rainforest again,' he decreed. Her taut mouth began to stretch into a helpless smile. She stole a glance up at him, irrepressible dimples indenting her cheeks.

'What's so funny?'

'You're just so bossy. Were you born domineering or did you get that way growing up?'

Joaquin reached out and very slowly tipped her back across the tumbled bed. 'The talent comes entirely naturally to me, *querida*,' he countered with immense cool.

Lucy laughed; she couldn't help it. Joaquin pinned her hands to the sheet in mock annoyance, his brilliant eyes intent on her animated face. The leap of instant awareness she experienced made her still. He smiled again, the indolent sensual smile of a male sure of his welcome, and bent his tousled dark head to kiss her.

Lucy turned over and reached out, only to discover that she was in bed alone.

Sitting up, she studied her surroundings in surprise. While she'd slept, Joaquin must have returned her to her own room. Discreet and sensible, she conceded, but she was uneasily aware that discretion had not been on his mind when he had first swept her off to bed. Suppressing a faint pang of anxiety, and refusing to acknowledge her disappointment at not waking up in his arms, Lucy got up.

As she showered, all she could think about was Joaquin. How could she have fallen so much in love in the space of a week? But then it had been a strange, intense and very eventful week, and Joaquin was really quite unique. As she donned a navy shift dress she was recalling her last memories of the previous night. It had still been dark the last time he had made love to her. His passionate urgency had set her on fire but burned her out. She had slept, and that must have been when he'd shifted her back to her own bed.

A yawn crept up on Lucy. But, tired as she was, she was determined to show up for the computer training which Dominga had mentioned. She didn't want Joaquin to think that she would try to take advantage of their new intimacy. It was ironic, she thought ruefully. It wasn't for her sister's benefit alone that she was now keen to prove that she was neither lazy nor unreliable.

Hopeful of running into Joaquin, Lucy went downstairs in search of breakfast. However, a maid showed her into a grand and imposing dining room where she found herself eating in splendid isolation. The bubbly sense of happiness she was containing was entirely new to her. She didn't want to examine how she was feeling too closely. She didn't want to let other more threatening thoughts intrude. *He doesn't even know who you are*, an unwelcome little voice whispered regardless at the back of her mind. In panic, she squashed the reminder and closed it out.

Dominga wasn't quite quick enough to hide her surprise at Lucy's arrival. Evidently the older woman had not expected her to show up for work again. She had definitely been seen with Joaquin in the courtyard the night before. How many of the staff suspected that she had spent the night in his bedroom? Lucy paled at those all too realistic concerns and hurriedly shelved them. Somewhere in the back of her mind she was painfully aware that she had broken every rule she had ever respected, but the intoxicating happiness which filled her whenever she thought about Joaquin was far more powerful.

A young male whizzkid arrived to give her the basic training she had been promised on the computer. But Lucy found it incredibly hard to concentrate. Should she have sought Joaquin out before breakfast? Or would that have seemed too pushy? Was she supposed to wait until he came looking for her?

Late morning, Joaquin finally put in an appearance by coming in to speak to his secretary. The instant he entered Lucy's heartbeat speeded up. She almost rose from her seat before she recalled that they had an audience. Feeling bound to stay where she was and allow him to make the first move, she pinned her gaze to his tall powerful figure. His dark grey business suit was superbly tailored to his athletic frame but very formal. For perhaps the first time Lucy recognised *who* Joaquin Del Castillo was. He was a powerful and wealthy industrialist, light years distant from her in status, and finally facing that reality dismayed her.

But, just as quickly, Lucy recovered her confidence. She remembered Joaquin laughing with her the night before, hugging her close with the easy physical affection that was so natural to him and so powerfully appealing to her, and she lifted her head high again.

She waited for him to finish speaking to Dominga. The seconds passed, her tension steadily climbing. His bold bronzed profile looked remote and serious. She wanted to see his eyes. She was just desperate to meet his eyes. But it didn't happen. A moment later Joaquin had strolled back out again without so much as a glance or nod in her direction.

Lucy sagged. He hadn't seen her...of course, he hadn't seen her! She was barely visible seated behind the computer monitor, she told herself ruefully. He might even think she was still in bed. He wouldn't ignore her, would he? Could that be his idea of being discreet? Sort of *super-super-discreet*?

Tortured by such uncertainty, Lucy found that the lunch break seemed to be a long time in coming. But, as soon as it did arrive, Lucy headed straight up the corridor towards Joaquin's office. However, several yards from the ajar door of his office, she realised Yolanda was back; the girl was shouting at the top of her voice. She paused, winced at the chilling timbre of Joaquin's no doubt withering response.

Just as she was about to move on and abandon any attempts to see him, the door flew back on its hinges and Yolanda stalked out, slamming the door shut behind her again. Her stunning face was flushed and streaked with tears. 'I might as well be a *slave*!' she gasped on the back of a distraught sob. 'Joaquin's threatening to take my allowance away. Even my money is not my own. I feel so humiliated!'

'Oh, Yolanda, please don't get so upset…' Without hesitation, Lucy closed a comforting arm round the weeping brunette's waist, which was about as high she could comfortably reach. 'I'm sure he doesn't mean it—'

'Then you don't know my brother,' the brunette whispered raggedly. 'He says that it is his *right* to tell me how to live my life and that I have had too much freedom—'

'Too much?' Lucy was surprised, for on the face of it it didn't seem to her that Joaquin's sister had any freedom at all. Except perhaps in the matter of her fairly noticeable wardrobe.

'Now I am to go nowhere without a chaperon,' Yolanda shared with shuddering mortification. 'At my age! I'll be a laughing stock!'

As the brunette pinned her quivering lips together and turned away, Lucy's heart went out to her. A *chaperon*? In this century? Lucy wasn't surprised the other woman was distraught. Even allowing for cultural differences, Joaquin was treating his sister like a wayward child who had to be kept down and controlled. It was natural for Yolanda fight for independence.

Her brow furrowing on that straying thought, Lucy knocked on the door of Joaquin's office. When there was no response, she went in. Joaquin was standing with his back to the door. Even his well-cut jacket couldn't conceal the powerful tension etched into his broad shoulders. As she entered, he swung round, blazing anger in his shimmering green eyes.

Intimidated, Lucy stilled and watched his darkly handsome features freeze, his brilliant eyes narrow and shutter.

'How may I help you?' Joaquin drawled flatly.

That distant invitation, which carried not a shred of intimacy, made Lucy's cheeks burn as if she had been guilty of some awful *faux pas*. 'Maybe this isn't the best moment to…well, er—'

'Why wouldn't it be the best moment?' Joaquin enquired even more coolly.

Lucy worried at her lower lip, nervous perspiration dampening her skin. She was so tense her muscles ached. Suddenly her attempt to see him seemed like a dreadfully forward move and the ultimate in mistakes. 'I know that you and Yolanda have just had a bit of an argument,' she admitted awkwardly.

'That is no concern of yours,' Joaquin countered with chilling reserve.

'Of course not, but…' Lucy's voice petered out; she honestly didn't know what to say. This was not the passionate teasing male who had held her in his arms and made love to her only hours earlier.

The silence lay like a dead weight between them.

'You thought sharing my bed last night gives you some special privileges?' Joaquin enquired with smooth derision, an ebony brow slanting.

Every scrap of colour drained from Lucy's face. That contemptuous question hit her squarely where it hurt. In the same moment she lost her naive faith in what she had believed they had shared and she was badly shaken. She felt her knees tremble, her tummy perform a sick somersault.

'Well, possibly one special privilege,' Lucy framed with

strained dignity as she backed towards the door. 'That you would have the good manners not to throw that in my face!'

Suddenly Joaquin unfroze and strode forward to intercept her. 'Lucy…' he grated.

She didn't want to look at him, but she couldn't stop looking at him. Shock was trammelling through her in stricken waves. A faint line of colour accentuated the taut slant of his superb cheekbones. His lean strong face was all angles and tension, a tiny muscle pulling at the corner of his sensual mouth. He had partially lifted one brown hand as though he intended to touch her, but he dropped it back to his side.

'This situation is untenable,' he murmured with harsh clarity. 'Stop playing games, Lucy. Accept defeat, sign that agreement and go back to London.'

'But I—'

'*Por Dios*…I will not conduct an affair with you while my sister is under the same roof,' Joaquin stated with distaste, his strong jawline squaring. 'Last night was complete madness!'

She saw that too now. All of a sudden it was clear as crystal. Surely only temporary insanity could have convinced her otherwise? And it added a whole new dimension to her suffering to appreciate that he had reached that decision long before she had. Without another word, for she wasn't capable of saying anything more, she walked out of his office again.

CHAPTER SEVEN

LUCY found herself back in her bedroom without any recollection of having actually taken herself upstairs.

She lowered herself shakily into a chair and stared into space. She had behaved like a idiot, she decided. Joaquin had called their intimacy complete madness, but he didn't know the half of it, did he? Joaquin still believed she was Cindy Paez, heartless fraudster and goodtime girl. She plunged upright again, suddenly desperate to reclaim her *own* reputation, her *own* identity by telling him the truth. Then shame and reason reclaimed her and she dropped back into the chair again to cover her face with her hands in a gesture of frustration.

She had promised that she would protect Cindy. She had promised that she would not betray her. Cindy needed time to sort out her finances and time to work out how and when she would tell Roger about the fix she was in. Lucy had promised her twin that breathing space. In any case, only a fool would imagine that Joaquin would greet a confession to the deception Lucy and her twin had engaged in with anything other than even greater outrage and disgust.

Whichever way Lucy looked at the situation, she saw that her boats had been burnt the very first day she had met Joaquin Del Castillo and allowed him to believe that she was Mario Paez's widow. Since the moment she had met Joaquin she had been lying her stupid head off! Tough luck that she had then fallen head over heels in love with him. But she needn't kid herself that Joaquin would find her any more attractive as Lucy Fabian. In thinking along that line she was being pathetic and trying to avoid the real issue, which was…

Joaquin had *dumped* her.

Joaquin had *ditched* her.

Joaquin had *rejected* her.

The fantasy world she had allowed herself to live in for the past eighteen hours had, as a result, just collapsed round her ears. She had been a one-night stand. Not even one full night, she reflected in even greater mortification. He had tossed her out of his bed before dawn and now he wanted her out of his house *and* his country as well. A man couldn't make his feelings much clearer than that!

She had brought it all on herself too! Had she imagined that sex would be the magic way to Joaquin's heart? She cringed, bitterly angry at her own weakness. All the regret that she felt she should have experienced earlier in the day now filled her. She had allowed Joaquin Del Castillo to use her for an evening of entertainment. But how did she blame him when she had virtually offered herself on a plate? It wasn't as if he had even pretended that he wanted a real relationship or anything like that. No one single lie had he told her. And yet *still* she had gone to bed with him! How was she ever going to come to terms with that humiliating truth?

A maid knocked and entered with an envelope.

Rising to reach for it, Lucy turned it over and frowned, registering that it had not come through the post. Only when she had opened it did she realise what it was. The wretched repayment agreement which Joaquin had first faced her with in Fidelio's tumbledown home! What the heck was she supposed to do with it when she *couldn't* sign it?

She had to phone her sister again: she had no other choice. Leaving her bedroom, she just walked straight across the corridor. The door of a guestroom opposite her own was lying wide, clearly in the process of being aired. Lucy dialled Cindy's London apartment.

'I thought you weren't going to ring again!' Her twin gasped accusingly.

'Have you spoken to Roger yet?' Lucy frowned momentarily as she was distracted by a loud click on the line.

'How am I supposed to do that when he's in Germany?' Cindy demanded.

Lucy had totally forgotten that fact. Only now did she remember her sister complaining about the fact that Roger's firm was sending him to Berlin for a fortnight and that he wouldn't be back until just before their wedding. 'Sorry, I—'

'Look, there's been a cash offer of the asking price on your flat and I've accepted it. I intend to tell Roger that I'm giving *you* the money.'

Lucy tensed in disbelief at the news. 'But—'

'When really I'll be transfering the funds to Fidelio's bank in Guatemala. OK? Are you satisfied now?'

'You need to tell Roger the truth, Cindy,' Lucy protested.

'No, I don't,' Cindy snapped angrily. 'All *you* have to do now is convince Del Castillo that that is *all* I can afford to repay.'

'I don't think Joaquin will accept that.'

'How can you be such a wimp when I'm depending on you?' Cindy condemned. 'In fact, it strikes me that you've already made one hell of a mess of things out there!'

Lucy paled, her stomach knotting. 'I've done everything I could, Cindy—'

'*Everything but tell her where to get off!*' The unexpected intervention of another female voice on the line gave Lucy such a shock that she dropped the receiver as if she had been burnt by it. Yolanda?

Lucy looked on aghast as Joaquin's sister strolled into the room, cool as a cucumber. She had a cordless phone clamped to her ear, a phone which she was still actually talking into. 'You've got some nerve, Cindy Paez...sending Lucy over here like the sacrificial lamb, so that you can save your own precious skin!'

'Yolanda?' Lucy gasped, grabbing for the receiver she had dropped to see if her twin was still on the line. *'Cindy?'*

'Who...was...that?' Cindy mumbled, sounding as aghast as Lucy felt.

Across the room the brunette made a production out of lowering her phone to show that she had said all she intended to say.

'Never mind,' Lucy said shakily. 'Bye, Cindy.'

'Let's go for a walk,' Yolanda suggested with an amused look, as if discovering that Lucy was an imposter was of no serious importance.

In a daze, Lucy followed her downstairs. Yolanda walked into a magnificent drawing room, closed the door and settled herself down on an antique sofa.

'How did you find out?' Lucy fixed strained eyes on her companion and stayed upright.

'Easy-peasy. Before you came back upstairs I went into your bag, dug out your passport and *looked*! Then I checked your travel wallet and found this sweet mini photo album. Inside it there's a picture of twin baby girls, and another of you and your sister as grown-ups.' Yolanda rolled her eyes with decided scorn over such sentimentality.

'So now you're going to tell your brother—'

'Not necessarily...'

Lucy blinked and focused with widened eyes on the young Guatemalan woman. 'But—'

Yolanda shrugged. 'Joaquin's sure to find out eventually. Why should I get involved? Why should I be the one to blow the whistle?'

Lucy breathed in deep, thinking fast. Right now, Yolanda was at daggers drawn with her brother. Did it give the volatile brunette a kick to know that she had found out the truth about Lucy while *he* was still in the dark?

'I mean one way or another your silly sister will end up paying, because Joaquin doesn't quit.'

'Cindy's not silly...she's just *scared*!' Seeing Yolanda stiffen at that contradiction, Lucy sighed. 'All right, let me tell you the whole story, and then maybe you'll understand.'

Yolanda listened with keen interest, but demonstrated not the slightest sympathy for Cindy's plight. 'I still don't see why *you* should be taking the heat for *her*.'

'Cindy didn't plan it that way.'

'But she's anything but sorry that it's turned out that way!' Yolanda scanned Lucy's troubled face and shook her head in apparent wonderment. 'You're just too nice to fight your own corner. You let everybody walk all over you.'

'No, I don't—'

'What am I doing right now? You didn't even shout at me for going through your handbag!'

Lucy gave her a rueful smile, thinking that for all her sophistication and self-confidence the other woman could occasionally sound very naive. 'I've got more important things to worry about.'

'No, you just need a fast-track escape from Joaquin and I can give it to you,' Yolanda announced.

Incredulity at that announcement blossomed in Lucy's eyes.

Her beautiful companion reddened. 'Well, what's the use of you staying on here? You can't sign that agreement and you can't leave without help.'

'But you're Joaquin's sister,' Lucy heard herself mutter helplessly.

'Half-sister,' Yolanda qualified, tossing her head, her full mouth compressing. 'I'm not being disloyal; I'm just suiting myself. Big Bro will be on your sister's tracks no matter what happens, and there's nothing you can do about that.'

There was an awful truth to that assurance and it made Lucy shiver. She could only hope that that bank transfer of cash which her twin had mentioned would be sufficient to put Joaquin Del Castillo in a more reasonable frame of mind where Fidelio Paez was concerned. But she still could not understand why Yolanda should be offering to help her.

'How would it suit *you* to help me to leave?' Lucy asked with wide eyes.

'That's my affair. But you have only a few hours to make up your mind. Joaquin's leaving for a business meeting in New York later this afternoon, but he'll back by tomorrow night. I certainly couldn't help you to vanish while he's still around!'

Joaquin's half-sister rose and glided with fluid steps back to the door. 'So it's up to you, Lucy. Seems to me you haven't got many options, because if you *don't* decide to go I will probably feel that I have to tell Joaquin that he's got the nice twin instead of the nasty one!'

Lucy's tummy clenched at that unashamed threat. She hurried to the door, but Yolanda was already heading back upstairs. It was clear that as far as the brunette was concerned the interview was at an end. So what *was* Lucy going to do?

Not knowing whether she was on her head or her heels, she wandered back down to the office. As the staff were taking the long lunch break favoured in hot climates, it was empty. She sat down at her workstation and drew in a deep breath, trying to calm herself down. If she didn't sign that repayment agreement Joaquin would get really, really furious, and Lucy felt that she had already made enough of a fool of herself without being forced to hang around where she most definitely was *not* wanted.

At the same time, however, if she performed a vanishing

act without signing she might well bring down Joaquin on Cindy's head before the wedding. But wasn't Roger safe in Germany right now? If she left a letter behind promising that bank transfer her twin had mentioned, wouldn't that satisfy Joaquin for a week or two at least? He was a hugely important and busy guy. How likely was it that he would drop everything and race over to London immediately?

The door opened. Joaquin stilled on the threshold.

Lucy collided with his spectacular eyes, watched them narrow and veil. It hurt, it really hurt her to see the cold distance in his gaze. And right at that minute, when she herself was aware of him with every fibre of her being, the pain felt just about unbearable.

'What are you doing in here?' Joaquin demanded with sardonic bite.

'I didn't feel like lunch—'

'*Por Dios*…you would put up with *anything* sooner than agree to strip yourself of your ill-gotten gains!' Joaquin condemned with slashing contempt. 'However, if you're determined to play this charade out to the bitter end, you might as well make yourself useful.'

'Useful?'

Joaquin settled a sheet of paper down on the desk beside her. 'Turn up that file and print it out for me.'

Her teeth plucking at her lower lip as she struggled to utilise what she had learnt earlier and perform the task, Lucy found herself wondering why she was bothering. Who was she trying to impress? Where was her pride? He was behaving like an absolute louse. She was rigid with the force of her pent-up emotions. She shifted on the seat, reminded by the intimate ache of her body that Joaquin had enjoyed a most thorough acquaintance with it before developing convenient but *very* belated regrets.

'Are you planning to take all day over this one minor request for output?' Joaquin demanded icily.

Her hands suddenly lifted off the keyboard and balled into fists which she slammed back down on the keyboard again. 'Stop talking to me like that!' she practically shrieked at him as she jumped out of her seat, temper erupting from the emotional turmoil she had been fighting to contain. 'I've got the message...OK?'

'You'll have got the message when you sign that agreement,' Joaquin countered, with a cool that she would have found formidable had she been in a calmer frame of mind.

'For goodness' sake—'

'Once you sign, I may...I just *may* consider calling on you the next time I'm over in London,' Joaquin imparted flatly.

Totally disconcerted by that assurance, Lucy blinked. 'I don't understand—'

'Don't you?' Joaquin vented a cynical laugh, his lean strong features hardening. 'You appeal to the very worst side of my nature, *querida*. If I can contrive to withstand temptation, you won't ever see me again.'

Lucy's soft mouth opened and closed again in slow motion.

Joaquin's jewelled eyes wandered in a leisurely appraisal over her slight slender frame, lingering on the firm swell of her small breasts and the highly feminine curve of waist and hip so well defined by the deceptively simple shift dress she wore. By the time he had completed that increasingly bold evaluation of what they both knew he had an infinitely more intimate acquaintance with, Lucy's cheeks were scarlet and her hands were knotted into defensive fists.

But at that moment it was herself she was fighting rather than him. His potent magnetism was firing the atmosphere between them. That suggestion that he might see her again in London had thrown her, leaving her in no fit state to muster her defences. Her mouth was dry and her heartbeat had accelerated.

Spiky ebony lashes semi-screened his slumbrous green gaze, his beautiful mouth taking on a sensual curve which was all too familiar to her. 'On the other hand,' Joaquin mused in a husky undertone roughened by all-male satisfaction, 'I'm single and I can afford you. Why should I deny myself the occasional indulgence?'

An indulgence? Lucy thought of chocolate as an indulgence, but she had never thought of herself in that line. *I can afford you.* She could not credit that she had sunk low enough to be faced with such an offensive statement. That Joaquin even felt confident enough to say that to her appalled her. Then she met those brilliant knowing eyes of his and she paled to the colour of parchment and finally understood. Joaquin Del Castillo was supremely well aware of his power over her. It was the final humiliation and it chilled her physical response to his presence.

'You think I...you think I care about you,' she said unsteadily.

Joaquin spread fluidly expressive hands in a gesture that was anything but an indication of humility.

'And you are ready to *use* that to make me do what you want?' she framed, in quivering disbelief that any male could be that cruelly manipulative.

Joaquin gave her a measured nod of confirmation.

Lucy folded her arms in a jerky motion. She thought of the way she had behaved the previous night. She was no actress, and had had no idea of playing it cool. She had probably betrayed herself a hundred times over in the way she'd looked at him and what she had both said and done. At the very least, he knew that she was keen. No longer could she meet his eyes. She was deeply shaken by the degrading proposition he was outlining to her.

'I *do* understand your shocked sense of injustice, *querida*,' Joaquin murmured silkily. 'How many times have you run rings round men crazy for you? But this time around it's going to be different.'

Lucy stepped out from behind the workstation separating them, two coins of high colour adorning her taut cheek-bones. 'If you think for one moment that I'd be stupid enough to let you reduce me to the level of some tramp you spend the night with whenever you feel like it—'

'Such emotive words,' Joaquin sliced in, smooth as glass. 'Yet you set no boundaries last night. You wanted me too much to be sensible or calculating and it paid dividends, *es verdad*? For what I am now offering you is an arrangement to which you are uniquely well suited—'

'No, I'm not!' Lucy gasped in stricken outrage.

Shrugging a wide muscular shoulder in a very Latin dismissal of that protest, Joaquin continued to rest his incisive green eyes on her angry face. 'In this life we all end up settling for the best we can get. So choose between me and the money you conned out of Fidelio. You can have one but not *both*. And if you choose me, it will be only on my terms.'

'I just can't believe you're talking like this to me!' Lucy confessed with raw honesty.

'Isn't it marvellous that you should still possess that endearing little streak of almost child-like innocence when things don't pan out quite the way you planned them?' A grim smile flashed across his devastatingly handsome features as he paused by the door. ' No man in his right mind would keep you in an office, *querida*. When you punched the keyboard you crashed the whole system. I'll have to contact my head office in London to get those figures now.'

In a daze, Lucy focused on the monitor, which had gone all blurry and now bore a large error message. The other two computer monitors bore similar messages as well. Momentarily she closed her eyes to get a grip on her seething emotions. But Joaquin had knocked her sideways. He had a head office of some kind in London? How often *was* he in London? Dismayed by thoughts that should have no place in her head, she experienced a burst of self-loathing. Even if Joaquin Del Castillo was in London every blasted week she would never willingly set eyes on him again! He was so sure of himself, so certain he had her where he wanted her. Well, he would soon find out that she learnt from her mistakes!

Lucy went off in search of Yolanda, and with the assistance of a maid eventually ran her to earth in a custom-built gym where the gorgeous brunette was doing what appeared to be graceful ballet exercises at a bar.

'I've thought over what you've said,' Lucy proclaimed, coming to a breathless halt several feet away. 'I'll take your help...I want to go home!'

As that last phrase emerged, more in the nature of an over-emotional wail, Yolanda stilled to stare at Lucy. 'So Joaquin's been spreading his special variety of joy and happiness in your direction as well.'

'This has got nothing to do with your wretched brother!' Lucy snapped, rather foolishly in the circumstances.

Yolanda's attention had already strayed. Her lustrous brown eyes glowed with satisfaction. 'I'd love to see Joaquin's face when he realises that we've *both* done a vanishing act!'

CHAPTER EIGHT

BY LATE evening of the same day, Lucy had learnt just how hard and embarrassing it could be to perform a vanishing act in which Yolanda Del Castillo played a leading role.

Noting with relief that the volatile girl was now asleep, Lucy subsided back into her own comfortable seat on the plane. Just an hour into a flight to London, Lucy was counting the cost: her nerves were in shreds and she was exhausted. Yet Yolanda had engineered their departure from Hacienda De Oro with remarkable efficiency.

While Lucy had sweated blood over the writing of an explanatory letter to Joaquin concerning the cash transfer which Cindy had promised for Fidelio, Yolanda's maid had packed for Lucy and whisked away her suitcase. She had then been shown down to a rear exit. Outside had sat a four-wheel drive with Yolanda in the back seat.

'Lucy, hurry up and drive off before we're seen!' she had urged.

That was when Lucy had discovered why she had been so essential to Yolanda's plans. Yolanda had seen Lucy's driving licence in her handbag.

'Of course I do not drive myself,' the brunette had responded when Lucy had voiced her surprise. 'I am always driven, but if I ask one of the staff to take me to the airport Joaquin will find out long before I get there!'

Lucy had found that long drive a nightmare. She had never driven such a huge car before, nor had she had prior experience of driving on a different side of the road. Then there had been the horrors of the busy traffic in Guatemala city, the wrong turns she had made, the cars that had hooted furiously at her. Lucy had been a nervous wreck by the time they'd finally reached the airport. But there had been worse to come…

Even two hours after the event, Lucy just cringed at the memory of the dreadful scene Yolanda had thrown when she'd been told there were no seats left on the flight she wanted to board. She had proclaimed that she was Yolanda Del Castillo at the top of her voice. She had ranted and raved until she'd got what she wanted. She had also insisted that Lucy's economy class ticket be upgraded.

'Joaquin is held in huge regard in my country. They will bump other passengers off the flight for my benefit,' Yolanda had forecast smugly. 'After all, it is a great honour that I, a Del Castillo, should travel on their airline!'

That forecast had proved correct. Then Yolanda had thrown *another* tantrum on boarding, to ensure that they secured the most spacious front seats in the first class section. Two middle-aged businessmen had scuttled into other seats like mice. Worst of all, Lucy had received censorious glances from other passengers, as if they somehow imagined she ought to be cooling Yolanda's outrageous behaviour.

No longer was Lucy surprised that Joaquin had been playing the heavy big brother with his demanding sister. Yolanda was immature—outright uncontrollable if she was crossed—and terrifyingly unscrupulous. More like a nightmare teenager than an adult, Lucy conceded inwardly. Had great wealth and too much indulgence made Yolanda that way? Had Joaquin been trying hard to straighten his sister out?

'I really like you, Lucy,' Yolanda had confided before she'd gone to sleep. 'When I've set up my own apartment in London you can come and visit me if you want.'

Lucy just couldn't understand why she was feeling so

responsible for Yolanda all of a sudden, but it seemed to her that in spite of her stunning looks and seeming sophistication Yolanda was woefully unsuited to the independence and freedom she craved.

With every airborne mile that carried her further from Guatemala and Joaquin, Lucy got more and more miserable. How would Cindy feel about her coming home without having sorted out her twin's problems in the way she had hoped and expected? Joaquin would be even more furious that Lucy had vanished along with his temperamental sister. It just seemed that no matter what she did, she did it wrong…

'I'll call you when I have time,' Yolanda promised as her cases were loaded into the cab which Lucy had procured for her outside Heathrow. 'Don't expect to hear from me *too* soon, though. Socially, I shall be very much in demand.'

Lucy went straight to her sister's apartment. Cindy was stunned to find her on the doorstep, but her first reaction after she overcame her astonishment was to give Lucy a relieved hug. 'Thank goodness you're home! Did you get everything settled?'

'Not quite—'

'You didn't sign that agreement, did you?'

Lucy shook her head and explained the situation she had left behind. While engaged in making a welcome cup of tea for her twin, Cindy listened anxiously and then began to look perplexed.

'Why do you keep on saying his name that way?'

'Whose name?'

'*Joaquin*…'

Lucy flushed. 'I'm not saying it *any* way. He was just pretty central to events, that's all.'

Her twin refused to be sidetracked. 'Are you telling me

that you went and *fell* for the guy who's trying to wreck my life?'

'With a little bit of luck it won't come to that if you settle this business with Mario's father once and for all.'

'I *will*. I saw a solicitor yesterday and he'll handle it. But right now it's *you* I'm more interested in.'

'I just want to forget I ever went to Guatemala,' Lucy muttered truthfully.

Silence lay for a second or two.

Then Cindy shrugged. 'Well, if Del Castillo comes here looking to cause more trouble, he won't find me. I've been hired by a film unit that starts shooting in Scotland this weekend and I have to be at the studios in another hour!'

'Sounds like fun…' Lucy concealed her disappointment that her twin was leaving almost as soon as she herself arrived.

'But it means I won't be here to help you get your flat packed up. The buyer wants possession as soon as possible. And the sooner he gets in, the sooner Fidelio gets his cash,' Cindy pointed out. 'I haven't decided yet what I'm going to tell Roger.'

'You know…I thought you'd be furious with me for just coming home.'

Cindy grimaced, her colour heightening. 'Yolanda fairly put me in my box with what she said on the phone. Why *should* you take the heat for me? I'm sorry that I got you into this mess in the first place,' she admitted ruefully. 'My sins have come back to haunt me and I'll just have to handle the fall-out as best I can.'

With that one brief and effective little speech, Lucy felt the difference between her twin and her more impressionable and anxious self. Cindy might have panicked when she'd first learnt about Fidelio's predicament and Joaquin's demands, but ultimately Cindy rolled with the punches and took each day as it came.

Thirty minutes later, seated in the cab which would take her back to the flat she had once shared with her mother, Lucy sighed. The crowded city streets and the cold dull winter weather seemed a poor exchange for the lush beauty of a colourful country like Guatemala. But she had her sister's wedding to look forward to, and then Christmas, she reminded herself. Hadn't she always loved the festive season? But Roger and Cindy would still be away on their honeymoon and Christmas would be rather lonely...

Two busy weeks later, Lucy moved into her sister's apartment. Cindy was still not home. Her twin had finished working with the film unit but she was currently in Oxford, staying with Roger's parents, to where he would return from Germany. Their wedding was now only three days away and, thanks to the organisational skills of Cindy's future mother-in-law, her sister had virtually no last-minute details to check.

Within ten minutes of sitting down in her sister's lounge mid-morning, to take a break from unpacking, Lucy fell asleep. When she woke up again, she was exasperated with herself. Why was she so tired all the time? In addition, her tummy was out of sorts and she had had a couple of minor dizzy spells as well.

As she had tried to explain to her doctor forty-eight hours earlier, it wasn't that she felt exactly ill, more that she just didn't feel quite *right*. Had she some infection which she had yet to shake off? Her doctor had done some tests. She was to phone later to get the results, she reminded herself ruefully.

The intercom buzzed as she was making up a bed for herself in the spare room. Walking out to the hall, she caught her reflection in the full-length mirror on the wall. Gosh, she looked drab and washed out! After the experience of wearing her twin's designer garments, she had become uncomfortably aware of how dowdy her own clothing was. Her blue tunic sweater and long skirt might be warm and comfy but they had neither shape nor style.

However, she was stuck with the wardrobe she had. Right now, she was poor as a church mouse, and she had more pressing priorities. Although she had managed to find a temporary job as an assistant in a toy store over the Christmas period, and was starting work the day after the wedding, she still needed to find somewhere of her own to live.

'Yes…?' she said into the intercom.

'Buzz me up…' Joaquin drawled in the most lethally intimidating tone.

Lucy froze. Instant recognition of his dark deep drawl sent her into a mindless tailspin. 'B-but—'

'*Now*, Lucy!' Joaquin thundered without hesitation.

In a total daze, she hit the button. There was just no stopping the soaring sense of joy and excitement washing over her. *He was here in London!* All right, so he didn't sound as if he was in the best of moods, but any minute she was going to see him. She opened the door and turned in a dizzy little circle and then stilled in guilty dismay. What the heck was she thinking of?

Laying eyes on Joaquin Del Castillo again would put her right back to the beginning of the recovery process. Not that she had travelled that far along the road to recovery, she conceded reluctantly. After all, she still thought about Joaquin at least once every five minutes, and in particularly weak moments almost constantly. But, like it or not, Joaquin did not feel the same way about her. So it would be foolish for her to feed her craving for him with further exposure.

Just as she heard the lift doors whirring back on the landing, Lucy went to close the apartment door again.

'Sorry, I just don't think this is a good idea, but you could always phone me—'

Joaquin took her totally aback by forging forward regardless. Thrusting the door wide enough for entrance, he simply lifted her out of his path and set her down again before she could offer any further objection. 'Right, where is Yolanda?' he demanded with raw impatience.

Disconcerted by his aggressive attitude, and flustered by being lifted off her feet like an exasperating but minor obstruction, Lucy just gaped at him. Joaquin looked as if he had been through hell since she had last seen him. His brilliant eyes were shadowed. His stunning cheekbones were sharper and fierce lines of tension bracketed his taut mouth as he studied her with charged expectancy.

Yolanda! Lucy was sharply disappointed and felt that she should have been better prepared for that demand. Naturally he was angry that his sister had left home in defiance of his wishes. And, being Joaquin, an autocrat to his fingertips, he obviously wasn't going to let the matter lie. Even so, Lucy was jolted by the sense of rejection she experienced at the reality that his visit had nothing to do with her personally.

She was very pale. 'I really don't think I can tell you where your sister is without her permission—'

'Either you tell me or you tell the police!' Joaquin shot back at her without hesitation.

'The p-police...?' Lucy repeated in a wobbly burst of incredulity at such a threat.

'I am outraged by your behaviour in this business,' Joaquin informed her, his strong jawline clenching hard. 'How could you help Yolanda to run away from home? She left me a letter telling me that she was returning to school. Fool that I am, I was so relieved that I did not even check her story! Then I waited a week to let the dust settle before I tried to call her.'

Like a woman turned to stone, Lucy mumbled thickly, 'School?'

But Joaquin was still talking. He drove an angry hand through his thick black hair and focused on her with shimmering green eyes full of condemnation. 'When I discovered that she hadn't returned to school I assumed that she was with you. This apartment has been under surveillance ever since then. I have been awaiting your return.'

'*School?*' Lucy said a second time with greater stress as Joaquin strode past her into the lounge. She followed him. 'Why are you talking about Yolanda going back to school?'

'Where else should a sixteen-year-old be?' Joaquin demanded wrathfully.

'A *sixteen*-year-old…she can't be…no, there is no way she can be just sixteen!' Lucy protested, gazing back at him with disbelieving eyes.

'Where the hell *is* she?' Joaquin launched at her again.

Shock and the most appalling feeling of guilt assailed Lucy. The depth of his anxious concern for his sister's welfare was patent. She had been taken in by a teenager playing a role that had come easily to a young girl raised in the lap of luxury and indulgence. Aware that Lucy was impressed by that act, Yolanda had ensured that she stayed fooled. When Lucy had finally got around to asking what age the brunette was on that drive to the airport, Yolanda had lied and said she was twenty-one. But why, when she had actually witnessed the other girl's wilful moods and immaturity, had she not put two and two together and at least *suspected* the truth?

'I honestly didn't know what age she was, Joaquin. Oh, my goodness, what an idiot I've been!' Lucy exclaimed, biting at her lower lip and shaking her head.

Joaquin closed lean hands round her forearms. 'All I need to know right now is *where* my sister is. Much will be forgiven if she is safe and unharmed.'

'She phones me most days.' Lucy dashed the sudden rush of tears from her strained eyes. 'Last week she flew to Paris to visit some friend called Loretta—'

Releasing her, Joaquin produced a portable phone. 'What is Loretta's surname?'

'I don't know, and it hardly matters because Yolanda is back in London again. For goodness' sake, she spent most of yesterday with me!' Lucy confessed. 'She said that she was in a hotel, but she didn't say where and I never thought to ask. She seemed rather lonely, and I would've asked her to stay here with me, but—'

'It might have cramped your style?' Joaquin slotted in with fierce derision.

Lucy paled at that crack. But she could not explain that the apartment was not hers without admitting that she was *not* Cindy Paez, and at that moment there were more important things to worry about. Genuinely agitated by what Joaquin had divulged, and feeling very much to blame, Lucy sank down giddily into an armchair.

'Have you a contact number for Yolanda?' Joaquin shot at her.

'No…she's always called me,' Lucy admitted heavily. 'Joaquin, I *swear* I hadn't a clue how young she was!'

But Joaquin was no longer listening: he was on his phone talking in urgent Spanish. His bold bronzed profile stood out in sharp relief against the pale wall behind him. He moved one hand expressively as he spoke, spreading his long fingers, closing them again while restively pacing the floor. She had forgotten his vibrant energy, the way he seemed to take over and dominate a room the minute he entered it. A tide of tormented awareness which she would have done anything to suppress washed over her.

'What phone number will Yolanda be using to contact you…the one here?' Joaquin swung back to her to demand.

'No…' Lucy breathed in deep to explain, but embarrassed colour now put to flight her previous pallor. 'Yesterday was my birthday and she gave me a mobile phone as a present. She said she was fed up not being able to get hold of me when she wanted me...she hasn't called me on it yet, though.'

'Then, you and your phone can come back to *my* London home with me! *Por Dios*...don't you dare try to argue with me!' Joaquin warned with ruthless bite as her lips parted in dismay. 'I'm not letting you out of my sight until I get my sister back and you are the only lead I have right now!'

Feeling as responsible as she did over a situation which she had helped to create, Lucy got up without argument. 'I'll get changed.'

Joaquin scrutinised her slender taut figure, a deep frown line slowly forming between his dark brows. 'Why are you dressed that way?'

'What way?'

'Like some older woman who doesn't care how she looks any more,' he extended with a questioning slant of an ebony brow.

Lucy edged out of the lounge without responding. Joaquin had finally had the opportunity to see her as she *really* was and he wasn't exactly thrilled by the view. Shorn of her twin's fine feathers, she had lost any claim to glamour. On that galling thought, she hurried into her sister's room. There she picked out a black skirt, a soft turquoise twinset and a pair of high heels. She refused to think about why she was raiding her twin's wardrobe in the midst of a crisis in which her appearance should be the very last thing on her mind.

Joaquin tilted back his arrogant dark head to study her as she made her breathless return, clutching a small travel bag. She could feel her face burning as he appraised the snug fit of fine wool over her breasts and the slim length of leg now on view. Suddenly wishing that the floor would open and swallow her, Lucy turned away. Talk about being obvious! Rushing to put on a more flattering outfit had to have given him a very clear message as to her susceptibility, but to her relief he made no comment as she locked up the apartment.

Out on the street, a limousine awaited them. Lucy settled back into the rich leather upholstery, striving to act as if she travelled in similar style every day.

'You're lucky that I didn't involve the police in this,' Joaquin delivered without warning, throwing her a grim glance that made her back into the furthest corner of the seat. 'My sister is a very rich young woman. Had you not accompanied her back to London, I would have been afraid that she had been kidnapped when she failed to show up at school. But, though I have little faith in your moral principles, I did not believe that you would put Yolanda at risk.'

'For the last time,' Lucy groaned ruefully, 'I didn't realise she was only sixteen!'

'Isn't it strange, though, that in spite of that age-gap the two of you seem to be very much on the same wavelength?' Joaquin drawled in a sardonic aside.

Lucy decided to ignore that crack. 'Is Yolanda's mother over here with you?'

Joaquin vented a cynical laugh. 'No, Beatriz isn't in London. She has no interest in what her teenage daughter does.'

Lucy frowned. 'Why?'

'Beatriz was my father's second wife and very much younger.' Joaquin murmured drily. 'When he died, he made my sister an heiress, but his will decreed that Beatriz would lose much of her income if she remarried.'

'Which she did?'

'Beatriz and her new husband then had the responsibility of handling my sister's trust fund. However, gross financial irregularities persuaded the trustees to make other arrangements when Yolanda was nine years old,' Joaquin explained with sardonic cool. 'When Beatriz was no longer in a position to rob her daughter blind, she chose to send her off to an English boarding school and more or less forget about her.'

Lucy was shaken by that unemotional rendering of unpleasant facts. 'I'd already gathered that she and her mother weren't close, but—'

'Beatriz resented having a daughter so much richer than she was herself.' Joaquin made no attempt to conceal his derision. 'Yet her present husband owns a very large and successful construction company and they are by no means poor.'

'Did you have much contact with Yolanda while she was growing up?'

'Not enough to establish the relationship which her mother was determined to discourage. But when my sister's school suspended her as a punishment—'

Lucy winced. 'What did she do?'

'She sneaked out to a nightclub and got her face splashed all over the tabloids. Where do you think the It Girl fantasy came from?' Joaquin enquired drily. 'Beatriz said she could no longer cope with her and sent her to me. When the suspension was up, Yolanda then refused to return to school.'

'So that's what the arguments were about,' Lucy sighed. 'I got hold of entirely the wrong end of the stick.'

The chauffeur opened the door beside her. Lucy blinked in disconcertion and scrambled out. She had been so involved in her conversation with Joaquin that she hadn't even noticed that the car had drawn to a halt outside an imposing Georgian house in a quiet residential square.

The spacious hall was beautifully furnished and very elegant. A manservant spread open the door of an equally impressive drawing room.

'Where's the phone Yolanda gave you?'

Lucy dug the cerise pink phone out of her bag and extended it.

Joaquin removed it from her hold. 'It's not even switched on!' he shot at her incredulously.

Lucy reddened. 'I haven't read all the instructions yet, but I did charge it—'

Joaquin flicked through the buttons and then set the phone down on the coffee table. 'You haven't missed any calls.'

She took a seat in an armchair. She studied the beautiful wool rug fixedly, felt her stupid eyes sting with tears. How pathetic she had been, rushing to borrow her sister's clothes like an over-excited teenager invited out on a hot date! It was so obvious that there was just nothing there for him any more. But then weren't a lot of men supposed to be like that? She was no mystery now. She was not outstandingly beautiful either. Why, she hadn't even bothered making use of the cosmetics which Cindy had painstakingly taught her to apply! That passionate night at Hacienda De Oro had been a mistake as far as Joaquin was concerned. And now, more than two weeks on? The way *he* was behaving, she might as well have dreamt up the entire encounter.

'You realise that you can't tell Yolanda I'm here when she rings,' Joaquin spelt out.

Lucy nodded.

'That you have to find out where she's staying and arrange either to go over there or to meet up somewhere? I don't want her vanishing again,' Joaquin completed.

Lucy nodded a second time.

Where were her wits? What was going on inside her head? *This* was the guy who had suggested he might call in for the occasional night of recreational sex when he was in London. Suggestions didn't come much more offensive.

In fact, if he was to lay a single finger on her she would scream and tell him exactly where to get off! Only it didn't look as if she was about to get the opportunity to demonstrate her aversion to him.

The manservant reappeared with a tray of coffee. Joaquin moved his hand in a negative motion signifying disinterest. Lucy poured a cup for herself while he paced the floor in preoccupied silence.

'*Infierno!*' Joaquin bit out, half under his breath. 'What the hell am I supposed to say to Yolanda when I *do* get hold of her?'

That driven demand touched Lucy's heart and chipped away at the barriers she was striving to raise for her own protection. She watched him spread his hands and drop them again in an expressive gesture of frustration. In his dark navy pinstriped business suit he looked so cool and elegant and distant, but his crystalline green eyes betrayed the depth of his anxiety.

'I think your sister needs to know that you love and care about her—'

'She *must* know that!'

'I'm not sure she does,' Lucy sighed. 'And try not to be confrontational. If she doesn't want to go back to school, there have to be other options that could at least be discussed.'

Joaquin elevated a derisive ebony brow. 'You want me to sit down with a big smile and tell her she can be a wild child if she wants to be?'

At that crack, Lucy abandoned her coffee and stood up. 'No, just let her know that you're willing to listen. A lot of what Yolanda says is just *talk*. She hasn't even gone to any nightclubs.'

Joaquin raised both hands in an impatient motion of dismissal, his darkly handsome features hard with resolve. 'I know what is best for my sister—'

'You've already admitted that you don't know her very well, so how *can* you know?' Lucy asked him ruefully.

He tensed and lost colour beneath his bronzed complexion, but he didn't lower his arrogant dark head one inch and his brilliant eyes reflected ice-cool scorn for that reminder.

'OK...you asked, and now you're putting me down for answering, but that attitude won't work with Yolanda. She's as stubborn and hot-tempered as you are!' Cut to the bone by that silent derision, Lucy turned away.

His lean hands came down on her rigid shoulders and slowly turned her back. She focused on his smooth gold silk tie. Long fingers curved under her chin to make her look up. 'I'm sorry, *querida*. I've never been very good at taking instruction.'

The sound of that familiar term of endearment closed Lucy's throat over. She gazed up at him, strained eyes wide and wary. 'I was tactless—'

'What you said was right. I've made mistakes...I can't afford to make many more with her...'

He was close, and she was so intent on him that she had already lost the thread of the conversation. Those beautiful eyes of his filled her with such a powerful longing to touch him that she clenched her hands by her sides to keep them there.

'Where have *you* been for the past two weeks?' Joaquin asked levelly.

'I told you in my letter...the flat—the one you said didn't exist,' she framed as a reminder. 'It's sold, but it had to be cleared for the new owner.'

'No such property appeared in the list of your assets.'

Lucy was having a real struggle to concentrate. 'Someone slipped up—'

'So it would seem.' His dark rich drawl seemed to slow

down and lower in timbre, sending a delicious shiver down her taut spinal cord.

Her lower limbs untrustworthy supports, she trembled. In the charged silence, her heartbeat had speeded up to a mile a minute. The fierce tension of her taut muscles made her all the more aware of the swollen sensitivity of her breasts and the ungovernable ache building between her thighs. Nor was she so lost to all reason that she heard no inner voice urging retreat; she heard it but blanked it out, for the craving was stronger.

'*Dios mio…*' Joaquin sounded thickly, his fingers winding into her luxuriant caramel-coloured hair to tug her head back very gently. His scorching gaze raked over her face. 'Do you know how difficult it was to put you back into your own bed that morning? I didn't like that…I didn't like being that hungry, *gatita*. I didn't like aching to have just one more chance to feel you going wild under me…'

'No?' Her voice was a mere thread, for she was mesmerized by what he was telling her.

'No,' Joaquin breathed in roughened confirmation. 'Only a weak man lets desire come between him and reason. But two weeks has been enough of a deprivation for me to feel I have more than made my point.'

'You missed me…' Lucy muttered, hanging on his every word.

'Every hour on the hour…' Joaquin let his hands drop to her hips, to skim up her skirt and then hoist her up against him. 'More cold showers than I could bear. But I know now what it is that draws me. You're like a split personality, *querida*. I'm fascinated. How could I be anything else?'

Drawn only partially from her sensual abstraction, Lucy blinked, assuming she had misunderstood. 'A split—?'

Joaquin let his tongue delve between her parted lips with an erotic expertise and promise that was not best suited to enabling her to hold up her end of a sensible conversation. She jerked against him, a stifled moan breaking low in her throat as the feverish hunger he had already ignited took fire in excitement.

'Of course, I *know* what you are…I know exactly what you're capable of,' Joaquin murmured against her cheek-bone while she was fighting to get back the strength to breathe. 'But you've honed your camouflage skills to the level of an art form.'

'I don't know what you're talking about—'

Both arms banded round her, Joaquin settled fluidly down on to a sofa with her astride him. One hand closing into her hair to tip her head back, he pressed his lips to the delicate skin just below her ear. Suddenly it felt like the most erotic spot in her whole screaming body. She gasped out loud, clutched at his hair, feeling the burn of her own excitement in sensual shock.

'Don't you?' Joaquin prompted almost roughly, framing her flushed cheekbones with both hands and holding her entrapped, scorching green eyes delving into passion-glazed violet-blue. 'You're like a chameleon and you're very clever. You give every man what he wants: in fact you *become* what he wants.'

'Joaquin, I—'

'*Silencio, por favor.*' He rested a warning fingertip against her lips.

'B-but—'

'It's the secret of your success, *querida.*' Joaquin scanned her shaken expression with satisfaction and lowered his hands again. 'Where did you swot up on Mayan ruins to impress me? In my *own* library? That romantic little dip you took in the forest, knowing that I was on your trail—'

'No…you're wrong!' Lucy was appalled by the suggestion that she had planned everything that had happened between them, had indeed waged a campaign to attract him.

'And that night in my bed you gave me the shy but eager virgin that every Latin American male fantasises about. It was an illusion, *naturally*, but it was a brilliant performance,' Joaquin assured her appreciatively as he let his sure hands stroke caressingly from her slim hips along the extended length of her taut slender thighs.

The arousing glide of his hands on her over-sensitive flesh made her tremble, but she was taken aback by the rock-solid conviction with which he spoke.

'If I didn't excite you quite so much, you would be white with shock,' Joaquin forecast with galling amusement. 'Did I neglect to mention that you can continue moulding yourself into being exactly what I want with my full support?'

'You're calling me one big fake!' Lucy condemned strickenly, and then she froze on the awareness that *that* was exactly what she was. Fake name, fake appearance, fake everything!

'Big hurt eyes and cue for tears that well up,' Joaquin labelled silkily, throwing his arrogant dark head back to study her with intense concentration while retaining his imprisoning hold on her. 'And, even though I know it's a superb act, I feel like a bastard for hurting your feelings.'

'Let go of me!' Lucy wailed, anchored to his muscular thighs in what now seemed to her to be the most mortifyingly inappropriate position.

'No…' Joaquin told her, taking her soft mouth with a sudden dark passionate force that caught her totally by surprise.

She brought her hands thumping down on his broad shoulders but somehow forgot to coil them into fists. And then that moment of resistance was gone. Her need for him was greater. Within seconds she was kissing him back with the same drugging intensity he was teaching her. Raw seething excitement gripped her. She pressed herself as close as she could get, which wasn't close enough, and with a husky growl Joaquin started rearranging her, an operation complicated by his apparent reluctance to separate from her for a single moment.

'*Por Dios*...you can set me on fire with a kiss, *querida*,' Joaquin breathed raggedly.

Lucy looked up at him, vaguely wondering how they had got to be lying down full length on the sofa, but considerably more aware of how incredibly good it felt to have the heavy masculine weight of him against her again. And then she heard a curious little metallic rendition of what sounded remarkably like the opening to the 'The Teddy Bears' Picnic'...

Just as suddenly, Joaquin thrust himself away from her and vaulted upright. He snatched up the mobile phone and extended it to her with a hand that was noticeably unsteady. 'Yolanda, it must be...make the lies good,' he urged unevenly, dulled colour lying along his taut cheekbones.

But as it turned out Lucy had no need to tell a single lie. Indeed, during the brief conversation which followed she had more trouble getting a word in edgeways. Yolanda had had her purse stolen from her bag in a shop and was in floods of tears. 'I've got no money...what do I do?' she asked brokenly.

'We'll be right there...OK?' Lucy promised soothingly.

On the way back out to the limousine, Joaquin said incredulously, 'You said only *four* words and yet you betrayed my presence—'

'She's far too upset to worry about who "we" stands for,' Lucy muttered shakily, still in shock at her own behaviour—and his. Her wanton body was still all of a quiver. She was desperate to put some distance between herself and Joaquin while she dealt with her emotional turmoil, but she also felt the need to rush to Yolanda's side, because somehow she had become fond of the younger girl.

And Yolanda, touched for the first time in her life by crime, only froze for a split second when she saw her brother approaching a step in Lucy's wake. Although she was relieved to see Lucy, it was self-evident that the arrival of a strong male figure on the scene was even more welcome after the shock the Guatemalan girl had suffered. As bursts of rapid Spanish were exchanged and Yolanda turned instinctively to her bossy big brother for support, Lucy felt very much like a third wheel.

Since there was little hope of its recovery, Joaquin suggested that the stolen purse should be reported to the police immediately, any credit cards cancelled, and that later they would go straight to Yolanda's hotel so that she could pack.

'You can come in with me, Lucy,' the brunette told her more cheerfully.

'I'd like to, but I'm afraid I have an appointment this afternoon,' Lucy responded uncomfortably, still not having met Joaquin's eyes once since they had left his townhouse.

'But I need some company,' Yolanda protested with reproachful eyes.

'Come back to the house with us and join us for dinner,' Joaquin murmured smoothly, adding his voice to his sister's.

'I'm sorry, but I really do need to get home. I'd be grateful if you could just drop me off at the nearest bus stop,' Lucy stated tautly.

After all, Joaquin thought that she was a fake and she *was* a fake—indeed a much bigger fake than he could ever have guessed. He was a clever guy. How could she have been so foolish as to imagine that he would not sense on some level that she was not quite what she appeared to be? And what other interpretation could he have put on behaviour that just didn't match what he believed he knew about her background and lifestyle? After all, her twin *was* very different, in personality and presentation. Cindy was confident, occasionally even aggressive in her outlook on the world, and nobody's fool. Cindy was not shy or awkward or naive.

It was time that she cut loose of *any* connection with Joaquin and Yolanda Del Castillo, Lucy conceded heavily. Cindy had put a solicitor in charge of any further communications with Joaquin concerning the repayment of her former father-in-law's savings. There was no further need for Lucy to play any role, nor any requirement for Joaquin to be told that she was, in fact, Cindy Paez's sister. In any case, sooner or later his *own* sister would inform him of that fact and probably laugh her head off at how he had been fooled.

As neither Del Castillo was accustomed to having their wishes ignored and their invitations refused, there was a distinct coolness now in the atmosphere.

'I'll call you…' Yolanda said sullenly, when the limo stopped to let Lucy alight. Ironically the brunette finally both looked and sounded her age.

Joaquin flashed Lucy a darkling glance of censure but Lucy evaded it. He would have invited a chimpanzee home for dinner had he believed it would keep his volatile sister happy, she thought bitterly. She caught the bus and went shopping for food. On her walk back to the apartment she found herself passing within yards of her doctor's surgery and decided to call in for her test results in person.

The receptionist checked the card, which had a note attached. 'You need to make another appointment.'

'Another?' Lucy queried anxiously. 'Does that mean something came up in the tests?'

'I expect it's just the norm for a first pregnancy,' the young woman said blithely. 'I'll check with the doctor now. I can never read his handwriting.'

CHAPTER NINE

PREGNANT?

No, there was no doubt, no room for error, Lucy's doctor had assured her in the five minutes which was all the busy older man had been able to spare her before his next patient arrived. Tests were now so advanced that they could pick up a pregnancy at the very earliest stages, even before the menstrual cycle was noticeably disrupted. Lucy had stumbled out of his surgery again like an accident victim.

The possibility that she might be pregnant had not even occurred to Lucy. In retrospect she was shattered by the realisation that she hadn't once thought of that risk. Not that night she had been with Joaquin and not afterwards either. She had never had any reason to think about contraception, having always naively assumed that she would be in a long-term serious relationship before she became sexually involved. On the face of it, what *did* that wild passionate and romantic night of lovemaking with Joaquin have to do with the production of a little baby nine months down the line?

Only now the connection between those two events was painfully obvious to Lucy, and she was deeply ashamed that she had behaved in such an immature and irresponsible way. A baby…Joaquin's baby. Not a piece of news she could picture him greeting with anything other than outrage. But then hadn't Joaquin, with considerably less excuse, been equally careless of consequences? Lucy's bowed shoulders straightened a little on that conviction. Was she supposed to believe that a male of his sophistication and experience had been so overwhelmed with desire that he had forgotten to use contraception? Well, she might have conceded that excuse had Joaquin only made love to her *once*, but when she finally finished counting up how many times Joaquin had made love to her she stopped marvelling at the reality that she had conceived a child after one abandoned night. Had Joaquin been industriously set on creating a baby, he could not have made more effort to that end!

After a sleepless night, Lucy was tidying the kitchen early the next morning, taking refuge in keeping herself busy in an effort to keep herself calm, when she heard the front door open.

'Lucy...?'

She stiffened in astonishment because it was her future brother-in-law's voice. 'I'm in here, Roger!'

Roger Harkness appeared in the doorway. He was a big, thickset young man, with light brown hair and deceptively bland blue eyes set into lean, sun-tanned features. 'Cindy warned me to shout first in case I gave you a fright.'

'I thought you were staying in Oxford until tomorrow?'

'Cindy and my mother *thought*...and Cindy had to stay because my folks have invited a pile of guests round this evening,' Roger grimaced. 'But my firm didn't send me to Germany for two weeks just to have me roll back last minute, get married and go off on honeymoon without reporting back somewhere in between!'

'It's a shame, though—'

'I have to write up a detailed report and present it first thing tomorrow morning to the senior partners. I'll get it finished quicker here.'

'I didn't move any of your stuff in the spare room,' Lucy hastened to assure him, reminded that the room she was currently occupying was the same one which Roger, having given up his own flat before he went to Germany, had set up as a home office in which he could work.

'I wouldn't have worried about it if you had,' Roger

assured her with a rather strained and unconvincing smile. 'I'm really tired, so I'm going to hit the sack for a couple of hours and then start work.'

As he trod off down to the bedroom, Lucy bit anxiously at her lower lip. The sooner she found herself a bedsit the better. She didn't want to be playing gooseberry to a newly married couple. Even using the spare room she would be inconveniencing them. Roger had seemed tense and awkward with her, unlike his usual genial self.

Poor Cindy, Lucy reflected sympathetically, her thoughts turning to her twin, who had been so much looking forward to her reunion with Roger, only now to find it cut short. Roger had only got back from Germany the night before. He must have driven straight to Oxford, spent the night and got up at dawn to get back into London so early. Certainly her twin wouldn't have had the opportunity to make any serious confessions to Roger. But then *when* her sister chose to tell Roger about the financial hot water she was in was really none of her business, Lucy reminded herself.

Didn't she have enough problems of her own to worry about? Exactly what was she planning to do about the fact that she was pregnant? She wasn't prepared to consider a termination. She would have her baby...Joaquin's baby. No matter how *he* felt about it. But how would she live? It was all very well making airy-fairy plans to raise a child on her own, but Lucy was already foreseeing how difficult it would be.

She wasn't capable of earning a salary big enough to cover the cost of childcare. In some circumstances government help was available to assist single mothers to stay in employment. Only she didn't have a clue whether she would qualify for help, didn't have a clue where she would live, how she would live...*anything*!

And at that point of rising panic, the doorbell went. Rushing to answer it, while being surprised that it hadn't been the intercom which had sounded a warning of a visitor first, but too preoccupied to put on the security chain, she just opened the door.

'Allow me to tell you that the security is useless in this building,' Joaquin informed her with grim disapproval. 'The main entrance door downstairs was lying wide open. Anybody could just walk in!'

But *he* had. And in that first time-suspended moment of recognition Lucy was overwhelmed by happiness. Thought had nothing to do with it; instinct reigned supreme. There he stood, looking breathtakingly, stunningly handsome in a black cashmere overcoat worn over a faultlessly cut dark business suit. But then her brain kicked back into functioning again and she went rigid.

'Joaquin…?' The birth of sheer panic turned Lucy pale enough to make his keen gaze narrow in his inspection of her now startled face. But she couldn't help but be aghast at his arrival. Roger was in the apartment! Roger had never even heard of Joaquin Del Castillo but Joaquin had certainly heard of Roger, and if the two men were to meet and Joaquin learnt how he had been deceived what else might be said in Roger's hearing? If Roger *had* to find out what his bride-to-be and her sister had been doing while he was safely out of reach in Germany, the very worst way he *could* find out would be from a male who had as low an opinion of Cindy as Joaquin had!

'Why are you looking at me like that?' Joaquin strode smoothly past her into the hall.

'Sorry…I wasn't expecting you,' Lucy muttered in a stifled undertone, her shaken appraisal pinned to his tall powerful frame while she tried feverishly to work out how to get rid of him again.

'Are you normally this slow on the uptake in the morning, *querida*?' Joaquin teased with husky amusement as he thrust the door shut behind him.

She was discovering that she could not meet those extraordinary green eyes without being intimately aware that she had conceived his baby. It was bad enough that she was terrified that at any moment Roger might appear to find out who was visiting, but to be burdened with yet another big guilty secret where Joaquin was concerned was all of a sudden just too much for Lucy to handle. Sheer nervous tension made her tummy lurch with nausea.

'Are you ill?' Joaquin began to question with a frowning look of concern.

With a stifled moan of chagrin, Lucy raced for the bathroom, but she had the presence of mind to close and lock the door behind her. She was sick. In the aftermath, the loud thumping on the door demanded her attention.

'Lucy…don't be stupid, open this door!' Joaquin urged with considerable impatience.

Hurriedly freshening up, capable of considering nothing but the reality that she felt absolutely awful, Lucy went dizzily back out to the hall.

'Suppose you'd collapsed in there?' Joaquin curved a supportive arm round her slim shoulders and then with a muttered curse in Spanish lifted her into his powerful arms to carry her into the lounge opposite and lay her down on the sofa. 'I'll get a doctor. You're just not a very healthy person, *querida*. I think you need a really thorough medical examination—'

'No, I—'

'Lie there and keep quiet,' Joaquin instructed, standing over her clutching his mobile phone with an air of serious purpose. 'How could I have taunted you with the amount of time you have spent out of work in recent years? It is obvious to me now that you suffer from a great deal of ill-health.'

'I really don't need a doctor,' Lucy began, trying to sound forceful enough to stop him in his bossy tracks.

'Allow *me* to tell you what you need.'

'But you don't know—'

'I know it's not normal to look green,' Joaquin slotted in crushingly.

'I'm pregnant...' The confession just escaped her in a weary burst of resentful frustration at his refusal to listen to a word she was saying.

But this time Joaquin *had* listened, and the phone dropped clean out of his hand as he involuntarily loosened his grip on it. His lush ebony lashes lifted, revealing stunned green eyes. But then the oddest thing happened. He screened his gaze again, threw back his wide shoulders as if he was squaring up to a challenge, and said only the slightest bit unsteadily, '*Sí*...so you *still* need a doctor.'

'Talk about interrupting at the optimum wrong moment...' another male voice groaned from across the room.

In all the excitement, Lucy had totally forgotten about Roger. She was still caught up in the drama of having told Joaquin she was pregnant without actually having intended to tell him. But the sound of Roger's apologetic intrusion was an even greater shock, and she reared up off the sofa just in time to see her sister's large bulky fiancé backing speedily into the hall again, looking almost comically embarrassed by what he had overheard.

'*Por Dios*...no wonder you acted so weird when you saw me at your door!' Joaquin framed thickly, his accent growling along every carefully enunciated syllable. His bronzed skin had an ashen quality as he studied her with seething contempt.

'I think...I think it's time that I explained something to you,' Lucy muttered tautly, thinking frantically fast and seeing that full confession was the only option left. 'But could we go somewhere else to talk about it because it's kind of private?'

'Roger Harkness...what need is there of privacy to explain his presence here in your apartment?' Joaquin demanded with volcanic force, spreading both arms wide with the sort of volatile expressive body language that was extremely intimidating. 'You got back into bed with your ex-fiancé after sleeping with me. I neglected to offer you an option sufficient to keep you *out* of other men's beds! You came back here to *him* last night...you slut!'

Lucy turned pale as death. 'It's not like that, Joaquin, because—'

Joaquin focused on her with a dark blistering fury that only seemed to heighten with every second which had passed since Roger's hasty exist. 'And now you're pregnant and you can't possibly know *which* of us is the father...I'll get DNA tests done when the baby's born. In the meantime, he's welcome to you, if he still wants you, but only *after* I've beaten the living daylights out of him!'

For a staggered instant, Lucy was paralysed to the spot by that unashamed threat of violence. Joaquin strode out of the room like a man on a mission. Lucy regained the use of her limbs and surged in his wake. 'Joaquin...for goodness' sake!'

But Joaquin was throwing wide every door he came to in search of a fight, indifferent, it seemed, to Lucy's efforts to prevent him. Nobody was more surprised than Lucy when Roger failed to appear. She reckoned that her future brother-in-law must have walked straight out of the apartment to give her and Joaquin peace to talk.

'Infierno!' Baulked of his prey, and incredulous that Roger had evidently just gone out and left them alone together, Joaquin grated in wrathful frustration, 'What sort of coward is he that he runs away from a fight?'

'Please just calm down for a moment and listen to me,' Lucy urged feverishly.

Joaquin turned ferociously bright green eyes full of condemnation on her. 'Listen? Listen so that you can whisper lying explanations into my ears and try to convince me that the child you carry is mine?' he countered with savage derision. 'It will snow in hell before I *listen* to you again!'

And with that highly emotive smouldering condemnation, Joaquin strode out of the apartment.

Lucy was in a sobbing heap on the sofa when Roger reappeared. 'So that was Joaquin Del Castillo,' he remarked as Lucy crammed a tissue to her mouth and sat up, struggling to pull herself together again. 'I feel really sorry for that guy.'

Stunned by that most telling admission from her sister's fiancé, Lucy gaped at him.

'Yes, I know the whole story. Cindy kept me up until dawn talking about it,' Roger revealed. 'I'm more or less beyond being shocked now, but she didn't mention that *other* matter...the one I really would rather not have overheard.'

'Cindy doesn't know and I'm not going to mention it just yet,' Lucy muttered tightly on the subject of her pregnancy. She realised that she was kind of beyond shock as well, after the distressing encounter she had just had with Joaquin. The guy she loved, the father of her baby, had just walked away, thinking all sorts of crazy horrible things about her.

'I want to thank you for looking out for Cindy while I was away,' Roger said flatly. 'I owe you...we both owe you on that score.'

Lucy gave him a blank look.

'Come on, Lucy. Your common sense prevented her from making a bad situation ten times worse. If she'd lost her head and dug her heels in, she most probably would have ended up in court accused of fraud,' Roger stated tautly, his frank open face stiff. 'Quite frankly, it's fortunate it *was* you in Guatemala!'

Lucy was embarrassed. She could see that he was still angry with her sister.

'With my help, Cindy will pay back every penny with interest to that old man,' Roger told her squarely.

'But she didn't *mean* to hurt anybody,' Lucy pointed out hurriedly, before he left the room, still looking really grim.

Her thoughts turning to her own situation then, Lucy accepted that she had got herself into an awful mess. No matter which way she broke the news, Joaquin would be outraged by the manner in which she and her sister had deceived him, and Lucy knew with a sinking heart that she would have to wait until the wedding was over before she risked telling Joaquin the truth of her identity.

Roger's faith in Cindy had been shaken. The very last thing Roger needed now was to see her twin confronted by Joaquin in a righteous rage. That might just be the straw that would break the camel's back. Lucy already suspected that Roger had used this report for his firm as an excuse to put some distance between himself and her twin while he came to terms with what he had been told. What if Roger decided to call off the wedding? Lucy saw for herself that the situation could still go either way. Right now, marooned with Roger's parents, forced to go on pretending that she was a happy bride-to-be and entertain visitors, poor Cindy *had* to be really suffering.

So, although every instinct Lucy possessed was urging her to track Joaquin down without further loss of time and tell him that she was *not* Cindy Paez, she didn't feel that she could dare take that risk in case it rebounded on her twin. But, at the same time, it really hurt Lucy to leave Joaquin believing that she had already turned to another man and that she couldn't be sure of *who* had fathered their child. Right now, Joaquin truly believed that she was a slut. Hadn't she been in his arms yesterday? However, in about forty-eight hours she could get in touch with him and sort it all out, she promised herself wretchedly.

In the afternoon, Lucy went out and walked round the shops, with their wonderful festive displays. Roger had been pacing restively round the apartment, looking increasingly uncomfortable at her presence. That had worried Lucy even more. Naturally he would start feeling awkward if he was toying with the idea of dumping her sister two days before their wedding.

Yolanda called her on the mobile phone she had given her. 'Have you still got Joaquin with you?' she asked brightly.

'No, he's long gone…I mean, he didn't stay long,' Lucy rephrased hurriedly.

'Did he offer you the job?'

'What job?'

Yolanda proceeded to tell her that she was prepared to go back to school but only as a day girl, not as a boarder. Joaquin had pointed out that, although he could spend more time in London, he was often abroad and she couldn't stay alone in the townhouse with just the staff for company.

'So I suggested that he could give you the job of being my companion,' Yolanda completed with satisfaction.

Lucy looked heavenward for inspiration. Even if Joaquin hadn't received the impression that she was a bed-hopping wanton earlier in the day, he would not have offered her such a position. Yolanda's idea had never been destined to make it off the drawing board.

'Thanks, but it wouldn't have been a good idea for me—'

'Lucy,' Yolanda scolded. 'You're crazy about my brother and I like you. If he saw enough of you, he might be attracted to you.'

'I think a little of me goes a long way with Joaquin right now,' Lucy muttered, not knowing whether to laugh or to cry.

'Why haven't you told him you're the *other* twin yet?' Yolanda demanded. 'Do you want me to do it for you?'

Lucy paled to the gills at the offer, and felt even worse about what she had to go on to say. 'Please don't do that, Yolanda. I promise I'll tell him in a couple of days. I'm very sorry that I've involved you in keeping a secret from your brother.'

'Get real, Lucy,' Yolanda groaned, sounding her world-weary best. 'Do you think I tell him *everything*?'

Lucy climbed out of the wedding car, clutching her posy of flowers, and followed the other three bridesmaids, composed of Roger's three chattering sisters.

All of them wore beautiful white silk brocade dresses, for Cindy had reversed the more conventional colour choices and chosen a wedding gown that was her favourite shade of pink. They congregated in the big church porch and then surged forward to greet the bridal limousine drawing up. Looking radiant, Cindy emerged and took the arm of Roger's father who had offered to give her away.

'You're too early.' One of the ushers came out to warn them. 'Roger's been held up.'

Cindy went white. 'Where is he?'

'Panicking in a traffic jam!' the usher teased. 'Should be here in five minutes.'

The day before, Lucy had spent a great deal of time trudging round the shops. In the early hours, Cindy had returned to London to mend fences with Roger. Lucy hadn't the slightest idea of what had passed between the couple, but Cindy was still a nervous wreck, convinced that her bridegroom had come close to changing his mind about marrying her.

A long low-slung black sportscar shot to a halt in front of the church steps, where nobody was supposed to park. Lucy saw it first because everybody else in the porch was

too busy talking. With shaken eyes, she watched Joaquin
Del Castillo vault out of the car as if he was jet-propelled,
his darkly handsome features fiercely set.

Having heard the sound of the car, Cindy hurried forward
to her twin's side. 'Is that Roger arriving?' she asked anxiously.

Like somebody just waiting for the roof to fall in on her,
Lucy watched Joaquin heading for the steps. Her heart was
racing so fast she was afraid that she was about to faint. It
seemed that Joaquin had finally found out that she and
Cindy had deceived him. What else could he be doing here?
But how had he found out? Had his sister told him? Was
he now prepared to confront Cindy in front of all these
people on her wedding day...*would* he be that cruel?

'Oh...no,' Cindy whispered in horror, having read her
sister's face. 'That's Del Castillo...isn't it?'

Joaquin mounted the steps two at a time. But he stopped
dead when he saw Lucy, frozen on the top step and looking
almost as pale as her dress. *'Por Dios,'* he exclaimed
hoarsely. 'This cannot be. You cannot do this...I will not
allow it—'

'Please...please go away,' Cindy pleaded tearfully.

Only when Cindy spoke did Joaquin take the time to
glance at the woman who stood by Lucy's side. He frowned
as he focused on Cindy, the look of disbelief in his glittering green eyes instantaneous. He stared at the two sisters.
*'Infierno...*there are *two* of you?'

It was the longest moment of Lucy's life. 'We're twins,'
she muttered unevenly. 'I'm Lucy—'

'I know you're Lucy!' Joaquin gritted. 'Do you think I'm
so blind I can't tell you apart?'

'I think what my sister is trying to tell you is that I'm
the one who ripped off Fidelio Paez,' Cindy told Joaquin
tightly. 'I'm the one who married Mario and the one who

persuaded Lucy to go to Guatemala in my place and pretend that she was me.'

So intense was Lucy's concentration on Joaquin's stunned stillness she was conscious of nothing else. She couldn't even concentrate on what her sister was telling him.

Cindy just kept on talking, as if by talking she could keep any threat Joaquin might offer at bay. 'Lucy didn't want to do it but I made it very difficult for her to refuse...I took advantage of her—'

Joaquin cut right across her. 'Which one of you is the bride?'

'Me...Cindy,' Cindy responded, in visible bewilderment at such a question.

A dark line of colour flared over Joaquin's fabulous cheekbones. The silence smouldered for what felt like for ever. 'Enjoy your wedding day, Cindy,' he murmured without expression.

Cindy backed away like someone who very badly wanted to pick up her skirts and run but who was afraid that any sudden movement might provoke exactly what she most feared. 'Thank you,' she whispered unevenly.

Only now was it dawning on Lucy that Joaquin had thought that this was *her* wedding day!

'And for your sister, that selfish, frivolous user and abuser of other people, you lied to *me*,' Joaquin breathed in a terrifyingly quiet voice.

The buzz of the chattering bridesmaids in the background might as well have been a million miles away. Lucy's world had stopped spinning and flung her off into frightening freefall when she least expected it. It was as if a pool of rushing silence enfolded her and Joaquin.

'I believed it was *you* who was marrying Roger Harkness today. Your sister's neighbour laughed when he saw me outside the apartment. ''All away to the church,'' he said.'

Joaquin breathed in very deep and studied the pale oval of her stricken face with cold hard eyes. 'I cannot abide lies, and every word you have ever spoken to me has been a lie, every single moment has been based on deceit.'

At that harsh condemnation Lucy made a tiny instinctive movement with her hand, as though she would have touched his sleeve. But Joaquin's distaste and anger was a potent barrier and her hand dropped weakly back to her side.

'No...no, it wasn't,' she attempted to protest.

'I don't even know your name...' Joaquin flung back his proud dark head and surveyed her with speaking contempt.

'Lucille Fabian,' she framed chokily. 'Joaquin, *please*—'

'This is not the place. My presence is not welcome here. Surely you did not sacrifice so much just to cloud your sister's wedding day?' Joaquin said very drily, and he swung on his heel to stride back to his fabulous car.

If Lucy had been in freefall prior to that moment, she now felt as though she had hit the ground with a bone-jarring crash. After an instant of hesitation, Lucy flew down the steps in Joaquin's wake.

'There's Roger's car!' someone exclaimed behind her. 'They're coming in by the side entrance.'

Before Joaquin could get back into the Ferrari, Lucy caught at his sleeve with desperate fingers. 'I'm sorry!'

Ice-cold green eyes clashed with hers. 'You're making an exhibition of us both.'

Lucy fell back from him. A slow, painful surge of pink washed her cheeks. Turning away, she walked back up the steps, horribly conscious that the little drama being played out before their eyes had finally attracted the attention of the rest of the bride's attendants in the porch.

Cindy hurried forward and closed an arm round her twin. 'I'm sorry...I am *so* sorry,' she whispered shakily.

'It wasn't going anywhere anyway,' Lucy framed, trying

to force a smile and relieved when, a few minutes later, the church doors were opened and it was time to get into place with the other bridesmaids.

Joaquin had come to the church believing that *she* was the bride. Had he had some mad idea of preventing the wedding from taking place? 'I will not allow it,' he had said. Well, what did his motivation matter now? She had never been able to believe that her relationship with Joaquin Del Castillo could have a future. But her failure to tell Joaquin the truth the day he saw Roger in the apartment had probably been the finishing blow. Right to the bitter end she had kept loyal to Cindy—but shouldn't she have had a greater sense of responsibility towards the baby she had conceived? Ensuring that Joaquin despised her would scarcely benefit her unborn child.

At the beginning, pretending to be Cindy had been like a game she'd played, she saw now. Exotic travel and fancy clothes had been seductive trappings for a young woman bored with her own dull and uneventful life. Nor could she blame Cindy for persuading her into that disastrous masquerade. Her twin had had no suspicion that Joaquin Del Castillo had sent the plane tickets to snare a woman he believed to be a con-artist.

Yet Joaquin had had right on his side in what he'd been trying to do. She had even recognised that reality. She had tried to persuade herself that she was still lying for her sister's sake, but by then hadn't she been just as afraid that telling Joaquin the truth would wreck any chance she had with him? Not until she had witnessed Joaquin's absolute revulsion had she registered just how inexcusable her continuing deception had become. Like many other people, Joaquin couldn't stand liars. And Lucy had never felt so miserable in her life.

Outside the church after the ceremony, when the photographer had almost finished his task, Roger strolled over to Lucy's side, bent his head and said to her with a grin, 'Have I got a surprise for you!'

Her brow furrowing, she turned to ask her new brother-in-law what he meant, but Roger and Cindy were already heading for the car which would ferry them ahead of their guests to the reception. However, Lucy did not have very long to wait to discover the surprise in store for her. The very first person she saw when she walked into the hotel function room was Joaquin!

Sheathed in the dark suit that fitted his wide-shouldered, slim-hipped physique to perfection, his white shirt and elegant silver-grey silk tie accentuating his bronzed skin and black hair, he looked stunningly handsome. But what shocked Lucy even more was that Joaquin was with Roger, and the two men appeared to be conversing with all the ease and familiarity of old friends.

Breaking away from a group of guests, Cindy made a beeline for her twin. 'When Roger arrived at the church, he saw you outside with Joaquin. He guessed who he was and he jumped out of the car before Joaquin could drive off and persuaded him to come to the reception. Roger trying to play cupid...I still can't believe it!'

'Yes, well...' Lucy was all too well aware of why Roger had made that effort on her behalf. Roger knew that she was carrying Joaquin's baby, news that she still had to share with her sister.

'And Roger didn't even tell me what he'd done until we were on the way here, and now, for goodness' sake, they're getting on like a house on fire!' Cindy marvelled with a rueful but accepting laugh. 'Isn't that just like men? They just ignore all the drama and start talking about sport!'

One of the bridesmaids settled a drink into Lucy's hand. Across the foyer, Joaquin finally took note of Lucy's presence. Brilliant, unreadable green eyes rested on her taut face, and with a final word to Roger he strode over to her.

'Well, this is a surprise,' Lucy began awkwardly.

Joaquin elevated a sardonic brow. 'Is it? Roger stepped into the breach with admirable common sense. Fidelio's problems may be at an end but your brother-in-law knows that ours are *not*. Even if I wanted to, I'm not in a position to just walk away now.'

At that grim assurance, Lucy's chin came up, her violet blue eyes furious. 'You can walk away any time you like! OK?'

So the baby was a problem. Well, what other attitude had she expected from Joaquin? Few men would welcome being saddled with the consequences of a one-night stand! At least he was being honest, she tried to tell herself, seeking some saving grace in that blunt admission, but she still felt cut to the bone. She hadn't asked to be pregnant and she didn't want to be pregnant. In fact, right at that moment, the knowledge that there was a baby growing inside her just filled her with fright. She felt more like a teenager than the adult she had believed herself to be.

Joaquin closed long fingers over hers as she attempted to move away. 'We'll talk later,' he spelt out warningly, tightening his grip when Lucy engaged in a covert tug of war with his hand, and then disconcerting her entirely by using his other hand to separate her from the wine glass she was still holding. 'I'll get you a mineral water. I seem to recall that alcohol is not recommended, *es verdad*?'

'Will you just keep quiet about my condition?' Lucy hissed at him out of the corner of her mouth, seething emotions washing about inside her to such an extent that she believed she might explode from the pressure.

'My apologies,' Joaquin breathed with icy hauteur. 'But at this moment I can think of nothing else.'

Quelled by that confession, which was a most ironic match for her own troubled state of mind, they headed for the top table where a place had been made for Joaquin. As she passed by her sister, Cindy broke off her conversation with her father-in-law, rose from her seat with a beaming smile and enfolded Lucy in a sudden effervescent hug. 'Congratulations, sis! Doesn't Joaquin move fast? I'm so happy for you I could cry!'

A bewildered look stamped on her face as Cindy dropped back into her seat, Lucy muttered, 'What on earth...?'

Joaquin urged her further down the table and into a chair. 'Naturally I informed Roger of my intentions.'

'What intentions? Roger?' Lucy questioned in a daze, still struggling to work out what her twin had been congratulating her on.

'*Dios mio*...he is your closest male relative. To whom else would I have spoken?' His crystalline green eyes veiled from her view by lush black lashes, Joaquin sank with fluid grace down into the seat beside her. 'But never before have I been so aware of the gap between your culture and mine. Had Roger been Guatemalan, he would not have waited for me to approach him. He would have demanded the same result with a gun to my head and the church already booked!'

'J-Joaquin...' Lucy whispered shakily, her throat closing over as what he was saying began to make sense. But she was hampered by the reality that she just couldn't credit the 'result' he was talking about. 'Exactly what are you saying?'

His beautiful mouth hardened. Tilting back his arrogant dark head, he dealt her a cool, unimpressed glance that questioned her apparent inability to follow his meaning. 'That we will be married just as soon as I can arrange it, *querida*. What else?'

CHAPTER TEN

AT THE same instant, Roger stood up to make a speech. But Lucy was welded to the formidable challenge in Joaquin's cool gaze. Her mouth running dry, she tore her shaken eyes defensively from his.

Strange how a proposal she would have received with joy just a few days ago now filled her with a deep sense of hurt and humiliation, Lucy conceded painfully. No wonder Roger and Joaquin had got so chummy so fast! But what did Joaquin expect from *her*? Applause? Grovelling gratitude? He had not even proposed to her! Although nothing had yet been discussed between them, although many explanations had yet to be made on her part, Joaquin had decided all on his own that there was only one solution. An old-fashioned shotgun marriage with a bridegroom set on doing what he felt he *ought* to do rather than what he *wanted* to do!

Lucy thrust up her chin. 'With reference to the proposal you put before my brother-in-law before you even thought to mention it to me,' she countered tartly. 'No, thanks!'

At that point, Roger insisted on giving a toast to 'Cindy's just-got-engaged-sister, Lucy.' Lucy shrank in her seat, face flaming with self-consciousness and growing outrage. What was wrong with everybody? Without one word of personal assent from her, her relatives were happy to assume she was getting married. Of course, it would certainly get her out of their apartment. The minute she thought that silly petty thought, she suppressed a groan and struggled to get a rational grip on herself.

155

'Let's dance,' Joaquin suggested when the meal was at an end and the floor had filled.

'Forget it,' Lucy snapped, after maintaining the longest and most sullen silence in history.

'You're behaving like Yolanda!' Joaquin lowered his head to give her what felt like the ultimate put-down, brilliant green eyes exasperated.

Lucy reddened, stood up, and fought off an overwrought urge to both hit him and burst into tears. Joaquin tugged her into his arms. The achingly familiar scent of him enfolded her and did something crazy to her pulses and her heart. She closed her eyes, shaken to find that her wretched body was indifferent to her mental turmoil. The lure of that hard muscular physique against hers and the tantalising heat of him was almost impossible for her to fight. Little quivers of darting warmth glanced through her taut limbs, stirring up the hunger she would have done just about anything to stamp out. She trembled.

'"No thanks"?' Joaquin husked in effective repetition of her refusal an hour earlier, his silken derision sliding along her sensitive nerve-endings and then striking like a whip. 'If you were in my bed now you would give me a very different answer, *gatita*.'

At that crack, she stiffened, and missed a step. 'That's what you think—'

'That's what I *know*, for your desire for me is the only honest thing you ever gave me!' Joaquin breathed in a harsh undertone.

Lucy paled. 'All right… I should've told you the truth sooner—'

'You did not tell me the truth *at all*,' Joaquin slotted in with crushing precision.

'I was scared you would confront Cindy and cause more trouble between her and Roger before the wedding,' she argued feverishly.

'Poor little Lucy, always sacrificing her own best interests for those of others,' Joaquin countered with deeply sardonic bite. 'But isn't it remarkable that instead of becoming my mistress you will now become my wife?'

Her teeth gritting at that comeback, Lucy saw red. She stretched up on her toes to gasp into his ear, 'I wouldn't be your mistress if you *paid* me.'

'*Por Dios*…did you think I expected you to share my bed for nothing?' Joaquin enquired, smooth as glass. 'I cut my teeth on women considerably more calculating than you. I expected a price, but even I could never have dreamt that it would be a wedding ring!'

'Rot…in…Hades!' Lucy hissed the last word like a spitting cat and stalked off the floor to take refuge in the cloakroom.

That louse was the guy she thought she loved? She rinsed her hands under cooling water and shivered with angry confusion and a deep, deep sense of loss. Why was it she was now remembering his teasing warmth that morning he had called, before everything had gone catastrophically wrong? Though now she knew what the warmth had been angled at achieving, didn't she? Joaquin had still been planning to make her his occasional bed partner. So if she was in shock right now, so was he.

She clutched the edge of the vanity unit and breathed in deep on that latter acknowledgement.

Joaquin was still—quite understandably—seethingly angry with her. He might be putting on a show of cool for the sake of appearances, but just a couple of hours ago Joaquin had discovered that she had engaged in a really massive deception and that virtually everything he had believed he had known about her had related to her sister Cindy instead! Then Roger had seized probably the worst possible moment to persuade Joaquin into attending the reception. Why the heck had Joaquin agreed?

'Even if I wanted to, I'm not in a position to just walk away now,' Joaquin had said. So Joaquin had allowed Roger to smooth things over in the aftermath of all the bad feeling over Fidelio simply because Lucy was going to have his baby. But why had he immediately informed Roger that they were getting married? Relieved to see such a tidy conclusion to an impending drama, Roger had naturally been delighted to hear and share that news.

So what was she going to do? Stick her nose in the air and walk away just to show that she could do it? Or recognise that right now Joaquin had a perfect right to be furious at the games she had played in Guatemala? But had he really planned to make her his mistress? Recalling her visit to his London home, and the passion which would very probably have plunged her back into bed with him again, she flushed with embarrassment.

If making her his mistress had been Joaquin's ambition, he had been progressing well on that score. She might have found herself involved in a heartbreaking affair in which she was always waiting for his next phone call. Lucy spread thankful fingers across her still flat tummy. If there was a choice…and it was by no means certain that there *was* a choice—for she didn't want a reluctant bridegroom—she knew she loved Joaquin, and that she would rather be his wife than his mistress…

When she returned to the table, she saw Joaquin standing with Roger and Cindy. She watched his charismatic smile flash out, but noted that it didn't quite reach his eyes. For a male in the mood he was in, he was, however, putting on a heck of an impressive show. And why not? He was rich, he was sophisticated, he was the original Mr Cool on the surface…but underneath? He absolutely fascinated her. A secretive smile brought a dreamy curve to Lucy's mouth as she kept her distance and mingled with the other guests.

When it was time for Cindy to change so that she and

Roger could head for the airport, her sister took her up to the hotel room with her. 'So my former worst enemy is going to join the family...only you could have pulled that off in so short a time!'

'It's not quite as simple it sounds. I'm going to have a baby,' Lucy finally told her twin.

Cindy was dumbstruck. 'But of the two of us you're supposed to be the cautious, sensible one.'

'Human, too.'

'But you were only over there a few—'

'Long enough,' Lucy slotted in ruefully.

Cindy grinned. 'So I'm going to be an aunt and get to see what it's like being a mother before I try it for myself.' She hesitated, her face colouring. 'I guess Joaquin will bring you up to speed on the other business.'

Lucy frowned. 'What other business?'

'Never mind now. It's not something I want to think about any more,' Cindy gabbled in a rush, but she gave her twin a rueful glance. 'But I can tell you one thing... Joaquin's a really decent guy!'

On the way downstairs again, having refused to satisfy Lucy's curiosity as to what she had been talking about, Cindy paused to throw her bouquet. A crowd of young females gathered but Cindy threw her flowers wide and high and with deadly accuracy at Joaquin. 'I wanted *you* to have it,' she whispered to her twin.

Ten minutes later, the bridal couple having departed, Lucy climbed into Joaquin's Ferrari. 'I suppose we're about to talk,' she said tautly.

'Not a good idea while I'm endeavouring to hold on to my temper, *querida*,' Joaquin drawled in succinct warning.

'Feeling like that, it's just insane to talk about us getting married,' Lucy sighed.

'I don't see it in that light. I have a duty to my child *and* to my family name. There is no choice about how we handle this with my sixteen-year-old sister in the same house-hold. We'll be married within three days.'

'Three days?' Lucy echoed in disbelief.

'If I cannot get a special licence for us to marry here within that time-frame, I will fly you back to Guatemala and have the deed done there.' His bold bronzed profile grim, Joaquin filtered his car somewhat aggressively into the traffic flow. 'The sooner we are married, the better. If I can contrive to shield my sister from the consequences of my own stupidity, I shall do so.'

Lucy hadn't thought of Yolanda, but now she did and she cringed with discomfiture. An out-of-wedlock preg-nancy was not the way to impress a teenage sister with the principles which Joaquin would wish to instil.

'I...I could go away somewhere... I mean, obviously, I wouldn't keep in touch with her—'

'Don't be foolish. A child cannot be hidden for ever. Or perhaps you are thinking that the child should not be born. It is my wish that it should be!' Joaquin shot at her in a harsh but anxious undertone.

Lucy paled. 'It's my wish too.'

'*Por Dios*...then why are you arguing with me?'

She closed her aching eyes. Joaquin wasn't giving her a choice, but she still knew that she *had* a choice. Did she marry him because she loved him and she was carrying his child and hope that somehow, some way, they could work a miracle together? It could not be said that Joaquin was in a mood to be easily persuaded. It could not be said either that working miracles was on his mind.

'Why don't you just talk out how angry you are with me for pretending to be Cindy?' she muttered ruefully. 'I can take it...'

The silence just sizzled. He had so much emotion, but it was all under firm lock and key. He thought strictly in shades of black and white. She was pregnant. For him, that was a problem. He seemed to believe he could solve that problem as if it was any other everyday problem. He took no account whatsoever of emotions. Did he feel *anything* for her apart from anger?

Lucy surfaced from sleep and slowly pushed herself up on her elbows to find herself lying on a bed in an unfamiliar but decidedly masculine bedroom. The light by the bed gleamed over a silk tie lying across the arm of an antique chair. The last thing she recalled was being in Joaquin's car.

She checked her watch. It was almost midnight. As she sat up, the door opened and Joaquin entered. When he realised she was awake, he stilled and studied her with veiled eyes. Self-conscious beneath that scrutiny, Lucy pushed her tumbled caramel hair back from her face and tucked her feet beneath the white dress pooled around her.

'Your sister didn't choose that gown,' Joaquin commented. 'It's too elegant.'

Taken aback, Lucy coloured, but he was right. Cindy had stipulated the colour but her mother-in-law had chosen the style.

His penetrating gaze still glittering over her, Joaquin vented a roughened laugh. 'You look the very picture of Victorian innocence. In Guatemala, you wore only revealing clothes designed to attract male attention. Too short, too tight, too provocative.'

'Considering the way your own sister dresses—'

'But *only* in the privacy of her own home, in an effort to shock and annoy me,' Joaquin interposed wryly. 'I looked at you and I read the message in the clothes you wore.'

'What message?' Lucy was now taut, flushed and discomfited.

'That you were sexually available, that you knew the

score, that you wanted me to look and desire you,' Joaquin supplied with a raw edge to his dark deep drawl. 'I got the *wrong* message, *es verdad*?'

Lucy dropped her head, for there was a certain amount of truth in what he said. Cindy adored being the centre of male attention. Cindy always dressed on the edge of provocation. 'They weren't my clothes.'

'Did you think I hadn't worked that out yet?' Joaquin spread one lean brown hand in an angry movement. 'Just like you fondly imagined outside the church today that I might *not* be able to tell you and your twin apart?'

'A lot of people say they can't—'

'Then they're playing to the gallery. Cindy looks older. Same features, but different expression and cynical eyes.'

'I wouldn't have been too happy if you hadn't been able to tell us apart,' Lucy conceded.

'I would have been happier had I found out my mistake before you left my country,' Joaquin admitted, his beautiful mouth curling. 'I only ever intended to spend the one night with you—'

'Let's not talk about that,' Lucy cut in uncomfortably.

Joaquin dealt her a gleaming glance, his hard jawline squaring. 'I have never brought a woman to Hacienda De Oro. It is my family home. Out of respect for my female relatives I observe certain standards there, but desire overcame my fine principles,' he stated. 'I had nothing with which to protect you. I believed you had recently been living with a man—'

'I understand that.' Lucy just wished he would drop the subject.

'Do you? Precautions did cross my mind, but my hunger was stronger than my caution,'' Joaquin confessed curtly. 'So now we both pay the price.'

A wash of prickling tears hit the backs of her eyes. 'It doesn't have to be like that, Joaquin.'

'Do you think I'm whingeing like some teenage boy faced with his obligations?' Joaquin laughed with what sounded like genuine amusement, and that made her glance up in sharp disconcertion. 'Now that I have spent all afternoon and most of the evening counting the costs, let me count the benefits.'

'Benefits?' Lucy queried in surprise.

'I shall have you in my bed whenever I want. I shall have a child, and I like children. I will also get a keeper for my very troublesome sister.' As he spoke Joaquin closed the distance between the door and the bed and reached for her hands to pull her to him with easy strength. 'Yolanda's too old for a substitute mother figure, but just ripe for a big sister with a sympathetic manner. She likes you. You certainly made a hit there!'

Still trying to adjust to that volatile change of mood which had so taken her by surprise, she felt her mouth run dry as Joaquin just lifted her against him like a doll. Her heart hammered, the most wanton sense of anticipation rising as she collided with his shimmering green eyes. But Joaquin did not kiss her. Instead, he flipped open the door again, and she belatedly appreciated that he was actually taking her *out* of his bedroom.

'But maybe it's not Yolanda whom I most want and need to be a hit with...' Lucy confided in a sudden rush, the awkward sentence tripping off her tongue, ill-considered but honest in sentiment.

'It is all that is on offer, *querida*. Unlike you, I do not tell lies. If you did not have my baby inside you, you would not be here now.' Further down the well-lit corridor, Joaquin thrust open another door and carried her over to the bed.

'But I couldn't live with you feeling like that!' Lucy confessed, so great was her recoil from that blunt statement.

'I do not have one of those tolerant forgiving natures that

everybody is supposed to have these days,' Joaquin delivered in a driven undertone. 'I have a very strong sense of what is wrong and what is right, and what you did to me was *very* wrong. Do not ask or expect me to pretend otherwise.'

Having shattered her with that speech, he laid her down on the bed with careful, even gentle hands. '*Buenas noches*, Lucy.'

Lucy stared at the ceiling until her vision clouded with the strength of her stare. Tears trickled out of the corners of her eyes and stung her taut face. Well, she had asked how he really felt about her and he had told her. He had told her, with the kind of sincerity that scorched, exactly how he felt. She had been judged and found wanting and he did not believe that he would ever manage to forgive her. She couldn't possibly marry him. She couldn't possibly!

She tossed and turned all night, but eventually she weighed every possibility in the balance and that was when she decided that she *would* marry him. First and foremost their baby deserved that she made that commitment and try to make their marriage work. She would have to be patient where Joaquin was concerned, but with time and opportunity on her side mightn't he start seeing her in a different light? All right, so he didn't love her, but nobody got absolutely everything they wanted, did they? She was willing to compromise.

On the way downstairs next morning, Lucy could not help noticing the absence of any form of seasonal decoration, yet in little more than a week it would be Christmas day. Probably Joaquin and his sister always spent the Christmas period in Guatemala, she reflected.

Joaquin lowered his newspaper when she entered the dining-room for breakfast. Still clad in her bridesmaid's dress, because she had nothing else to wear, Lucy felt a little foolish.

'The special license will be granted for the day after tomorrow. I expect my diplomatic status helped.' Casting aside the newspaper, Joaquin rose to his full, formidable height, his well-cut charcoal-grey business suit accentuating his wide shoulders and lean muscular physique.

He took a lot for granted, and Lucy stiffened. 'I haven't said I'll marry you yet.'

Cool green eyes set in a darkly handsome lean male visage arrowed into hers. 'Will you?' he said drily.

Her colour heightened. 'Yes.'

'I never doubted it for a moment, *querida*,' Joaquin murmured silkily. 'One of my staff is handling the arrangements. The application requires a copy of your birth certificate.'

Anger and embarrassment claimed her and she bit down on her tongue before she said something she might regret.

'I suggest that you move in here today,' Joaquin continued evenly. 'Yolanda's school breaks up for the holidays tomorrow and she'll be home in the afternoon. I'd be obliged if you were in residence by then.'

Taking her seat at the beautifully set table, trying not to seem sensible of the attentions of the manservant pouring a cup of coffee for her, Lucy asked, 'Won't you be here?'

'I'll be in Paris by this afternoon.'

She worried at her lower lip. 'Tomorrow?'

'I'll be back in London late tomorrow night.'

As he headed for the door, Lucy scrambled up again. 'You're leaving now?'

'Tell me, am I likely to get forty questions *every* time I leave you?' Joaquin enquired drily.

Lucy reddened, but she nodded with unapologetic certainty.

His brilliant eyes shimmered over her face and then narrowed. He caught one hand in her hair and pulled her mouth under his in an onslaught that was so unexpected that a tiny cry of surprise escaped her. It was a devouringly hungry kiss that sent her reeling. The stabbing thrust of his tongue sent a wave of excitement hurtling through to her to the extent that his equally abrupt withdrawal felt like a punishment.

Dark colour scoring his proud cheekbones, Joaquin released her and expelled his breath. 'I almost forgot. The ring…'

Still recovering from that explosive kiss, Lucy watched him lift a small jeweller's box from a side-table and extend it to her. 'Ring?' she questioned, her heart starting to beat even faster, her reddened mouth to curving into a smile.

'A betrothal ring.' Joaquin frowned, his beautiful mouth harshly compressed as he made a positive production out of glancing at his watch like a male severely pressed for time. 'My sister will expect it. Take her shopping with you for a wedding gown.'

'A wedding gown?' Lucy clutched the box in one hand and made a speaking gesture with her other at what was she actually wearing. 'But I could wear this—'

An expression of distaste crossed his lean strong face. 'No Del Castillo bride would wear a second-hand dress!'

He reached the door and then swung back to murmur reflectively, 'Choose something white…a white dress. Full-length and traditional.'

He was thinking of Cindy's bridal apparel, which had been pink and short, she registered dully. 'Anything else?' she asked, not really expecting a further response.

Joaquin contemplated the wall rather than her, hard jaw-line set in a stubborn thrust, apparently deep in thought on a subject which she had not expected him to take one iota of interest in. 'A veil…and perhaps a tiara…I'll have my mother's jewellery flown over. You'll need a bouquet…white roses,' he stipulated without hesitation. 'And don't put your hair up.'

Lucy absorbed the surprising detail of his instructions with ever-widening eyes.

Joaquin sent her a slashing sidewise glance and his strong jawline set even harder. 'I'm thinking of the look of things for my extended family and friends…on film, you understand. We'll throw a big party and show the film at it when we return to Guatemala to see in the New Year.'

'So we'll be spending Christmas here?' Lucy gathered. 'May I order a tree?'

For the count of five seconds Joaquin looked as though he had not a clue what she was talking about.

'A Christmas tree…' she extended awkwardly.

'Do as you wish,' Joaquin said, with all the enthusiasm of Ebenezer Scrooge, his impatience palpable.

And then he was gone.

'The look of things'? For the sake of appearances alone? Lucy was very pale. She opened the jewellery box and caught her breath at the glittering diamond ring formed in the shape of a flower. It was exquisite and very unusual. An engagement ring, or as *he* had called it, a betrothal ring. 'My sister will expect it'. That stabbed her to the heart, and she couldn't help but think how painfully ironic it was that Joaquin should condemn her for the deception she had practised on him but then make it crystal-clear that he expected her to put on another dishonest charade where their marriage was concerned.

CHAPTER ELEVEN

'FOR a cheap dress that had to be bought off the peg, it looks really good,' Yolanda conceded forty-eight hours later as she appraised the wedding gown which Lucy wore from all angles.

'It was a very expensive buy!' Lucy protested.

'Lucy…you have a new scale of expense to learn now that you are about to become a Del Castillo. Anything that hasn't been specially designed for you is cheap!'

But it was *still* a dream of a dress. Alone, Lucy would never have entered the couture salon to which Yolanda had taken her only the day before. By that late stage, fretting at her failure to find anything which would be worthy of the tiara which Joaquin had mentioned, Lucy had been getting really desperate. The gown had been a sample, in a tiny size. Without a murmur about the inconvenience, it had been shortened to fit her last night and delivered first thing that morning, a delicate confection of rich fine fabric, its bodice and long slender sleeves overlaid with a very fine tracery of seed pearls.

'I think it is so cool that Joaquin just can't wait to marry you,' Yolanda confided with a grin, helping Lucy to anchor the magnificent diamond tiara to the lace veil. 'Yet when he followed us to London, whenever I mentioned you he changed the subject! I suppose that means that when a guy is really, really crazy about someone he doesn't want to talk about it like a woman does.'

'No,' Lucy agreed hurriedly, bowing her head.

She had not even seen Joaquin since he'd left for Paris. He had returned very late the previous night. With Yolanda in the house, determined that every tradition should be followed, Lucy had found her efforts to go down to breakfast blocked and had ended up eating off a tray instead, while being lectured on what bad luck it would be for her to see Joaquin before they met at the altar.

Following the ceremony, Yolanda was spending a few days with a schoolfriend. She and her brother had finally reached an agreement on her future. The teenager would board during the week but come home to the townhouse at weekends. After she had sat her exams in June, she would have the option of completing her education in Guatemala.

A limousine ferried Lucy and Yolanda to a little church on the outskirts of London. Lucy couldn't believe her eyes when she saw the equivalent of a whole camera crew in place, awaiting their arrival.

'This will make the television news at home,' Yolanda pointed out to her, surprised at Lucy's surprise.

In fact the whole ceremony was taped, but Lucy, who would have been very nervous about that idea had she known about it in advance, took account of nothing and nobody but Joaquin from the minute she walked down the aisle. And from the instant she entered the church his attention was on her. Joaquin was sheathed in a superb pale grey suit which threw into prominence his devastating dark good-looks. As his bright eyes met hers Lucy was conscious only of an intense sense of happiness, and every other concern just fell away.

The ceremony complete, the ring on her finger, Lucy floated back into the limousine on Joaquin's arm.

He gave her a slow smile. 'You look superb, *querida*.'

'Yolanda said it was a cheap dress.'

Joaquin laughed with rich amusement. 'The term is relative when used by my sister!'

'Oh, my goodness!' Lucy suddenly clamped a hand to her mouth in dismay. 'May I borrow your phone?'

'What's wrong?' he demanded, extending the carphone with a frown etched between his straight ebony brows.

'I was supposed to start work today and I totally forgot to ring and tell them that I wouldn't be taking the job after all!' While Joaquin looked on in apparent astonishment, Lucy called directory enquiries to get the number of the toy store and then rang to offer profuse apologies for not having informed them of her change of heart sooner.

'Why are you looking at me like that?' Lucy asked self-consciously when she had replaced the phone, her conscience at peace again.

'It *is* your wedding day. I'm amazed that you took the trouble to make that call.'

'I don't like letting people down.'

His lean strong features had hardened. 'Isn't it a shame that you couldn't afford me the same consideration?'

'If you're talking about me having pretended to be Cindy,' Lucy responded tautly, 'that is an entirely different matter.'

'*Por Dios*...you have a talent for understatement.'

Lucy breathed in deep. 'But I might have told the truth sooner had you not made so many unpleasant remarks about my sister's past and then gone on to suggest that her future husband ought to be warned about what she was like.'

'So that's your excuse. I was very angry about what the old man had had to suffer.'

'Cindy never intended *anybody* to suffer! She may have written stupid letters asking for money, but she honestly believed he could afford to be generous. That's not the same thing as being a con-artist.'

Joaquin shot her a darkling glance. 'Nor is it acceptable behaviour. And you do my image of *you* no favours in trying to imply otherwise.'

'I'm sorry. She's my sister and I love her...flaws included,' Lucy stated, tilting her chin. 'People can change, Joaquin. Finding happiness with Roger changed Cindy and I didn't want to see her lose him.'

'*Infierno!*' Joaquin slashed back at her with a sudden raging incredulity that wholly disconcerted her. It was much as though she had thrown a match on a bale of hay: the conflagration was instantaneous. 'Yet you had little concern for what I might think of *you!*'

'That's not true,' Lucy began shakily, paralysed to the spot by the blaze of dark fury brightening his extraordinary eyes.

'You let me call you a whore!' Joaquin condemned, off-balancing her even further with that outraged reminder. 'You lied to me. Even the night we made love you were still lying. But the worst, the most unforgivable of acts, was to leave me believing that you were sleeping with another man and that you might not know whose baby you were carrying!'

Lucy sat there like a little stone statue, heart thumping in the region of her dry throat, motionless with sheer shock.

'I might have gone away…I might *never* have come back. I might have abandoned you for ever. And did you count the cost? Did you care? *No!*' Joaquin thundered in a splintering crescendo of accusation, his lean strong face rigid.

'I…I would have contacted you.'

'*How?* Do you think I would have taken your calls or accepted your letters or even believed anything you said or wrote?' Joaquin demanded with raw contempt. 'A woman who let me believe such filth about her for longer than a moment is not a woman I can be proud to have as a wife! I can only hope you have more loving concern for our child when it is born than you had for me!'

With that wrathful conclusion Joaquin sent the privacy panel separating them from his chauffeur buzzing back and rapped out something in Spanish. She soon knew what it was. The big limo came to an almost immediate halt and Joaquin thrust open the door and sprang out.

'Joaquin!' Lucy gasped. 'Where are you going?'

'I need some fresh air,' he gritted in a driven undertone, and closed the door on her again.

Fresh as opposed to the air she was polluting with her presence, she translated in a daze as the limousine pulled back into the traffic again. Joaquin vanished into the busy crowds of Christmas shoppers. She looked at her watch. They had been married for forty-five minutes. She blinked and slowly filled her lungs with oxygen again.

Suddenly she was faced with the acknowledgement that she had carelessly glossed over something huge as if it was no more than a molehill. Behind her the molehill had mushroomed into a volcano. She, who prided herself on her soft heart and her sensitivity, had behaved in the cruellest way imaginable, and as she sat there numbly attempting to justify herself she found that she could not.

There *was* no excuse for her having allowed Joaquin to spend two entire days believing that Roger was her lover, most particularly not when she was pregnant. Just because she had known it wasn't true; just because she had been afraid to come clean and admit who she really was there and then. She had hidden behind the defence that she *still* had to put Cindy first, but that was no defence at all. Yet she had tried to make Joaquin listen and he had refused to listen. He had been in such a temper she had let herself be rebuffed.

When she got back to the townhouse, she was too disturbed by the awareness of her own less than presentable behaviour to be embarrassed by the reality that she was alone. Joaquin was furious with her and she understood why. How could she have treated someone she loved as she had treated him? She knew how volatile he was.

Suppose he had just decided right then on the spur of the moment that even for the sake of their child he could not stand to be married to such a selfish, insensitive woman? Recognising what a state she was working herself up into, Lucy stopped pacing the floor and decided that she would be better occupied doing something with herself.

The twelve-foot tree which had been delivered the day before now stood in the hall waiting to be dressed. That evocative pine scent brought back hazy memories of Christmases when Lucy had been a young child. Before her parents had divorced they had always had a real tree, as opposed to an artificial one. Entering into the spirit of the occasion, Joaquin's urbane manservant had produced boxes and boxes of vintage decorations from the attic where they had lain almost twenty years, since Joaquin's mother's death. Apparently Joaquin and his late parents had once spent every Christmas in England.

Reluctant to remove her wedding dress, but determined to keep it clean, Lucy borrowed a large apron, donned it, and began to burrow into the boxes. Her enthusiasm increased with every box she opened, for she found beautiful handmade decorations which had more than stood the test of time. She was standing on a low set of steps fixing an exotic feathered bird to a branch of the tree when the front door opened two hours later and Joaquin reappeared, with a gaily wrapped parcel in his hand. She froze. Three feet into the hall, he froze too. He appeared transfixed by the sight of her.

'*Madre mia!*' Joaquin suddenly exclaimed, and setting aside the parcel in haste, he strode across the hall to close both arms round her. He lifted her down from the steps much as though he was reclaiming her from grievous danger on the edge of a cliff.

'Are you crazy?' he demanded tautly. 'The staff should be doing this.'

Lucy focused on his lean, dark devastatingly handsome face, a tide of sheer heady relief washing over her. 'I love dressing the tree—'

Joaquin elevated an ebony brow. 'On your wedding day?'

'I needed something to do.' Lucy snatched in a steadying breath. 'And before you say anything, I've got something to say. I wish I could give you some magical explanation of why I let you go that day Roger barged in without making you listen to me, but I *can't*! I think I had just got so used to pretending to be Cindy, to being passive on my own account—'

Joaquin reached out and linked his hands with hers in a feeling movement. His brilliant green eyes held hers. 'I can't stand passive.'

'Well, I swear that if you hadn't come to the church on Cindy's wedding day I would have come to you to explain!' Lucy broke in urgently. 'I was really upset that you should think those things of me.'

Joaquin was now gripping her trembling hands very tightly. Dulled colour marked his proud cheekbones. 'I shouldn't have abandoned you in the limo,' he conceded in a driven undertone. 'But I was afraid of what else I might say...the damage I would do.'

'But you were right. I didn't think of how you might have been feeling.'

'*Por Dios*...I felt like I was being ripped apart that day at your sister's apartment!' Joaquin admitted grittily. 'But the crowning nightmare was believing that you were marrying Roger. I came to the church intending to do whatever I had to do to prevent you marrying him but very much afraid that I would be too late.'

'And instead you found out that I wasn't even who you thought I was,' Lucy filled in, shamefaced. 'Joaquin, I'm so sorry—'

'No, your concern for your sister was understandable.' Poised very straight and tall, Joaquin lifted one wide shoulder in an eloquent shrug that dismissed his own previous anger. 'In the heat of the moment in Guatemala I *did* make a most dishonourable threat. How were you to know that I would never have carried it out? I am *not* the kind of man who would sink to the level of carrying disreputable stories about a woman to another man.'

Recognising the distaste stamped in his lean strong face, Lucy sighed. 'I should have known that too.'

His beautiful mouth compressed. 'How could you have? From the instant I laid eyes on you I was strongly attracted to you. That angered me, and in an effort to remind myself of who and what I believed you to be I made several offensive remarks. I cannot excuse myself for having said such things to a woman.'

'I was shocked,' Lucy recalled ruefully.

'*Sí*...I saw that too, and marvelled at it. Then, when you condemned my lack of courtesy, I was outraged—but you were right to reproach me.'

It was balm to Lucy's ragged nerves to learn that Joaquin had been strongly drawn to her from the moment he met her, and she looked up at him and gave him a rather tremulous smile, for the extent of her relief had brought her emotions very close to the surface. 'I'm just glad you're home now. I was scared you were halfway back to Guatemala!'

'I can be hot-headed, *gatita mia*,' Joaquin conceded, his full attention pinned to her lovely smiling face with an intensity that made her incredibly aware of his powerful masculinity. 'But I assure you that even in the grip of all my stubborn pride and fury, I could not be that big a fool!'

'I was worried...' Belatedly becoming aware of the ludicrous apron she was wearing, she tugged her hands from his, only to find herself looking in dismay at her grimy hands. 'My goodness, I need to wash…I seem to have got more dust on me than the duster!'

Turning away in some chagrin at how she must look clad in her silly apron and with her childishly grubby hands, Lucy started up the stairs.

'For causing you concern—I apologise…' Having tracked her up to the landing, Joaquin caught one of the hands she was keeping well away from her gown in his, to plant a kiss almost defiantly into the centre of her palm.

Her knees went wobbly as she collided in shock with his shimmering crystalline gaze. 'I love your eyes,' she heard herself mumble.

'So you told me many times when you were ill…' His wolfish grin flashed out with charismatic brilliance.

Dredging her attention from him again with the greatest of difficulty, Lucy sped down the bedroom corridor, only to find herself forestalled by Joaquin, saying very decisively when she headed for the guest room she had been using, 'Wrong door.'

Feeling ridiculously self-conscious over that reminder that they would now be sharing the same bedroom, Lucy hurried further down the passageway and across his bedroom, straight into the *en suite* bathroom to wash her hands.

'You are still so shy, *querida*,' Joaquin murmured with a rueful amusement that made her cheeks burn as he came to halt in the doorway. 'Only *now* do I recognise what a lousy actress you were in Guatemala. I told myself that the innocence I kept on sensing was a good act. I could not bear to want you so much and believe that you were out of reach. For of course, had I known the truth, it would have been dishonourable for me to take advantage of you.'

'You didn't do that.' Grabbing up a towel, Lucy hastily dried her hands.

'I *did*. Don't you know it's asking for trouble to go to bed with a man who tells you not to fantasise about a future? It was a line and you swallowed it,' Joaquin imparted in a seriously pained tone. 'You should have told me to get lost.'

'But I didn't want you to get lost,' Lucy answered truthfully.

'You were a virgin...'

Looking anywhere but at him, Lucy nodded her head in embarrassed confirmation.

Joaquin groaned out loud. 'All that nonsense you spouted to conceal that reality! I would have waited for our wedding night—'

'Joaquin...this is one of those subjects when cultivating a short memory would be the very nicest thing you could do for me.' Now frantically engaged in a struggle to untie the knot of the apron strings, so that she could shed the wretched garment and once more look like a normal bride, Lucy found herself receiving help. Joaquin edged her backwards out of the bathroom, spun her gently around and had her out of the apron in two seconds flat.

'The fault was mine. I was too proud to accept that I could be so much in love with a woman who seemed to be the total opposite of my every ideal,' Joaquin breathed ruefully.

'So much in love...?' That was all Lucy heard, and that confession just pinned her to the spot with a dry mouth and a madly racing heartbeat.

'Which is why I came to the church on your sister's wedding day. The minute I realised I might have lost you to another man, *nothing* else mattered!' Joaquin shared in a raw-edged admission. 'Not that you might have slept with him, not that the child might even be *his*...I still wanted you to be mine.'

'Oh, Joaquin,' Lucy muttered, her eyes glistening with helpless tears. 'I can't believe you loved me that much—'

'Didn't I rush to the church to tell you so?' A forgivably

grim smile of recollection momentarily curved his firm mouth. 'Only to discover that you were not Cindy Paez and not the bride either. Never have I been made to feel like such a fool! In anger with you, I almost let my pride destroy us then.'

Lucy touched his hand with uncertain fingers. 'You were allowed to be angry—'

'But I might have driven you away. I wanted to punish you for having deceived me. Yet, when I thought about it, I had always known the *real* you,' Joaquin stressed, spreading both hands in speaking emphasis on that point. 'The whole time you were just yourself in Guatemala. Honest in every way you could be. Very shocked to hear of Fidelio's situation, always attempting to show me that there were *two* sides to every argument—'

'You know...' Lucy broke in, so eager was she to share her own feelings at that moment. 'I love you very much too!'

Joaquin surveyed her with shimmering eyes full of appreciation, and his smile became one of unalloyed satisfaction, his brilliant gaze softening to tenderness. Nothing was said. In that instant nothing more *needed* to be said. He pulled her into his arms with unconcealed impatience and kissed her with the most explosive hunger he had ever shown her.

There was nothing remotely cool about the way in which he got her out of her wedding gown, nothing measured or smooth about the manner in which he stripped off his beautiful suit. They were both on an emotional high of sheer relief and happiness that all the misunderstandings were now behind them. From that first drugging kiss she was on fire, aching for the glorious fulfilment that only he could give.

In the aftermath of that wild passion, which swept them both to the heights and then dropped them down gently to share a wonderful sensation of togetherness, Lucy recognised that she had never felt so happy in her life. And that sensation was made all the more intoxicating by the quiet awareness that Joaquin felt exactly the same way.

His bright gaze, semi-screened by his lush black lashes, smouldered over her with possessive intensity and then his mouth quirked. 'There's something I should tell you... I will personally replace the remainder of Fidelio's savings. He will never know that the money did not come from your sister.'

Lucy could not conceal her total disconcertion at that announcement.

Joaquin smiled ruefully and skated his fingertip over her full lower lip. 'Roger argued with me, but I insisted that clearing the debt would be my wedding present to them both.'

'But why...why did you change your mind and decide to do that?' Suddenly registering that this must be what her twin had referred to but refused to discuss before she'd set off on her honeymoon, Lucy was genuinely amazed that Joaquin had decided to make so generous a gesture towards her sister and her husband.

'I now believe that Fidelio and Cindy were *both* victims, in their own way. If Mario hadn't died, it would never have happened.' Joaquin sighed. 'But Mario was using my hotel suite when he met your sister. He was a very nice guy, but it is possible that in a desire to impress Cindy he somewhat exaggerated his circumstances and misled her entirely.'

Lucy nodded very slowly at this re-rendering of possible events. She had the tact not to comment. She saw that Joaquin had been realistically reappraising what he recalled of his former friend's character. A nice guy, but possibly not above the kind of boastfulness which might have come close to actual lying, she translated for herself.

'It is not a good idea for Roger and your sister to start

their life as a couple with a substantial debt still hanging over them. They had already lost the value of that flat which was sold. Your sister is going to have a hard enough time living within their income,' Joaquin pointed out wryly. 'It occurred to me that to saddle them with so great a burden might put considerable strain on their relationship in the future.'

'Yes.' Lucy had been trying not to worry about that angle herself, but there was no denying that Roger would have had good reason for resentment when he found himself under such financial constraint. After all, he had not even known Cindy when the debt was incurred. Suddenly she was just filled to the brim with gratitude that Joaquin had had that much foresight and generosity.

'It means so little to me, but so much to them.'

'I just love you ten times more than I did a minute ago!'' Lucy told him exuberantly, for he was every bit as clever as she had ever thought he was.

Joaquin lay back against the pillows and let her cover him with kisses. He gave her a wry smile. 'Fidelio will also profit more from this less punitive way of resolving the situation. We will invite Roger and Cindy to Guatemala to meet the old man and that will make him very happy.'

'You're brilliant,' Lucy assured him, even more impressed and quite unable to hide the fact.

'I told you that you were made for me.' Joaquin studied her rapt face with tenderly amused eyes. 'The Latin male ego thrives on appreciation.'

Much later they ate by romantic candlelight in the dining room and Lucy unwrapped the gift which Joaquin had set aside and forgotten about when he returned earlier that afternoon. It was the most exquisite crystal angel.

'I saw it in a store. It made me think of you,' Joaquin confessed silkily.

'An angel?' Lucy queried a little tautly.

'Not quite,' Joaquin countered teasingly. 'But I can see through you the same way I could see through crystal.'

After their meal they finished decorating the Christmas tree, which had to be just about the very last thing Lucy had expected to share with a male of Joaquin's sophistication. But Joaquin, it turned out, was no more proof against the lure of happy childhood memories than she was, and he was drawn into the task the instant he recognised some of the vintage decorations which Lucy had already hung.

His mother, who had died when he was ten, had adored London. Christmas had never been the same after that for him. And Lucy had had much the same experience with her mother, after her parents had parted.

'It made me sort of crave all the festive trappings while I was growing up,' she confided ruefully. 'Mum just had no interest after my father walked out.'

'If you want to put a giant Santa Claus on the roof and cover the whole house in naff lights, you can, *gatita mia*,' Joaquin promised, appreciatively hugging her to him with all the affection and warmth she revelled in. 'Yolanda will come in the door and groan about how sentimental you are, but secretly love it all.'

Actually, he got that wrong. His sister came through the door on Christmas Eve, took one look at the gorgeous tree and gushed with unhidden excitement, 'Oh, wow, Lucy... you're going to do the whole *family* Christmas bit! Are we having a turkey for dinner, like British people do? Crackers to pull? Silly games? Do I get to hang a stocking? Open my pressies at midnight?'

'No, you'll have to be seriously cool and control yourself until dawn breaks on Christmas morning,' Joaquin delivered with gentle irony.

Yolanda gave him an amused look. 'Joaquin...I'm adult enough now to be in touch with my inner child.'

On Christmas Day Yolanda left a happy trail of wrapping paper right round the drawing-room, glorying in every gift right down to the cute and cuddly teddy bear in her stocking, and then went into seclusion with her phone to amuse herself talking to her friends.

'Next year will be our child's first Christmas,' Joaquin whispered huskily, banding his arms round Lucy, who was still dazedly studying the huge mound of gifts which had more than made up for all the disappointing Christmases in her past.

'Yes…' She sighed dreamily, thinking that the little inflatable Santa Claus which Yolanda had included as one of her jokey presents would no doubt be exactly what their child would like to poke and pummel.

'Not many women would appreciate a teenager around within a few days of their wedding.' Joaquin studied her contented face with deeply appreciative eyes. 'But you don't mind, do you?'

Lucy smiled. 'I like the feeling that I'm part of a family just as much as she does.'

He kissed her breathless, and her heart sang and her pulses raced. Sensible talk receded for some time, until Lucy recalled that they were supposed to be attending a church service before lunch. Aghast at how late it was, she leapt off the sofa with pink cheeks, shocked at herself. 'Joaquin…we nearly forgot about the service!'

Joaquin studied her with amusement and he laughed. 'Did we warn Yolanda that tradition is going to bite even deeper today than she appreciated?'

Upstairs, Yolanda groaned in mock suffering on her call to a friend. 'You have no idea how *soppy* they are—always holding hands like kids. And Joaquin is just *so* clueless it's painful to watch. He's given poor Lucy all these dreary, dreadful books on the Maya…and as if that wasn't enough to bore her to death, he's dragging her off on some ghastly mega-tour of ruins next month. As if what we've got at the foot of the garden isn't enough for him!'

'Yolanda!' Joaquin called.

A week before Christmas, almost a year later, Lucy settled her infant son into his bouncing cradle in the drawing room of the townhouse.

Cindy and Roger were coming for lunch in about an hour and a half. Lucy was wearing an elegant blue dress, purely and simply because Joaquin had remarked on how that shade matched her eyes. She smiled to herself now at the memory of how Joaquin had once described exactly how she should look at their wedding. She had been awfully dim not to immediately grasp that a guy who could even picture what flowers she should carry to the altar was a hopeless romantic and very much in love.

Jaime Enrique Del Castillo yawned to regain his mother's attention. He had black hair and blue eyes and he was the most peaceful laid-back baby ever. But then their first child had absolutely no reason to be anything other than happy and content, Lucy conceded with a grin. He was first and foremost the most important little person in the household, and he received an incredible amount of attention from his parents, his aunt Yolanda and the staff.

Having left school and gained reasonable results in her exams, Yolanda, now seventeen, was attending a London art college. She was showing some talent and was now more interested in becoming a famous artist than attaining fame as an It Girl. Lucy had had quite an input in that development and, having attained the greater freedom of being a student, Yolanda was growing up fast.

Lucy had experienced a truly blissful first year of marriage, and she could not have been happier. Soon after their wedding Joaquin had swept her off on a leisurely three-week exploration of the ruined cities of the Maya. Although visiting some of the less accessible sites had been ruled out by Joaquin, on the grounds that such exertion was unwise for a woman in the early stages of pregnancy, they had had the most fabulous time on that trip. Lucy was now learning about conservation methods and Joaquin was convinced he had found his soulmate. Yolanda had been known to remark that as company went her brother and Lucy could sometimes be a challenge, particularly when they got stuck into what she deemed 'that boring stuff'.

Cindy and Roger had visited Guatemala over Easter, and had been invited out to Fidelio's refurbished ranch. The old man had greeted Cindy with open arms, and Roger with equal warmth, counting them both as relatives and delighted that they should visit him. Fidelio Paez was every bit as sweet as Yolanda had once said he was, and, no longer hampered by her guilty conscience, Cindy had genuinely warmed to the older man.

Lucy and Joaquin's first child had been born late enough after his secret due date for the uncritical to assume he had been born only slightly early. Their blushes had been spared. Now, crouching down to watch her baby Jaime stare at the lights shimmering over the glittering ornaments on the Christmas tree with round, fascinated blue eyes, Lucy studied the beautiful eternity ring which she had received on her last birthday and decided that she was the luckiest and most spoilt woman in the world.

Joaquin strolled in, dark and devastating in a beige suit. He laughed as Jaime stretched out a tiny hand in the direction of a swinging bauble further out of his reach than he could yet calculate. 'He would swarm over that tree like a miniature demolition man if he could!'

'This time next year he'll be a trial,' Lucy forecast with fond anticipation.

Joaquin bent down and slotted a rattle into his infant son's empty hand. Jaime relaxed again. 'He'll be even more entertaining than he is now. He's got a real tough-man grip on that rattle...do you see that?'

Lucy nodded agreement and tried not to smile.

Joaquin straightened and snaked out a powerful arm to catch her to him, brilliant green eyes scanning her amused face. 'You're laughing at me again.'

'Jaime just doesn't look that tough to me yet,' she confided chokily. 'But I'll take your word for it. Both being guys, I guess you have a special link.'

'*You*,' Joaquin filled in with hungry appreciative emphasis, claiming her parted lips with his own in the kind of long, slow drugging kiss that always left Lucy reeling and dizzy and which was very much a major feature of their lives. 'A very, very special link. I adore you, *querida*.'

'*Sí...*' Lucy sighed dreamily.

'*Sí...*' Joaquin confirmed a little raggedly.

Jaime, who enjoyed a thoroughly undemanding itinerary, and who had not the faintest notion of being a chaperon or even being a tough guy at that moment, just went back to sleep and left his parents in peace.

Michelle Reid grew up on the southern edges of Manchester, the youngest in a family of five lively children. But now she lives in the beautiful county of Cheshire with her busy executive husband and two grown-up daughters. She loves reading, the ballet, and playing tennis when she gets the chance. She hates cooking, cleaning, and despises ironing! Sleep she can do without and produces some of her best written work during the early hours of the morning.

A SICILIAN
SEDUCTION

by

Michelle Reid

CHAPTER ONE

GIANCARLO CARDINALE arrived in the doorway of Knight's executive dining room to the surprise discovery that some kind of function was taking place. The remains of a gourmet-style lunch still lay in evidence amongst a scatter of empty wine bottles, and the twenty or so people who were gathered there were now standing around in small groups talking while they sipped at champagne.

'What's going on?' he asked the man beside him.

'Lunch between presentations to one of our best clients,' Howard Fiske explained. 'And Edward really should have made the effort to be here for it.'

His anger was clear. If it wasn't bad enough that the corporate chairman himself should have turned up here unexpectedly, to have done so on a day when Edward should have been presiding over such an important meeting, annoyed Howard intensely.

Giancarlo said nothing, but he sympathised. He knew all about Edward's irresponsible streak, after all. In fact Edward's flagrant lack of responsibility on all fronts was the sole reason for his being in London. He had come to deal with it once and for all, and the sooner he got it over with the better it was going to be for everyone. Which left him with only one question he needed answering before he got down to the nasty business of dealing with the problem.

Which one was she?

As he stood there, still unnoticed by the rest of the gathering, his gaze began moving over the newly refurbished ultra-modern room with its beech-wood surfaces and flashes of so-called inspirational colour—all paid for with his money in an attempt to haul Knight's out of the dark ages.

But it was not so easy to revamp the people, he observed, seeing the same starched collars and the same grey faces, with their grey little minds which collectively helped to keep the company in a state of near peril.

His teeth came together on a snap of irritation. Edward had promised to restructure his workforce last year when they'd discussed merging Knight's into the Cardinale Group. In fact, Giancarlo had insisted upon it before he would agree to ratify the deal. Edward might be his brother-in-law but the Cardinale Group was not run as a charity. As a venture capitalist Giancarlo looked for potential in any proposed merger before he even considered putting together a rescue package.

Edward had been told this, had understood it, and had agreed to all the provisos at the time. So—other than for laminate flooring and some splashes of colour on the walls—where had all the money he had been steadily shelling out to Edward gone? For none of these grey, slightly bored faces he could see in here showed a hint of a change in attitude.

Which was why Giancarlo had no problem at all picking out his quarry, since she was the only one that fitted the description his source had provided him with, of a young, very nubile, bottle redhead, with an inherent ability to distract any man.

If this really was Natalia Deyton, then Edward could certainly pick them, Giancarlo decided as he stood watching the way she worked around the room like a true professional.

Professional in what? he then found himself pondering

cynically as his darkly lashed gaze shifted from her admittedly exquisite profile to the revealingly flushed one belonging to the young man she was talking to at present. Her job description had her down as the personal assistant to Knight's namesake and managing director. But with a face and a figure like that, it wasn't surprising that Edward Knight had given her job title a whole new twist.

Anger suddenly began to bite as he stood watching the provocative way she was teasing that blushing young fool. Tying him in knots, he saw. Making it plain that she was open to suggestion.

Brazen bitch, he thought sourly. Then—

Brazen *bountiful* bitch, he found himself extending when the crowd suddenly shifted and he got a glimpse of what it was that was hooking their attention. She had the kind of cleavage a man could dive into—as her skimpy white top with its dipping neckline was blatantly advertising!

No wonder half the men in here looked hot about their starched collars. And no wonder Edward couldn't keep his damn hands off her, Giancarlo added harshly when he felt even his own more discerning loins give him a stinging kick that actually forced him to draw the muscles in around his sex to stop the obvious from happening.

'*Dio,*' he breathed, when as if sensing his scrutiny she suddenly turned to look straight at him.

Those eyes, those amazing eyes! He had never encountered anything like them! Blue, they were blue. A smoky, steamy, sultry blue that had his imagination shooting into overdrive as he began to wonder what happened to those eyes when she was beneath a man and in the throes of an orgasm.

Did Edward already know? Was he still man enough to acquire that heady kind of knowledge? Giancarlo's sister said no. In fact his sister had been quite disconcertingly open about Edward's recent inability to satisfy her on that front. But this was different. The woman standing here could incite a dying man to take one last sip of the nectar.

Without any warning, a new kind of emotion was suddenly overwhelming him. It was a hot, tight, primitive emotion that sank its roots deep into his possessive psyche, where it lashed him with the burning message that he did not *want* Edward to know what Natalia Deyton was like in bed. He didn't want any other man but *himself* to know what, in that single blinding hot flash of a moment, he knew he fully intended to make his exclusively...!

Oh, good grief! Natalia found herself gasping inwardly as she caught the full heat of the stranger's expression. In all her life she had never encountered a look quite like it. Men looked at her and wanted her, she was used to that. She would be lying if she tried to deny an effect she had been having on the opposite sex for most of her adult life.

But the way this man was looking at her was something else entirely. It was hot and compulsive and so very possessive that she actually felt as if he were crawling right inside her skin and claiming total occupancy.

Stunned and shaken by the whole experience, she quickly dragged her eyes away. But too late to stop a tight, breathlessly excited feeling from permeating her blood, and, although she tried very hard to concentrate on the conversation taking place around her, she was really hearing nothing but a strange roaring taking place in her head. Her eyes had glazed over, leaving only a mirror image imprinted on her retina of a tall, lean, very attractive stranger with black hair, olive skin and dark, dark compelling eyes that even now, while she wasn't actually looking into them, still made her feel as if she were being invaded. Who was he? What was he? Why was he standing there looking at her like that?

It was almost impossible not to look back at him—just to check that he was real and the small sip of champagne she had allowed herself hadn't started her hallucinating.

It was most definitely a relief to find Howard Fiske had claimed his attention. But the power of the physical man still seriously disturbed her. Everything—everything about him from the long, slightly hooked shape of his nose that should have spoilt his playboy good looks but didn't, to the lean tight structure of his body clothed in the finest Italian tailoring, affirmed the man's sexual appeal. He oozed it, pulsed it, threatened and promised it.

Oh, my God—she looked away again, so appalled by her own lustful thoughts that they made the sexual way he had been looking at her fade into insignificance.

'Are you feeling all right, Natalia?' a voice from what seemed like a long distance off managed to squeeze its way into her consciousness.

'Yes,' she replied, though it took all she had in her to find the light, reassuring smile to go with the answer. 'But I think the champagne is beginning to get to me.' Another passable smile—a rueful one—and she placed her glass down on the nearest table. 'Never could take alcohol during daylight. Another sip and I would probably end up snoring for the rest of the day.'

'You would never snore...' Very intense, deadly serious—it was almost a relief to look into Ian Gant's besotted eyes because his boyish attraction to her was so easy to deal with.

'Tell me about your lovely fiancée,' she urged, glancing briefly to his left as she did so. 'The wedding is only a few weeks away, I believe?'

It was enough. He took the hint. The flush of attraction

changed to a flush of embarrassment when he recalled the presence of Randall Taylor, his future father-in-law who, hearing weddings mentioned, turned to join in the discussion.

After that she was able to put the stranger out of her mind while she concentrated on the business in hand. Which was, in part, supposed to be an exercise in public relations because Taylor-Gant were threatening to take their business elsewhere if Knight's did not improve their overall performance.

A grave step—a tough step when you took into consideration that Taylor-Gant had been using Edward's marketing skills since for ever.

The sudden tap on her shoulder had her turning with a smile at the ready for whomever it was who wanted her attention.

But the smile died the moment she found herself looking down at Howard Fiske. Cold-eyed, mean-mouthed, and with the naturally aggressive manner that seemed to come along with his short, thin stature, he drew her apart from the others with a set of fingers on her arm that dug in just a little too tightly for her liking.

'Your presence is required,' he said, flicking his eyes to her cleavage with an insolence that made her grit her teeth. 'Edward's office. As of now.'

Edward—the magic word. 'He's turned up at last?' she exclaimed, so relieved she couldn't contain it. But she had been worrying about him throughout the whole morning when it had become clear that he'd gone missing without telling anyone. It wasn't the first time he'd done this recently, but this particular day it had been important that he be here to soothe the Taylor-Gant ruffled feathers. But Edward wasn't thinking too clearly at the moment, due to a struggle he was having with himself. *Many* struggles, she then extended painfully. To him his whole life was in a mess and he just didn't know what to do to make it better.

'Just excuse yourself and go,' Howard Fiske tersely instructed. And as he removed his fingers from her arm she was almost positive they brushed against the side of her breast quite deliberately.

It made her want to shudder, though she contained the need, having learned very early on in her six-month conflict with Howard Fiske that a response—any kind of response to his blatant touching—was just what gave the nasty man his kicks.

So with a blank face she nodded in silent acquiescence, then turned to make her excuses.

'That girl is a credit to this company,' Randall Taylor remarked as he, too, watched the way she took her leave of each person in turn before eventually escaping through the door.

You wouldn't be saying that if she were bedding your future son-in-law behind your daughter's back, Howard thought with a smile that hid his real contempt for Edward's so-called *personal* assistant as he watched her slip quietly out of the room.

Suddenly he felt almost happy, because he had a very good feeling that Natalia Deyton was about to meet her Waterloo—or Giancarlo Cardinale was not the man he was reputed to be...

Natalia, on the other hand, was too busy worrying about Edward to think about anything else as she took the direct route across the dove-grey carpet covering her own office floor on her way to Edward's office.

The door was firmly shut, but it didn't deter her. With only a cursory knock to warn of her arrival, she opened it and sailed right in there with all guns blazing. 'Edward—you have to know that I am very angry with you,' she announced. 'I really can't believe that you've let everyone down like this! Where have you been all morning? What is it you—'

'It's not Edward,' a smooth, deep, totally unfamiliar voice with the merest thread of a foreign accent inserted.

In the process of closing the door behind her, Natalia spun on her slender heels then froze, totally stunned to see the tall dark stranger from the dining room comfortably ensconced in the chair behind Edward's desk, and looking as if he had every right to be there!

He had even removed the jacket to his dark suit, so the bright white of his shirt stood out against the black leather back of Edward's chair, adding extra emphasis to the width of his shoulders and the breadth of his chest, which set that same tight, tense breathless feeling that had attacked her earlier stinging through her system.

It was awful—stifling and confusing because she didn't understand what was happening here! Not the tingling sensation, nor the baffling fact that some total stranger seemed to have taken up residence in Edward's office. And what was just as bad was the way he was running those eyes over her again as if he had every right to do that also!

'Who are you?' she demanded. 'What right have you to be in here?'

He didn't even bother to answer. Instead he just continued to inspect her from the top of her gleaming head to the tips of her shiny black leather court shoes. It was like being stripped to the bare skin by a pair of black lasers, she likened, automatically stiffening up in outright objection.

'I asked you a question,' she snapped out.

'Actually, you asked two,' he drawled in a soft, dry,

husky tone that had her stomach muscles curling in on themselves in response.

A sensual response, she noted in helpless confusion. What was wrong with her? Who was he, and why was he making her feel like this?

It was deliberate too; she was at least functioning sharply enough to be aware of the hint of calculation behind his lazily seductive regard.

'I'm going to call Security,' she announced, turning back to the door again.

'Three questions, if we include the one you thought you were asking Edward,' he tagged on very silkily.

And like a trigger that had the power to control her every movement, his use of Edward's name had her freezing yet again as a few very salient points began to filter into her stunned brain cells at last.

She'd first seen him standing with Howard. Now he was installed behind Edward's desk. And he had removed his suit jacket, which suggested that he intended to be there for quite some time. The jacket to his *Italian*-made suit, which went so well with his rich, dark *Italian* accent.

Oh, no. Her heart sank as full understanding finally hit her, and her skin began to prickle for a completely different reason. 'Giancarlo Cardinale,' she breathed out unsteadily.

'Well done,' he commended with a smile she didn't like. 'Now, please...' he waved a hand towards the chair opposite him '...come and sit down, Miss Deyton. We need to talk, I think, and we may as well be comfortable while we do so.'

But now she'd had his identity confirmed, she had no wish to move another inch away from this door until she had a few important answers. 'What's happened to

Edward?' she asked in a short, tense voice that revealed her anxiety. 'Is he all right? Has he taken ill?'

Anger leapt to life so abruptly in those lazy dark eyes that it took her completely aback. 'Nothing has happened to Edward,' he clipped out. 'Edward is *never* ill—as I am sure you are already aware of.'

Natalia didn't like his tone. It stiffened her backbone, as did the cold cynicism suddenly hardening his expression.

So what had happened to bring about a change in his attitude? And where *was* Edward? It was a question that sent a sudden cold little chill chasing down her spine. 'His wife, then,' she prompted, too anxious to realise that she was treading a very unstable line here. 'Has your sister taken ill or something?'

From anger, Giancarlo Cardinale turned to ice. 'You ask a lot of questions for a lowly clerk,' he incised.

'I am not a lowly clerk,' she denied.

'What are you, then?'

If it was possible her backbone went even straighter— and seemed to become a live conduit for the warning shot of electricity that went tingling down its full length. He couldn't know, could he? Warily she studied his dark face for any clues as to what exactly was going on because something dire certainly was, or he wouldn't be here like this.

Had he found out about her relationship with Edward...?

Sitting there watching the play of emotions taking place on her face, Giancarlo was experiencing a quiet sense of satisfaction for having so quickly brought her to the point where she was considering the frightening prospect of full exposure.

And who would not be frightened in similar circumstances? he allowed. If she had managed to work that much out, then she had also remembered that the blood that ran in his veins was Sicilian, and to a Sicilian family honour meant everything, which meant that she was in deep trouble.

Yet—oddly—he didn't want her afraid of him, though barely an hour ago he had been walking into this building looking forward to frightening the life out of Natalia Deyton—before he kicked her out of here.

Now things had changed. His game plan had changed. He had looked into her eyes and seen a sensual heaven beckoning him that he could not ignore. He wanted to experience that heaven. He wanted to touch it, taste it, lose himself in it. He wanted to spend days and nights and long exquisite weeks exploring all its possibilities to the exclusion of none—before he kicked her out.

Which also meant that he needed her to see him as her hero not as her enemy if he was going to convince her to let *him* in her bed instead of Edward.

Not that Giancarlo doubted for a second that this was exactly what she was going to do, because, no matter how beautiful she was to look at, he had not forgotten that a cold and calculatingly mercenary woman lurked beneath all of that beauty. Why else would she choose a paunchy middle-aged man like Edward for her lover if it weren't out of avarice?

Or was money her big turn-on? he then wondered cynically. Well, if it was, he decided, then he possessed more of that spicy commodity than Edward could ever hope to offer. Nor was he middle-aged or paunchy...

But his time was limited. He had put six weeks aside in his busy work schedule to be here in London. Six weeks to woo her, thoroughly slake his lusts in her—then redress family honour in a way that Natalia Deyton would never forget in a lifetime.

Still, first came the sweetness before the vengeance, he told himself, recognising the tight sting of anticipation for exactly what it was as he prepared to make her fall on him in undying gratitude.

'My apologies, Miss Deyton,' he murmured suddenly. 'I have clearly upset you, and I had no wish to do that. Please, come and sit down, and I will explain to you why I am here.'

She blinked and went pale but began moving towards him. Watching her do so was a pleasure in itself. The graceful stretch of her legs, the sway of her hips, and the unbelievable amount of sensuality she displayed from slender shoulders to beautiful feet. Even the way she lowered herself into the chair on the other side of the desk possessed a kind of poetry. And her hair was not bottle red but a natural burnished copper that caught fire in the weak sunlight seeping into the room from behind him, enhancing her amazing milk-white skin.

He missed none of it—wanted all of it. Especially that mouth, he decided. That soft, gorgeous mouth which was already parted and trembling slightly as if inviting him in.

But the eyes were no longer looking sultry. They looked scared. He wanted sultry. To get it, he leaned forward in the chair, using sexual body language to grab her attention. It worked; her lashes flickered slightly as her gaze dropped from his face to his shirtfront as it came closer. The hairs covering his chest began to prickle in indication of his own sexual arousal.

The spice of life, he named it dryly, noting the way her breathing quickened and her breasts lifted and fell beneath the fitted white top, as her own indication of sexual arousal. Deciding to consolidate on that, he got up and walked round to settle his lean hips on the desk only a few short inches away from her.

'Edward is well,' he assured her, watching the way her eyes slid down the length of his legs—then quickly away again. 'My sister Alegra is also well,' he added. 'In fact they are at this moment enjoying a well-deserved holiday cruising the Caribbean.'

Surprise brought her eyes up to clash with his. 'But—Edward never said—'

'Because Edward didn't know anything about it.' Giancarlo smiled. 'The cruise was arranged as a surprise present from me for their silver wedding anniversary,' he explained. 'You did know that Edward and my sister have been married for twenty-five years?' he then slid in silkily.

She shifted uncomfortably. 'Yes,' she confirmed.

Yes, he repeated silently. Of course you know. This was supposed to be the point where he duly informed her of what *he* knew about her affair with Edward—before he told her to get the hell out of his brother-in-law's life while she still had a chance to do it in one piece. He even had the fat cheque already made out and waiting in his pocket, to give a little impetus to her departure.

But the cheque remained where it was, and he no longer wanted Natalia Deyton to escape in one piece. He wanted to retain certain parts of her, the secrets of her beautiful body for one, the key to her heart for another.

Vengeance, sweet vengeance, he named it poetically. The Sicilian in him had no difficulty at all squaring his intentions with his conscience.

'The trip was planned in complete secrecy, and dropped on them both without warning a mere hour before they had to leave for Heathrow airport,' he expounded with a wry look that acknowledged the necessity to give neither of them the time to think about it. 'The surprise also came with my personal assurance to Edward that I would come and take care of things here for him while he is away, so he could have no excuse to protest the speed with which he and Alegra were rushed off to catch a flight to Barbados, from where they will begin their cruise.'

'On one of your cruise-liners?' she asked as a glimmer of understanding began to hit her blue eyes.

They weren't sultry but at least they were no longer frightened. 'What else?' He smiled. 'Honeymoon suite, royal deck, no luxury spared. Your concern for their well-being does you proud, Miss Deyton,' he then said with blatant flattery. 'But my own concern for their well-being would not offer them anything less than the very best to help them get over the tragic year they've had.'

Another magic word, he made grim note as she came jerking to her feet at the mention of the tragedy. Her eyes began changing again, clouding over—though not into the sultry expression he had been aiming for. What he saw was guilt. It showed she possessed a conscience, he supposed, though what that guilt was confirming to him did his resolve no favours.

Maybe he should just revert back to his original plan and throw her out of here! he considered on a sudden rise of black anger that hardened his expression, when he recalled the terrible year his sister had just endured since the violent death of her son—her only child—in a car accident. Marco had been the shining light in Alegra's life. When that light had been snuffed out, the family had feared she would never survive the darkness that had followed.

So to discover her husband had found solace from his grief in a woman half the age of his wife was a sin no self-respecting Sicilian could forgive. As he stood there, staring into Natalia Deyton's pained blue eyes, he had a dreadful urge to reach out and choke the very life out of her!

It therefore came as a complete shock to have her reach out and gently touch his shoulder. 'I'm so sorry for your loss,' she softly murmured. 'Edward told me how close you were to Marco. It must have been a terrible time for all of you.'

She had seen his anger and was mistaking it for pain, Giancarlo realised. And her touch on his shoulder was making the taut flesh beneath it crawl with revulsion.

Liar, he then immediately scoffed at his own interpretation. His flesh was tingling with pleasure, not revulsion. Just as his heart was beginning to beat that bit harder because her eyes were sultry at last! And the idea of reverting back to his original plan suddenly lost its appeal because there was much more satisfaction to be gained from slaking and slaking and slaking himself in this woman—before he tossed her onto the heap she belonged upon.

Though that *heap* at this precise moment had taken on the shape and form of a bed of tumbled linen. He could see her stretched out on it, naked and aware, inviting him with those amazing eyes to take anything he wanted from her.

A much more satisfying form of vengeance, he decided, knowing, even as he told himself that, that he was responding to the weakness of his own burning flesh rather than to the incisive intellect he was much better known for.

It didn't stop him, though, from reaching up to touch a gentle finger to the corner of her beautiful mouth. 'Thank you,' he murmured. 'For your understanding.'

The mouth quivered beneath his touch. Her eyes were growing darker, her cheeks slightly flushed, and he felt himself being drawn slowly downwards until his mouth was within a mere hair's breadth of tasting pure heaven.

Abruptly she jerked away, and with a rather dazed shake of her head took a couple of unsteady steps backwards, almost falling over the chair she had been sitting in, in her haste to put some distance between them.

Giancarlo watched and said nothing, in this case deciding that silence was golden when only a fool would misread the signals passing between them.

Having placed what she seemed to believe was a safe distance between them, Natalia composed herself then—quite bravely, he thought—looked him directly in the eye. 'How long will Edward be away?' she asked.

He almost smiled at that cool little voice, but managed to control the urge. 'Six weeks,' he replied, watching her lovely skin take on that milk-white pallor again as she took in this last piece of shocking information.

She was seeing six weeks of hell ahead of her while she tried to fight her own feelings, he suspected. He gave her a week—at the most. And made no effort whatsoever to hide his own sexual awareness. His eyes remained dark and his expression intense, the message he was conveying so clear that she blushed and had to look away again.

'Edward assured me of your *full co-operation* in his absence,' he informed her dulcetly, ruthlessly piling innuendo on innuendo with all the masculine charm at his Sicilian fingertips. 'And I do not see us having a problem getting on with each other—do you?'

'N-no, of course not,' she agreed with as much professional cool as she could muster. But she was looking quite satisfyingly flustered as she turned her back on him to stare at the door in a rather desperate need for escape now. 'Is—is there anything I can get for you?' she asked as desperation became an uncontrollable desire and she began walking on unsteady legs towards the door.

'Coffee would be nice,' he said. 'Black, preferably Italian if you can lay your hands on any.'

She nodded and kept walking.

'Plus all the files on Edward's major clients,' he added more briskly. 'Specifically the clients you were busily...*charming* during lunch today.'

'Taylor-Gant.' She supplied the name with her back still towards him so her frown was for her eyes only at the odd way he had used the word *charm*. 'We market their designer lingerie.'

'Do you wear it?'

He saw the flinch, was absolutely sure she was standing there with her eyes screwed shut—probably cursing herself for falling into that one? 'No,' she answered curtly, and opened the door.

'Then buy some,' he instructed. 'To market a product one should know exactly what it is you are marketing.'

'It isn't my job to know,' she protested.

'It is now,' he replied. 'I expect by the end of the week for you to have an opinion on their full range. And that, Miss Deyton,' he added for good measure, 'is exactly the kind of information the personal assistant to a corporate chairman is supposed to know.'

The door opened and closed, leaving him alone to smile at her hurried departure, very satisfyingly aware that she had left here feeling more confused than she had felt when she'd first walked in and found him here instead of Edward.

The game was on. He was in control. He didn't doubt it for a single moment. Natalia Deyton was his for the taking. He was actually enjoying himself—and within a week he intended to be enjoying himself a whole lot more...

CHAPTER TWO

STANDING on the other side of that closed door, Natalia was attempting to come to terms with what had just happened in there. It wasn't easy, simply because she didn't *know* what had happened—if you didn't count the disturbing impression that she had just indulged in the thorough seduction of all the senses.

And with Giancarlo Cardinale, of all people.

Her skin gave a flutter on a small inner shudder that helped release some of the tension out of her body. Not that she felt any better for it, she noted as she made herself walk across her office and then sank weakly down on the edge of her desk while she tried to get herself back together.

Giancarlo Cardinale. The name was playing over and over inside her head like a mantra, frightening, disturbing—exciting, alluring.

Oh, dear God. She closed her eyes only to find that, once again, his image was firmly imprinted on her retina. The dark hair and skin, the compelling brown velvet eyes that had held her captive even though she desperately hadn't wanted them to. Then there was his mouth—that terribly sensual mouth she could see drawing her own mouth towards it like metal to a magnet.

She could still feel the effects, still feel a warm, soft pulsing of needy flesh that brought her fingers up to cover her lips in an effort to stop the sensation. It didn't work, and if anything only seemed to make matters worse when

22

she felt her blood begin to heat in the mere memory of what she had wanted his mouth to do to hers.

Then—no, she amended that. Her blood wasn't just growing hot, it was searing through her veins like pure radiation. Poisonous.

Poisonous? The word brought her hand snapping away from her mouth and her eyelids shooting open in shocked realisation of what she had just unwittingly done.

She had given the whole crazy experience a very accurate label, because, yes, Giancarlo Cardinale had to be poison—to her at any rate. Poison by passion, poison by desire, poison because she knew there could be no future in letting him come close. Yet she had a terrible feeling that she was going to let him close. That she simply was not going to be able to help herself.

The next shudder became a shiver, which brought goose-bumps standing out on her skin. The man was her enemy, she grimly reminded herself. *Any* member of the Cardinale clan was her enemy. But this one, this tall, dark, frighteningly sexy head of the house of Cardinale had the power to completely demolish her newly found belief in herself if he ever discovered just who it was he was dealing with.

Then there was Edward, she moved on to link one problem neatly with the other. Edward, of all people, knew the danger this situation was putting her in! So why had he done it? What the hell did he think he was playing at setting her up like this—and without any warning?

She jumped up, began pacing the floor, arms crossed, head bowed, eyebrows puckered by a frown as she tried to work out just what was going on here. It simply made no sense. Edward was her life. Both had sworn more than once that they couldn't bear to be without the other now. So why was he putting their relationship at risk like this?

A sudden thought had her spinning back to her desk. Hitching her behind onto its pale beech-wood top, she stretched over and tapped a button on her keyboard, which would activate her voice-mail. Surely Edward would not have gone blithely off on his cruise without leaving her some kind of explanation for all of this?

It was a real relief to hear his deep, rather hurried voice filling the room. 'Natalia, my dear. I have some news.'

In the very act of opening the door, Giancarlo Cardinale went perfectly still...

'I have very little time to explain this, so bear with me and concentrate,' Edward Knight instructed. 'Surprise— surprise!' He sounded tense and just a little anxious. 'Alegra and I are in Barbados, would you believe? And about to embark on a second-honeymoon cruise, care of— Giancarlo! The point is, he's arranged everything so right and tight that I hardly have time to make this call. But I had to warn you—he's coming there. He will be looking after the business while I am away. So you're going to have to watch your step with him. Watch what you do, watch what you say—and for goodness' sake don't fall in love with him! I need to know that my girl will still be there in one whole piece, waiting for me when I return.'

Natalia laughed, though it was a rather thick, self-deriding sound. Giancarlo on the other hand heard nothing even vaguely amusing in what Edward had said. His mouth was tight, his eyes hard. If Natalia had glanced round and seen him standing there, she would have run screaming for her life.

But she didn't turn, and Edward was still talking. 'Also I need you to do a few things for me before he arrives,' he explained.

'Too damn late,' she muttered.

'I have some personal papers locked in the safe—you

know the ones I mean,' he added brusquely. 'I would prefer Giancarlo not to set eyes on them. You know the combination—and so does Giancarlo now, because I was stupid enough to give it to him without thinking. So get all my private stuff out of there before he has a chance to find it, and keep it safe somewhere else for me until I come home. Got to go now,' he announced hurriedly. 'Alegra is glowering at me. I'm going to miss you. Be good while I'm not there—'

The connection was broken. Behind her the door to Edward's office was silently closing again, leaving Natalia alone to mull over everything Edward had said—none of which made her feel any happier with the situation. He'd offered too little much too late and put their secret at risk in the interim—which also told her that he still hadn't got around to breaking the news about them to his wife.

'Oh, hell,' she sighed. When was he going to learn that keeping secrets from the people you loved only made you miserable?

Only in this particular case she had to concede he had a valid reason for keeping silent. Alegra had taken enough over the last tragic year—as Giancarlo himself had pointed out. To discover that her husband was harbouring a dark, dark secret was not the best silver wedding present he could give his wife.

Then there were the papers he wanted her to get out of his safe! How was she supposed to do that now the great man was already firmly entrenched in Edward's office?

In Edward's office, she repeated and felt the dizzying sway of her heart as it took her off on another tangent. A tangent to do with Giancarlo Cardinale and Edward's other instruction. Don't fall in love with him, he'd said. Well, she saw no danger in that actuality happening.

But falling into bed with him was an entirely different thing.

Giancarlo was at Edward's desk working on a portable desktop computer when she took his coffee in. Freshly ground, Italian blend, just as he'd requested. He didn't look up, and she didn't speak as she carried the tray over to place it down by his elbow.

But just the sight of him sitting there was enough to make her nerve-ends crackle. I'll get over it, she told herself, using Edward's advice to strengthen her backbone. Like all surprise situations, the novelty always wears off after a while. It just requires overexposure.

Outside the bright February sun was just beginning to stream in through the window behind him now. And she couldn't resist pausing to watch the way the pale gold sunbeams poured light onto his black silk head and over his broad shoulders before filtering down his arms to the neatly kept tips of his long brown fingers.

Was there nothing about this man she didn't like? she wondered helplessly. Even the view of his nose from this new angle didn't seem to make it any less appealing. Her fingers itched to follow its arrogant contours, then slide lazily towards his—

Oh, stop it! she scolded herself and, without giving a second thought as to why she was doing it, she walked over to the window and angled the blinds so the light no longer hit him.

'I like the sun,' he remarked with an abruptness that had her turning to frown at the back of his bent head. 'My Sicilian blood has an unquenchable need for it.'

'Is your computer screen Sicilian too?' she quizzed, making light of his remark because she could see no reason for the sudden change in manner.

He didn't get the joke. 'Open the blinds,' he clipped, a

long finger stabbing almost angrily at a button on his keyboard that sent off into cyberspace a document he couldn't possibly have been able to read on his sun-blanched screen.

Without a word, she did as she was told, grimacingly aware that the atmosphere had most definitely turned frosty, though she hadn't the slightest idea as to why it had. See, the novelty is already wearing off, she told herself as she turned away from the window, feeling absolutely no chemical reaction at all to that particularly autocratic tone.

'Any messages?' he queried.

She had taken one step only and was suddenly freezing to the point that she actually stopped breathing. 'No,' she answered, having to force the lie up through her thickened throat.

'Not even from Edward?' he prompted. 'I expected him to put in one call at least, to check everything was all right here…'

Her pulse began to race. 'No, no call from Edward,' she denied.

Without any warning he sat back in the chair, then swung it round until he was facing her. With the sun now hitting him full in his face, his narrowed eyes seemed to glitter accusingly as they raked over her. Tension began to rise—a hard, tight, prickly kind of tension that had nothing to do with the man's sensual pull, but with the air of menace he seemed to be transmitting from every perfectly constructed cell.

'But if he rings, you will inform me immediately, hmm?' he probed, so softly that she hoped it was her own guilty conscience that was making her feel as if she was on trial here—and not that silken tone.

'Yes,' she lied yet again. 'Of course,' she then added

for good innocent measure, trying desperately to sound like the coolly detached and businesslike assistant she was supposed to be.

'Good.' Giancarlo smiled, but it wasn't a real smile—in fact it sent an icy chill chasing through her. Then without another word he swung back to the desk to continue with what he had been doing.

It was a silent dismissal she was more than happy to comply with, considering the huge lie she had just told him. Setting her tingling legs moving, she walked around the desk and began treading the expanse of grey carpet, which seemed to spread like a mine-infested ocean out in front of her, threatening to blow her lies up in her face each time she put a foot down.

She hated liars, she always had ever since the day she'd discovered how much her own mother had lied to her for most of her life. So to find herself doing it actually hurt a very sensitive part in her that she knew she was going to find difficult to pacify.

'What is Howard Fiske's extension number?'

This second question reached her at about halfway across the room. She told him. He murmured a thank-you. She walked on, thinking only of getting away so she could sit down somewhere away from prying eyes and grimly justify—if only to herself—what she had just done.

'And the combination to Edward's safe,' he then prompted. 'Do you know that also?'

At which point the excruciating tension she was beginning to feel threatened to swallow her whole. 'Don't you know it?' she asked, frowning because she was recalling what Edward had said.

'Edward wrote it down for me,' he confirmed. 'But I do not have it on me right at this moment.'

Relief fluttered through her. If he hadn't got the combination with him, then she had time to get Edward's papers out of harm's way—so long as she could grab the opportunity to do so.

'I can't help you there, I'm sorry,' she apologised, comforting herself with the weak excuse that her reply hadn't been a full lie—only a half one. She *couldn't* help him, and she *was* sorry. But she was feeling as if the combination were presently burning itself in block letters across her guilty face and all he had to do was get her to turn and face him so that he could read it!

'Maybe Howard knows it,' he murmured.

'Maybe he does,' she agreed, sure in the knowledge that Howard *didn't* know. Then she whipped quickly through the door before he could come up with any more uncomfortable questions...

Giancarlo Cardinale watched her go with his head fizzing on the very edge of a violent eruption. Lying little witch, he was thinking angrily. Lying, cheating, *beautiful* witch! he tagged on hotly as he watched that tight rear-end disappear through the door and felt his fingers itch to go chasing after it.

'You will get yours, Miss Deyton,' he promised. 'One day soon you will most certainly get yours.'

Picking up the phone, he punched in Howard Fiske's number. Five minutes later he was putting the phone down again and feeling downright miffed on so many fronts that he couldn't make his mind up which took priority.

Howard didn't know the combination to Edward's safe, which didn't really surprise him, or the deceitful Miss Deyton would have gone to pieces, he was sure. But Miss Deyton had not gone to pieces. She had tossed off her airy replies with guileful ease! Which meant he was going to have to keep a very keen eye on her if he didn't want that safe opening today without him knowing it.

And Howard himself was another problem he was going to have to deal with. Having fed Giancarlo all the ammunition he needed to do something about Edward's little office affair, Howard had expected him to come here and get rid of Natalia without any compunction. Now the mean-mouthed swine was angry because Giancarlo was refusing to play it his way.

What was it with Howard, anyway? he suddenly asked himself as he got up to go and stand by the window. Did the man fancy Natalia himself—was that it? Was his attitude sour grapes because Edward was enjoying something Howard would like to enjoy himself?

Something hot began to burn in his stomach, and he knew exactly what was causing it. It was the sudden image of not one, but two, middle-aged lechers pawing her smooth white flesh, while she let them—because she liked it.

His hand snaked up, and with a violent tug on the pullcord he cut out that image by snapping shut the blinds he had insisted Natalia opened.

Petty or what? he asked himself. Petty—yes, he admitted. Angry—yes. With Edward, with Howard—with *himself* for all wanting the same woman!

Well, one third of the competition had already been removed from the picture. And another third could go the same way quick enough, he decided as he turned to snatch up the phone again.

Ten minutes after *that* particular call, and he was beginning to feel back in control. By tomorrow Howard Fiske and his filthy mouth would be flying to Milan to spend a couple of weeks smouldering in frustration beneath the wing of Giancarlo Cardinale's second in command, learning how his job should be done. By the time he was due back, Natalia Deyton would be so much Giancarlo's woman that Howard would only have to glance at her to know that the problem had been dealt with—Giancarlo's way.

Yes, he felt a whole lot better about that little scenario...

She'd forgotten to take the requested files in to him. Seeing them sitting there, still neatly stacked on her desk where she had placed them before taking in his coffee, made her want to hit something in utter frustration—because it meant she was now going to have to go back in there.

And she just didn't want to. She didn't want to face another barrage of awkward questions, or face the man himself, for that matter! Giancarlo was like a ride on a roller coaster, she likened. One minute rocketing her into a steep dive through all the senses, the next he was hurling her into a corkscrew twist, making her struggle with her own guilty secrets. It was all so very precarious that she dared not so much as breathe in case she caused the whole thing to come crashing down around her!

The intercom on her desk began to beep. 'Those files, Miss Deyton?' drawled her tormentor with a coolness that did nothing to ease her turmoil.

That sexy voice should be X-rated, she decided as she flicked a switch to acknowledge the reminder with what she hoped was a matching cool. Then, taking a deep breath, she gathered up the armful of files and began walking back towards that connecting door, which was beginning to resemble the entrance to a torture chamber...

The moment she stepped through it, she sensed the change in the atmosphere. The blinds had been drawn, blocking out the shafts of sunlight which had given the room such a sharp edge before.

And he wasn't where she'd expected him to be, she realised, glancing at the empty chair behind the desk before beginning to scan the new softer light until she located him over on the other side of the room. He was sitting comfortably stretched out on one of Edward's soft grey leather sofas with his dark head thrown back, his eyes closed and with his feet propped up on the low beechwood coffee-table. The tray she had brought in earlier now resided beside his feet—and, like his jacket, his tie had now disappeared and the top couple of buttons on his shirt had been tugged free.

Was he intending to complete a full strip before the afternoon was over? she found herself speculating sarcastically.

Then wished she hadn't thought such a stupid thing when, on a sudden rush to the head, she found herself picturing him stretched out there naked. Brown skin, long, powerfully muscled legs, a hard-toned, superbly built masculine torso, she saw in that single fevered flash of a moment. But it did not stop there. Oh, no, because she was also picturing the look in his eyes as he waited for her to join him in the self-same naked state.

'Come and join me,' he murmured.

She almost jumped out of her skin! As it was she reacted violently enough to send the top file sliding off the pile so it slithered to the floor in a spill of white paper. In a flurry of pure wit-scattering dismay, she bent to place the rest of the files on the floor then began gathering together the papers with fingers that had lost the ability to co-ordinate.

How could you—how *could* you? She was railing at herself, relieved to have the diversion so she could hide her flaming cheeks, which she knew without a doubt were displaying every naughty thought running through her wicked head!

Never *ever* had she indulged in wild fantasies over any man—so why start now with this one of all the men she could have chosen?

'Here, let me...'

A pair of black leather shoes appeared in her vision. Then a pair of dark silk worsted-covered knees as he bent into a very male squat. She felt ready to self-incinerate when her eyes began flickering along his inner thighs. Dragging them away again, she made a reckless grab at a piece of paper—as a long brown hand did the same.

Skin touched skin. Electricity went crackling up her arm with such clamouring speed that it almost knocked her right off balance! She let out a gasp; there was no containing it, nor the sharp way that her head came up. Blue eyes clashed helplessly with deep dark brown.

After that there was stillness, a complete and utter stillness with hand touching hand and eyes holding eyes, swapping a knowledge that neither was doing anything to disguise.

No, her common sense was trying to advise her. Don't let this happen. It's wrong, it's dangerous, it's too darn complicated to warrant taking the risk.

But he's so irresistible, her weaker self whispered. Exciting, beguiling, utterly compelling. She even felt herself leaning closer—just as she had done the last time she had looked deeply into his eyes...

Somewhere in the distance a phone began to ring. It was her salvation. And, good grief, but she needed saving! she acknowledged as, on a flurry of embarrassment, she withdrew her hand and scrambled to her feet, then fled back into her own office, leaving him still squatting there, with his dark eyes following her every single step of the way.

The call was an internal query that took all her powers of concentration to answer without sounding drunk. By the time she came back, the files had been stacked on the coffee-table and Giancarlo Cardinale was poring over the contents of one of them.

'Come and sit down,' he instructed without a single inflection in his tone to so much as hint at what had just passed between them.

She moved on legs that were still feeling weak and unsteady, over to the sofa on the opposite side of the table.

'No, not there,' he said. 'Sit here, next to me so we can look at these together.'

Together, she repeated to herself. What a buzzword. What a provocatively tantalising buzzword. And as she moved to perch herself stiffly on the cushion next to his she found herself wishing that the man were as ugly as sin.

'Coffee?' he offered.

'I don't drink it,' she politely refused.

An eyebrow tweaked as he scanned the typed print on the piece of paper he was reading. 'What—never?' he asked, but she had a feeling the raised eyebrow was mocking the stiff way she was sitting there.

'Sometimes—after dinner maybe.' She shrugged, stubbornly deciding that it was time to take every single word he spoke at its absolute face value. No hearing hidden meanings, no looking for anything other than a professional boss-assistant relationship.

'A cup-of-tea girl,' he presumed, placing one piece of paper aside to pick up another.

'I prefer water, if you must know,' she told him.

'A woman with simple tastes, then.'

'Yes.' She nodded—very firmly because she *was* a woman of simple tastes. And Giancarlo Cardinale was not simple at all. He was a rare delicacy only the very rich or the very reckless would consider trying. She was neither rich nor reckless. In fact, she was the most cautious person she knew!

Which only made her reaction to Giancarlo Cardinale all the more perturbing. It just wasn't like her.

'Now...' he said on a complete change of manner '...explain to me why this company needs the skills of marketing experts when the product they produce virtually sells itself...'

Peering over his arm, she saw the famous Fillens logo, and smiled ruefully at his comment. 'Geoffrey Fillen and Edward were at school together,' she explained. 'Fillens have been using Edward's marketing skills for as long as he has been in business.'

'Ah, the old school network.' Giancarlo grimaced understandingly. 'Lucky Edward. Does the business from this company also come via the same route?' he asked, indicating towards a different file.

After that, she became engrossed in a lesson on the astuteness of this man's business mind as he began picking out the base-root foundation upon which Edward had built his company.

And as the afternoon wore on she found herself becoming more and more fascinated by Edward's brother-in-law as he displayed qualities that by far outweighed the merely physical. He was shrewd, he was quick, he was incredibly logical when it came to matters of business.

He possessed a low-pitched and easy telephone manner that clearly kept his listeners safely assured that, though he might not be where they wanted him to be, he was still accessible and in control, with his finger most firmly on the pulse of everything beneath the Cardinale Group umbrella.

She even knew when he was talking to his secretary because his tone grew firmer, sharper, more commanding—though she didn't understand a word because he was speaking in Italian. A language that worked on the senses like alcohol, sluicing out tensions and replacing them with warm, soft feelings of—

Oh, no, not again. With a jerk she fixed her attention on the stream of notes he'd had her taking. The phone went down—and rang again almost immediately. Without a pause he switched from Italian to English, and began a discussion about corporate profit projections that left her completely flummoxed.

Dynamic was the word she was toying with when he suddenly sat down beside her again. Heat sizzled between them, but she grimly ignored the stomach-curling effect it had on her.

By five o'clock, open files lay scattered all about them and the coffee-table, and the lights were on to supplement the loss of sunlight seeping in through the blinds.

Natalia was beginning to fade a little, but Giancarlo wasn't. Like a human dynamo, the more he found to delve into, the more invigorated he became.

So another hour went by, and she was kneeling on the carpet by the coffee-table, carefully feeding paper back into the files he had scrutinised and finished with, when yet another phone call took him striding back to the desk.

The moment he began speaking Natalia was aware of the difference in this call from all of the other calls, no matter what language he was speaking. This one was being carried out in Italian—a warm, soft, intimate Italian loaded down with so much sensual promise that she didn't doubt for a moment just whom it was he was speaking to.

A lover. It had to be. And as she sank back onto her ankles feeling very odd suddenly, as if someone had just punched her in the stomach, she couldn't believe that she hadn't so much as considered the prospect of his having a lover in his life.

Well, that's fine. It's okay, she tried telling herself. In fact it suited her very well that he had someone else to concentrate his sexual interest upon! But inside she burned and squirmed with that nasty hot thing called jealous resentment, which only got worse the more '*cara mia*'s and '*mia bella amore*'s she caught interspersing his husky-toned conversation.

It seemed a good point for her to make her exit, she decided, slamming the last file back down on the stack with more violence than was necessary.

The sound it made had him glancing up, but his dark gaze was hazed by distraction, the kind of distraction that set her heart thudding on a burst of good old-fashioned anger. The kind of anger that had her coming to her feet and walking towards the door without bothering to announce her departure.

'Going somewhere?' his silken voice came sliding after her.

She glanced back, saw him leaning there against Edward's desk, with a hand clamped over the telephone mouthpiece—and a glint in his eyes that she just didn't like.

It came too close to sexual arousal for her fastidious sensitivities. Couldn't the man wait until he had his privacy before indulging in that kind of conversation? He was even daring to peruse her figure as if it belonged to the woman who was arousing him, she noticed in affront.

'It's late,' she bit out. 'In case you haven't noticed. We seem to have finished here, so I'll leave you to it.'

With that she walked out, firmly closing the door behind her with absolutely no suspicion that the man she had left on the other side of it was now slowly replacing the phone on its rest, with a smile on his face that could only be described as—triumphant...

He was getting to her—really getting to her! It felt pretty good. He even gave the phone a light tap as if in thanks for its help. Then the smile cracked into a full-blooded grin when he thought of Serena, his best friend's wife, who had just laughingly threatened to tell Fredo if Giancarlo didn't stop speaking to her in that seductive tone of voice!

The phone rang again. He picked it up, knowing exactly who was going to be on the other end of it. 'Fredo—all is fair in love and war,' he announced before the other man could get a word in. 'And before you ask, no, my war is not being waged against your beautiful wife...'

CHAPTER THREE

'*BUON GIORNO*, Miss Deyton,' Giancarlo greeted briskly as he strode in the next morning. 'You had a pleasant evening, I hope, and are feeling rested enough to begin a whole new day?'

No, she hadn't, and no, she wasn't, but it was all too obvious that he'd had more than enough of both, she noted, viewing his irritatingly upbeat manner through heavily jaundiced eyes.

Everything about him appeared thoroughly revitalised from the brightness in his tone to the healthy sheen of his olive-toned skin. Clearly burning the candle at both ends had only an invigorating effect on him. Even his clothes looked sharp enough to draw blood if you touched them, she thought as she ran those same eyes over his steel-grey suit with its matching colour shirt and silk tie.

Whereas she felt wrecked because she had done nothing but wage war with herself right through the evening and into the night. Troubled by her lies, troubled by her attraction to him and more than troubled by the uncontrollable way her imagination had insisted on drawing lurid pictures of him locked in the arms of some gorgeous Italian who possessed all the sensual expertise a man like Giancarlo Cardinale would expect from the woman he allowed into his bed!

'A Ms Delucca just called,' she informed him frostily. 'To complain about you leaving this morning, without saying thank you.'

'Ah, Serena,' he murmured smilingly—a smile that became a disgustingly rakish full-blooded grin, which showed no sign whatever of any embarrassment at having his private life put on show like this. 'I will apologise later. But first we have some things to do that will—'

He stopped. Went still, seemed to stiffen slightly, then suddenly lost all of that rakish humour. 'How long have you been in?' he demanded suddenly.

'About five minutes,' she replied, suddenly very aware of how finely she'd timed getting Edward's papers out of the safe before Giancarlo had arrived. The day did not officially start for another half an hour and she'd really thought she'd had plenty of time. As it was, the darned man had virtually caught her with her hand in the safe!

But as far as *he* was concerned, she might not have got around to removing her coat yet, but she *had* collected the post and checked for emails—plus taken a call from his current mistress!

'Do you have a problem with that, Mr Cardinale?' she demanded, having already come to the decision at some point in the early hours of the morning that she was not going to let him turn her inside out for two days on the run!

He didn't answer, but he was frowning darkly. And if she could glean any consolation from that frown then it was in the knowledge that his irritatingly upbeat mood had so obviously collapsed.

'Take your coat off and come into my office,' he instructed, jumping into autocratic mode with a snap to his tone that sent her hackles up.

'Yes, sir,' she replied, using frost to his bite.

He muttered something she didn't catch, then strode through the connecting door before slamming it shut behind him.

She allowed herself an exaggerated wince, then began

removing her camel-coloured full-length cashmere coat
and soft lilac scarf at a speed that confirmed her determination not to be bullied. So she took her time settling it
on its hanger, then took another few moments to smooth
down the fabric of her calf-length black pinstriped suit.
She had chosen to wear this particular suit because it
showed less leg and the tailored jacket fastened right up
to its mandarin collar. Her hair was up as usual, neatly
secured by a black shell clasp, and her make-up was so
underplayed it might not even be there.

If anyone could look at her and even vaguely suggest
that she was asking for the kind of looks Signor Cardinale
had treated her to yesterday, she would call them liars! But
she was not seeing that all she had done with her severe
cover-up was incite the imagination to wonder what was
being hidden…

Which was exactly what Giancarlo began thinking about
from the moment she stepped into his office. Natalia's hair
glistened like polished copper, her skin sheened like a
pearl. Her body moved with the sensual grace of a born
siren—and her eyes would be cutting him into two pieces
if he were made of glass.

The woman was not of this world, he grimly decided.
She was all fire and ice and dangerous witchery. She filled
him with the primitive urge to go over there, pull her into
his arms and kiss her senseless.

And she knew it. Look at her! he growled to himself.
Standing there with her chin up, just daring him to try it!

'We are changing location,' he announced right off the
top of his head and with no idea of what he was talking
about. All he knew was that he wanted her out of this place
before she found a way to get her sticky fingers into
Edward's safe. It had almost ruined his day to come in

here this morning and find that she had got here before him. He seemed to have misplaced the piece of paper with the combination number that Edward had given him, and six long weeks of wondering when she was going to grab enough time away from him unseen to crack the darn safe were more than he was prepared to cope with. Though he was going to have his work cut out trying to come up with a valid excuse for making such an impulsive announcement, he admitted.

Still, it had been worth it just to see that cold, haughty expression she was wearing this morning collapse into a flurry of confusion.

'What?' she choked out as if he'd spoken in a strange language.

If he could have any wish granted right now, it would be to have that sensational gasping mouth fixed permanently to his own hungry mouth.

'I have decided I cannot work here,' he continued, thinking on his feet and glad he was good at it. 'It is too complicated trying to run this company as well as my own from here. You saw yourself how much time I spent on the telephone yesterday when I should have been devoting my energies to what is wrong right here.'

Wrong right here... Natalia stared at the hand he was using to punctuate the point with long fingertips stabbing into Edward's desk, and felt a horrid little flutter of alarm slither down her backbone. 'Wha-what's wrong here?' she stammered out warily.

'Everything,' he replied. And she wasn't even wearing any lipstick, he noted. Did she know he couldn't stand the taste of lipstick? 'Even the little information I gleaned from the files yesterday was enough to tell me that this place is in deep trouble.' She blinked, and he grimaced because that part at least was the ugly truth. 'The premises may have been thoroughly modernised but its business practices are positively archaic, so I am about to do something about it.'

'But—you can't do that!' she protested. 'It isn't your place to mess with Edward's business!'

'I can do anything I want, Miss Deyton,' he corrected her with a haughty incision. 'I own controlling stock here, in case you have forgotten. When I injected a large amount of cash into this place last year, Edward's brief was to completely modernise. He seems to have gone as far as refurbishing the premises—and no damned farther.'

'His son died…'

'I am aware of that,' Giancarlo clipped out. He felt his face harden when he recalled where Edward's energies had gone to salve his grief for his dead son, when they could have been salved by continuing the job he had begun right here, where it mattered. But he hadn't done that, and everything at Knight's had simply stagnated while Edward indulged himself in a bit of womanly comfort.

This woman's womanly comforts. Fire flared up from his heart, diverted to his eyes and spat sparks out over Natalia Deyton. 'Grief is no excuse for tardy business practices,' he proclaimed with what even he knew was a gross lack of sympathy.

'So what is it you intend to do?' she asked in a tone meant to slay him for his insensitivity.

'Bring in my team of experts,' he said, glancing down at his watch and wondering if he could pull this off in the time space he was gunning for. 'They will arrive late this afternoon and set up a six-week re-educating programme that will haul the staff here into this century. Howard Fiske already knows about it,' he added with what he now saw as a clever bit of unwitting pre-planning. 'He is, as we speak, flying to my head office in Milan, to begin his own re-education on how I expect my executives to conduct themselves.'

'I thought you were Sicilian,' Natalia murmured, so out of context in his point of view that it stopped his train of thought completely.

'What has that got to do with anything?' he demanded.

'You said Milan,' she explained with a shrug meant to convey mild indifference. But in truth even she didn't understand why she said such a stupid thing. 'I just presumed you lived and worked in Sicily. Edward said...'

She faded out, seeing by his sudden narrowing expression that he didn't like what was being said here.

'Edward said—what?' he prompted grittily.

Another shrug and she was beginning to feel just a little hunted. 'I only remember him remarking once, about your home in—in Trápani, I think he said,' she answered warily. 'He m-made it sound very—beautiful.'

If she'd been looking for a diversion with that last remark, she didn't achieve it. 'Quite cosy little chats you two must have indulged in to reach the point where they included me,' he remarked. 'Maybe we should sit down and compare notes some time. See if his references to you were as—interesting...'

His tone was cold, and she'd gone quite pale. But the very thought of her having this kind of conversation about him with Edward set his teeth on edge...

Natalia, on the other hand, was kicking herself for starting this at all. She knew his comment about comparing notes was merely his way of getting back at her, because Edward would *never* have discussed her with Giancarlo. Not during this lifetime anyway.

But she was genuinely regretful for invading what Giancarlo clearly saw as his privacy. And despite knowing she should leave it alone, the words of explanation came anyway. 'Edward was missing his son,' she gently explained. 'He seemed to need to talk about him so I let him. Your home in Sicily came up because I gained the impression that Marco used to spend a great deal of his time there with you. So it was perhaps natural for Edward to refer to that.'

He had stopped looking at her, his eyes becoming hidden beneath the long sweep of his lashes. Anxious because she was concerned that she'd only managed to upset him further, she took an impulsive couple of steps closer to the desk behind which he was standing. 'Please don't think he discussed you personally, because he didn't,' she assured.

To her surprise, he smiled, albeit grimly. 'I was ten years old when Edward married Alegra. Two years later Marco arrived. We were more like brothers than uncle and nephew. When he died last year, we all—went to pieces a little. I have not been back to Sicily since he died there, for instance. Alegra sank deep inside herself, while Edward...' he paused, seemed about to say something else, then, on a short sigh, changed his mind '...Edward found his own means of escape,' he clipped out. 'Which is why this place has been left to stagnate over the last year. But now it's time to do something about it,' he added on a firmer, brisker note. 'So we will begin by getting in my team of experts to knock his staff into shape while Edward himself devotes some long-overdue time to patching up his ailing marriage.'

Why it seemed as though he had turned that last comment into a threat, Natalia didn't understand. But as for the rest of it—oh, she understood it all far more than he would ever know. Marco had been visiting Giancarlo in Sicily when the tragic accident had happened. Young, reckless and with his whole life ahead of him, Marco had taken Giancarlo's Ferrari out without permission, lost control of the powerful machine, and crashed it, killing himself as he'd done so.

Those of his family left behind were inconsolable. Directly after the funeral in Sicily, Giancarlo had flown off the island and disappeared for weeks somewhere no one could find him. Alegra had gone into deep mourning. No one had been able to get near her. She'd spent hours in Marco's bedroom here in London. It had become a shrine, Edward told her once. A sad, torturous, sacred shrine.

And Edward? Well, Edward's story was equally as sad though not quite as wretched as the others. Because he'd found her, Natalia admitted. In her he'd found a link with his son and someone into whom he could divert all that painful love he had festering inside him.

'He doesn't even have a picture of Marco in here,' Giancarlo grated, with a contempt aimed at Edward that hid a lot of his own pain, Natalia suspected.

'It's in the safe,' she said. 'He couldn't bear to look at it, so he put it away...'

The safe, Giancarlo repeated bitterly to himself. What else had Edward got hidden in his damned safe that he didn't want him to look at? Pictures of his wife in happier times? Pictures of his lovely mistress who'd helped him to live again while the rest of them still floundered in guilt and misery?

The phone began to ring. It was a relief to have something to take his mind off the black anger suddenly consuming him. To hell with Natalia Deyton, he decided as he snatched up the receiver. To hell with his seduction plan! He'd had enough. She was out.

And as soon as this call was over. He never wanted to set eyes on Edward's mistress again if he could help it!

It was his second in command calling from Milan, wanting to know what he was supposed to do with Howard Fiske when he arrived. As he began biting out orders, Natalia turned as if to leave him to it.

'Stay,' he growled.

She stopped, then turned her head to look at him questioningly over her shoulder. The eyes were sad, the blue irises darkened mirrors that reflected the distress of what they had been discussing.

Had Edward received that same look when he'd opened up his grief to Natalia Deyton? If he had then it was no wonder he'd used her as his escape from misery, Giancarlo decided. Because he could feel himself being drawn towards the same exquisite means of escape.

For vengeance, he added, recalling why all of this had started. Vengeance for putting at risk what was left of his sister's broken heart, by seducing her husband. Well, an eye for an eye—the Sicilian way, he reminded himself. Or, in this case, seduction for seduction. It was so very appropriate...

The game was back on. He suddenly felt better, and sat down in the chair to begin a more lazily sarcastic conversation with his caller, while casually waving Natalia into the other chair.

She didn't comply. He wasn't surprised. He had seen by her body language, from the moment he'd walked in this morning, that she had decided to take him on.

He liked the idea of that. It added spice to the chase and gave his mood another lift that did wonders for his testosterone levels. And he even set himself a rather titillating deadline, which involved him tasting her lovely mouth before the day was over.

'Right, that's it,' he said, switching from Italian to English the moment he put down the phone. 'All the arrangements are confirmed. My people will be here by late afternoon. What I need from you now is a tour of all departments, so I can make the initial assessment on what they are going to be required to do.'

'I still don't think this is right without Edward's agreement,' Natalia informed him.

'Your protest has been noted,' he coolly acknowledged, and glanced at his watch before coming to his feet. 'Time to move,' he announced. 'We have a lot to get through before we stop for lunch. Then we should, with a bit of luck, have some new premises to look over this afternoon.'

'We?' Natalia prompted. 'What has your choice in new premises got to do with me?'

'Since you will be relocating right along with me—' he shrugged '—I automatically assumed you would like to look your new workplace over.'

But Natalia didn't want to relocate with him! In fact the very suggestion filled her with utter dismay! 'But my job is here!' she protested. 'I am *needed* here! Edward—'

'Your job, Miss Deyton,' he cut in coldly, 'is wherever or whatever I decide it is. And why do I get the impression that you suspect my every move is designed to actually harm this company?' he added grimly.

When he put it like that she began to feel rather stupid, because he was right and she did suspect him of—something, though she had to confess she didn't know what that something was.

'I'm sorry,' she sighed, making a climb-down she knew she really had no choice about. 'But you've been here for less than twenty-four hours and already you're planning to turn the place upside down!'

'Upside down is better than the way it stands at present,' he returned with contempt, then released a sigh of his own because her climb-down had made him realise that his confrontational stance was not helping his cause. 'Listen,' he said, aiming for a more conciliatory tone. 'Allowing me to turn this business around while Edward is safely out of the way where he can't worry is doing him a favour, believe me. And to make it work in the short time allowed, I need you to work with me, not against me. Is that too much to ask—for Edward's sake—?'

Her stubborn stance was faltering. He could see it happening in the frown that clouded her face. 'Okay,' she said heavily. 'What is it you need me to do?'

With a surrender like that, he didn't hesitate in consolidating it. 'I need someone I can trust working alongside me, and, since Edward clearly trusts you, then you have to be my obvious choice,' he explained, watching his carefully chosen words work their expected magic.

She was hooked. He had her...

'So,' he continued, 'while my people come in here and turn this place around, you and I will move out so they can do their job without feeling me breathing down their necks. What I need from you is your secretarial skills and your input on any decision-making I may be required to do regarding Knight's.'

'What about *my* re-education?' Natalia questioned dryly, trying to make light of what had turned out to be yet another heavy interview. But the moment she saw that gleam enter his eyes she knew she'd said the wrong thing.

'You think I am not up to the task?' he probed silkily.

And it was back, just like that. From clever negotiator to lazy seducer in one smooth movement. His eyes feathered over her and her skin began to flutter. He paused at certain relevant locations and caused absolute mayhem.

Stop it! she wanted to snap. But 'stop it!' would only encourage him into being more provocative. So she

clamped her lips shut, gritted her teeth tightly together behind them and said absolutely nothing.

Though what really made her teeth grit together was the
warm, soft laugh he emitted as he walked around the desk.
'Coming?' he queried innocently and strode towards the
door with that smile still working.

She followed because she really had no option. But she
couldn't say that she was pleased with what had transpired
in here today. As she entered her own office the telephone
began to ring. Diverting towards her desk, she picked up
the receiver. Ten seconds later she was gritting her teeth
yet again, and holding the receiver out to him.

'The lady who rang you earlier, sir,' she announced with
frosty formality.

The mocking smile on his face warmed into pure pleasure. He took the phone and Natalia only just escaped their
fingers brushing by a fine hair's breadth. 'Ah, *buon giorno,
mia bella amore…*'

The rest she shut her ears to and instead walked out of
the room and into the executive washroom, where she
spent a few seething moments bringing her composure
back into line. By the time she entered her office again,
he was busy scrawling something on her note-pad, and the
telephone was back on its rest.

Arrangements for their next date? she wondered acidly,
watching him tear off the piece of paper, fold it and slide
it into his jacket pocket.

'Right, that tour,' he said, and began walking straight
towards her.

She held her ground out of sheer cussedness. It was a
stupid stand to make because he simply slid a hand around
her waist and turned her to walk with him. Her breathing
failed, her body started singing, and her mind went blank
in response.

That hand—that hand…was the only chant playing over and over in an empty chasm of dark self-awareness.

'Where do we begin?' he enquired so innocently she could have screamed because he knew exactly what the feel of his hand on her waist was doing to her!

'The accounts department seems a good place.' She was rather pleased by how smoothly her voice came out.

'Before we go in—' he said, swinging her deftly up against the wall, then coming to stand directly over her. She was suddenly faced full on with his wide chest, and it took all her control not to start breathing faster.

'This is a delicate situation,' he murmured, seeming to have no idea how appropriate she was finding the comment. 'It is essential that you and I present a united front when we begin breaking the news to the staff here about what is about to happen. We must be relaxed, congenial and seem as one in our confidence that what we are proposing will be for their good as well as the company. This way there is a chance that they will be a help to my staff when they arrive and not a hindrance, you understand me?'

Natalia nodded, and wished he would move back a bit.

'We will not give the impression that I am here to scrutinise or criticise,' he continued. 'But all the same we will be doing both. You can do this, do you think?'

'Play the cheerful spy?' she said, making the fatal mistake of lifting her chin to send him a rueful smile. A smile that died on her lips when she caught his expression. She looked away again quickly, but not quickly enough to save herself from the disturbing glow she had seen burning in his eyes. 'I can't say it's my favourite role,' she added distractedly.

'But for their sakes, you will do it anyway?'

Their sakes. 'Yes,' she said, accepting that she was going to have to trust him to do what he had said he was going to do here, while taking into consideration the feelings of the people he would be dealing with.

'Good.' He moved back. Her relief to have no part of him touching her was so profound that she almost wilted into the carpet.

For the next couple of hours they paced from department to department. She introduced him to everyone individually, and, in typical Italian style, he charmed them all from the junior receptionist upwards. And in the charming gleaned so much information out of each and every one of them that Natalia was rather shell-shocked, by the end of it, as to how many people working there had been willing if not desperate for the changes Giancarlo was proposing.

'Right, let's get out of here,' he said eventually, and began striding across the reception area towards the doors, without waiting to see if she was following.

He was angry, she acknowledged, and couldn't really blame him for feeling that way. The long list of personal grievances, which had been aired here this morning, was enough to incense anyone with a reasonable grasp of good business practice. And whatever else she doubted about Giancarlo Cardinale, she did not doubt his business integrity.

Poor Edward, she thought sadly as she stepped outside to find Giancarlo had already hailed a cab and was opening the door ready for her to precede him into it.

Edward had no idea how low morale was amongst his staff and would have been deeply hurt if he'd been here today to discover what Giancarlo had so slickly uncovered.

So maybe it was right that Edward wasn't going to be here to see the transformation of his precious company, she concluded.

He waited until they were driving towards Kensington

before making any comment. 'Things are even worse than I envisaged,' he said.

'I know,' she agreed. There was nothing to be gained from pretending otherwise.

'How long have you known?'

Her shrug conveyed her reluctance to answer. 'Don't ask me to criticise Edward because I will not,' she told him and turned her head to stare bleakly out of the cab's side window.

'You admire the fact that he has run his own company into the ground?' The snap in his tone was laced with sarcasm.

Natalia kept her face turned away and said nothing in answer. For what could she say in Edward's defence that would not be betraying his darkest secrets? She couldn't. It was as simple as that. Edward's pride was just too important to her.

Strange, she mused, how one person could become the axis your life revolved around in such a short length of time. This time six months ago she hadn't even known of Edward's existence. This time six months ago she had been alone and sad, and seeing nothing bright in her future to make her feel any better, then—wham—everything had changed with one single glance across a café table.

It could still make her heart leap just to think of him, think of his loving face and his loving eyes, and that silly expression that would come over both, which would say without words—I still can't believe that you belong to me.

But she did, and nothing—nothing in this big world was ever going to take that away from her.

So her silence remained a wall she maintained between them as they travelled. Whatever Giancarlo was thinking about that silence did not really affect her. The man professed to care about Edward. And she did trust him to do what was best for his brother-in-law's company. But she would never trust him with Edward's heart, for it would take another man who had been hurt as deeply as Edward to understand its secrets.

The restaurant was a small, smart, popular place serving Italian cuisine. And Giancarlo was known there. The proprietor himself escorted them to their reserved table conversing with Giancarlo in their native language as they went. But she could tell the man beside her was in no mood to share polite conversation with anyone right now.

The proprietor helped her into her seat. Giancarlo sat down opposite. Menus were produced. A bottle of sparkling water appeared from seemingly nowhere. And the telling fact that Giancarlo must have ordered it, since no other table had the same thing, made her aware that, whatever else was going on inside his head, he could still call up the short, throw-away conversation about her drinking preferences, which they'd had yesterday.

At last the proprietor took his effusive leave. Giancarlo heaved out a sigh that made her smile in wry understanding of its necessity. He saw the smile—and matched it with one of his own. 'He is Sicilian; I supposed you guessed it. We come from the same village.'

Only you lived on top of the hill while he lived at the bottom, she presumed simply because of the proprietor's constant if metaphorical cap-doffing.

'Don't expect to use that,' he warned, arching a mocking brow at the menu she was holding. 'For I think we are about to be treated to the full repertoire of Sicilian cuisine.'

'Good or bad?' she asked, made curious by his rueful expression.

'Edward hates it,' he replied and instantly had her withdrawing back behind her protective wall...

*   *   *

Giancarlo saw it happen, sat back in his seat with a heavy sigh and lifted a long-fingered hand up to his tie knot as if he was going to loosen it with an impatient yank, then changed his mind and dropped the hand to his lap instead. 'Your loyalty to him becomes you, Miss Deyton. But have you tried to consider that loyalty in this case may well be misplaced?'

'You clearly don't like him very much. I do, which means we have a conflict of opinion that does not encourage an exchange in confidences.'

'You are mistaken,' he corrected. 'I am very fond of Edward. I just dislike the fact that he seems hell-bent on destroying everything he used to hold so dear.'

'Grief does that to some people,' she replied, having no idea that, in making that comment, Giancarlo was talking about more than just Edward's crumbling business.

'You said that with the conviction of experience,' he remarked, following the shadow which crossed her face.

'My mother died fourteen months ago,' she confessed, keeping her lashes lowered so he wouldn't see the pain in her eyes. 'Unexpectedly, like Marco,' she added. 'And even you know the kind of effect that shock and grief can have on you.'

'I didn't use it as an excuse to neglect my responsibilities,' he grimly pointed out.

Well, I did, and Edward did—as did Giancarlo's own sister, Alegra—though she was sure he didn't want to hear that, Natalia mused grimly, and reached for the bottle of water, mainly for something to do to hide the sudden heaviness of heart she was feeling.

'And your father—?' he asked, wondering what he had to say about his twenty-five-year-old daughter's affair with a man almost twice her age.

To Giancarlo's surprise her skin went as pale as the cloth covering the table.

'My mother never married.'

He beat her to the water bottle by a mere hair's breadth brush of their fingers. She snatched her hand away to place it on her lap where her nails curled into a skin-piercing fist while she concentrated on the sparkling water he was pouring into two wineglasses in the taut hope that he wouldn't ask any more probing questions.

He didn't. Being as astute as any red-blooded man deeply interested in the woman he meant to thoroughly seduce in the very near future, he realised her reply was her polite way of saying that she never knew her father.

So, with her mother gone, had she begun casting her eyes around looking for someone to fill the hole that had opened up in her life, and found the perfect substitute in a never-known father-figure like Edward?

It all seemed very plausible suddenly—forgivable even—though he had no intention whatsoever of going down that road simply because it would lead him away from what he was now wanting for too many reasons to count.

Not quite liking what that admission was saying to him, he picked up the wineglass and took a deep swallow—forgetting what was actually in the glass!

His expression was so comically disgusted that Natalia forgot to stay aloof and found herself laughing. 'You didn't have to have water just because I do,' she gently pointed out.

'I was trying to impress you with my temperance!' he threw back accusingly. 'And all you do is laugh!'

'I don't need impressing,' she told him with the laughter still warming her eyes.

His own grew still. 'Oh, yes, you do,' he insisted, and

watched her jump straight back behind her wall as the
temperature between them came back to a steady simmer.

I'll have you, Natalia Deyton, he vowed. By fair means
or foul, I *will* have you...

CHAPTER FOUR

THE meal was a rather quiet affair after that, mainly because Natalia had put herself on guard against Giancarlo Cardinale's irresistible charisma. But the food was surprisingly light and pleasant, which made her realise that he'd had more control over his Sicilian friend than he'd led her to believe.

He also controlled the small bouts of conversation they slid into, with what she read as his deliberate intention to keep the atmosphere light between them while they ate. So he talked, she listened, offered up a reply when it was absolutely necessary and in general tried very hard not to let herself become more fascinated with him than she was already.

But it was difficult when the man himself was a fascination even without his smooth, quiet, deeply sensual voice washing over her like a hypnotist's drone aimed to keep her trance-like.

Her eyes rarely left him so they missed very little: the way he lounged in his seat, the way he ate sparingly, the way he sipped at the half-bottle of crisp dry white wine he had ordered to suit his palate rather than the water...

'Are you sure you wouldn't like to try some?' he offered, tipping the bottle of wine towards her invitingly.

Natalia shook her head. They had reached the point in the meal where she was sitting over her empty plate with her elbows resting on the table and her glass suspended close to her mouth between her fingers. Her eyes had darkened, though she wasn't aware of it, and there was a softer look about her which to him made her seem not of this world again.

Young, lovely, most definitely sexy, yet she gave off a conflicting aura of innocence. That aura bothered him, because it only helped to prove how good she was at projecting herself as something she wasn't.

Like most seasoned liars, he grimly concluded.

'A sip of white wine isn't going to compromise your ability to function efficiently, you know,' he heard himself snap in irritation.

Irritation at whom? he then asked himself. Her for being what she was or himself for wanting what she was?

'I'll fall asleep,' she said, offering a light shrug of her narrow shoulders when he flicked a sceptical glance at her. 'It happens,' she insisted. 'So I've learned to be careful.'

'You were drinking champagne at lunch yesterday,' he reminded her. 'And I don't recall you falling asleep afterwards.' In fact she was too feisty if anything, he added silently.

'Sipping sparingly at it,' she corrected. 'As I suspect everyone else was doing.'

'Apart from the rather impassioned young man you were with, who seemed to be downing it rather—feverishly.'

'Each to his own.' She shrugged again, refusing to take the bait he was offering her.

He smiled. He watched her watch the smile materialise with the kind of concentration that set his juices flowing. 'He fancied you like hell,' he inserted softly. 'And had to gulp champagne to stop himself making a grab for you.'

Her blue eyes began to flash a warning of anger. 'If you noticed that, then you should also have noticed that I didn't take him on,' she pointed out.

'With a face and a figure like yours, Miss Deyton,' he

derided, 'you should never need to take any man on because they will do all the running for you.'

'With cynicism like yours, Mr Cardinale,' she countered, 'I am not surprised that you hold that opinion.'

'Giancarlo,' he said, making those amazing eyes blink. 'My close friends call me Giancarlo…'

He sat back to watch lazily the way her spine began to straighten and the glass came carefully down upon the table—most effective body language, he determined.

'I'm an employee, not a friend,' she asserted, glancing pointedly at her gold wrist-watch as she did so.

She was preparing to back off again. He took his chance and snaked his hand out to capture one of hers as it began to slide away from the glass. Like a butterfly struggling in his palm, he felt her fingers flutter, then go perfectly still.

'You will call me Giancarlo from now on,' he repeated. 'And I will call you Natalia—you understand me?'

Yes, he saw that she understood very well what he was saying, but he also saw by the guard she'd placed on her eyes that she was never going to admit that. So he explained it more fully. 'I don't mind doing all the running when I am interested. In fact I rather enjoy it,' he admitted. 'But I mean to catch. So be prepared, *mia cara*,' he warned with smooth, sensual emphasis, 'for the time when *I* drink champagne with you. For it will not be to drown out my desires, but to inflame them. And you will drink and be inflamed also.'

Her cheeks were growing warm, her eyes darker. He watched her lean towards him over the table, and waited to see what she was going to come back with.

'It is not going to happen, *signor*, so forget it,' she said in hot rejection. Then she snatched her hand away and rose to her feet and, without another word, simply walked away from him.

*   *   *

He let her do it too! Natalia could feel him sitting there, burning mocking darts into her back as she wove her taut body between the restaurant tables on her way to the door.

Outside she paused for a moment to suck in some deep breaths of cold February air. Her cheeks were burning but her flesh felt like ice. And why not when she hadn't even got a coat on? The way she was shivering had nothing to do with him and what he'd dared to say to her! she told herself crossly.

But she had to get away from here, she decided, taking a few jerky steps before she pulled to a stop again. No coat, she repeated. No purse either. When he'd hurried her out into the taxi to come here, she hadn't given a thought to her personal items all still waiting where she had left them, in her fifth-floor office, which had been such a haven to her for the last six months—until Giancarlo Cardinale had decided to invade it!

Or invade her, she then amended with a squeezing sensation deep down in her body. An arm looped around her waist. She almost groaned in frustration. He stood at least six inches above her and was crowding her like a great grizzly bear!

Only he was no bear—grizzly or otherwise. He was smooth and sleek and tormentingly masculine. 'I don't want you to want me,' she told him in a thin, tight little voice.

'Too late,' he said. 'I already want you. All we need to do now is get you to admit that you want what I want, then we can place this affair on an even footing.'

'I don't have affairs,' she threw back. And *affair* just about said it for Natalia. Not relationship or even emotional involvement, but an affair of the body. Physical, basic.

She thought she heard him huff out a sound of scorn,

though she could have been mistaken because he was hailing down a passing black cab at the time. But even the suggestion that he was scorning her statement was enough to keep her tense and distant as he hustled her into the taxi.

Long, lean, and as lithe as hell, he sat down beside her, then proceeded to stretch his body so he could fish in his pocket for something while her body went into tension overload as she watched him, and the cabby waited for him to say where they were heading for next.

A piece of paper appeared. She recognised it as the same one he had been scrawling something down upon after his girlfriend had telephoned this morning.

If he's intending to take me to meet her, she thought hysterically, then he really is as crazy as I'm beginning to suspect!

He relayed an address on the other side of the City, then settled back beside her while the driver began feeding the cab into the traffic.

'I would prefer to go straight back to the office,' she told him frostily.

'We will, later,' he replied. 'We have things to do first…'

Which instantly shot her to pieces. 'I don't want to *do* anything with you!'

He looked at her, she looked at him, lightning flashed— and they fell on each other. It was that quick, that hot, and that torrid. Mouth straining against mouth, breathing fast and fevered. It was shocking, a terrible dive into absolute abandonment…

Giancarlo couldn't believe this was actually him! But he wanted her—badly—and he wanted her now! And it had to happen in the back of a London black cab, of all places, with no privacy and no hope of taking it where he desperately needed it to go!

But her mouth really did taste of heaven, as his senses had been telling him it would from the first moment he'd set eyes on her. The sheer exquisite I-can't-get-enough-of-this pleasure of it was completely taking him over. And while he devoured she let herself be eaten, denying him nothing—nothing.

She was his for the taking...

This shouldn't be happening, Natalia was telling herself over and over. It made no difference. She loved the taste of him too much, the tight masculine domination with which the kiss was being sold.

He tasted of wine, and hot desire. She was dizzy on one and burning up on the other.

Oh, someone save me! She groaned when his hand came to curve over one of her breasts and the flesh beneath came alive in a burgeoning thrust that must have left him in no doubt as to what she was feeling.

This was it, the point of no return for her. She knew it and she suspected that he knew it. She either stopped him now or she surrendered completely.

It was the taxi pulling to an abrupt standstill that had them both breaking apart. They had arrived, apparently, though Natalia was too dazed to know where they were.

To give him his due, if the cabby had noticed what they'd been doing in the back of his cab he made no sign of it as Giancarlo paid him, adding a rather large tip, she suspected, going by the pleasant way the driver responded.

Opening the door, Giancarlo reached for her hand, then stepped out on the pavement trailing her with him as he went. Neither had looked directly at the other since the kiss. But she could feel its heat on her lips still and the hand he had folded round one of hers was very possessive.

He was gazing at the frontage to a large building built in stone which reminded her of just one of many Victorian office blocks that dotted this area of the City. But when they stepped into its luxurious foyer, she began to realise that this was no ordinary office block, but a block of highly exclusive City apartments, with a concierge who rose to his feet behind his workstation and smiled politely as they approached him.

Giancarlo gave his name and was handed a plastic card, then was directed towards the lifts and told to use it in the lift to gain access to the top floor. Natalia managed to take back her hand as they walked towards the lift. He said nothing. They still hadn't looked at each other.

No surprise there, she thought tensely, when you think what happened the last time.

The lift doors slid open, and Giancarlo waited politely for her to precede him inside. It was lined from ceiling to floor with tinted mirror glass, and she went to stand in the far corner and kept her face lowered because she just didn't want to see what her reflection was going to tell her if she did dare look up and catch a glimpse of herself. The lift began to rise. Giancarlo had taken up a position in the other corner across from her. She sensed his brooding study but refused to meet it. The silence was stifling, the tension so fraught it began lifting the hairs all over her body. If something didn't break it soon she had a horrible feeling she was going to burst out crying.

Maybe he knew it. 'Natalia,' he murmured, using her name with husky intimacy that ran through her blood like mercury. 'You can look at me; I am in control now.'

Well, bully for you, she thought with acid satire. Now ask me if *I* am in control! But despite the inner quip, she found herself lifting her head with a defiance that burned in her eyes as they hit him.

'Who owns this place?' she asked, using the first non-provoking question to pop into her head.

'A—friend of mine,' he answered with his voice—while his eyes most definitely brooded on other things. 'He is into property development. This building has only recently begun letting its space.'

'*Office* space?' she sliced sweetly at him.

'No.' He shook his dark head—and her fingers itched to grab hold of it and pull it down until his mouth hit hers.

Oh, damn, she cursed…

Damn it… Giancarlo was cursing silently. If she continued to look at him like that it was likely he would stop this lift and show her how much it was costing him to remain this passive.

'Apartments,' he answered levelly. 'I need a place to stay while I am in London as well as a place to work from, and this will be the ideal solution.'

'You've been here before? Last night, for instance?'

Ah! He began to get an idea as to what was really eating at her. Not the serious risk of torrid sex in a rising lift—but the risk that she was about to be walked into his busy den of iniquity.

He allowed himself a small grimace, seeing that the hook he had used to concentrate her mind on him had now become a hindrance to the developing situation.

So, 'No,' he replied. 'Last night I stayed with the property developer himself and his lovely wife—Serena Delucca,' he placed succinctly, watching carefully as her expression began to show the slow dawning of full understanding.

'Playing games, *signor*?' she grimly mocked him.

'Don't we all, *signorina*?' he dryly returned.

Her breasts began to ache. They had no right to do so when the conversation could not be even vaguely considered sexual.

No? a little voice inside her head scoffed. Every single thing the two of you do or say is so sexual it should be X-rated!

The lift stopped. They both straightened away from the walls. The doors slid open. They stepped out together into a wide, light, square inner foyer with shiny white-tiled flooring and magnolia walls, and no doors but wide, deep-set, angular openings that linked room to room in a way meant to convey the impression of space and light and freedom of movement.

It also came pre-furnished, in a style designed to complement its open planning. Nothing stood out, nothing glared back at you, just a clever blend of natural shades and fabrics that were so easy on the eye you could almost miss them.

'Nice,' she said, not sure if she liked it.

'Bland,' he replied, showing he felt the same as she did. 'Serena's choice, if I am not mistaken. Being a black-haired, black-eyed witch, she likes to make an impression in any given situation. And she would make an impression in here,' he said.

Then he turned to look at Natalia.

'No,' she gasped when she saw his expression. But it was already too late. His hand snaked up, pulled the clasp from her hair, then stood back to watch the silken strands tumble in a glistening copper flow down her neck and over her shoulders until they settled like a caress to the curve of her breasts.

'Now that,' he drawled, 'is what I call making an impression.'

Copper-fire hair, white skin, rose-coloured lips, wide, shock-darkened lover-blue eyes, he listed covetously. Long black suit hugging a slender body, breasts that wanted to feel his touch again—and a pair of amazing legs which were taking her backwards in a useless bid for escape.

She'd missed her only chance, he saw, as her wary reversing took her right away from the open lift. Which left her with nowhere else to go but deeper into the apartment, treading bright white tiles on slender heels that made tiny tapping sounds as she went.

He began to track her, his hand snaking out to flick the button that would send the lift away. Watching him do it, she realised her mistake, her lips fell open and began to tremor, and his chest began to beat to the drum of the chase.

'Th-this isn't funny,' she stammered on a constricted flow of air.

'I am not laughing,' he pointed out, lifting his hand up to the knot of his tie to slowly begin pulling at it.

If it was possible her eyes grew wider, flickering from his fingers to his eyes in a slightly wild stare of disbelief.

He said nothing else. He didn't need to. The tie came loose and he began sliding it leisurely from around his throat. He let it fall in a snake-like slither to the floor, then began unhooking shirt buttons.

She went stock-still—then jerked a hand up to press it against her upper chest, and he smiled as he came to a standstill, because he knew she had picked up the same beat he was feeling.

'Going to stop me?' he taunted softly while his fingers

continued slowly slipping open buttons. 'All you need to do is say the word, and it stops right here...'

The big test. The acid test. Natalia knew she was hovering on the edge of a rather large precipice. She either backed herself right off it, or she held her ground. It was her choice. He was giving her the choice.

Her mouth was dry, her throat tight, her body pulsing to its own hectic rhythm. There he was, standing there, no longer looking quite so razor-sharp any more, with his tie gone and his shirt buttons half open down his front so she could see tantalising glimpses of golden skin and dark body hair—and even smell that illusive scent she recognised on an another level of consciousness as utterly seductive.

Pheromone, they called it. The sexually aroused male putting out messages to the sexually aware female.

But *this* male and *this* female—? She lifted her gaze to his dark, compelling eyes and saw the capital red letters DANGER gleaming warningly there. Think of the complications, she told herself. Think of Edward—the lies! Think what you could be risking here!

Think of that mouth fixed on your mouth, her foolish heart suggested, sending her eyes flickering again on a downward path over a face she didn't seem to be able to look at enough. Then onto his hands, which made her flesh tingle with excitement, and his body, which filled her with such clamouring hunger.

And what was it but sex? she tried telling herself. I can do that! I can live with that! I can enjoy this man then let him go when it's time to call a stop to it before it has a chance to hurt other people! I can do it, she insisted, and felt her heart give a heavy thump at the decision, then start racing furiously as if it knew something she didn't...

What was she thinking? What was going on inside that beautiful head to make her stand there looking at him like that? Indecision? Uncertainty?

Loyal thoughts of Edward?

The very suggestion made something violent wrench inside of him, and in angry response to it he began striding forward. He didn't want to hear Edward's name falling from her trembling lips, so he was going to make damn sure it didn't happen!

Reaching for her, he fed his fingers into her glorious mass of hair, used his thumbs to cup her chin so he could keep that exquisite face turned up to his—then lowered his head and kissed her. The sheer heat of her response reached right down to the very core of his manhood. He heard himself groan. She let out a little whimper that told him she was experiencing exactly the same as he. The knowledge soared like a phoenix rising out of the fire of his anger to consume him with the need to make her catch fire too.

He altered his stance, inviting her closer. She came without hesitation, sinking into him and lifting her hands to fold them around his neck while he sent his sliding slowly downwards. Over her shoulders, down her back, feeling the hectic pulse of her heart as he passed over her ribcage, then on down until finally they settled against the curving firmness of her hips.

And through it all their mouths strained against each other. Warm and hungry, soft and deep. He was back in control. The seduction was on. They had only one place to go from here.

Yet—what did he do?

He broke the kiss, looked deep into her passion-glazed, most definitely sultry blue eyes which held all the promises of life's rarest pleasures just waiting for him to tap into them—and he changed his mind.

'No,' he said, quietly and very calmly.

She began to frown, her softly parted, gently pulsing mouth still feeling his mouth against it. 'No?' she replied in sweet confusion.

'No,' he confirmed, but kissed her again to soften the blow before he added huskily, 'We will not do this now. The timing is bad. We have an apartment to view. I have an important meeting to attend in less than an hour. I should be ashamed of myself. You deserve better than a quick roll on the nearest bed we can find. I beg your forgiveness. Next time I will show a little more—finesse, I promise you.'

'Finesse,' she repeated, seeming to register only that one word out of everything he had said. Her eyelashes fluttered down, making the tip of his tongue tingle with a desire to reach out and follow their gently curving spread against her cheekbones. Her body drew back, her fingers trailing very slowly from his nape to his chest, where his gaping shirt proved no barrier against the burning touch of her palms as she flatted them against him—then pushed him away.

He had hurt her, he could see it. She felt humiliated and cheap. But he couldn't change the unpalatable fact that having suspected that she was thinking of Edward just when he'd kissed her had effectively ruined what had been promising to be a mind-blowing experience for him.

Because no woman, he vowed with an inner harshness that narrowed his eyes when she flicked up those lashes to look at him again—no woman thinks of another man when she should be thinking of Giancarlo Cardinale! In fact, the next time he brought Natalia Deyton to a point of complete surrender, he would make absolutely certain that she did no thinking at all!

So, 'Unless, of course, you prefer the quick roll?' he offered with just enough of a taunt in his tone to make her eyes flash.

'Why?' she came back like the flick of a whip. 'Is that all that's on offer?'

Oh, very good... He began to grin. The English had a saying for this, he mused, something to do with being foisted or hoisted on one's own petard. He began to laugh. He was enjoying himself again.

While she looked ready to attack him like a deranged cat.

Well, that was okay. He could deal with that. In fact, he would look forward to it. Only this particular cat would be purring for him by the time the deed was done...

I'll swing for him. I promise I will! Natalia vowed as she turned and walked stiffly away. When she'd managed to calm down a little she would begin to appreciate what a lucky escape she'd had!

For the man was a tease—an arrogant tease. He ought to know better at his age. Unless, of course, leading women on then backing off once he had them where he wanted them was the way Giancarlo Cardinale got his sexual kicks!

And she had surrendered. That telling little truth shuddered through her on a shaft of self-disgust as she stepped through the first opening that she came to—then stopped dead in utter surprise at what her eyes were being treated to.

Because she had never seen anything quite like it. The room—if you could call it a room—opened out into a square-shaped arena with a high white ceiling and a polished maple floor, which went down in steps to a sunken seating area furnished with soft cream leather sofas and chairs. In its centre sat a slab of marble that was supposed to be a table, she assumed. And the walls were painted in the palest yellow, the long plain hung curtains of lined white voile.

'I think we have found the sitting room,' a sardonic voice murmured behind her.

She would have stiffened in revolt, but she was just too overcome by what she was seeing. 'You're really going to live here?' she asked, unable to imagine anyone actually using this place!

'Looks like it,' he answered, stepping past her to walk down into the seating area, where he shoved his hands into his trouser pockets and began to look around.

He'd done up his shirt, Natalia noted. In the short walk from where she had left him to him joining her here, he had tidied away all the evidence of his little after-lunch diversion. Even his tie was back around his neck, though hanging loose there, at least.

'Come down here and take a look at this,' he said, unaware of the bitter thoughts going through her head.

She went because it was easier to do that than argue. 'Some bachelor pad,' he drawled, nodding towards one of the walls where another doorless opening led straight into a bedroom. You could even see the bed—a vast low-slung thing covered in snowy white linen. 'I even have the sacrificial altar on which to lay out my victims.'

He was amused, but as she looked at the slab of marble posing as a table through a new set of eyes she felt herself blushing like an idiot.

'Not yet,' he whispered close to her ear, sending her nerve-ends screaming for cover.

But before she could retaliate with something really cutting, he was frowning at his watch and already turning away. 'We are running out of time,' he clipped out as if the other provocative remark had never been uttered. 'Let's see the rest of the place. We need to find somewhere to set up operations before a team of technicians arrive to connect us up.'

The idea of having to work here with him on a daily basis was becoming less palatable by the minute. But she followed him through room after room of minimalism gone mad. The dining room, for instance, almost matched the living room in style and texture. The kitchen was more white floor tiling, more maple wood, with more marble and some stainless steel thrown in as a feature.

As he'd said. The perfect bachelor pad.

There was even a room set up ready as a designer office. 'Ah,' Giancarlo said, glancing round them. 'At last I begin to see why Fredo suggested this place.'

So could she. Thinking of it from a strictly business point of view—and she was determined to keep her view of this situation *strictly* business from now on—this was absolutely ideal for what she assumed was required of the busy venture capitalist wanting to work from home.

All it lacked at the moment was its communications hardware to link him into anywhere he wanted to go. The rest was already provided for. The workstations, the chairs—even the sunlight he professed to need for his Sicilian blood to run smoothly through his veins was managing to filter in through the voile-covered window.

It was her own needs which were beginning to trouble her because there was no separate office for her to escape to for a bit of relief from his relentless personality.

Also, it was right on the other side of town from Knight's—and her own home in Chelsea.

'What's the matter?' As sharp as a needle, he picked up on her concern.

'Nothing,' she said, turning away from him, suddenly feeling so weary she just wanted to sit down in a dark corner somewhere and sulk. 'How soon do you intend to move in here?' she asked, looking for a diversion, and finding it where she did not want it to be.

'Now,' he announced. 'We will do it now. I will make a few phone calls to get things started, then leave you here to oversee the installation of everything we require while I shoot off to Knight's to meet with my staff.'

'But I need to go back there myself!' she protested. 'I've left my things there—my coat, my purse, my—'

'No problem. I will collect anything of yours and bring it with me when I return,' he insisted, not even seeming to see her look of angry dismay at the way he was completely taking her over like this! 'By the time I get back, I expect this place to be up and running,' he warned, already lifting a mobile phone from his pocket and punching in numbers while Natalia sank into the nearest chair in an air of defeat.

It was like being in the presence of a human dynamo and she just didn't have any energy left with which to keep up with him. So she didn't bother—the chair was as good as any dark corner to sulk in at this precise moment. So she sat there and simply let his voice waft over her head as he made call after call and she pondered the miseries of crossing London on a daily basis just to endure more of—this.

'Okay. Everything is organised,' he said eventually. 'The technicians will be here in half an hour. They know what I want. Make sure that everything is up and running before you let them leave.' He glanced at his watch, frowned and began heading for the door that wasn't a door.

'Give the concierge a call,' he instructed over his shoulder. 'Find out the name of the nearest supermarket and get some provisions delivered here. I will be back—when-ever.' He was already at the lift. 'Until then—make your-self at home…'

CHAPTER FIVE

MAKE yourself at home…

Well, Natalia decided to do just that. Giancarlo wanted provisions? He got provisions. He wanted his office up and running by the time he got back? He got his office up and running by the time he got back. He even got the office drawers and cupboards stocked with every miscellaneous item known to the nearest office stores suppliers she could locate as soon as the telephone line was connected.

Efficiency was her middle name, she decided. No one could fault her organisation skills! Everything was neatly filed, everything had its own neatly printed tab. In fact, in the few hours she'd had, she'd brought Signor Cardinale's nice new workplace to life with an absolute vengeance.

And vengeance felt like a very good word to her at this precise moment while she sat in her chosen chair at her chosen monitor screen, in her chosen corner of the room, doing exactly what she was paid to do, which was dealing with all the neglected business of the day that had arrived in her network-linked work-folder while she had been otherwise engaged.

In fact she was just finishing up when the sound of the lift drawing to a halt alerted her to his return, so even her timing was super-efficient, she made a very satisfied note, glancing at her watch as she did so.

Seven o'clock, it told her. Which made her a very dedicated personal assistant with super-efficient secretarial skills! she mocked herself grimly as she shut down her network-link to Knight's.

Outside it had been dark for hours, so it was a long time since she'd gone round the apartment switching on lights and drawing curtains. But although the place had taken on a more appealing image with the subtle use of artificial lighting, she was heartily glad to be getting out of it.

She stood up as she heard his footsteps sound in the white-tiled foyer. By the time he appeared in the opening she had stepped around her chair and was just unhooking her suit jacket from its backrest. Glancing up, she found herself looking into a lean dark face that was beginning to look a little jaded round the edges. He needed a shave, his shirt was open at the neck again, the tie knotted but hanging loose as if tugged like that by impatient fingers. Over his arm lay her coat, her soft lilac scarf, and he was holding a plastic carrier bag in which, she presumed, was her handbag.

The desire to voice a polite greeting to him was not even an option. She was angry, and if it weren't for her loyalty to Edward she would have walked out of this apartment hours ago, gone to collect her own things from Knight's, then walked out of there too, with the intention of never returning!

But as things stood regarding her commitment to Edward, she merely demonstrated her anger with Ginacarlo Cardinale by flicking her eyes away from him, then completely ignoring him as she finished pulling on her jacket.

But that did not mean she wasn't hotly aware that his eyes were sliding over the dark red top she was in the process of covering up...

Red on red, he was thinking, wanting to voice some deep, dark, sensual question as to why the red of her wonderful hair was not clashing with the red of her very sexy top.

But he was too alive to the silent warning that any comment at all from him was not going to be appreciated.

She was back behind her frosty wall, he made note, then grimaced because—hell, who could blame her? Separated, isolated, and infiltrated were the buzzwords which came to mind to describe what he had done to Natalia Deyton.

Then he'd left her alone here to stew on it all for hours upon end with the deliberate intention of keeping her balanced on an emotional edge, ready to tip over whenever he felt like making it happen.

So, no wonder she looked frosty. No wonder her chin was up and her mouth pulled into that flat little line of stiff disapproval meant to convey a warning to him that if he said just one word out of place she would most probably kill him.

But, *Dio*, she looked sensational in her anger with her hair streaming down her back like a proud defiance in her absolute refusal to redress what he had arrogantly undressed earlier.

'Your luggage has arrived.' She spoke suddenly.

His loins gave him a vicious kick because that icy voice was just begging to be melted.

'I had it placed in your room for you to deal with.'

Her fingers were busy fastening buttons on the severe black jacket that did nothing to hide the body beneath and, even if it had, he would still have been able to feel the firmness of her breast against his palm so it wouldn't have mattered anyway.

'Also, a car was delivered.' She pointed to a set of keys lying on the workstation set up near the window. 'You will find it parked down in the basement. Black, I believe,' she added with just the merest hint of acid. 'Of the Italian variety. Not easy to miss, I should think…'

And that, he read, had been a deliberate strike at his

masculine ego for his choice of car in a traffic-blocked city like London. She would have been more impressed by a small nondescript run-about than his brand new phallic-symbol Ferrari, he judged, and almost sent her a provocative challenging smile—but the conditions didn't advise it.

Because, despite all the frosty defiance, she looked tired and a little pale and the finest hint of bruising was beginning to darken the sockets of her beautiful eyes. Oddly, he didn't like to see it. For all he was aware that his siege tactics were a deliberate part of his divide and conquer war of attrition, he had no wish to lay to waste that part of her which had fired his motives in the first place.

So he did absolutely nothing as he watched her turn to walk towards him with her jacket buttoned up to her stiff neck, and her eyes as cold as the Arctic. Coming to a stop in front of him, she reached out to take her scarf first, sliding it off his arm and looping it around her neck before reaching for her coat. He said not a thing as the warm cashmere-wool mix settled across her shoulders, its long length reaching way beyond her slender calves. Nor remarked when, with a careless grace, she slid the long pelt of her hair out from inside the coat, then reached out to take the carrier bag containing her handbag.

'Goodnight,' she said, and walked proudly away from him.

It really was a sensational performance. Shame it was all spoiled by the distinct threat of tears he had glimpsed in her eyes just before she'd turned away...

Nothing, she was telling herself as she walked. No words, no expression, no attempt to thank her for the hours she had put in here for his benefit—not even a hint that he was aware of everything else he had put her through today! She hated him, she really did!

But what really hurt was that he'd let her walk away just now. Why should it hurt? she asked herself as she stabbed an angry finger at the lift-call button. What was the matter with her? Was she an absolute sucker for punishment or something? The man was cruel, he played cruel games like a cat would with a mouse before it gobbled its victim up and spit out the bones. Was that what Giancarlo Cardinale had in store for her? A final gobbling up of her before he spit out what was left and walked away?

'Oh, come on—come on!' she begged the lift, feeling the tears begin to threaten for real now.

She went to hit the button again—found her fingers clashing with another set of fingers and glanced up to see through a veil of tears—him standing beside her.

Her hand snapped away. 'Forgotten something?' she asked, meaning to sound sarcastic, but she only managed husky and wished she weren't such an emotional fool.

'No,' he replied, quietly, levelly. 'It was you who forgot me.'

The lift arrived. She frowned, not understanding his meaning. Then decided she didn't *want* to understand it as she stepped into the lift and turned to press for the ground-floor foyer—when once again his hand beat her to it.

He pressed for the basement. 'I am driving you home,' he explained.

Standing there, not half an inch separating her from his whipcord lean, muscle-hardened, *arrogant* stance, she noticed the bunch of car keys dangling from his lean dark fingers, looked up at his carefully neutral expression, and said, 'Go to hell,' thickly, succinctly. Then reached out *again* to press for the ground-floor foyer, and had her hand firmly captured, stopping her from touching anything—but him.

Sensation hit her in a crackling rush that fled round her system. She tried to break free, got herself pinned for her trouble against mirror-lined walls that sent back reflected images of the two of them from just about every angle. It was mad, compelling. Dark face—white face. Black hair—copper hair. Flashing blue eyes—steady brown velvet. And two mouths coming closer as if unable to resist the hypnotic pull of the other.

'Don't...' she whispered in a last-ditch attempt to save herself from disaster.

He drew back. She hated him for it. 'Do you allow me to drive you home,' he levelled quietly, 'or do we return upstairs to—discuss the matter?'

What a choice. The ultimate ultimatum, she recognised, for, despite his level voice, the quiet, calm manner, she knew what was being put on offer here. Escape, the chance to live another day—or capture, in its most consummate sense.

The silence sizzled with hesitation. It ate at her senses and burned in her breasts. His hands were locked on her upper arms, hers were flattened against his rock-solid chest, so she could feel the steady pound of his heart, and the even spacing of his breath. But she could also feel her own heart rattling around as if in a whirlpool—panicking because she wasn't breathing at all.

The decision was that difficult to make...

If she chose to go back upstairs, he would be the loser here, Giancarlo told himself, because she would be coming to his bed still fighting him, and by tomorrow she would hate him for it.

But he didn't want her hatred. He wanted her warm and

willing and believing that to be with him in his bed was
the only place she wanted to be. In fact, it was essential
she feel like that. For what good was a single night of
passion going to do him when it came to seducing her right
away from Edward?

It was the long-term seduction of Natalia Deyton which
was the real goal he had set himself—making her want
him enough and trust him enough to need him more than
she'd ever needed anyone.

But if she chose to go home, he wasn't sure he could
let her go that easily either. She had no idea what her eyes
were telling him, he thought tensely. No suspicion that he
was being eaten up inside. She was tying him in knots, he
freely admitted it. Sensual knots, emotional knots. Greedy,
compulsive, frustrated knots that made a complete mockery of the offer to drive her home.

He'd meant to be kind, show her another side to himself
that was thoughtful and caring because she'd looked so
tired and stressed out. He'd discovered he didn't like it—
didn't like knowing that her strain was entirely his fault.

'I need to go home,' she whispered throatily. And the
tears were still there! He wanted to kick himself for making them happen. He wanted to say to hell with it all and
simply take her back to his apartment anyway!

They came to a stop and the doors slid open, revealing
two fellow tenants waiting to enter, their polite expressions
trying hard not to notice the buzz of sexual tension bouncing off the mirrored walls of the lift-car.

Giancarlo straightened away from her instantly. Natalia
quickly slid herself past both him and the two others with
her head lowered so they couldn't see her pained embarrassment.

He joined her as the lift doors closed again, leaving them

alone in the softly lit car park with a double row of expensive cars.

The Ferrari still stood out as different, squatting low and sleek in its reserved slot, like a black cat waiting to pounce the moment it was given the opportunity.

Deactivating its state-of-the-art security, he walked round to the passenger door and opened it for her. She didn't say a single word but just folded herself into the plush leather seat and waited for him to close the door.

She was staring directly ahead when he climbed in beside her. He adjusted the seat to accommodate his long legs, clipped home his seat belt, and then fired the engine. The car had been parked front end out so all he had to do was put it in gear and they were moving with a low purring growl that made his teeth clench with pleasure because, no matter what Natalia felt about this car, he was Italian, and his Italian blood revelled in that sound like no other.

Except the purr of a woman, he ruefully considered. Then he shut down that line of thinking before it took him places he couldn't afford to go right now...

Outside in the street it had started raining. Natalia sat watching heavy sheets of the stuff slating down from a leaden sky, and knew she would have been soaked through to the skin before she'd walked ten feet in this kind of downpour.

Which made rather a mockery out of her stiff-faced bid for independence earlier, she acknowledged. Doing it her own way, she would have arrived home looking like a drowned rat and feeling more miserable than she already did!

'Where to?' he asked.

'Chelsea,' she told him shortly. Then, because she was beginning to feel the unfair sting of her own churlish manner, especially when she remembered that he had arrived at his apartment looking tired, yet here he was, driving her home in weather not fit for dogs, she lightened her tone to add, 'It's on the other side of the river. If you—'

'I know where Chelsea is,' he cut in levelly.

She floundered into silence again, realising she should have remembered that he was quite familiar with London. Edward had told her once that Giancarlo had worked here in the City for a few years when he'd been just beginning to strike out on his own 'playing the hot-shot City broker and cutting quite a dash with the ladies,' Edward had fondly described the Giancarlo of those days. But then, Edward was deeply fond of his wife's younger brother, she recalled heavily. Which made this other situation that was so quickly developing all the more impossible.

Oh, Edward, she thought sighingly. What am I going to do? What *am* I going to do—?

No answer came back because Edward wasn't here, but she was and so was Giancarlo, driving together, through a rainy London evening in a car that turned heads even in this kind of weather—and with an atmosphere inside the car that sang with sexual tension, even though they were both trying to pretend it wasn't there.

She began feeding him directions once they were nearing their destination, her voice sounding huskily intimate, even to her. The rain stopped quite suddenly as they turned into her street. She directed him to a parking spot by the kerb outside her house and inside she was beginning to tremble slightly as the car stopped and the engine died.

For it was, she realised, the beginning of yet another dangerous situation: the point where she said a polite thank-you and goodnight—or invited him inside.

'Nice house,' he commented, pre-empting her need to say anything. He was peering out of the car at the row of tiny cottages. 'It must cost you something to live here,' opined the astute banker in him. 'How many of you share, to rent a place like this?'

Casually said, merely curious more than anything, but still Natalia felt herself stiffening as a hint of warning went chasing down her spine. 'I don't rent,' she answered warily. 'And I don't share...'

She doesn't rent, and she doesn't share, Giancarlo was slowly repeating to himself, and suddenly felt himself going cold. He wasn't a fool, he knew the price of property in London, especially in a fashionable area like this. So how did a young woman trained as nothing more than a secretary, earning the salary he knew Natalia Deyton earned, afford to live here?

The answer came back like a stab in the chest. She couldn't afford it—but Edward could.

He was sitting here with another man's mistress, staring at another man's love-nest! And for a terrible moment he thought he was going to be sick!

Edward in there, with Natalia. Edward in there, cheating on his wife—cheating on Giancarlo's sister—with Natalia! His eyes began to burn into the brick frontage as if he could see every salacious thing they did in there.

'M-my mother passed away about fourteen months ago, if you recall,' Natalia was telling him huskily.

His black eyes flashed to her profile on a flare of hope. 'And you lived here together before she died?'

She went pale. 'I...n-no.'

The answer gutted him.

'Sh-she left me well provided for,' the little liar embroidered her tale of deceit. 'I just prefer to live alone. W-would you like to come in, h-have some coffee be-before you start back?' she offered—as a diversion tactic perhaps, to stop him probing any deeper into her financial arrangements?

Well, no, he would not like to come in! They would not carry him dead over the threshold of that—den of sin! he thought through the roaring in his ears. 'It is late,' he refused, amazed at how even his voice sounded. 'And it has been a long day. I think we are both tired…'

She looked so relieved that he had to presume she'd been terrified of him walking in there and discovering some little piece of evidence that would lead him to Edward.

'Then I'll say thank you, for bringing me home.' She didn't push the issue, found a brief smile—and was reaching for the door catch when he stopped her.

'Have dinner with me,' he said gruffly. 'Tomorrow night.'

She turned a puzzled frown on him. He didn't blame her—he was confused himself! All he knew was that things had changed. He wanted her out of that house and in his bed in *his* apartment before another day went by!

'I will be out all day tomorrow,' he went on, thinking on his feet again. 'I have meetings to attend in the City, so I won't see you unless you wait for me to get in tomorrow. So I am asking you to have dinner with me,' he repeated.

'What—like a date?' she asked, looking into his eyes with her own so wide and seductively vulnerable, he hated himself for the blast of heat he felt where he shouldn't!

'Yes, a date,' he confirmed, gruffly and suggestively. 'One where we get to know each other outside the work environment, and explore the—possibilities to what we know is already here…' He touched her soft and crushable lower lip with a finger. The warm flesh pulsed in instant response. 'Bring a change of clothes with you tomorrow, change at the apartment to save us some time…' In a minute, he thought fiercely, she will be licking that finger, and *Dio*, but he was burning for her to do it! 'It will be good, hmm?'

She knew what he was saying, the sultry look in her deceitful eyes told him so, as did the sensual pulse in the air surrounding them. And as his body throbbed and his anger roared and his eyes burned with his intentions, he felt that softly pulsing lip move on her answer.

'Yes,' she said.

Triumph sang in his blood. After tomorrow night she would not be sleeping in Edward's cosy little love-nest ever again! She was his for the taking, and he was going to take her! By the time this thing was over Natalia Deyton was going to belong to *him* body and soul, Giancarlo vowed.

Body and wretched lying soul…

CHAPTER SIX

BY SEVEN-FIFTEEN the next evening, Natalia was standing in the bedroom of Giancarlo's apartment, hurriedly putting the finishing touches to her make-up before she found herself somewhere to go to wait for him that wasn't so—thought provoking.

She couldn't believe an apartment of this size and class had only one bedroom and bathroom in it! A bachelor pad, he had dryly described it. One with hardly any doors and no locks on the few that it did have!

He had not arrived yet, and her tummy was fluttering with a nervous anticipation that was making it impossible for her to put her lipstick on straight. Sighing, she grabbed a tissue to wipe it away, then tried again.

It had been a strange day all told, she reflected. Disturbingly quiet without him here, yet she'd been feeling his presence everywhere from the moment she'd stepped out of the lift this morning.

No, before that, she amended, recalling the private taxi-cab that had arrived at her front door early this morning, arranged by him, to transport her here with the minimum of fuss and the maximum of comfort. The man certainly knew how to make an impression, she mused dryly. First with the door-to-door transport, then with the concierge waiting in the foyer to hand her the necessary security access card so that she could activate the lift, and an apology from Mr Cardinale for not being here today. 'I am instructed to inform you that he will be here to collect you at seven-thirty...'

Seven-thirty had seemed a comfortingly long way off then—but the man himself hadn't. From the moment she'd stepped out of the lift she had felt him everywhere she went in the apartment. Here in the bedroom, for instance, where she'd come first to hang up the suit bag carrying her clothes for tonight. The first thing to hit her had been the clean-scented smell of his soap permeating out from the connecting bathroom. And the evidence of his occupation lay everywhere she happened to look, like the loose change on the bedside table and the black cotton robe tossed casually on the bed.

A bed she couldn't so much as glance at without feeling her skin prickle as her mind shot off to places it shouldn't.

'Oh, heck,' she cursed softly, and made herself finish the job she had started before her nerves completely got the better of her. It had been bad enough taking a quick shower in his bathroom, hurrying herself through the chore with her senses on edge, tautly aware of the lack of a lock on the door and listening out for the sound of him returning early, terrified he would catch her there naked yet wickedly turned on by the idea at the same time. In fact she'd shocked herself by how vivid that fantasy had been.

She ought to be ashamed of herself. The note he'd left her had invited her to feel free to use the apartment as her own—but it had not given her permission to weave fantasies about him in his shower!

But then, it had been a week for heightening the senses. Yesterday she had spent in a constant state of high anxiety not knowing what he was going to come at her with next. Today, even though he had been physically absent, he had hovered silently in the background of everything she'd done, like the warm breath of a prospective lover on her nape, making his desires felt.

Oh, stop it! she scolded herself and began feeding her

cosmetics back into their bag with impatient fingers. It was the sheer volume of work he'd left for her to do that made it feel he were breathing down her neck! she told herself crossly.

So much work, in fact, that she decided he must have stayed up all night to produce it! Letters to type. Memos to create and wing off to all the separate departments in Knight's, carefully spelling out his directives and what he expected back from each and every one. Then there was the pin number he had left her, to enable her access to the Cardinale Group computer mainframe. A long list of jobs regarding all his other business interests had given her a daunting insight into how powerful a man he actually was.

No wonder she had become so obsessed by his presence, she told herself. He'd even emailed her at precisely one o'clock, ordering her to stop and make herself some lunch!

Then, halfway through the afternoon, the package had arrived by special courier. Her fingers went still, her eyes flickering up to catch their darkened expression in the mirror as she replayed that moment when she'd been handed the glossy white garment box—with the Taylor-Gant name inscribed in gold on the lid—and instantly known what had been inside it.

'Consider these homework,' the accompanying note said, scrawled in his bold black mocking hand. 'I trust your good judgement as to which set you choose to wear tonight.'

Inside the box had been no less than three different sets of underwear. A sheer black lace set, a flimsy white silk set and a daring set in come-and-get-me red. All of which were so sensually provocative that she'd actually blushed as she'd visualised him choosing these things for her to wear!

But she was wearing the white set, which was telling her something she had no wish to dwell upon right now.

A telephone began to ring. Almost jumping out of her skin as the sound pierced the silence, she turned rather dazedly to look for the nearest extension line. She found it next to the bed, and went to answer it warily, knowing somehow that it had to be him.

'Did you carry out all my instructions?' his low, dark, huskily intimate voice murmured enquiringly, and made her instantly aware of delicate white silk lovingly moulding her body.

'I finished all the work you required me to do,' she replied coolly, refusing to take up the bait.

He laughed softly and the sound sent her legs weak.

'Where are you?' she asked, glancing down at her watch to see that it was exactly seven-thirty.

'Right here in the foyer,' he told her. 'Awaiting my date—are you coming down?'

Coming down? She frowned. 'Don't you need to change first?'

'Would you *like* me to come up?'

'No!' she cried, not understanding why she was being handed this reprieve from the one moment she had been dreading all day, but more than willing to accept it. 'I just need a few minutes and I will come down to you.'

Already beginning to panic, she put down the phone, then turned in an anxious daze to gather the last of her things together. She would have to collect them tomorrow, she told herself as she stuffed her day things into the suit bag with fingers that trembled in her urgency. For it wouldn't be practical for her to come back here tonight just to collect them.

Who needs a practical excuse to come back here? a little voice inside her head mocked.

Ignoring it, she turned to take a last quick glance at herself in the mirror. What she saw reflected back at her set her nerve-ends singing. Was that her—was it really her?

Her cheeks were flushed, her eyes were too bright—and the dress was an absolute disaster! It was too short, too tight, too—everything! she decided, giving a wriggling tug at the stretchy fabric in an effort to cover up some more leg. The dusky-blue silk-knit settled back to its original position the moment she let go of it—leaving her standing there staring at it in despair. She had deliberately chosen this particular dress because she'd thought it had all the right qualities to look elegant and demure with its long sleeves and what she'd remembered as a modest V neckline.

So how was it that she hadn't remembered how it clung to her body like a second skin? Or that the V dipped too low into her cleavage and her legs suddenly looked twice as long as they were!

And I should have put my hair up! she realised as panic put its foot on the throttle and went raging through her at full pace. Leaving it down to hang loose over her shoulders made her look—slinky, she saw in growing horror.

Had she time to stand here messing with it? The overriding fear of him losing patience and coming up here to find her told her she hadn't even got time to panic like this!

'Oh,' she groaned. This was all *his* fault! The wretched man had been slowly driving her out of her mind all day.

Then—no, she amended that as she shuffled her feet into three-inch high-heeled shoes and made a grab for her evening jacket. He had been driving her out of her mind from the first moment she'd set eyes on him two days ago!

Was it only two days? It felt like for ever, she thought

tensely as she snatched up her evening purse and left the bedroom.

She was hurrying past the kitchen opening when she spied the ice bucket sitting on one of the units with the bottle of champagne standing in it—and pulled to a stop, then closed her eyes on the unwanted reminder of this particular instruction he'd emailed her.

Five o'clock on the dot, she recalled with a tense little quiver. 'You may stop being the efficient Miss Deyton now and turn yourself into the very desirable Natalia for me. PS. Put the champagne on ice,' leaving her in no doubt as to his expectations later tonight.

But what really bothered her was—she'd done it. What did that tell her about her own expectations for tonight?

But—no. Grimly she blocked out that thought. They were going out for dinner, she told herself firmly as she stepped into the lift and pressed for the foyer. *Dinner,* she repeated. Nothing more, nothing less. When it was over she would go home to her own house and her own bed, and Giancarlo Cardinale would be drinking his champagne alone.

A promise she forgot the moment she set eyes on him. The lift doors came open as he was turning round to face them. She gained a very vague impression of subtle lighting and white tiled flooring, then—nothing.

He went still. So did she, the breath dying in her throat. He was wearing a dark suit, white shirt and a dark tie, all of which looked as if he had put them on only minutes ago. His face was clean-shaven, his hair as smooth as silk. He looked lean and dark and frighteningly special—and his eyes were so hot they made her flesh burn…

Had it worked? Giancarlo was asking himself tensely as he turned to watch the lift doors open. Had he managed to keep her mind so totally focused on him all day that she would not be able to think of any other man?

One look at her flushed, slightly guarded expression as the lift doors opened, and he had his answer.

Dio—yes! he exclaimed on a silent hiss of triumph that made his heart vibrate. She was his, those darkened eyes were seeing no other man but him, thinking of no other man—wanting no other man.

And this one wanted her with a craving that was threatening to take him over. She looked sensational. All fire and light and simmering senses, he expanded on a hot sense of masculine pleasure for the way those eyes were looking at him. Eyes that did things to him no other pair of eyes had ever done. The eyes, the hair, the wonderful skin, he listed. The body inside the sensually moulding fabric of her dress that brought vivid pictures to mind of what was going on unseen and did things to his libido that actually shocked him.

And then there was the mouth, he came to finally. It was a mouth to revel in, lose himself in, a mouth he had acquired a hungry taste for and intended to taste over and over again very soon.

In fact his driving impulse was to leap the gap between them and devour her right there and then in the lift on the way back upstairs. But there was also an overriding desire burning in him that simply wanted to enjoy watching her long legs bring her towards him.

His, all his, he claimed possessively. And stepped smoothly forward to gallantly take hold of her hand. *'Buona sera, signorina,'* he greeted softly. *'Non è bello quel che è bello, ma è bello quel che piace…'*

Somewhere in the background the concierge was watching all of this with smiling indulgence. Neither of them seemed to notice. Giancarlo was too engrossed in what was happening to her eyes again, and Natalia was trying to come to terms with the way his voice in its native Italian had affected her. She felt hot and stripped and touched all over!

'What did you say?' she asked, wary in case she was responding this violently to some bland remark about the time!

'Loosely translated?' he asked. 'Beauty is not for the one who is beautiful, but is beauty for the one who it pleases,' he huskily supplied.

She blushed; he smiled and caught her hand. 'You could reply here that I am good to look upon also,' he teasingly suggested.

But she shook her head. 'I'm not even going to try and compete with an Italian male speaking his own language,' she refused, then she smiled too, ruefully. 'You could have been telling me about the weather,' she confessed. 'It would still probably sound just as—sensual,' was the only word she could come up with.

The way his fingers moved around hers told her he'd liked her choice of word. 'Let me assure you, then,' he said, turning them towards the exit. 'No Italian male worth his salt would talk about the weather to a beautiful woman. It would be seen as a crime, believe me...'

Oh, she believed him all right. Didn't they say that the Italian male came out of the womb knowing the art of seduction?

'Where are we going?' She changed the subject. And tried not to notice how his body was brushing lightly against her own or inhale the same clean scent that had been tormenting her all day.

'Somewhere we will not be hovered over by an anxious compatriot,' he said with a dry clip to his tone as he pulled open one of the plate-glass doors and politely stepped back so that she could precede him through it.

He didn't relinquish her hand though. 'He was nice,' she defended the proprietor of yesterday's lunch. 'And the food was nice too.'

'I prefer to give my full attention to the woman I am with,' he replied, walking her across the pavement to where his car sat squatting on double yellow lines.

He opened the door, saw her inside and settled before walking around the long, low bonnet of the car to the driver's side. And through it all, Natalia was acutely aware that the ordinary conversation and the polite way they were treating each other were all just a front to cover up what was really happening here.

Giancarlo settled himself in the seat next to her, and she couldn't resist watching him as he did what was necessary to set them in motion. The suit was black, silk sheened and so obviously stylish that she didn't doubt for a second that it had begun life in the gifted hands of some famous Italian designer. In profile his face was even more attractive than it was full on—which surprised her when she thought about his less than perfect nose.

He turned his head, caught the intent way she was looking at him. 'What?' he asked curiously.

'Why didn't you come up?' The question came out as a low and husky quaver.

His eyes grew dark. 'You know why,' he replied. 'For the same reason I did not allow myself to do this, in the foyer.' Then he leaned across and kissed her.

It was the most beautiful moment she had ever experienced with him, nothing forced, no fighting—with herself or him—but a kiss conveying a promise she knew she would not attempt to resist when the moment finally came to her.

Their tongues touched, just once, then he was drawing away again, his eyes warm on hers as he brought up his hand and gently rubbed his thumb pad over her still parted, slightly pulsing lips, once, twice, three times, then he kissed her again.

'I prefer the taste of you to your lipstick,' he murmured when he drew away a second time.

After that she sat there while he drove, quietly coming to terms with the knowledge that something had just changed between them. She didn't know what it was, she only knew that she liked it.

He parked the car in a side street not far from his apartment, then took her in through a discreet door that led down into a basement club with low lighting and the kind of rhythmic blues music that kept pace with the throb of her pulse. They were shown to a table over in a corner with barely no more light than the candle in its centre where they ate seafood pasta from a plate they shared together, followed by chicken in a creamy sauce made in heaven.

And they talked, softly—carefully at first until they learned to relax with each other a little, their faces shrouded by a darkness lit only by the candlelight but no less alluring, because the mood was like that. Maybe the wine he insisted she have helped, even though he thoughtfully diluted it with sparkling water.

'I'm driving.' He smiled when she showed surprise to see him watering down his wine too...

But they both knew there was much more to it than that. He wanted her fully conscious and aware of everything they did tonight. He wanted no misunderstandings as to why she was going to allow him to make love to her. It was too essential to his plan that she came to him openly and willingly to place it in jeopardy by plying her with alcohol she had already admitted she didn't have a head for.

Then—hell, he thought. It was essential to *him* that she came to him clear-headed and knowingly!

'Let's dance,' he said on impulse, drawing her to her feet before she could argue.

He wanted to feel her close, run his hands over her body. He wanted to hold her into the cradle of his hips while they danced to something slow and easy, feel her moving against him, and just lose himself in the smoky promise in her eyes.

And he wanted to feel the sweet sting of desire build and build until neither of them could stand it any longer, then relieve the tension in hours of mind-blowing passion that would meld her to him so completely that she would never want him to let go of her again.

So he led her across the room to a tiny dance floor in front of the live blues band supplying the music, turned her into his arms and felt the instant tremor of electricity begin passing from her to him then back again.

It told him enough—for now. On a sigh that conveyed his pleasure in having her close, he used a hand on her waist to bring her against him, then began moving them to the swaying pulse of the music, with the feel of her breath on his throat, and his hands stroking the silk-covered framework of the most desirable woman he had ever held in his arms...

What made it all so much more sweetly tortuous was that she loved being this close to him. It was utterly intoxicating—more so than any mere glass of wine when the music seemed to throb to a beat she felt was being generated by the two of them rather than the live band on the podium.

She could feel the need in him talking to the need in her. It was all so compelling, even the way she let her fingers glide from his breastplate to his shoulders was an act compelled by a force she had no control over.

The action stretched her body, arched her back into closer contact with what was beginning to happen to him. Yet he didn't attempt to ease her away, and they swayed like that for what seemed like for ever, until she couldn't stand it any more and lifted her face up as he was lowering his to look at her.

What she saw written there held the air trapped in her lungs. It was desire, pure and simple, hot and tight.

'Let's get out of here,' he murmured, and even the rough-toned command had an arousing effect on her.

'Yes,' she answered. That was all, and she found herself being guided back to their table where he helped her into her jacket then walked her towards the exit, pausing only long enough to pay the bill.

Outside it was dry but cold and she stood shivering while he unlocked the car and helped her inside. He drove them away in silence, and headed for his apartment in silence. The fact that she wasn't voicing a protest told them both everything they needed to know.

The car swooped down into the basement then into its reserved bay. The engine died, he didn't look at her and she was glad because she didn't think she had the courage to look at him.

This kind of situation was so very new to her. She might not be a complete novice, but neither was she versed in the kind of artistry she suspected was required of sophisticated affairs.

And that was exactly what this was going to be, she told herself firmly—a sophisticated affair into which both partners entered knowing the eventual outcome.

A glorious time of loving, then the sad farewell.

She could do it; she knew the rules even if she had never played by them before! And those were the rules she *wanted* to play by. She had no choice. She could not allow herself to ever *hope* there was another choice.

He opened his door and climbed out. She did the same on the other side of the car. Then they walked together—yet oddly apart—into the waiting lift, and rode it all the way up to his apartment without either uttering a single word as to what was about to happen.

Strange, Natalia decided, understanding her own need to stay quiet in case she said something that would show him just how nervous she was feeling about this. But his silence worried her, for surely a man with his experience knew how important it was to keep the mood alive?

Yet he was standing there, frowning down at his feet as if something was bothering him but he didn't know how to voice his concerns.

Had he changed his mind? she wondered suddenly. Had the simple act of getting her to come here with him freely and willingly killed whatever it was that had been driving him to get her to this point?

The lift stopped; the doors slid open. Neither of them moved. Then he looked up—directly into her wary eyes. 'This is no game we are playing here, Natalia,' he said very seriously.

It made her frown because there hadn't been a single moment since she'd met him that she'd thought any of this a *game*.

'I am a very possessive man. If you stay with me now, you will belong to me. I will not tolerate anything less than your full commitment to me for as long as this thing lasts between us.'

He was talking more than a one-night stand here—

which was a relief because she hadn't been sure, not when their feelings had been running so hot and fevered from the beginning.

And 'as long as this thing lasts' suited her perfectly. Better than a one-night stand, but also better than a fear of something deeper developing. For that could never happen—could not be allowed to happen.

'I understand,' she said.

Relief tautened the flesh across his chest muscles. But it did nothing for the silent war he was having with himself. One part of him wanted to just tell her to go, get out of here while she still had the chance to leave relatively unscathed.

But another part of him was yelling at him not to be a bloody fool! Take what was on offer and let the future sort itself out!

He didn't understand himself, didn't understand what had suddenly altered inside him from the moment he'd begun the drive home. He wanted her, for goodness' sake! So, what was the problem?

Inviting her to leave the lift in front of him, he watched her body move with that sensual grace he had been watching for days now with a tightness around his loins.

Get yourself together, man! he told himself angrily. Then, 'Natalia,' he said.

She stopped, then turned. His heart skipped a beat, then began pounding in his chest. She looked frighteningly uncertain all of a sudden. He didn't blame her for feeling that way after the stupid performance he had just put on.

And why had he done that? He no longer knew because he was looking at that sensational figure draped in the same colour as her eyes, and the heat that went whistling through him put his mind right back in focus.

'The white,' he drawled lazily, relaxing his face muscles into a more seductive expression.

'White?' she repeated blankly. Then she caught on and blushed.

'The black was too provocative and the red was too— hot, so it has to be the white.'

Refusing to answer him, she turned away and stalked off towards the sitting room with her cheeks still on fire.

He was on fire again. He was even grinning as he paced after her. Without a word, he diverted into the kitchen, saw the champagne waiting in its bucket of melted ice, and the grin grew wider because he was perfectly happy again.

Edward didn't matter. Her *feelings* for Edward didn't matter—if that was what had been bothering him so much back there...

Natalia removed her jacket and draped it over one of the white leather chairs, then began pacing the sunken area with a tension that showed in her face.

She shouldn't be here with him. His strange attitude before had tugged a bit of sanity to the fore. It was wrong. It was dangerous. He belonged to the enemy camp. What happened if Edward ever found out? What would her being with Giancarlo Cardinale, of all men, do to him?

She should leave, she told herself. Now, while she had the chance to do it without having to explain herself. He'd disappeared, she didn't know where. She could just pick up her things and run.

Then what? asked the voice of reason. What happens tomorrow—do you hide away in your little house so he can't get you, and lose your job in the interim? How would you explain *that* away to Edward on his return without making Giancarlo look like the bad guy in all of this, when in actual fact it's you who is being bad here?

And—do you want him or don't you want him? she then asked herself impatiently. For those are the only two questions which should really count. After all, you can't go on for ever running your life to suit Edward's feelings. Especially when Edward was not willing to run his life according to yours!

So—do you want Giancarlo Cardinale, or don't you want him?

He appeared in the opening. He had done it again, was the first disturbing thing she thought. His jacket had gone, so had his tie, and the top two buttons on his shirt had been tugged undone. The wretched man had a habit of half undressing in her company that always managed to shatter her composure.

Or what bit of composure she ever possessed around him, she wryly expanded, noticing that he was also carrying the bottle of champagne and two fluted glasses which acted as yet another trigger, flipping her mind like a coin from one face to another.

Yes, I want this man, the new face said. Yes, I *need* this man! I can do this. I can love him and leave him when the time comes! I can—I *can*!

CHAPTER SEVEN

'HOLD that thought, whatever it is,' Giancarlo murmured lazily as he came down the steps to join Natalia.

He was smiling and relaxed, but the closer he came, the more tense she became, because, now it came right down to it, she didn't think she could carry this through with the *savoir-faire* he was probably expecting.

Maybe he sensed it, because there was a curious expression in his eyes as he came to stand beside her, and, although his attention was mainly involved in putting the two glasses down on the marble table so he could begin pouring champagne, he kept on sending her the odd glance, as if he couldn't quite make his mind up what it was that made her tick inside.

She wished she knew herself but sadly she didn't, or she would know how she should be behaving. Was she supposed to indulge in some light conversation to bridge the gap between this moment and the one where they moved on to the bedroom? Or should she be making certain moves on him to encourage along that second stage?

It didn't really matter because neither suggestion was possible for her right now. She felt too out of her depth, too tongue-tied by too little experience and especially with a man like him.

Picking up the two frothing glasses, he turned to hand one of them to her. She took it, eyes lowered now because that seemed the easiest way to get through these next few telling minutes.

'Sip,' he commanded.

Obediently, she sipped while he watched with a new kind of stillness that brought the colour streaking into her cheeks. The champagne tingled on her tongue, then did the same all the way to her stomach.

'Again,' he said and received mute obedience a second time.

He waited until she had made her second swallow, then his hand came to gently lift her chin—and he was no longer smiling. 'Last chance, *cara*,' he murmured quietly. 'I must be sure that this is what you want.'

Was it? she asked herself. Was jumping in the deep end when she barely knew how to swim what she really wanted to do? No, not really. 'Yes,' she whispered. 'This is what I want.'

'Then why the sudden look of anxiety?' he prompted.

'You told me to hold the thought,' she wryly pointed out.

'That belonged to a different thought,' he returned. 'I am now discussing the one that denies me your eyes.'

Lifting her lashes, she looked directly into his dark and sombre eyes and smiled a wry smile at his even needing to ask that question. 'I've known you for less than a week, and you wonder why I am anxious about this?'

'Would a few more days make any difference?' He put the question to her with genuine interest, she was sure, but it was mocking all the same, because he knew just as she knew that *this* had been written on the wall from the first second of their first glance at each other.

'No,' she ruefully replied.

'Then keep those beautiful eyes on me,' he softly commanded. 'I like to make love with *all* the senses, and your eyes make love to me more than any other pair of eyes I've known.'

'Known many?' she asked in a lightly mocking attempt to sound clever and witty and sophisticated.

His smile reappeared, teasing and warm. 'No, this is my first time,' he said.

And she laughed. It was such an outrageous thing to say—and she felt some of her awkwardness seep away. I love you, she wanted to say, but those words were banned to her every which way she looked at them, so she did the next best thing and reached up on tiptoe to brush her mouth against his.

'A lady has a right to be unsure of herself at moments like this,' she murmured as she drew away again.

'So does a man,' he countered. 'Now—take a sip of your champagne again and hold it in your mouth.'

Intrigued by the instruction, she did as he bade, her eyes still fixed on his as he did the same thing with his champagne. Champagne bubbles began to fizz on her tongue and the roof of her mouth, and the air between them stirred as a new level of awareness took precedence.

Lost in the warmth of his eyes and the awakening of her own desires, she therefore didn't see what was coming until it was too late. With a smooth, slick move he slid a hand around her waist—then swooped on her mouth with no warning whatsoever.

The result was an explosion on the senses when his champagne-moistened tongue made contact with hers. It was the most erotic thing she had ever experienced. In a single moment she seemed to shoot from gentle awareness into full arousal with no gap in between. Her hand shot up, instinctively searching for support as pure sensation went racing through her on the flow of champagne bubbles that had entered her blood.

Her hand found a tightly muscled shoulder, and gripped. Breathing had gone haywire, mouth hot on mouth. Nervous barriers fell, uncertainties disappeared. The kiss deepened and became something else entirely—seduction at its most intense.

She heard the light tap of glass on stone but didn't recognise the sound for what it was until she felt her own glass being taken from her and placed on the marble table. Freedom to use both hands had her moving closer to him with her fingers sliding up the front of his shirt. She felt the warmth of living flesh, the hardness of well-honed muscle, and the slight prickle of chest hair, all of which sent a pleasurable little sigh whispering from her mouth into his mouth.

Why the champagne kiss should have caused this to happen, she didn't understand. All she knew was that it had happened—and that he'd known it was going to happen, which automatically said he had done this before.

'You're too good at this,' she murmured unsteadily when he eventually let their mouths separate.

'I get even better,' was his conceited reply. Then, with only that mocking remark to accompany them, he caught her hand and began leading her up the steps towards the waiting bedroom. As they passed by the wall switch he paused to dim the sitting-room lights. In the bedroom he did the same, shrouding them in a more intimate atmosphere, then taking her back into his arms.

She went without a murmur, her mouth welcoming him as if they were already lovers. The bed was several yards away, but neither seemed in any rush to get there, so it was reached in easy stages, the first stage being the caressing way he began to remove her dress. His hands skimmed her body, lighting fires as they went, then fed the flames on their way back up again. Long fingers slid beneath the silken weight of her hair swinging gently away from her back because of the passionate tilt of her head.

He found her nape, used his fingers to lightly measure its slenderness, then was moving again, finding the zip to her dress and drawing it downwards, while she merely clung to him, needing his strength when her limbs began to shimmer with a sultry kind of heat.

Then he was diverting her attention again by peeling her dress down her arms and her body until she stood in front of him in nothing but what she was wearing beneath. So now he knew his provocative guess earlier had been absolutely right, she realised as she watched his dark gaze skim over her white silk underwear with a look of triumph he did nothing to disguise.

'Homework?' he taunted softly, and she began blushing like crazy.

He just laughed huskily, and proceeded to make her feel utterly wanton standing there with her dress pooled around her feet as he explored every silk-smooth inch of her while retaining both his clothes and his dignity.

Not for long though, not for long. For it didn't take many seconds for her fingers to release the rest of the buttons on his shirt. He lost her mouth as the two pieces of fine white linen parted and a need to look at him overrode her need to feel his mouth seducing hers...

The last thing he expected her to do was to stroke him as he had been stroking her. The feel of her fingers against his flesh had his chest expanding on a fierce intake of air. The fingers paused, her eyes flickered upward to catch the intense pleasure reflected in his, then, with a sensuality that knocked him sideways, she moistened her softly pulsing mouth with the tip of her tongue, then lowered her gaze again and leaned forward to begin stringing clinging kisses from one tight male nipple to the other.

'*Dio, cara,*' he breathed in shaken reaction. And closed

his eyes as her mouth, her tongue and her caressing fingers locked him into his own world of burgeoning pleasure...

She'd been wanting to touch him like this for so long now it felt like for ever, Natalia was thinking hazily. And he was so wonderful to touch. She could feel his response in each ripple of flesh she so carefully explored. His breathing was tight, his heart thumping against his solid ribcage, and her fingertips felt enlivened by the rasping sensation of crisp body hair and satin tight flesh.

She wanted more. And more came with her lips joining in the banquet. At the first moist touch of her tongue on his skin he opened his eyes again, looked deeply into hers, then muttered something in his own language as she shook his hands free of the shirt so he could reach for her...

Mouths joined again, hotly, hungrily, her arms looped around his neck. Finding her slender hips, he eased her up against him, then leaned back against the wall behind to simply sink himself into the rousing heat permeating his body as she began to move against him in an erotic rhythm no man with blood in his veins could resist.

She was a born sensualist, and he couldn't believe his luck in finding someone like her. Inhibition seemed like a foreign word to her. She wanted him and was doing absolutely nothing to disguise that want. Did Edward know her like this?

No! his mind blasted angrily back at him. You fool, don't bring him in here!

'What—what's wrong?' Feeling the violent change in him sent her jerking back from him in confused reaction.

'*Niente*,' he rasped, didn't even know he had spoken in Italian, but saw her beautiful eyes darken into wariness and, on a grim act of black fury aimed entirely at himself for ruining the moment, he bent to scoop her up into his arms. 'I want you, that is what is wrong,' he growled. 'Have you any idea what you are doing to me?'

'Yes,' she said, and it shut down his anger like a plug being pulled on something destructive.

Because there it was—the look in her eyes he had first seen long days ago and had been searching for ever since. It was warm, it was soft, it was steamy and sultry and reminded him of the goal he had set himself to learn what happened to her eyes when he was deep inside her and she was toppling over the edge…

'Yes…' he agreed on a sensual hiss that made her tremble because she knew he was turning the answer right back on herself.

For he knew what he was doing to her, and as she gazed up into his velvet dark eyes, with their fires of desire burning inside, she knew she was about to be drawn into the flame.

He was taking over. He had been playing it passively for a while but now he became the man she'd expected, dark and demanding, holding her eyes by sheer strength of will as he reached for the hand she still had linked around his neck, and, being very deliberate about it, he drew the hand down between their two bodies and placed it on the clasp to his trousers.

It was a command to finish undressing him, and heat prickled along her skin. If he saw her uncertainty he wasn't letting her keep it. 'Do it,' he urged her and lifted his own hands to her shoulders, where long fingers hooked beneath narrow bra straps and with an agonising slowness he began drawing them down the curve of her arms.

It was a mutual undressing which heightened the tension to its nth degree. Tiny lace cups folded away from two high, firm, perfect breasts that clearly didn't need the support anyway. She released a sharp gasp when he first touched her there, running feather-like caresses over newly exposed flesh that responded by swelling and tightening with pleasure...

'Do it,' he repeated, keeping her mind focused on her own task, even if she didn't want it to be. 'Undress me,' he urged. 'Touch me. I want to feel what you feel...'

He could see what she was feeling because her head had tipped back and her mouth had parted and she was barely functioning on a conscious level. So when her fingers began to move against his waist, it felt like a small victory to be able to command her even while she was lost like this.

But it was a brief victory, he realised, feeling the muscles around his waist contract forcefully when her nails inadvertently rasped against his flesh. Sensation went raking through him, hot enough and tight enough to clench muscles all over him. *Dio*, he thought, and she hasn't even touched me where it matters yet...

It was all so erotic. While her fingers fumbled with the catch on his trousers, he was running tormenting forays across her acutely taut nipples with his fingertips. And her breathing was hectic; she couldn't think beyond the crazy notion that if this was making love the Sicilian way, then how did any woman survive it?

You don't know if you will yet, a little voice inside her head dryly taunted. This is only the beginning; wait until he decides to move to the really heavy stuff.

Stuff like lowering his dark head to kiss her hotly as she began to draw his zip down and felt the backs of her fingers make contact with a hard male erection covered by only the thin fabric of his undershorts. The experience made the centre of her sex begin to pulse to a beat of its own making, or maybe it was his beat, she was no longer sure of anything worth a damn. The whole affair was beginning to grow very steamy, his mouth hot and demanding on her mouth, his fingers tormenting her breasts and his manhood playing havoc with any preconceptions she might have had about his prowess in that area of his physical make-up.

She failed the major test though, because for the life of her she couldn't get herself to peel down those shorts. Or maybe he was the one that relented, she thought dazedly when, on a sudden decision that seemed to come from nowhere, he unclipped her bra, discarded it to the floor, then lifted her into his arms and carried her to the bed. Carefully lowering her onto it, he stood back to begin removing the rest of his clothes himself while she curled onto her side and lay there watching the deliberate stripshow taking place.

His shoes left his feet, the trousers were stripped away along with undershorts and socks in a few swift economical moves that quite simply took her breath away. But not as the sight of his body did, its leanness and its strength and the arrogance with which he displayed it all culminating in turning the excitement she was experiencing up another notch...

He saw it happen, saw the flame light her eyes and felt suddenly charged with sheer masculine pride in what she was seeing. But then, the feeling was mutual. She was lying here on his bed at last, and as he came down beside her his heart was thundering because she was the one who was reaching for him.

Everything merged into one long glorious coming-together after that. Her hands moved on his body, and his lips sought her breasts and the delicate round of her navel so exquisitely sensitive to the lap of his tongue. And she was anxiously kneading his shoulders when he began to slide the last flimsy scrap of silk down her hips.

'Kiss me,' she groaned.

It was such a desperate little command that he stretched up to take her mouth with a hungry passion that she simply sank herself into while he continued caressing each new section of flesh he was exposing. When his finger finally made contact with the soft mound of curls at the apex of her sex, he felt the fine, tight shudder of pleasure ripple through her, and was overawed by how good it made him feel.

And it wasn't all one-sided because her hands were moving over his body, tracing restlessly the length of his back, the lean tightness of his buttocks, his hair-roughened thighs, and he found himself willing her to put him out of his agony and take him in hand. It became a kind of battle, while their mouths clung and their bodies writhed, and their fingers hovered just beyond the goal both of them desperately craved.

Who surrendered the battle first it was difficult to say; maybe it was a joint surrender, because as he felt the tip of his finger slide that extra inch into sheer, sweet luxury her fingers closed around him with a delicate tenderness that rocked him to the core.

Her few scraps of clothing were an irritant now. With a rough sound of impatience he pushed himself up and completely rid her of her white panties. The stockings came next, sliding off silken legs which aided him by lifting and flexing in a way that almost sent him over the edge. He caught one long, slender calf in his hand and bowed his mouth to it, hungrily, sucking and biting his way upwards—until she stopped him by the simple act of pulling him by his hair back down beside her.

And in that one urgent movement, everything changed yet again. They looked deep into each other's eyes and it acted like a gentle calming, everything slowed to a long, lazy touch, feel, teasing medley. She kissed his eyelids, his cheeks, his arrogant nose, and smiled softly when he returned the honour.

'Beautiful,' he whispered, stroking his fingers through the silken spread of her hair. 'You take my breath away.'

'So do you,' she softly confided.

He laughed, softly. Then suddenly he wasn't laughing, he was kissing her hot and deep, and the whole thing became charged again, but with serious intent this time. Caresses became bold, more intimate, until they were touching each other with an urgency that could only be assuaged one way.

He came over her, she welcomed him, he settled his lean hips between her clinging thighs, and as he prepared to join them she seemed to know that he wanted her to open her eyes, and to keep on looking at him as that joining became real with the single deep thrust of his hips.

His eyes were black, glittering down at her, his features taut with desire. He began to move, slowly, deeply, watched the telling darkening of her own eyes as he built the pulsing pleasure at his own rich pace. Her legs had locked themselves around his body, her slender arms clinging to his back. And as the urgency grew in both of them still their eyes did not break contact; it was part of the loving, a necessary part, another point of total communication where they spoke to each other with every sense but without words.

Her eyes held no blue any more, only smoky swirls of grey and black, and even the grey was losing ground the closer she came to that final leap. And her mouth was open, the tense little gasps of pleasure growing thicker, more arousing when he'd thought he could never be more aroused.

But Natalia Deyton could make him feel things he had never felt before. She was warm and she was generous, and she held nothing in reserve. When his breathing grew tense and the rhythm became stronger, she simply came with him—all the way—stroke for stroke, shudder for exquisite shudder. Her hands shot up, grasped his face, her eyes spiralling out that final hint of grey as her body quickened. Then, 'Giancarlo,' she breathed.

That was all. Just his name in that soul-stripping way, then she leapt—*Dio,* she leapt, on a convulsion of muscle that completely shattered him—and shot him into the same wild place still echoing with his name as if she was pulling him with her into the kind of climax that took him way beyond anything he had ever experienced.

The woman was a witch. *His* witch, was the final fiercely possessive thought he had before he lost himself in the hot, dark bounty of their shared release...

Lying there beneath him with his face now pressed into the side of her throat and her body still pulsing gently around his possession, Natalia closed her eyes and just let herself float on a lazy sea of satiation. His weight was heavy on her but she didn't mind—she felt wonderfully invaded by his heat and his scent and an awareness that both of them were lying stretched out without a single bone between them that hadn't gone weak.

A smile touched her mouth, though she tried to stop it.

'Shh,' he breathed against her throat as if he was afraid she was about to speak and spoil the moment.

But that was her very last intention; she felt too good,

too at peace, too at one with this lover of hers who had given as much as he had taken. It was a beautiful knowledge. And just as beautiful to know from that lazy 'shh' that he was feeling the same way about it.

Eventually they moved, though, eventually with seemingly perfect sensory co-ordination he withdrew from her just as she reached the point where she needed to stretch her limbs to encourage them to recover some substance. With a lazy kiss pressed to her throat, he slid himself sideways, bent a knee across her thighs as if to make sure she didn't decide to stray, then came up on one elbow to look down on her gravely while gentle fingers carefully combed stray locks of her hair away from her face and throat and shoulders.

It was an act of tenderness she had not expected, and her throat tightened slightly on a tug of emotion as she lay there.

'You said my name,' he murmured suddenly.

Her long lashes flickered on a blink of surprise. 'I did?' she responded, having no memory of saying anything, she had been so lost to her senses.

He smiled an oddly satisfied smile. '*Sí,*' he confirmed. 'You called for me, Giancarlo, at your moment of ecstasy. It—pleased me.'

She could see that it did. But the remark still confused her. 'Who else did you expect me to call for?' she enquired with a little frown and teasing glint of amusement.

His response threw her. Instead of coming up with some answering tease to keep the same soft, intimate mood flowing, his face hardened and he growled something harsh in his own language, then swooped on her mouth with the kind of kiss that staked a claim she didn't think was necessary since he already possessed her.

'Mine,' he reiterated fiercely when he drew away again.

'You are *my* woman now, you understand me? You think only of me, you say only my name, and you dream only of me, *comprende*?'

'Oh, very possessive,' she mocked, not sure whether to be pleased by the burst of jealous possessiveness or angry at him for feeling he needed to stake his claim!

'*Sí*,' he confirmed, no shame, no apology. 'I am Sicilian,' he added with a lift of his chin that seemed to be conveying something portentous in that announcement. 'I guard what belongs to me.'

'And you think I now belong to you, is that it?'

'*Sí*.'

'And who do you belong to?'

'You, of course.' He frowned as if he didn't see the necessity for the question.

Which was Natalia's point, because neither did she see the necessity for this conversation at all! Unless this was his roundabout way of getting down to laying out the ground rules, she then thought on a sudden tight sting of understanding. 'How long for?' she asked huskily.

His frown darkened. 'For as long as it lasts, I suppose,' he answered. 'Who can say?' he added with what she supposed was a very Sicilian noncommittal shrug to go with his question.

But the shrug came too late, because Natalia was already ahead of him, ahead and walking along the self-same line. 'S-six weeks,' she heard herself say in a breathless tense little whisper, needing now to lay out the terms of this affair before he did it for her. 'When Edward comes back, you go home, and this will be over…'

Edward—? She dared to bring Edward, here, into *his* bed after what they had just shared? She dared to speak

Edward's name? Lay her rules about the length of their affair before him—in words that revolved around Edward?

Like a man who had just been attacked by a snake, he flinched right back from her, his eyes turning black as the vision in front of him changed from beauty personified in his eyes into Medusa—turning him into a pillar of stone where he lay.

Nothing that had ever happened to him before had made him feel as bad as he did right now. For here they were, having only just recovered from one of the most passionate interludes life could offer—and she was bartering terms like a whore in the market place. But with those terms revolving around *Edward*?

Anger suddenly roared, pumping the life right back into his frozen limbs to help throw his body round until he was looming threateningly over her. Unsure at this point if he was going to strangle her or kiss her darling Edward right out of existence, he reached for her shoulders.

She stiffened in alarm. 'What did I do? What did I say?' she begged in complete bewilderment as to why he was suddenly so angry. In her view, he supposed, she had just handed him the perfect excuse for dumping her and he should be damn well singing in elation!

But he wasn't singing, he was seething, because she had just confirmed every low, cheap, nasty thing he had ever been told about her. Brazen wasn't in it. 'You dare to set boundaries of time around me,' he bit out thickly, 'as if I am a stud bull in a field lingering with the female currently in line to be serviced—and then wonder why I am angry?'

She went quite white, and so she should do, he acknowledged as he watched remorse darken her beautiful eyes. 'I'm sorry,' she breathed. 'I didn't mean... I just thought you—'

'Well, don't think,' he growled. 'Not in my bed—ever!'

Then, because he couldn't stop himself, he buried his mouth in hers and wished to God he knew where this was going to take him, because something nasty was warning him that he was in too deep.

Natalia Deyton was beginning to get to him in ways he just hadn't expected...

CHAPTER EIGHT

NATALIA had offended Giancarlo and she hadn't meant to do that. In fact the last thing she ever wanted to do was spoil what had been the most beautiful experience of her life.

So when he kissed her she kissed him back hungrily. He was angry, so the kiss was rough, but the anger also ignited other emotions, which soon began to take them over.

For a second experience so soon after the first, it really should have been disappointing. But it seemed as if nothing this man could do would ever disappoint her. He drove deep and she welcomed his potency. He kissed hard and long and she fed it all back to him. They touched and tasted and lost touch with everything but themselves to an extent that it didn't even register that they were doing all of this without a single thought to protection.

That singularly terrifying occurrence happened when she was standing in his bathroom, carefully drying tender places after their shower in which their third wild coming together had taken them tumbling over the edge of sanity.

'Oh, no,' she whispered, going so still that it was no wonder he spun sharply to face her.

He was standing by the bathroom mirror with a towel looped casually around his lean waist while he used an electric razor, but the sound stopped abruptly when he saw her expression. 'What?' he demanded. 'What have you done?' His eyes dipped down to where her hand was tensely crushing the towel, then blackened in concern as they flicked back to her face again. 'Did I hurt you, *cara*?' he questioned jerkily.

She shook her head, her face so white it could have been porcelain. 'Y-you didn't use anything,' she managed to utter.

He froze, frowning, then slowly put down the razor to begin walking towards her. 'This is a joke, right,' he murmured.

But he had to know that it wasn't. She still hadn't moved and didn't think she dared to. Her legs felt strange, as if they were just about ready to give out on her, and her heart was labouring to find a steady rhythm.

'No,' she breathed, and began to shiver as shock thoroughly took her over.

Several Italian curses hit her eardrums, but he made a grab for a fresh towel and quickly wrapped it around her before grimly picking her up and carrying her back into the bedroom.

He sat her down on the bed, then swung round to sit down heavily beside her. He was in shock too, she recognised. Or maybe she should describe it as horror. 'How could we have been so blind stupid?' she choked.

'You are on the pill,' he bit out tautly. '*All* women take the pill!'

'Well, not this one!' she shot back, fiercely and furiously. 'God—' she jumped up. 'I should have known this was going to turn nasty on me! You're the wrong man for me! We shouldn't even have been doing this—!'

'I am *not* the wrong man for you!' he barked, instantly offended by the suggestion.

But he didn't understand and she couldn't explain it to him, so she began pacing the floor with the towel huddled round her, trying to come to terms with the dreadful fact that she might well already be pregnant with Edward's wife's brother's child!

'Oh.' The whimper was one of dismay and helplessness. 'Why didn't you think to ask?' she suddenly launched at him.

He was white behind the olive tint of his skin and his eyes were angry. 'Why did you not think to say?' he tossed back with biting derision.

'Because I did believe that most intelligent men thought safe sex a natural precaution!' she spat back, not knowing why she was attacking him like this when she knew she was as much to blame.

He jerked to his feet, and she instantly felt wretched because his cheekbones were no longer pale but dark with embarrassment. There seemed nothing left to say. As he walked off towards the bathroom again, she began gathering her scattered clothes together in a dazed kind of way that said she didn't know what she was doing.

By the time he came back a few minutes later he seemed to have himself back in control while she was just standing there staring blindly down at the few scraps of white silk she held in her hands, as if she didn't know how they'd got there.

'I'm sorry,' she whispered when she felt him in front of her. 'This is my fault. I should have thought...'

'Ditto,' Giancarlo replied and wondered why he wasn't feeling anything more than a rueful acceptance for his tragic lot.

Because she looked so adoringly pathetic? Because she was right and he should have been more careful—for his own health's sake if nothing else?

Or was it because her shrill claim that he was the wrong man for her had struck at the very heart of his ego and made it more important to him to prove her wrong about that than to stand about in a horrified stupor, wondering how the hell he was going to extricate himself from this potential disaster?

'What is the timing like?' he asked, gently extracting the bits of silk from her fingers while she let him because his question had made her pause and take stock of the situation.

'Good,' she murmured eventually. 'Good as in low risk,' she then extended, which made him grimace because *good* could only mean that—in this case anyway.

'Right,' he acknowledged. 'Then we have a wait-and-see situation on our hands,' and he smoothly whipped the towel away from her shoulders.

'What are you doing?' she cried, making an attempt to grab it back again.

Too late, for he was already tossing it to one side along with her clothes. 'Taking you back to bed,' he said so casually that it even surprised him how calmly he was behaving. He grasped one of her hands. 'It is three o'clock in the morning and we both need some sleep.'

'Sleep?' she repeated.

He turned a grin on her that had her eyes widening. 'Sleep,' he repeated. 'You've ravished me enough for one night.'

'But—' she was floundering and he liked it '—I should be going home and—'

It was the simplest thing in the world to swing her down on the bed then follow her. 'Home is here now,' he smoothly decreed. 'For the next few weeks anyway until we know one way or another.'

'What are you talking about?' she protested. 'I don't need to live here with you just because we have both behaved recklessly!'

'Yes, you do,' he insisted, stripping the towel from his hips and tossing it aside before he reached for the sheet to cover them. 'I am Sicilian. I take care of my own. And until you prove otherwise, you now belong to me—so don't even think about taking a morning-after pill. And also,' he added with husky promise, 'I want you here. Can you tell me honestly that you do not want to be here too?'

She couldn't. He knew it. She might claim he was the wrong man for her, but when it came down to it he was the one she wanted.

The only thing she said was, 'I had no intention of taking a morning-after pill. I don't agree with them.'

Reaching across her to put out the light, he kissed her delicious mouth as he settled down beside her, then pulled her into his arms.

'Tomorrow we move your things in,' he said softly into the darkness.

She didn't say another word.

He had her. She didn't know it yet, but he had Natalia Deyton just where he wanted her and, despite the stupid risks it had taken to get her here, he had never felt so good about anything...

To her own surprise, Natalia slept heavily, waking up to find herself alone in the bed as a weak sun began seeping in through the voile-draped windows. She lay there for a while, listening to the warm quietness surrounding her, reluctant to let herself begin thinking of the calamitous events of the night before.

Though not all of them had been calamitous, she admitted, feeling an accompanying warmth filter into those places in her body that had known only pleasure last night. In fact some of those moments had been so intense that it was impossible not to soften and allow them to replay themselves for a little while.

But only a little while, she accepted when a sound from somewhere beyond the bedroom alerted her to the fact that she was not alone here. Giancarlo must be around somewhere, waiting for her to put in an appearance.

A sigh whispered from her, dragging her out of her relaxed stupor and forcing her to get out of bed where she padded off to use the bathroom before going in search of her suit bag, so she could put back on the clothes she had arrived here in yesterday.

They seemed more appropriate somehow, now that daylight was back and with it reality. The slinky blue dress and the sexy underwear belonged to another time and most definitely another person than the one she was seeing in the mirror this morning.

And just who was she seeing? she asked herself as she stood, carefully pleating her hair with the knowledge that she was using the severe style as a piece of armour.

A very foolish woman, she informed herself, who had made a huge mistake that was now clawing at her conscience and grating at worries she should never have put aside in the first place.

Namely—Edward versus Giancarlo Cardinale. Even the name made her feel chill now.

Not the man, though, she admitted as she watched her eyes darken simply by conjuring up his image. The man in his full and physical sense had never been the problem for her. It was his name and his relationship to Edward that caused this impossible conflict she could see no way round whichever way she tried to look at it.

Not that it really mattered now, she supposed, turning to pull on her clothes and make herself presentable. The whole thing had turned sour from the moment she'd realised that neither had thought about contraception.

Oh, he had been good and kind and said all the right things a woman he had just made love to would expect from a real man. But there was no way in the cold light of day that she was going to hold him to any of them. She could only hope that in the cold light of the same day he, too, had thought better about bringing his new lover here to live with him when surely the quick exit and a lot of inner praying was the best way to be dealing with this?

With those very wise thoughts in mind, she slipped her feet into low black court shoes and made herself go in search of him. She found him lounging at the kitchen table with the *Financial Times* spread open in front of him and a pot of coffee at his elbow.

He looked different this morning, she noted as she paused in the doorway. His clothes were different. Casual chinos and a long-sleeved polo shirt in a dark red colour that for some crazy reason reminded her of the red underwear he had provided yesterday and almost had her blushing.

Luckily the blush didn't arrive when, sensing her standing there, he looked up, and it only took him a few moments to run his eyes over her prim hairstyle and her equally prim slate-grey suit to know exactly what mood she was in this morning.

'Standing in guarded territory, I see,' he drawled, sitting back in his chair to view her more thoroughly. 'Tell me,' he appealed, 'that this does not declare an end to a beautiful friendship.'

'Don't be so trite,' she snapped, walking forwards and going to the fridge to get herself a carton of juice she had stashed in there yesterday, then opening cupboards until she found the glasses.

'Then don't try pulling any neat tricks on me, *cara*,' he replied with a sudden grimness. 'You belong to me now. We reached that agreement at some point in the early hours of this morning when we both knew what fools we had been.'

So, he was angry. She'd suspected as much by now—though she had expected the opposite response to it. 'Do you have any appointments today, or are you working from here?'

As a change of subject, she was rather pleased with the smooth way she did it—considering the butterflies going mad in her stomach. She even managed to pour the juice into the glass without spilling any of it onto the worktop.

'We are taking a day off,' he announced. 'So we can move your things in here.'

She put the juice carton down, and picked up the glass, aware that his angry eyes were still following every single thing she did as if he expected her to make a sudden run for it, and was not going to be caught napping when she did. 'I am not moving in here with you,' she told him quietly.

'After that we will do something really domestic, like supermarket shopping for provisions,' he went on as if she hadn't spoken.

'You can do that just as easily over the Internet these days,' she told him.

'Then there are a few things this place needs to make it more—homely,' he persisted unrelentingly. 'Like a television set and a decent music centre, and some cushions or something to make that soulless sitting room more inviting to relax in. And if you tell me that those can be ordered over the Internet,' he added with a silken snap, 'then I will probably have to stand up and come over there, and show you a few things that most certainly cannot!'

'Why are you so angry, for goodness' sake?' she turned to throw at him bewilderedly. 'You should be pleased I'm not keeping you to what you said last night...'

Giancarlo just glowered at her and said nothing, because how could he tell her that dear Edward had already been on his mobile asking where the hell his Natalia was? He was supposed to be patching up his marriage—the love-struck adulterer! Not worrying about his mistress because she wasn't exactly where he expected her to be!

So he'd lied to Edward and enjoyed doing it. He told him he'd sent her off on a fact-finding mission to some bloody place he couldn't even recall now. But it had served a dual purpose of reassuring Edward that not only was *his* Natalia safe, but she was also *safely* out of Giancarlo's influence!

The two-timing swine had actually said as much. And it stuck in his own throat that he couldn't just say— 'Go to hell, Edward. She is with me and staying with me! So keep your lecherous emotions in check from now on!'

But he couldn't say it, because he knew Edward. Let Edward know that he was aware of his little bit on the side and the stupid man would have a fit of panic and feel the need to confess all to Alegra just in case Giancarlo decided to do it before him! Edward knew how close brother and sister were and that any Sicilian male worth his salt would not remain silent in the face of such dishonour to one of his family!

But Giancarlo also knew that Alegra could not cope with the truth about her beloved Edward. She adored him—had adored him from the day he'd walked into her life at the tender age of eighteen, and no other man had ever come close to reaching her since! Unless you included Marco, he added with an ache that set his anger blazing.

For it was bad enough that she'd had to lose her son. To place in front of her the truth that she could be in danger of losing her husband would finish her. No doubt about it.

And to really top it all off nicely, he raged on within his own throbbing silence, he now knew, without a single doubt in his head, that if Edward had kept his lecherous hands to himself then he, Giancarlo, could have met Natalia Deyton and been free to explore the possibilities of their attraction with openness and honesty instead of having deceit and lies poisoning everything!

And the bottom line to that? he asked himself as his brain threatened to stall completely in response to his heated fury. He would not have rushed her into bed. And he would not have done it without even the most basic of sexual precautions!

So now he had a woman standing here who belonged to him in more ways than any woman had ever belonged to him, while she—

Hell! He stood up violently. She believed half of her still belonged to Edward! She even lived in Edward's house, damn it! Wore clothes bought with Edward's money!

Well, not for much longer, he vowed, his eyes hardening with a determination he could see was alarming her. But he had her. He had Natalia Deyton just where he wanted her. All he needed to do now was convince her of that!

'You could be carrying my child,' he reminded her thinly.

'There is just as much of a chance that I'm not!' she instantly replied.

'One chance in a thousand is good enough for me,' he returned. 'I am Sicilian,' he reiterated, knowing he was using his nationality like a damned hammer to beat her into submission. 'To a Sicilian, family is everything. While

the small chance exists that you could be carrying my
child, it makes you the mother of *my* Sicilian child! So
stop arguing,' he said with the flick of a hand gauged to
draw her anger. 'Accept your fate—for the near future anyway.'

'Why, you arrogant *bully*!' She gasped in wide-eyed disbelief that she was actually hearing any of this.

She was right and he was.

'I don't need to stand here and take this!'

Try moving, his eyes challenged. 'Drink your juice,' he
prodded, saw the anger flare, saw the eyes change to warning bright diamonds, and was bracing himself for action
even before the glass went sailing past his shoulder…

She couldn't believe she had just done that! Natalia stood
staring in horrified amazement as the glass of juice went
flying past his shoulder and smashed against the opposite
set of wall units.

Trying to blink away the sense of shock, she ended up
focusing on Giancarlo—then immediately wished she
hadn't when she saw the expression his face was now
wearing.

Retaliation was coming, she saw with a telling little
quiver that had nothing to do with alarm. 'You asked for
that,' she murmured unsteadily, feeding water onto burning
oil when all he did was start striding towards her. 'Have
you any idea how arrogant you sound? How self—' he
reached her; in height and breadth and dangerous attitude
he really intimidated enough to make her swallow ner-
vously before she could carry on '—s-self-opinionated and
just downright pompous?'

'Pompous,' he repeated, softly, smoothly, so succinctly
she felt her fingernails digging into the underside of the
unit top.

She nodded, swallowed again when his hand came up to rest on her shoulder, and stubbornly pretended that it wasn't there. 'Nobody th-these days goes around s-spouting such old-fashioned r-rubbish!'

'Rubbish,' he repeated that word also. And the hand moved from her shoulder to her nape. Natalia straightened her spine ever so warily. 'You think it is both rubbish and pompous to show a respect for family values?'

Values like his, she did, when she knew for an absolute fact that if he ever discovered her little secret he would soon forget those same family values. For there was no way that he would want to make *her* a part of his *Sicilian family* with or without his child inside her!

A point that didn't do her any favours at all because just thinking about it brought the sting of tears to the back of her eyes. 'You might pay my wages, Giancarlo—that does not give you the right to run my life!'

'No?' he said, and the hand at her nape tightened perceptibly, sending warning signals tingling down her spine. 'What about sex, then? Will the great sex be a big enough incentive to make you live with me?'

Live? That's a joke! she scoffed silently. He just wanted a convenient live-*in* sexual convenience! 'What, more studding for the prize bull?' she taunted. 'I thought that scenario offended your ego.'

'Well, let's just see, shall we?' he drawled lazily. And using his hand as a brace to lift her mouth up to his, his own swooped down and took…

Took without mercy, took by storm—took her shooting off to a place she didn't want to go to then never wanted to come back from.

Took her right there in the ultra-modern kitchen, with

her clothes gaping and her skirt ruched up around her waist and the rest removed by very quick fingers.

And he took her with his mouth, nothing else. He took her lips and her tongue and made him their master. He took her breasts and teased and sucked until she cried out in exquisite agony, and he took her down a dark, sensuous road she had never ever dared to visit before when he bent to her thighs and took the ultimate intimacy of all.

Which was when he took her will to fight him, right there in the kitchen with her fingers laced into his hair and her mind lost in a swirling sea of sensation.

'Giancarlo,' she begged. 'I'll do anything you say, but, no more—please. I'll stay—I'll stay, but please make love to me properly...'

And that was the point where she took something from him. It was in his eyes when he rose, then picked her up to carry her to the bedroom. She saw pain and remorse for the tactic he'd used to gain her surrender. Then she saw him begin a terrible battle with himself that she feared he was actually going to win.

But he didn't. And, strangely, their lovemaking then was the sweetest, gentlest, most deeply felt experience they had shared to date.

Later, he dropped her off at her house with the promise to be back in an hour to collect her. 'You won't come in and wait?' she asked.

He looked at the house, then shook his dark head. 'No, I won't come in,' he answered. 'I—have things to do,' he excused himself. But the way he said it hurt her somehow, though she didn't know why it did.

Once inside, the little house felt different. As if the soul had been taken out of it. Even her telephone didn't seem to be working, she discovered, hearing only a constant high-pitched beep when she picked it up. Neither did the answering machine show any new messages since the last time she'd been here, which led her to suspect that the phone had been out of order for quite a while.

Frowning, she made a mental note to call the phone company to get them to see to it, as soon as she got back to the apartment. Then went off to pack for a long stay with her new lover.

Strange, she thought, even after what they'd shared, those words didn't seem real…

Giancarlo pulled up outside the small Chelsea townhouse, right on the appointed hour, and was relieved to see the door already standing open and her cases stacked neatly in the opening.

With a bit of luck, he wouldn't need to go inside. He had no wish to see inside Edward's love-nest. In fact he harboured a deep abhorrence for going near anything Edward and Natalia had shared.

As he got out of the car she appeared in the doorway. He found a smile from somewhere but it was hard. He was still involved in a struggle with himself where one part of him stubbornly justified his tactics this morning and another derided them as a man's reaction to another man pacing around his territory.

Walking across the path, he leant over to kiss her before bending to lift the cases. 'Is this it?' he asked, and noticed that she already had her coat on.

She nodded, and to his further relief stepped out behind the cases, then turned to shut the door securely before she joined him at the car.

They didn't speak as they drove away. In fact they didn't speak all the way back to his place, and the mood was heavy. He didn't like it. It worried him yet he couldn't seem to come up with anything to lighten it.

In the end he made a snap decision, and felt better for it because this was more like the man he always liked to believe he was, thinking on his feet and acting on instinct. So, instead of taking the car down to the basement, he stopped outside the front entrance.

'Stay there,' he told Natalia, then disappeared into the boot to get her luggage, took it into the foyer and told the concierge to deliver it upstairs. By the time he climbed back in the car he was beginning to feel more like himself—though he couldn't say the same for Natalia.

'What's going on?' she demanded warily.

'We're going out somewhere,' he said, gunning the engine.

'Where?' she asked.

He didn't answer simply because he had absolutely no idea other than they both needed a complete change of scenery...

They ended up in Brighton. Natalia couldn't believe it. Yet, he couldn't have come up with a better idea to help blow away the stresses and strains of the last twenty-four hours.

It was cold and the wind was sharp, and Giancarlo had to buy himself a sheepskin coat from the first shop they saw selling menswear. But they walked the beach for hours, and ate lunch in a sea-front fast-food café then walked the beach again on their way back to the car.

By the time they were driving back towards London, she'd relaxed, he'd relaxed—enough to actually look at each other without guarding their eyes.

Only once did he mention what had happened that morning, during dinner at a small restaurant they found as they hit the outskirts of London. He looked up from his plate and found her watching him. Not knowing what she was thinking tightened the muscle around his heart.

'I apologise if I—offended you this morning in the kitchen,' he said sombrely.

'Edward said you could be ruthless when you wanted to be.' She smiled a little wryly. 'I should have remembered that.'

'Edward would say that,' he returned very grimly—and changed the subject. Apology over, she noted. Time to move on and leave the rest behind.

Well, she had no argument with that—not any more anyway. It was a decision she had come to when she'd watched him drive off down the street after dropping her at home, and she'd been suddenly drenched in the terrifying idea that she was not going to see him again.

Scares like those focused the mind remarkably, she'd discovered. She had been offered the chance of a few weeks of nothing but Giancarlo. After that—nothing, no matter what else might or might not transpire.

But she was determined now to enjoy those few weeks, and not allow anything whatsoever to spoil them.

So she smiled at him across the table, then very gently asked if they needed to buy a bottle of champagne on their way home...

CHAPTER NINE

THE stock market was having a bad day. Share prices were jumping all over the place, figures flashing blue and red on the screen with no clear reason as to why they were doing it.

Sitting there, staring at the screen in front of him, Giancarlo saw nothing. His eyes were glazed. He just wasn't interested in what the world was panicking about.

For he had his very own panic button sitting not ten feet away. One quiet swing of his chair and he would be able to see her, happily getting on with her work with no idea what was going on inside his head.

Their time was up. Any day now—any moment, come to that—Natalia was going to turn to him and tell him that she was or was not carrying his baby.

Either result was going to cause problems, he knew that. But at least the former took care of itself to a certain extent. They would just have to get married. He could deal with that. Okay, so he would have to square it with Edward. Tell him the truth, and then seriously warn him off so much as remembering that Giancarlo Cardinale's new bride had once been *his* mistress.

But—*Dio*, he cursed silently, that was not a conversation he was looking forward to! He might end up killing Edward just to remove those memories from his head!

And there was Alegra to consider. What self-respecting Sicilian introduced his sister to her husband's ex-mistress? If Alegra ever discovered the truth about Natalia, she would never forgive any of them. It was in the genes.

Forgiveness was not a word a Sicilian recognised, and, although Alegra might have been living in England for the last twenty-five years of her life, she was still a Sicilian.

He would lose his sister; he didn't doubt that he would.

But even the prospect of that painful loss did not worry him as much as the prospect of a negative result to his and Natalia's wild night of unprotected sex. For—where did they go from that point on? The positive result removed the need to make choices, but the negative provided a whole new set of problems he had no answers to.

Because he didn't want to let Natalia go. Not today or next week or any week come to that—with or without their baby growing inside her. His problem here was trying to convince her of that, making *her* believe that he wanted to be with her—with or without a pregnancy.

But he had no idea if she was thinking the same thing. She was a closed book as far as her feelings for him were concerned. Oh, she loved the sex, he acknowledged cynically. He would have to be suffering from a real crisis of self-confidence if he couldn't tell that what she experienced in his bed was pretty damned special.

But was it special enough for her to want to stay with him no matter what? he pondered as he gave in to the urge to swing his chair around so he could look at her sitting there with her hair tied back in that prudish knot and wearing that skimpy red top again that did not know the meaning of the word prudish.

Did she care—really care for him?

Sensing his attention on her, she looked up and smiled. It was a smile that always made him ache. Surely no woman smiled at a man quite that way without being in love with him at least a small amount?

Who knew? He then mocked that. Remember her background. Remember Edward and what brought you here to

London in the first place. A woman with a secret lover knows how to lie with smiles, just as she knows how to lie in other ways.

Was the smile a lie?

You should detest her for what she is, a hard voice inside told him as he swung back to his busy screen again.

But he didn't detest her; he was falling in love with her. He had known that bleak fact for many days now and no amount of sensible conversation with himself was going to change that fact.

But he needed to know what it was he was dealing with and the waiting was slowly killing him...

What was he thinking while he sat there pretending to concentrate on market fluctuations when she knew he wasn't seeing a single figure flickering in front of his eyes? He was too still, too—tense, and that brief smile he'd offered her just now had been forced, Natalia was sure of it.

Was he worrying about the same thing she was worrying about? Was he sitting there wondering what the heck he was going to do if she was pregnant?

She wasn't a fool; she knew that Giancarlo was not the marrying kind. She knew he adored her body and what she could make him feel, but that didn't mean he wanted more from her than a few weeks of this sexual bliss they had managed to create for themselves. Take away the fear of an accidental baby and offer him back the life he'd had before he'd decided to play cupid for Edward and Alegra, and she was sure she would not be seeing his heels for dust as he disappeared into the sunset back to reality.

For this wasn't reality. Not for him, not for her. They'd both been living in a tightly closed cocoon in which sex was all and everything, and feelings were not so much as discussed.

Was he worried that, when it came to it, she was going to cling to him like a vine and refuse to let go? Was he worried that he was going to feel duty-bound to offer more than he wanted to give, if they discovered that she was pregnant?

Oh, please, God, she prayed fervently. Don't let me be pregnant, because I *can't* marry him. I can't stay with him beyond these next few weeks whether I am pregnant or not!

The stress in not knowing either way was beginning to get to both of them, she was acutely aware of that. So aware in fact that she didn't dare tell him that they should have known yesterday. Didn't dare think about it herself…

On a sigh Giancarlo gave up trying to appear absorbed in what he was supposed to be doing, and got up, then strolled over to brace his arms either side of her as if he were checking on what she was working on at the moment.

She smelled delicious, of something so delicate it teased his nostrils every time he came near her.

Stirred up his senses. 'How about an early lunch?' he murmured huskily, moving in to brush his mouth against her cheek.

She blushed; he felt the heat beneath his lips. It amazed him how she could still blush like that, especially after the weeks they'd spent being so intimate with each other.

Was the blush a lie too?

'You're insatiable,' she condemned him—but she didn't put up any kind of a fight as he pulled her to her feet.

'I adore you,' he replied, not even bothering any more to hold the endearments back. But then, he had stopped doing that a long time ago. She just hadn't noticed. 'Come to bed with me, *cara*,' he commanded grimly. 'I need you…'

*   *   *

I need you. Those three little words were like manna from heaven to her love-starved ears. He needed her, and when had she ever been able to deny that she needed him?

'I seem to recall you *needing* me this morning,' she reminded him as he began leading her along the hallway.

As arrogant as always, and so gorgeous it wasn't fair, 'I will take that as a challenge, *signorina*,' he warned without pausing in his stride. He trailed her behind him down the hall and across the sitting room they rarely bothered to use, into a room they used all too frequently—but she didn't demur.

For she knew she would rather be doing what they were about to do than what they had been doing, which was sitting there worrying—separately.

So, without a murmur she reclaimed her hand and took a few paces away from him. Then, with her back proudly facing him, she began to undress, coolly and unselfconsciously, aware of his eyes dark on her, and that the tension of earlier would be melting away in favour of this more appealing diversion.

So the top she was wearing came over her head, then she kicked off her shoes and shimmied out of her skirt, and, as a final touch, loosened her hair to let it flow over her shoulders before she turned to face him.

'*Dio,*' he breathed as enlightenment hit. 'You provoking little witch, you knew this was coming!'

'Homework.' She grinned, because she was wearing the red lace underwear he had bought her.

He started towards her with his fingers already at his shirt buttons and his eyes promising revenge.

But she even took control of this. 'No, I want to do that,' she said, and knocked his hands away to replace them with her own...

* * *

It was easy to stand here and let her undress him. It was, in fact, the easiest thing in the world for him to lose himself in the pleasurable touch of this beautiful woman as she kissed and stroked his shirt from his body, leaving him to enjoy the gentle quiver of white flesh cupped in provocative red lace as she worked her way down his torso.

He didn't touch her; he didn't attempt to help. He just stood there feeling the blood of life begin to pump the fire of passion into him as she dropped to her knees to remove his shoes and socks before reaching up to tackle his trousers.

This was what he wanted, he told himself. In fact he needed this display of sensual worship to help soothe his vulnerable ego. As he stared down at her golden head with its hot copper lights, and watched her slender white fingers efficiently strip away the rest of his clothes, he heard himself murmur lazily, 'Be gentle with me, *cara*.' Because in this game he knew exactly where he stood with her.

High on the plinth of passionate lovers—if there were such a thing.

'Why?' she questioned, looking perfectly cool as she ran her eyes over what she'd exposed. 'Nothing I see here looks that fragile.'

And to prove her claim she closed her fingers around him. The air was sucked into his lungs on a shuddering gasp that forced his eyes closed on a shaft of fierce inner response, and for a long moment he just hovered there, waiting, wanting, knowing what was coming—

Then, 'No,' he rasped on a rough-toned denial, and was suddenly pulling her to her feet so he could close his arms around her.

'Why not?' she wanted to know, and he understood her confusion, because he didn't usually stop her when she was in this kind of mood.

But he had suddenly discovered that he needed to be the one in control here. It was the only way he was going to cope with the lowering knowledge that somewhere, somehow he had become this woman's sex slave.

If anyone had told him two weeks ago that he, Giancarlo Cardinale, would one day find himself in this invidious position, he'd have laughed in their face!

The next few hours drifted by utilising the best remedy he knew for easing stress. It made for a long and languorous lunch-break. With bodies entwined they built the magic, with touch and taste and sensual caresses that helped cocoon them once again in the warm, moist-honeyed sweetness, which culminated in her lying beneath him. Limbs wrapped with limbs, and with him moving deep inside her, with his eyes and his mouth and the gentle touch of his hands, he made a different kind of love to her.

It was a small piece of heaven.

The same remedy came into play again late that same evening. And another day went by, and another, until nothing was easing his stress levels—because she still wasn't telling him anything he needed to know.

Unable to stand it any longer, he took a different kind of evasive action.

'Go and get dressed up,' he said one evening. 'We are eating somewhere special tonight...'

There was nothing that unusual in them eating out—they ate out quite frequently, in fact. So what felt different about this evening? she asked herself while her fingers scrambled through her jewellery case in search of her watch, which she had mislaid somewhere.

A sign of distraction in anyone's book, she mused, feeling Giancarlo's eyes lazily watching her as he lounged on the bed, dressed and ready to go and just waiting for her to finish getting ready.

It was what he was wearing that was making tonight different, she admitted. The black dinner suit and bow-tie turned him into a different person—a hard, sharp, breath-catchingly sophisticated person she felt very much out of her depth with.

'Have you seen my watch?' she asked, trying to sound perfectly normal when in actual fact she was feeling quite strange beneath the wrap she had tied loosely round her.

'What does this look like?' he murmured teasingly, reaching into the case to slide a slender wrist-watch out from beneath a thin red silk handkerchief it had been hiding beneath.

'Oh…' she gasped…

The strangled little sound sharpened his interest, sending his lazy gaze off to check what it was he was holding casually between finger and thumb—and felt himself floundering on the rocks of a mind-sizzling fury.

'It—it's very old,' she told him shakily, trying for a dry little laugh that didn't quite make it. 'It doesn't even work. It-it's an heirloom of m-my great-grandmother's.'

'*Your* great-grandmother?' he repeated, waiting with gritted teeth for her confirming nod. It came, and his inner anger soared to a place it had never visited before.

For he knew this watch. He had even been allowed to handle it very carefully once when Edward had shown it to him years ago—and explained to him that the delicately worked, enamelled diamond-set cabochon wrist-watch had belonged to *Edward's* grandmother! It was the only thing of value she had managed to bring with her to England after the fall of Imperial Russia.

And it was a genuine Fabergé, unique and priceless. 'For

my first-born great-granddaughter,' she had instructed her grandson.

Giancarlo felt as if his skin were being lifted off his flesh by a rash of fury. For in the face of never producing a grandchild of either sex with the death of Marco, Edward, it seemed, had decided to pass the watch on to his mistress! Not even his wife of twenty-five loyal, faithful years—but his bloody mistress!

And she keeps it stuffed in a box with a load of worthless trinkets, he then added contemptuously. What does that say about the real person she is? he asked himself. If it means so little to her, then why the hell hasn't she sold it and made herself a tidy profit out of Edward's love?

'I'll have it fixed for you,' he offered.

'No!' she almost shrieked in her urgency. Then tried to calm herself. 'I t-tried once, but they said it w-would cost too m-much.'

I just bet they did, he thought grimly as he sent her horror leaping when he casually flipped the watch into his pocket. 'Let me try,' he offered. 'I know someone who takes great delight in restoring old watches...'

'I'd rather keep it exactly as it is,' she said, needing to moisten her lips as she held out her hand. 'In f-fact it means too much to me to w-want to risk letting it out of my sight.'

'I'm not going to lose it for you,' he assured. 'Just get it—'

'No, Giancarlo!' she snapped—in more ways than vocally, he noted cynically as she made a sudden dive towards his pocket in her desperation to get the watch back! 'Give it to me! Please—!'

His response was to lift her up by the waist and drop her down on the bed, then to follow her. 'Make me,' he taunted, feeling anger flip him over into some other place entirely that literally set his teeth on edge. His eyes were hot, his body hard and—God help him, but he wanted her!

Wanted her so badly that it took him by storm.

His only consolation to that, he supposed later when he stood beneath the ice-cold jet of the shower, was that she had been affected as badly as he.

But when he came back into the bedroom, he found his clothes waiting for him on the neatly remade bed—and the watch was no longer in his pocket...

Natalia didn't know why he had brought them here. Glancing around her, she tried very hard to see what the attraction was in the most fashionable and therefore busiest restaurant in London right now.

After the small, more intimate places he had taken her to before, this place felt brash and noisy and over the top with its trendy decor and its trendy people all greeting each other with trendy kisses wrapped up in super-trendy smiles.

Why? she wanted to know. What is supposed to be so different about tonight, that he decided to bring me to a place like this?

You know why, the mocking little answer came back, sending her stress levels inching up another couple of notches. The man is straining at the leash with boredom while he waits to find out if he's going to be let off the hook by you.

Suddenly she wanted to be sick...

If she got any paler she would probably pass out! Giancarlo thought grimly as he fielded yet another greeting from someone whose name he didn't even remember.

They ate fashionable food from fashionable plates, with London's fashionable set milling all around them, and he hated every minute of it even while he kept his social smile in place, and pretended this was just what he wanted.

But it wasn't. Hell—he didn't know what he wanted any more! She tied him in knots, he admitted, glaring at her sitting there across the table from him looking so damn beautiful in her sparkling black dress that made him think of the black underwear she was probably wearing, and with her hair like silk against her shoulders—and that cheap gold watch, which reminded him of another watch, circling her slender wrist.

And he didn't like the way other men were eyeing her up, he added to his list of grievances, though she didn't seem to notice, he had to confess.

In fact, she couldn't look more unimpressed with a place if she tried to be!

Or maybe it was him she was unimpressed with, he pondered with a sting that made him snatch up his wine-glass. Did the urbane sophisticate in the bow-tie and the dinner suit, who drew the flattering attention of all the other sophisticates here, not reach her at all?

When was she going to give him the answer? he added on a restless shrug of his black-silk-covered shoulders that showed how Natalia Deyton was beginning to get under his skin in more ways than he wanted to deal with! She gave him nothing and he gave everything! he decided with an arrogance that tried to completely ignore that what he was getting from her was exactly what he'd aimed for!

Edward's mistress becoming *his* mistress. Nothing more, nothing less.

On paper he supposed he was a step or two up from a man who was twice her age and married with it, he allowed with a bitter kind of wit.

Though even he couldn't afford to give out Fabergé heirlooms as payment for services rendered! And—hell, he grimly extended on that theme. If he—Giancarlo—had found it easy enough to take her from Edward, then what was to stop her moving on as easily if a bigger catch came along?

An answer to one specific question, he reminded himself with a burning flash of his eyes in her direction. Yes or no, Natalia? he questioned silently. Surely she had to know something by now...?

He wanted out, she just knew he did. He was feeling so trapped by their situation that he was barely managing to contain his frustration with it any longer. She was going to have to let him off the hook. Yes or no to the question that was burning holes in both their heads. She was going to have to set him free, then disappear. It was the only thing for her to do even if the very idea was making her feel positively nauseous...

Why was she looking so down in the mouth and wan-faced? Giancarlo thought bitterly. As long as she had him over a barrel, she was sitting pretty!

Then it happened. No hint, no warning. She was just coming to her feet with some murmured excuse about going to the cloakroom, then she swayed and her eyes closed, and he saw her face turn deathly pale as her legs began to go from under her.

He was there to catch her. Anger forgotten, frustrations, resentments—everything sluiced away in that single swift move of his body from his chair to her side so he could take her weight for her.

'Okay?' he asked roughly.

'Yes,' she breathed, but he knew she wasn't. He could feel her trembling, and she was having to fight the need to lean heavily on him. 'Do you think we can go now?' she begged shakily.

'Of course.' Without another word, he carefully fed her slender frame beneath his shoulder and began carefully guiding her between tables with curious eyes following them...

Natalia couldn't really blame them for their curiosity. Giancarlo was holding her so close that she was finding it difficult to put one foot in front of the other. He continued to hold her like that while he paid the bill, and only released her for as long as it took to help her into her coat. Then she was back beneath the protection of his arm before she had a chance to move a single step.

'You can let go of me now,' she told him when they eventually made it outside.

'No,' he replied, that was all. It was gruff and it was tight and it declared no room for argument as he herded her down the street to the nearest taxi rank, and helped her inside a black cab.

She wasn't sure why they had come by taxi tonight, unless it had something to do with the amount of wine Giancarlo had drunk through dinner. She had a horrible feeling he had come out with the specific intention of getting himself drunk. And his mood had been so short and surly she hadn't known quite how to deal with it.

It didn't help that she had been feeling under the weather for most of the evening—ever since he'd noticed her watch, in fact.

No, don't think about that, she told herself with a small shudder.

The shudder made him turn his head to glance at her sharply. 'I'm okay,' she assured him, but it wasn't the truth.

She felt weak and dizzy, and she knew she should have said something sooner. Her own quiet mood had affected his mood. But she had been worried and frightened of saying anything in case it forced the whole wretched problem right out in the open.

Now the problem didn't need forcing out, because it was sitting here between them like a great lump of rock just waiting to be shattered by one tiny comment—I think I'm pregnant. Or—I think you are pregnant, depending on which one of them decided to say it first.

Yet neither of them said a single word all the way back to the apartment. He was grim-faced and withdrawn and she felt her heart sting every time she dared a quick glance at his profile. Handsome didn't even begin to cover what made Giancarlo Cardinale the compelling force he was to her. She adored every lean, hard, noble feature, every flicker of his lashes, every twitch of his flat-lined, sensually moulded mouth. She even adored the way he was being very careful to keep his eyes away from her eyes because it showed that he was as aware as she was that the moment of truth was too close for comfort.

And she adored the way his hand was gripping her hand so tightly, even over that imaginary lump of rock which had trouble stamped all over it...

He couldn't say a word. He didn't dare. Not until he'd had time to think—though what that meant he had been doing for the last few weeks made it anybody's guess, he grimly admitted. Because *this* was thinking, which just went to show how suspicion could fool you where reality could not.

'*Incinta...*' he murmured, feeling a whole new set of powerful emotions grab a tight hold of him by the sheer weight of her condition.

'What?' Natalia prompted.

'Nothing,' he said, not realising he'd spoken out loud, and glad she didn't understand his language.

The taxi drew up outside the apartment then, saving either of them the need to speak again while he paid the driver and climbed out himself before helping Natalia down onto the path beside him.

She still looked pale, and her hand gripped his arm with enough force to tell him that she still felt frail. Without a word he folded her back beneath his arm to take her into the building. The concierge was there, they all smiled politely at each other, and the lift waited at the ready to transport them into privacy.

He needed that, he acknowledged. Privacy to think with this brand-new clarity of mind he was now experiencing.

Keeping her close to him while he activated the lift, he then spent the time it took to reach their floor in silent communion with the top of her head, thinking, feeling— *Dio*, feeling more than he could actually believe was possible just because one small suspicion had become hard fact…

God, she felt awful. Sick in the stomach and light in the head. If he didn't say something she was going to start crying! She just knew she was because, if it wasn't enough that his silence was killing her, then this gentle, protective way he was treating her was enough to make the tears flow.

Did he have to crowd her into the corner like this? she thought on a sudden bout of breathlessness that had her sinking back further into the lift corner. He was all brawn and bone and familiar scents that were beginning to make her feel really dizzy.

'*Stai bene?*' he enquired, clearly sensing something.

'What's happened to your English?' she snapped at him in an effort to dispel whatever it was that was happening to her.

'It is here,' he replied, as calm as anything.

'Then try using it if you want to be understood,' she advised, sounding waspish but not even caring any more. The lift doors opened then. Maybe it was timely, because she'd seen the way his chest had lifted and fallen. He was controlling the desire to retaliate in kind.

Aware that she was stupidly treading the fine line to destruction, she slipped out from beneath his overpowering stance and walked quickly out of the lift and across the lobby on legs that were threatening to collapse—

The telephone was ringing. She stopped and frowned as she turned instinctively in the direction of the nearest extension which happened to be in the office.

'I will get it,' he said, striding towards the office. She didn't demur, for it had to be for him. The life of a venture capitalist didn't recognise time zones.

She was just removing her coat when she heard his voice make its usual deep curt acknowledgement to whoever was trying to contact him.

Silence followed. Something about it made her go still. Then his voice came, hard and tight, and as she stared at him he spun his back to her, his body bristling with tension as he became involved in a question and answer session in thick deep Italian with whoever was on the other end of the phone.

Then the phone was slammed down. Silence hit. For the space of ten excruciating seconds, he just continued to stand there staring at the wall in front of him while she waited with bated breath, somehow knowing that something dreadful had just happened.

When he did move, she found herself taking an unsteady

step backwards as he strode towards her. 'W-what's wrong?' she asked anxiously.

'Nothing,' he clipped, but he was lying. 'I have to go out,' he announced, striding right by her. Then he was gone, disappearing back into the lift and sending it downwards without even offering her a single glance!

Whomever he had been talking to had given him an excuse to get away from here before they had a chance to talk—and, good grief, but he'd taken it with wings on his feet!

It hurt. She couldn't pretend it didn't. In a daze filled with bitter new experiences tonight, she walked into the office, draped her coat over a chair, then sat down without really knowing she had done it.

A flickering red light suddenly intruded on the edge of her vision. As she turned towards it, it was purely instinctive to press the play-back button on the answering machine.

Almost immediately a shrill, near-hysterical voice came whipping into the room with her. And even though it spoke in an agitated mix of Italian and English, she got the drift of what it was saying.

'Where are you, Giancarlo?' it was demanding urgently. 'I have been ringing and ringing—' It was his sister's voice, Natalia realised as Alegra suddenly switched to Italian. She recognised it because she had spoken to her several times while working with Edward.

Then—'Edward.' She picked out his name from the garble. Followed almost instantly by another couple of recognisable words that had her going cold inside.

It was the link between Edward and the name of a famous hospital right here in London that really shook her.

Edward was ill. She knew it without a hint of a doubt in her head!

Natalia got up and ran...

CHAPTER TEN

GIANCARLO felt sick. Standing here with Alegra weeping in his arms and talking wildly, all he could think was—I am going to be sick.

'He made the confession, Giancarlo,' Alegra sobbed out in shrill broken English. 'He starts acting strange. Then he suddenly insists we leave the cruise and fly home. We are almost here when he has the attack. He thinks he is going to die, so he decides to tell all! But what does this confession do for me?' she choked, so utterly distraught it was wretched. 'He took another woman to his bed! He made a child with her! He betrayed me and defiled me and now he is going to die on me!'

'He will not die, *cara*,' he murmured, finding the comforting words from somewhere, but he didn't know where from because his brain had crashed, the sheer scale of the horror unfolding before him just too much for it to take in. 'Shh,' he soothed. 'He will live—he will live.'

And he *will*, Giancarlo found himself vowing angrily. Because he wanted Edward very much alive so he could personally kill both him and Natalia Deyton!

Natalia. His heart suddenly wrenched, the pain and the anger shooting out in all directions and holding him stock-stone still. Natalia the witch. Natalia the bitch. Natalia the lying, cheating, artful deceiver, who had knowingly and calculatingly lured him into bed with her—so she could foist Edward's bastard off on him!

'But then he deserves to die for doing this to me!'

153

Alegra burst out. 'A child, Giancarlo! He made a child with another woman! I will never forgive him!'

The Sicilian promise. His bones clenched at the sound of it. Yet he understood it—hell, did he understand!

A sound by the waiting-room door caught his attention. Looking up, he immediately began to burn inside because—there she was, standing in the doorway as if his own wrath had conjured her up, and looking achingly, destructively beautiful in her sparkling black dress, which somehow reminded him of the Fabergé watch.

A watch she'd probably filched out of Edward's safe along with everything else he'd asked her to get out of there. As her own idea of payment for services rendered—to both Edward and himself?

And now she had the cheek to turn up here, when she must know that the game was up, looking all pale and ethereal and—

Dio! 'I am going to make you pay for this,' he hissed at her his own Sicilian promise from between tightly gritted teeth.

She blinked as if he'd slapped her. Yet the very idea of laying another finger on her traitorous flesh had his stomach reeling all over again. At the same dizzying moment his sister broke free from his arms and saw her standing there.

'It is she!' Alegra exclaimed shrilly. 'She is the one, Giancarlo—she is the one! I know the hair, I know the eyes!'

'Edward...' Natalia whispered shakily. 'H-how is he? What—?'

'Get out!' Giancarlo blasted at her, losing touch with himself as the sound of Edward's name quivering on her lips sent a shaft of burning black anguish thrusting its way through him. 'You are not wanted here. Get out of my sight!'

Now she had gone as white as a sheet, he saw. Her beautiful eyes so dark, it could be anguish colouring them like that. But it was not anguish. It was the look of horror at being found out!

'I just need to know how he is,' she insisted. 'I d-don't want to make trouble, b-but I must know if he—'

'You are the trouble!' his sister fiercely responded, diverting Natalia's attention away from him…

Natalia saw the other woman start towards her with her eyes spitting out the kind of hatred and venom Edward had always predicted she would see.

'Edward would not be in here if it was not for you!' Alegra cried. 'You could not leave well alone! You had to seek him out and play on his broken heart!'

'He loves me,' Natalia whispered in her own defence. 'Love doesn't break hearts, it helps to heal—'

Derision lanced across Giancarlo's hard face, and his sister almost jumped on her in her rage. 'How dare you say that when it is you who has poisoned his mind?' the older woman launched at her shrilly. 'You put yourself in my dead son's place and fed on Edward's grief and pain until he could bear it no longer and made himself ill!'

Alegra lifted up a hand. Thinking she was about to be attacked, Natalia stiffened up warily, her eyes blinking in rapid confusion as another, larger hand appeared in her vision, also raised as if ready to strike. But all Giancarlo did was capture his sister's hand before it could throw the expected blow.

After that Natalia just stood there shaking with shock and pain, feeling as if she was being bombarded by hatred from two different sources. With Alegra it was with the words that were still spilling from her lips. With Giancarlo it was simply in his expression.

And Edward was right, she realised painfully. These people did not know the meaning of compassion.

Edward. Her heart lurched. 'Will one of you please tell me how he is?' she begged anxiously.

'Why do you want to know?' Giancarlo jeered at her. 'So you can make a judgement whether it is worth foisting his baby back on to him now that I know the truth about you?'

The truth? Her mouth went slack in disbelief. Was he saying what she thought he was saying here? Was he actually daring to suggest that any baby she might be carrying belonged to *Edward*?

Oh, God—the nausea came back with a vengeance when she began to really understand what it was that Giancarlo was thinking here. 'You believe I was Edward's mistress.' She breathed the terrible words out loud. He flinched as if she'd hit him. She wished she had done. 'You think I was trying to foist his baby onto you!'

'The truth always sounds shocking when spoken out loud,' he grated.

'*Your* truth, yes,' she agreed.

'What are you talking about, Giancarlo?' his sister put in bewilderedly.

He didn't even hear her, he was so busy despising Natalia. 'Oh, stop looking so damned bewildered!' he bit out in disgust. 'Edward has already confessed everything in sheer fear of dying with it all still festering on his soul!'

'Stop it!' his sister cried. 'Stop it, the both of you. This is wrong. It is—'

'The only person with a guilty conscience around here should be you for daring to believe such a filthy thing about either of us!' Natalia sliced over the top of her.

'Edward always said you came from crude stock,' she told him, taking great pleasure from seeing his arrogant face turn to rock. 'He was right! You couldn't have a more primitive view of life if you tried!'

'And trying to foist one man's child off on his brother-in-law is not crude?'

'Giancarlo!' Alegra inserted furiously. 'This has gone far enough!'

More than far enough, agreed Natalia, and with a final slaying glance at him she turned and walked out to go in search of the one who really mattered here.

Edward, leaving Edward's wife to put her brother's vile misconceptions in order. She even smiled in cold satisfaction as she heard the beginning of it before the door closed behind her.

'She is not the woman Edward betrayed me with!' Alegra was saying furiously. 'She is the *child* his betrayal spawned, you fool…!'

Giancarlo caught up with Natalia just as she was leaning over a distraught Edward and trying to calm him down. 'Shh,' she was soothing him—just as Giancarlo had been soothing Alegra not so long ago. 'Please, darling, don't do this, you're going to make yourself worse!'

But Edward wouldn't be soothed. 'I couldn't find you anywhere. I tried your house, the office, I even tried Giancarlo! But he said he'd sent you away on a fact-finding mission to Fillens in Manchester, and I believed him!' he choked out in self-disgust. 'I actually believed him and put you aside to worry about Alegra and myself instead.'

'As you should have done,' Natalia attempted to console him.

'No, I shouldn't,' Edward groaned. 'I should have

smelled a rat from the moment he said it! But it took me two whole weeks before it suddenly hit me—in Nassau of all the places—that there was no way he would send you anywhere like that unless he had an ulterior motive for doing so!'

'Shh,' she tried again.

'So I rang the firm,' Edward continued hoarsely. 'Got Howard Fiske who'd apparently not long come back from Milan. The swine was more than happy to tell me that you'd moved in with my brother-in-law within days of him arriving. And that's when it really hit!' he gasped out. 'Why Giancarlo had arranged the cruise and put himself in my place here in London. He must have found out about you and was doing the typical Sicilian thing by taking revenge for *my* sin out on you!'

'You mean—he came here to deliberately seduce me?' Natalia said, while Giancarlo stood there unnoticed, feeling the full weight of his own culpability land squarely upon his own rigid shoulders.

'Natalia...' he murmured, unable to remain quiet any longer.

She turned towards him, and for the first time Giancarlo looked into her eyes and saw Edward's eyes looking accusingly back at him. He looked at her hair and saw the colour Edward's hair used to be before the silver had overrun the gold. His stomach contracted, for what he was seeing was a terrible truth that had been staring him in the face from the very beginning, but he had been too blinded by prejudice to see it.

Sexual prejudice, he expanded sombrely.

Sex probably covered his blindness very well—in the beginning at any rate. He had wanted Natalia Deyton so badly from the first moment he'd looked into those eyes that to see then what he should have seen would have stopped his plans of seduction dead in their tracks. So he hadn't let himself see. For how did a Sicilian male seduce the daughter of one of his own family members? He didn't. It was as simple and neat as that.

And it was quite monstrous to know how low he had trodden in his *want* for Edward's beautiful daughter.

'You stay away from her!' Edward clearly held the same bitter belief. 'You've had your revenge, now get the hell away from both of us!'

It was the ugly scene in the waiting room playing itself out in reverse, Giancarlo noted. And he quietly tried again. 'Natalia—'

'Just go,' she cut in, having to use both hands to keep her father from getting up off the bed in his weak effort to protect her. 'You are making him worse.'

Could it get any worse? 'We need to talk,' he insisted, and saw by the sudden darkening of her eyes that she would rather slay him than speak to him. His grimace acknowledged her right to think like that—but he didn't back down. 'Talk,' he repeated warningly, and, with a final glance at Edward's angry struggle, he turned and walked away, taking the sight of Natalia's tears right along with him...

'He hurt you, didn't he?' Edward had seen the tears too. 'I'll never forgive him.'

'Nor will I,' Natalia agreed, but had to wonder why that knowledge wounded her so much.

You know why, she then mocked herself. Because you love him, cruel, hard, ruthless man that he is. 'Please stop fighting me, Edward,' she pleaded. 'Do you want me to lose you along with everything else?'

'I'm all right,' he snapped out impatiently. 'It was just

a little panic attack during the flight, that was all. Nothing worthy of all this fuss!'

He should have said heart attack but Natalia didn't correct him, because he was probably half right, and panic was what had helped bring it on in the first place.

'What did he do to you?' he muttered, falling back in frustration because he was too weak to even throw off a lightweight like Natalia.

'He thought I was your mistress,' she said, then smiled at her father's shocked expression because he just hadn't realised the twisted view others had had of their little deception.

After that she told him everything, quietly and unemotionally because there had been enough of that expended tonight. And also because the truth needed to be told from all angles if this muddled situation was ever to be sorted out.

But, 'God, I'm going to kill him!' Edward rasped when she withered to an empty finish, and he started trying to get up again.

'You will do nothing of the kind, you stupid—stupid man!' another angry voice commanded. 'Not when *you* are the one to blame for all of this!'

It was Alegra. Instantly placed on the wary defensive, Natalia straightened stiffly away from him while Edward sank with a groan back against the pillows.

'If you've come here to continue your family vendetta then you can turn about and leave again,' Edward grimly informed his wife of twenty-five years.

'I have not come to do anything,' Alegra replied haughtily, 'but be formally introduced to your daughter.'

Looking at her standing there, a diminutive figure dressed in blue, who held herself with a pride which gave her stature, Natalia had to admire just what it must be

costing Alegra Knight to say that. And for a moment—
just a moment—she saw Alegra's resemblance to her
brother, the same arrogant tilt to her head, the same darkly
challenging eyes, the same—

No. She shook the comparison away, not wanting to
think about Giancarlo right now.

'Not if you're going to start spitting out insults again,'
Edward refused harshly.

The eyes flashed once more, Natalia thought of
Giancarlo again—and again she thrust the comparison
away. 'The only person in this room who deserves insult-
ing is you,' Alegra hit back. 'So you may climb out of
that defensive hole you are trying to hide in and behave
like the gentleman I used to think you!'

To Natalia's surprise, Edward smiled—albeit wryly.
'You have the silken tongue of a Sicilian asp,' he dryly
informed his wife.

'I have the power to bite like one also,' Alegra returned.

And suddenly Natalia was beginning to feel definitely
in the way as something she had never been privy to before
began to fill the air space.

It was love. It was affection. Despite all the lies and
pain and anger, it was a deep and abiding togetherness
nurtured through years and years of tender loving care ad-
ministered from one constant soul to another.

Bearing witness to it brought the tears back to Natalia's
eyes because this was exactly what her father had been
protecting when he'd kept her a secret from everyone.
Now the secret was out, and she was afraid it was going
to spoil everything he had worked so hard to hold on to.

'I have been sent to instruct you that it is time to rest,'
his wife firmly changed the subject. 'So make these intro-
ductions so we two can go away and leave you to recover
from your sinful life.'

'I've told you before,' Edward said harshly. 'Natalia was born *before* I married you!'

'Two months?'

Natalia winced, understanding the curt thrust. So did her father, who became very weary suddenly. And for her the tears became harder to fight, because in the end, and once Alegra had time to think it all over properly, the fact that Edward had married her instead of standing by his ex-lover and child said a lot about his love for Alegra.

A nurse arrived then, insisting they leave now, and a few minutes later Natalia found herself outside in the corridor with her father's wife.

'Don't weep, child,' Alegra Knight murmured, and a gentle hand came to rest on her shoulder. 'We fight. It means nothing. We know that, even if you do not.'

'I never wanted to come between you,' she whispered painfully. 'I j-just needed to know him. It was...'

'I know.' The gentle hand squeezed her into a thickened silence. 'Edward has explained all. You do not need to justify yourself to me—or to anyone else concerned here, come to that,' she added carefully.

'He was never unfaithful to you after you married,' Natalia felt compelled to say. 'He never saw either me or my mother again, from the day I was born. If I've forgiven him for all the years of rejection, can't you forgive him too?'

The hand was removed. Alegra began walking. 'He was unfaithful during our betrothal,' she said coldly. 'Would you find it easy to forgive that?'

No, she wouldn't, Natalia had to admit.

'And while I was busy grieving the death of our beloved son, he was discovering he had another child to help salve his broken heart.'

'I didn't know about Marco until after Edward and I

met, or I wouldn't...' Her voice trailed away on a guilty thickening of her throat, which required her to swallow before she could try again. 'M-my mother had passed away, you see, and I found all these private papers relating to a father I never knew existed. It...'

This time she really couldn't go on. It had been one of the lowest points in all her life to discover that the mother she had adored had lied when she'd told her that her father was dead. Twenty-four relatively happy years suddenly soured on a medley of remembered conversations about a man called Nathaniel Deyton, a merchant seaman with eyes and hair the same colour as her own, who'd had the chance to meet his baby girl only once before the sea had taken him. There had never been such a person as Nathaniel Deyton. It was a name her mother had made up and taken up when she'd moved out of London with her daughter, to live the rest of her life in a quiet little village in Suffolk where nobody knew her so could not dispute her story.

From the moment Natalia had found out about her real father, she had made it an obsession to trace him and try to get to know him. It had taken several months to locate the right Edward Knight. Yet it had taken him mere days to reply to her tentative letter of introduction. They'd met in a crowded wine bar not far from his office building, and in minutes had been so at peace with each other that it seemed strange now to look back and know that first meeting had been only six months ago.

'He gave you the Fabergé watch, didn't he?'

Pulling herself back to the present, Natalia sucked in a thick breath of air and nodded. 'If you want it back, I'll be very happy to—'

'No, I was not asking for it,' Alegra responded. 'It belongs to you. You had a right to receive it. I just—missed it, that was all, several months ago, and Edward refused to say what he had done with it. So I began to worry—as wives do—whether he had found some other woman he preferred to give it to.'

'So you mentioned as much to Giancarlo,' Natalia murmured, beginning to see a whole new way of looking at the scene she and Giancarlo had had about the watch.

'But it was Howard Fiske who gave the silly imaginings of a grieving woman their hard substance,' Alegra added. 'He rang Giancarlo in Milan and voiced his—suspicions about your relationship with Edward. Giancarlo being Giancarlo—' she shrugged with true Sicilian understanding '—decided to put a stop to it before I had to find out.'

And the rest, as they said, was history, Natalia soberly concluded. 'He deliberately set out to use me.'

Alegra stopped walking. So did Natalia. They had almost reached the main foyer but neither seemed to notice. 'You need to talk to him about that,' she advised, and at the sudden freeze she saw encase Natalia's face she sighed and said, 'I am going back to sit with Edward, for I cannot leave here until I know the danger has surely passed.'

'Do you want me to stay with you?' It was instant and instinctive to make the offer.

But Alegra's refusal made its point. 'We need time alone together. And I need time to get used to the idea of you being a part of my family now.' A brief smile tried to take the sting out of her words.

Natalia smiled back in an effort to make it known that she understood, even if it did hurt. Maybe Alegra saw the hurt, because her cold expression softened a little. 'Go now,' she advised. 'I will find you if I need to but I do not see this problem he has caused his silly heart worsening now that the truth is out in the open.'

No, Natalia thought wearily. Neither did she. Edward

had been living under a terrible strain for the last year one way or another. It was no wonder his heart had finally insisted he give himself a break.

About to turn away, Alegra spoke again. 'Please forgive my rudeness to you before,' she intoned. 'It was a shock when he suddenly collapsed then began to confess all to me.'

'I'm sorry you had to find out that way,' Natalia responded, not knowing what else to say to make any of this better.

Alegra just smiled another of those smiles, then turned to walk back the way she had come, leaving Natalia standing there watching her go with tears in her eyes again, though she couldn't decide who they were for—herself or Alegra.

The whole situation had always had the potential to turn ugly. Now it had done, she found herself half wishing she had never contacted Edward, then there would have been none of this. No secret, no lies—and no ruthless Sicilian hell bent on waging a vendetta.

'Are you ready to leave now?' an all-too-familiar voice enquired.

A wave of pain washed over her, turning her around before she had a chance to think. Giancarlo was standing not three feet away. Big, dark, and with no expression whatsoever showing on his lean face.

She wanted to turn away again but found she couldn't. She wanted to hate him but found she couldn't even do that. So she ended up just standing there hurting all over, which made such a terrible mockery of everything...

She didn't know whether to hit him or hug him. Her mouth was vulnerable but her eyes were like glass, a dark grey glass with the blue lost behind a film of tears which, even as he looked sombrely into them, was quickly frosting into ice to shut him out.

But the quivering mouth was letting her down. She was hurting and she desperately needed someone to hold her right now.

Dio, he thought, so did he. But touching, he knew, was out of the question. Touch her now and she would probably never forgive him for violating that invisible barrier of self-defence she was standing beyond.

'I have a taxi waiting outside,' he told her, and was relieved to hear the words come out level because he certainly wasn't feeling level inside.

He expected the mute shake of her head in refusal. He even expected the cold shoulder she offered him as she altered direction so that she could walk by him without offering him a single word.

He didn't try to stop her, but as she went by him he fed quietly after her, 'I was deceived as much as you were.'

The claim stopped her, but she didn't turn, and his throat grew tight as he stood watching her hair and her dress glitter in the overhead lights of the foyer.

'No,' she said, that was all, just that small, tight denial, then she was walking again, beautiful head held high, slender spine as straight as an arrow, sensational legs long in their stride.

Grimly determined, he followed, drawing level with her, then adjusting his stride to hers. The gap between them was still there—not quite as wide but wide enough for her to feel her defensive barrier was not being breached. Neither did she turn to look at him and he did not look at her. The exit doors were automatic, swinging smoothly open as they reached them and they stepped out into the cold night air. She paused and shivered, her hands going up to cup her bare arms.

'Where is your coat?' he asked, beckoning the private taxi forward.

'I forgot it.'

He grimaced because he hadn't expected her to reply. The taxi drew up. It was a top-of-the-range black Mercedes promising warmth and comfort—if he could get her inside it.

Ignoring the car, she began searching the street for the nearest taxi rank.

'Money?' he prompted next.

She indicated with a shrug of one folded arm the sparkling black evening bag dangling from her wrist by its narrow strap.

It was communication of sorts, he supposed. 'Enough to take you to Chelsea—after midnight—when taxi fares go through the roof?'

The flicker of her lashes told him he'd hit the right button to achieve his aims. And, as if on cue, the driver stepped out of the Mercedes and jumped to open the rear door for them. Silently, Giancarlo thanked him for his perfect timing.

'Come on,' he invited. 'I will take you home.'

'My home,' she said, swinging her head round to look directly at him at last.

His hands twitched at his sides with a need to just grab her and kiss some healthy life back into her. But the frost went too deep and it might ruin his chances completely. 'If that is what you want,' he therefore agreed.

'It is,' she confirmed and without another word she stepped forward and slid into the back of the Mercedes.

With a grim nod of his head at the driver, he closed her inside, then he walked around to the other side of the car to get in as the driver sat behind his wall of tinted glass.

They moved away from the kerb with Natalia staring

fixedly out of her window and Giancarlo gauging that he had about five minutes before she began to realise she wasn't going to Chelsea.

'A Russian great-grandmother,' he remarked. 'Now I know where all the fire and the passion comes from.'

Her head flicked round, and it was as if a light had suddenly been switched on inside her. 'Don't you dare comment on my background!' she threw at him hotly. 'Don't you even so much as dare to make it any business of yours!'

'It is my business if you are sharing your genes with my baby,' he pointed out, quite happily fanning the flames.

'I am not pregnant!' she flashed.

'You cannot know that with such certainty,' he replied.

'Tomorrow will tell,' she muttered, and turned away again.

'Why tomorrow specifically?' he asked curiously, following every flash and restless quiver she made and loving every one of them because it meant he was beginning to melt the ice. Once the ice was gone he could begin dealing with the melting woman. A woman who was in for a big fight if she was foolishly allowing herself to believe that he was going to let go of her now.

Because he wasn't.

'I'll buy one of those test-kit things,' she informed him. 'First thing in the morning.'

'Good idea,' he said agreeably. 'We will watch the result with interest—together—'

'You won't be there to watch it!' she flung at him.

The caution brought her eyes back into contact with his—and this time he held on to them by sheer grim resolve. 'Oh, yes, I will,' he countered very seriously. 'For I do not think I should trust you to tell me the truth, you see...'

CHAPTER ELEVEN

IT WAS like waving a red rag to a bull, especially when Natalia had been intending to do just that if necessary and lie to Giancarlo! 'Will you want a DNA test done as well, if I find I am pregnant?' she enquired ever so, ever so acidly.

The dark eyes flickered, though they didn't release her eyes. 'Do you think it could be a possibility that such a test may be required?' he countered.

It was a clean hit. Natalia even found herself acknowledging it with a gasp, because she knew she had set herself up for that. They had known each other for a few weeks only. Not long enough to cover a full menstrual cycle, in fact. So even with his rotten suspicions about her relationship with Edward out of the way, she could quite easily be pregnant by some other imaginary guy, she supposed. How would he know that she hadn't been involved in an intimate relationship with any man for years?

She had been too involved in other things, such as a mother dying, and a newly found father to pour all her emotions into.

'No, a DNA test won't be needed,' she replied, resenting having to say it at all. Then she wrenched her eyes away to glare out of the side window while she waited for him to come back with some cynically disbelieving reply.

And why not? she asked herself bitterly. You fell into his bed like a woman who did that kind of thing all the time! Shame engulfed her, followed by a real contempt for the person she had allowed herself to become in her reckless desire for this man.

Then she stopped thinking. Her eyes blinked into focus on what it was she was actually glaring at. 'We're going the wrong way,' she announced, and was already leaning forward to knock on the glass partition so she could tell the driver—when another hand closed around her hand.

Suddenly the sparks were flying, crackling around the inner compartment and bouncing off all surfaces in a skin-against-skin chemical reaction that rendered her totally breathless.

Unable to stop herself, she glanced at him and felt her heart begin to race when she saw what was written in his eyes. He was going to kiss her—and she didn't want him to!—yet her eyes dropped to his mouth of their own hungry volition. It began to move, her throat locked, her own lips beginning to heat in preparation for what was about to come to them.

'Keys,' he said.

Lost in a daze of her own making, 'What?' she said.

'The keys to your Chelsea house,' he gently extended. 'Do you have them with you in that small bag?'

Natalia felt herself deflate like a popped balloon as reality pierced sheer fantasy. 'No,' she breathed.

Having made his point, Giancarlo let go of her hand, leaving her to complete the deflation by sinking shakily back into the soft luxury of leather, knowing now that, whatever else had been killed between them, the sex was still there, simmering quietly in the background waiting for its usual release.

'I'll just pick up my keys and go.' She seemed to feel it necessary to state her intentions.

He didn't even bother to reply, which to her stated *his* intentions far more ominously than an outright denial could have done. He had coerced her into getting into this car with him because he had been gunning for a complete showdown tonight even though he must know that it wouldn't be fair.

Not after the evening she had just been put through. Not after what she'd found out and hadn't had time yet to decide what she really felt about it all.

Yet she didn't persist with the point, and she didn't understand *why* she didn't. Which had her finishing the rest of the journey with the feeling of being trapped by herself as much as him.

The car stopped; the driver jumped out to open her door for her while Giancarlo got out on the other side. With a polite thanks to the driver, she walked off towards the glass-plated entrance to the apartment block leaving Giancarlo to tip the driver before following on behind.

The concierge was at his station, watching his portable TV set which sat beside his security monitor. He glanced up and smiled in recognition as he pressed the button to release the door lock. By the time the doors went swinging open Giancarlo was beside her and, with the usual exchange of polite good evenings with the concierge, they were making their way over to the lift.

As it took them upwards Natalia found herself making a comparison with this journey and the last one they had made together like this. Last time he had been crowding her into the corner, pulsing with suppressed emotion and ready for a different kind of showdown. Now they stood about as far apart as two people could get in such a confined space.

The lift stopped, the doors opened, she walked into the white-tiled private foyer, hesitated only for a moment before walking on again, passing the opening to the office on her left because she was no longer interested in doing that kind of business with this man. She walked by the sitting-room entrance because she'd never liked that room and if there was going to have to be a showdown then she wasn't putting herself so close to the bedroom when it happened. Which left only the dining room she liked about as much as the sitting room, and the kitchen, which was about the only place left.

Walking in, she went directly to the fridge and got herself a small bottle of sparkling water and a glass, then went to sit down at the table. She was just removing the plastic cap when Giancarlo strode in. Almost ghosting her actions, he went to the fridge to get himself a can of cola instead of water.

The tab went fizz. Her water hissed as it hit the glass. He walked over to stand staring out of the darkened window while she sat staring down at her glass. His arm lifted as he took a drink from his can. She took a sip of the sparkling water. Other than for those two relatively innocent actions nothing else stirred in the room if you didn't include the roaring speed with which two like-minded brains were working.

He began the battle. 'Will you marry me, Natalia?' he asked…

No answer, he noted. Did you really expect one? he then wryly asked himself. Only to wince when she suddenly started laughing, not loudly or hysterically but disdainfully.

'You've got a nerve,' she said.

Oh, I don't know, he silently countered, staring grimly down at his can. It is a lack of nerve that made me ask the question. I am in dire straits here or the shrewd gambler in me would not be putting my last card on the table first.

'You can't even bring yourself to ask me that to my face,' she added scathingly.

The jeer spun him round to face her. She was sitting there glaring an evil spell at him like the beautiful blue-eyed witch he always saw, and on a grunt of rueful surrender he threw himself in at the deep end.

'I fell in love with you at first glance across a packed company dining room,' he informed her. 'Is that in your face enough for you?'

He could see that it most definitely was not. She had turned white again, very white, and the eyes had gone grey, permeating the air with a frost of cold disbelief. 'You fell in *lust* with me, you mean,' she denounced in disgust.

'That too,' he agreed, adding a wry shrug because it was the truth, and he was determined that they would only deal with the truth from here on in. 'But at the time I believed you were my brother-in-law's mistress and the woman who was threatening to ruin his marriage.'

'Oh, that makes it all okay, then,' she mocked him bitterly.

'What else was I supposed to think?' He sighed out impatiently. 'Have you any idea what such a belief did to me?'

'I know what it did to you!' she threw back angrily. 'It turned you into a rat, and a deceiver!'

'That's great,' he derided. 'Coming from the woman who has been lying to me from day one.'

'At least I lied to protect someone I loved.'

'So did I,' he reminded her. 'Alegra is just as important to me as Edward is to you.'

'Only your way of protecting those you love was deliberately geared towards a bit of good old-fashioned Sicilian revenge at the same time,' she pointed out. 'My *reasons* for being with you were honest, Giancarlo. Whereas yours were only ever intended to cause me pain.'

He said nothing. The silence hung like a cloud between them because there really was no answer to her last bitter claim. So on a heavy sigh he changed tack, by ridding himself of his can and coming to pull out the chair beside her. Swinging it around, he then straddled it and sat down while she watched all of this with a distinctly wary look in her eye.

That was okay, he told himself. He could deal with wary better than he could deal with bitterness and pain. So he folded his arms along the chair back, placed his chin on the top of them, and, with her gaze held captive by her own wariness of what was coming, he repeated gently:

'Marry me,' and he smiled…

The smile hit dead centre, the proposal sent her head dizzy. And his wretched eyes were warming her right through! It was like being in the company of the world's most accomplished beguiler! It just wasn't fair—none of it! Did he honestly think she didn't know what he was trying to do?

'Listen to me,' she said, having to push the words up through a thickened throat because, really, she had no defence worth mentioning against this man, and she was beginning to weaken, she could feel it happening. 'Let's get a few things straight before this gets entirely out of hand,' she suggested. 'In the unlikely event that I am pregnant, I do not expect or even want an offer of marriage from you. It is neither necessary nor expected in this day and age. And I've been there,' she reminded him. 'I know what it's like to be a child of a single parent. There's no stigma in that label any more. If or when I need to do so, I will cope as my mother coped. I don't even mind!' she added in the hope that it would be of some help to him. 'So don't cut yourself up thinking you have to offer marriage to Edward's bastard daughter because you made a few mistakes about her. Especially when we both know we were never so much as heading in that direction before tonight's—mess came to light. What we had here was never very real, but just a window in time we both used to enjoy each other. But tomorrow or next week or—whenever, you can go back to Milan or Sicily or—wherever, and that window will close, as it should do. So don't try to keep it open out of some misguided sense of honour you feel you need to redress,' she begged. 'Nothing in this life is absolutely certain. We all make mistakes, change, move on. Let's not further clutter up the baggage we take with us, with a set of marriage vows neither of us wanted to make in the first place!'

To give him his due, he listened. He listened without comment and without expression as she rambled through her wise little speech. His forearms remained folded across the chair back, his eyes didn't move from her beautiful face. When she finally fell into an empty little silence, he simply allowed a small pause to hover after it, then repeated quietly:

'Marry me…'

Natalia erupted out of nowhere. 'Oh, stop it!' she cried, wondering just what it took to get through to this man! 'Why are you doing this? You know it isn't what you really want!'

'You don't *know* what I want,' he shot right back. 'Try asking me instead of telling me!'

'No,' she refused, because she felt she had already covered it as far as she was concerned.

She went to get up. His hand closing around her wrist stopped her. Electricity sizzled along her veins and she felt a wild rush of sheer excitement. Angrily she pulled free.

She had to get out of here, she decided urgently, before he really started getting to her! And she jumped to her feet, then immediately wished she hadn't done that when old dizziness dropped over her.

Seeing it happen, Giancarlo uttered a choice curse as he leapt up himself, then was impatiently kicking his chair aside so he could pull her against him. 'Don't go faint on me again,' he commanded harshly. 'This is no time for passing out. We need to deal with this!'

'I thought I was dealing with it!' she snapped, feeling so light-headed that she had to lean against him.

'No, you were talking utter rubbish,' he arrogantly opined. 'I just let you get it off your chest because you seemed to need to.'

Well, thanks, she thought grimly. 'Let me go, please.'

Instead he bent to hook his arm beneath her knees and the next thing she knew she was being cradled against his chest and he was striding out of the kitchen and down the hallway to the only room she expected him to take her to.

The bedroom. The bed, where he settled her down on the top of the covers then came to lie beside her. 'Sex isn't the way to solve this particular problem,' she drawled in acid derision.

'Sex isn't what I'm after,' he said, coming up on one elbow so he could look directly into her angry blue eyes. 'I simply wanted you safely horizontal just in case you decided to do something else stupid.'

I'm stupid. I talk rubbish, Natalia grimly listed. I can't be relied upon to take care of my own safety. And, he no longer wants sex from me.

'Now,' he said firmly. 'Ask me.'

'Ask you what?' she flashed, wishing she didn't just love having him this close to her.

'What I want from this relationship,' he provided, bringing the whole darn thing back to the last place she wanted it.

Oh, play the game and get it over with! she told herself frantically because he was too close and she was beginning to feel... 'What is it you want from this relationship, Giancarlo?' she enquired very wearily.

His eyes went black. It was like looking into some terrible place where her fate lay waiting. 'You,' he murmured huskily. 'I want you. I adore you. You are my life. So— will you marry me?'

'You're crazy,' she breathed, closing her eyes on a sigh of burning frustration. 'You just don't listen.' The eyes flew back open. 'You didn't even know who I really was until a couple of hours ago! So how can you know you want to marry this person?'

'Because she is the mother of my child,' he answered smoothly.

'I might not be pregnant!' she reminded him. 'Aren't you jumping the gun a bit?'

'That is not the point.' He smiled that electrifying smile again. 'In believing you could be pregnant, I discovered how much I loved the idea. So the rest does not really matter. You are the woman I want as the mother of my children. So—will you marry me?'

It was easier to close her eyes again and pretend he just wasn't there, she decided. A stupid idea when the man was lying right here beside her on a bed they had been sharing for weeks now, she mocked her own idiocy.

And to further mock the whole thing, his hand came up to brush a feather-light finger across the arch of her eyelashes where they lay flickering against her cheeks. 'I will cherish and adore you all of your life,' he promised huskily.

'Last week you were still plotting my ruin,' she replied.

He touched his lips to her stubborn mouth. 'I loved you even when I was plotting your ruin. Does that not count for anything?' he asked, moving on to nibble at one of her earlobes.

She had to move her shoulder in an effort to dislodge him—or start quivering. 'Is this the Sicilian way of being diplomatic?' she asked. 'If so, I have to tell you it doesn't work very well.'

He just laughed softly in his throat, which brought on the quiver anyway. 'I loved you even when I knew you were lying through your lovely white teeth to me,' he pointed out. 'Like the cool-headed denial you gave about not knowing the combination to Edward's safe, for instance…'

Her eyes flicked open. 'How do you know that I knew it?' she demanded.

His eyes were taunting, like his voice when he said, 'Because I listened in to the message Edward had left you on your voice-mail.'

'Is that why you asked me for the combination?' she gasped. 'Just to see what I would say?'

He nodded. 'It is also the reason why you have been working from here ever since,' he added. 'When you wouldn't give up the combination I decided I had to get you away from the safe. So I set up this place.' He glanced around them. 'So quickly you won't believe how much trouble I took.'

'But why?' she cried. 'Why should my father's private papers be so important to you?'

'Ah,' he drawled. 'But you are thinking like a daughter instead of a mistress,' he pointed out. 'I saw whatever was in that safe as your—payment let's say, for services rendered. And I enjoyed very much making sure you couldn't get your sticky hands on that payment.'

'Money, you mean,' she realised angrily. 'How cynical a mind do you actually have, Giancarlo?'

'Worse than you think,' he freely admitted. 'I had the safe opened by a locksmith the day after you came here to work. I found nothing inside it but Edward's private stock portfolio. And since I put that together for him, I presumed that whatever it was he didn't want me to see had already been taken—by his lovely accomplice—along with a genuine Fabergé watch, for instance.'

'You believed I'd actually stolen my great-grandmother's watch?' Natalia just stared at him, stunned by the depths his mind had her wallowing! 'Edward kept details of my birth in there,' she explained because she could see no reason not to now. 'I managed to get them out before you arrived in the next morning.' She now felt rather pleased with herself for doing that. 'Though I did so because Edward was so sure you had the safe combination somewhere—not because I expected you to resort to using a locksmith to get into it!'

'Machiavellian, that's me.' He smiled. 'You know I had mislaid the piece of paper he had written the combination on, so I had to resort to other methods.'

'Nothing is too low for you, is it?' she breathed.

'Will you still marry me knowing that?'

'I never said I was ever going to marry you,' she pointed out.

His answer was to swoop on her mouth. It just wasn't fair, Natalia complained helplessly. He was applying unfair tactics and she couldn't resist him and the fact that he knew that only made it all the more unfair!

'You said no sex,' she mumbled against his mouth.

'This is not sex,' he denied, moving his lips to her cheek then back to let them hover a hair's breadth away from hers again. 'It is showing my adoration for the woman who belongs to me.'

And to give his claim substance he began gently rotating the hand he had lying against her abdomen. Silk began to move sensually against her skin, the heat from his hand making it all the more pleasurable. She liked it, and didn't want to like it. And worst of all, his eyes were so dark and warm and incredibly tender that she felt herself starting to sink into them.

'Marry me,' he urged with husky softness. 'Let me be your husband, your lover and your devoted soul mate.'

'You're just hedging your bets in case I am pregnant,' she derided, but she made sure her lips made fleeting contact with his as she spoke. 'Come tomorrow when you find I am not, you'll be straining at the leash to escape.'

'Our child is growing in here,' he murmured softly. 'Just think of it. Or think of all the passionate nights we will have trying to put the seed there if it has not made it already.' And to punctuate his point his hand began to slowly ruche up her dress. She gasped in response; he rewarded the revealing little sound with another kiss.

'So, marry me,' he repeated.

'I can't marry you,' she breathed. 'I know you're only offering it because you feel some misguided need to redress an error.'

'Or because you don't love me…?' he softly suggested.

'Oh,' she choked, and brought up her fingers to place them against his mouth. 'Stop it,' she pleaded.

His eyes went so black she thought she could see right inside him, down as far as his pulsing heart. And he kissed the fingers, then reached up to remove them. 'Marry me,' he repeated.

Could she do it? she asked her weaker side. Could she dare to marry this man who had used her so appallingly…?

She was wavering; Giancarlo could feel her need to give in to him throbbing beneath his caressing hand.

'Marry me,' he said again, and felt that throbbing beat of desire pulse through him like an extra heartbeat.

She was his, he could feel it. The warmth of her lips told him, the tremor of her body. All she needed to do was whisper *yes* and the rest would take care of itself for now. 'What can be so wrong in marrying this man who wants you so badly, hmm? Marry me, *amore*,' he urged yet again, 'and I will promise to love you for ever.'

Love, the keyword, he noted as her blue eyes turned warm and dark and sultry. 'Yes,' she whispered.

Triumph filled his head, followed almost immediately by a different sensation entirely that lost them both the will to think at all for the next few exquisite minutes while he paid homage to that tiny 'yes'.

Then the telephone began to ring, bringing them both screeching back to reality with a jolt. He lifted his head, frowning in irritation because it was gone three in the morning and who the hell rang anyone at—?

'Edward,' Natalia said jerkily, and was trying to stretch over him to pick up the phone even as he snatched it up.

His arm wrapped around her, keeping her close. 'Yes?' he prompted, Natalia's fear becoming his fear when he heard his sister's voice coming back at him.

'Edward will not settle down and rest because he's worrying about his daughter,' Alegra snapped at him with failing patience with the man she loved. 'If Natalia is with you will you please put her on this telephone so she can reassure her father that you are not seducing her—again!'

'But I am seducing her,' Giancarlo drawled lazily, settling back onto the pillows and taking Natalia with him. 'You interrupted us, in fact,' he added, then coolly held the receiver to Natalia's ear so she could receive the full blast of his sister's anger instead of him.

From being white-faced with fear she was suddenly blushing. He began to grin, all wicked white teeth and Italian devilry. 'He—he isn't bullying me,' she replied to whatever Alegra had said. 'We were—talking,' she tagged on not very convincingly. Then— 'Edward!' she sighed out. 'Will you listen to me?'

Edward? The grin altered to a frown and he snatched the phone back from her ear. 'Edward,' he said, cutting the older man off mid angry flood. 'I would formally like to ask for the hand of your daughter in marriage.'

'No!' Natalia choked. 'Don't tell him that!'

'Yes, of course she has accepted me. Do you honestly think I am going to allow her to look elsewhere now?'

At which point Natalia sank back against the pillow and closed her eyes in an act of surrender. Seeing it happen, Giancarlo smiled to himself, and settled back to convince his angry brother-in-law that the woman in his arms was going to be so cherished that her papa had no need at all to worry.

'Okay?' he questioned when eventually he was allowed to replace the receiver.

'No,' Natalia replied. 'I feel like a hostile takeover. No trick too mean, no bribe too low. He did give you his blessing, I am presuming?'

'With the promise that he will be well enough to give you away at our wedding next week.'

'Next week,' she repeated as his arms looped round her and he pulled her into the crook of his body.

'You smell of woman,' he growled, nuzzling her earlobe.

'You said no sex.'

'I changed my mind.'

'What if I decide to change my mind about marrying you?'

'Too late,' he murmured, moving on to nibble at the corner of her mouth. 'We are officially betrothed in the eyes of my family. Pull out now and they will feel honour bound to avenge my broken heart.'

'You Sicilians have life all neatly packaged whichever way you want to look at it, don't you?'

'It is in the genes,' he explained, while stringing soft, light kisses across her full bottom lip now. 'We are very serious about family honour.'

Serious about other things, too, she thought as her body arched in response to what his hands were doing to her. 'And if I am *not* pregnant?' she asked on a last-gasp attempt to make sure everything was clear between them on this point.

'I will *make* you pregnant,' he declared, then set about showing her exactly how he intended to go about it...

The next morning she was sitting at the kitchen table drinking juice when he wandered in from the office. 'Well?' he said.

'No,' Natalia quietly replied. 'The test was negative.'

Giancarlo went still for a moment to take this in, while she sat there staring fixedly at her drink and hoping to goodness that he wouldn't see how frightened she was that this negative response was going to change everything.

Then a pair of hands came around her waist. Warm hands, strong hands, exquisitely familiar hands that firmly propelled her out of her chair, then guided her into the circle of his arms.

'Will you marry me, Natalia?' he softly proposed to her.

She looked up warily, wondering if this was some kind

of joke. 'You've asked me that question a million times already,' she mocked him.

'And you said yes, once, under duress. So now I ask it again. Will you marry me because you want to do so more than anything else? Will you marry me because I want you to do so more than anything else? And will you marry me because I love you more than anyone else?'

Her heart began to swell. Tears flooded her eyes. 'Yes,' she whispered. 'Because I love you more than anything else.'

'There.' He smiled. 'Now we both understand each other. It feels good, hmm?'

Oh, yes, she thought as she folded her arms tightly around him. It feels very good...

EPILOGUE

STANDING here on what felt like the edge of the world, Natalia gazed out on the silver-tipped navy-blue waters of a moon-kissed ocean, and wondered if a single day could ever be more perfect than this one had been.

Down there just beneath her she could see her father and Alegra strolling hand in hand along one of the many pathways that threaded through the terraced garden. Every so often they would stop and their two heads would come together over the tiny bundle Alegra held safely cradled in the crook of her arm.

Our son, Natalia thought tenderly, and felt her heart swell in her breast with the love Alessandro brought into all their lives. His arrival two months ago had been a blessing in so many ways. For her father and Alegra, Alessandro had been the final ingredient they'd needed to help heal old wounds and replace their grief for their lost son with a newfound joy who apparently looked so much like their beloved Marco.

If you didn't count the eyes, Natalia thought smilingly. For Alessandro's eyes were most definitely like her own eyes—as Giancarlo never ceased to complain. 'How am I supposed to be the strong father when he only has to look at me and I melt?' he liked to say to defend what a soft touch he was where his son was concerned.

He too had undergone a dramatic healing, she acknowledged, thinking back to the day she had tentatively suggested to him that his son should be christened in Sicily. She'd expected a knock-back—had even been prepared for

185

it with all her reasons at the ready to fiercely argue the point with him. But after only a few short moments of sober contemplation, Giancarlo had lifted his dark head to look at her, and it had all been there. The need, the hunger to see his homeland again, the readiness to heal that final part of him by taking happiness back to the place where only pain and grief had been left behind.

So here they were, all five of them fresh from a beautiful christening service in the same beautiful little church Giancarlo himself had once been christened in, followed up by a celebratory dinner shared in this beautiful place perched high on a Sicilian hillside, which overlooked a small piece of heaven.

She sighed happily.

'What was that for?' a deep voice enquired behind her.

'Come and look,' she urged, and felt a pair of familiar hands slide around her waist as Giancarlo joined her at the open window. As usual her bones melted at his closeness and she sank back against him. His chin came to rest on the top of her head and her hands drifted up to link fingers with his where they lay across her stomach. 'Do you see what I see?' she asked him.

'And what do you see?' he prompted.

'I see a beautiful night in a beautiful place, with two beautiful people and a beautiful child,' she softly confided. 'It was the right thing to do, wasn't it?' she then questioned anxiously. 'You all do feel much better for coming back here?'

His mouth brushed a kiss to the top of her head. 'Marco is no longer a ghost that haunts us, but a loving memory we have learned to cherish,' he quietly confirmed.

'Good,' she said, and sighed again in absolute contentment. 'Then everything is truly perfect.'

'Ah, you were wanting true perfection?' Giancarlo drawled.

His tone alone had her senses quickening, the soft feeling of contentment fleeing in the face of something much more elemental that was suddenly sizzling in the air.

'No, Giancarlo,' she firmly denied it. 'We can't make love now. Alessandro—'

'Is in the safest hands I know besides our own,' he inserted, then was reaching out to pull shut the bedroom window, before turning her to face him.

His eyes were gleaming with sensual promises; her body began to pulse in response. He bent down to kiss her, she sighed and let him because—when had she ever been able to resist this man? His fingers found the zip to her dress, and she quivered as it drifted down her spine.

'You really are incorrigible sometimes,' she informed him ruefully.

'You wanted perfection,' he countered innocently. 'I am the man who is so in love with you that he constantly strives to give you everything your beautiful heart desires.'

'I thought I *had* perfection,' Natalia dryly pointed out.

'No,' he denied. '*This* is perfection, *mia cara...*'

He was right and it was.

Jane Porter grew up on a diet of Mills and Boon® romances, reading late at night under the covers so her mother wouldn't see! She wrote her first book at age eight, and spent many of her high school and college years living abroad, immersing herself in other cultures and continuing to read voraciously. Now Jane has settled down in rugged Seattle, Washington, with her two sons. Jane loves to hear from her readers. You can write to her at PO Box 524, Bellevue, WA 98009, USA. Or visit her website at www.janeporter.com

LAZARO'S REVENGE

by

Jane Porter

PROLOGUE

"I DON'T kidnap women," Lazaro Herrera retorted grimly, his back to the plate-glass window overlooking Buenos Aires's fashionable Avenida Sante Fe boulevard. "I might have a reputation for being ruthless, but that's business, not personal."

"Sometimes I'm not sure if it *isn't* personal," Dante Galván answered, almost as an aside.

Lazaro turned sharply to face the man who headed Galván Enterprises, and the only man Lazaro answered to. Dante might be chief executive officer but as president, Lazaro was the acting manager. "Even I have scruples, and I draw the line at kidnapping."

"You're misinterpreting me. I never said *kidnap*. Zoe is my wife's younger sister. She's just twenty-two. All I want to do is to protect her."

Lazaro's gaze narrowed speculatively. "Protect Daisy, you mean." Dante didn't say anything and Lazaro's mouth twisted grimly. "Neither you nor Daisy like this American, Carter Scott—"

"For good reasons, mind you."

"So what you're really doing is shielding Daisy from unpleasant news."

Dante didn't immediately answer. His mouth pressed tight, his features pinched. Dark purple shadows formed crescents beneath his amber eyes. "Daisy can't lose this baby. She can't handle this right now,

5

can't handle more bad news, and I'll be damned if I let her suffer through another miscarriage.''

Pain throbbed in Dante's voice, pain and anger and helplessness. Lazaro knew about Daisy's two previous miscarriages. The second one occurred last year, and fairly late in the pregnancy. Daisy had been devastated by the loss and Dante had taken six weeks off from work to be with Daisy as she convalesced at the *estancia*. It was then Lazaro had completely taken over management of the corporation.

Unfortunately, Dante didn't know he was playing straight into Lazaro's hands. Dante didn't know that every move he made, every bit of power he relinquished, only strengthened Lazaro's position, and weakened his own.

''I'm lucky to have you,'' Dante said quietly. ''If it weren't for you, we'd all be in trouble.''

Lazaro tensed, his conscience pricked by Dante's earnest gratitude. He hated the tug of contradictory emotions within him and turned to face the window where Buenos Aires's skyline sparkled in the sunshine.

For the first time in a long time, he despised what he'd started here, with the Galváns.

He despised the secrets he kept buried in his heart, despised the thing that drove him to destroy Dante and the Galváns, but it was too late to change the course now.

Yet even as he stood at the window, weighted by memories of a dark past, he felt Dante's worry for Daisy, felt Dante's own burden, and longed to warn

Dante to be careful. *Don't trust me. Don't feel safe with me. Don't let me close to your family.*

But Lazaro didn't speak. He stifled the guilt and sense of obligation, telling himself that Dante's problems weren't his problems. Dante's pain wasn't his pain. Dante's loss wasn't his loss.

Lazaro drew a deep breath, hardened his emotions, and reminded himself that this wasn't a simple feud. It was revenge. More than revenge.

It was about one's soul.

His mother's.

Ice sheeting his heart, Lazaro turned from the city glittering with sunshine to face his secret arch rival. ''What's the plan?''

CHAPTER ONE

"BE quiet, do as you're told, and everything will be fine."

She'd been kidnapped—abducted in the middle of the day from Ezeiza International Airport in Buenos Aires in full view of airport security.

Zoe Collingsworth's stomach plummeted as the helicopter tilted sideways and flew at a peculiar angle to the earth below.

She gripped her boxy seat tighter, fingers clenched so hard that the knuckles ached. He'd told her not to talk and she hadn't, but she was very afraid. This couldn't really be happening…this had to be a bad dream…

"We'll be landing in a few minutes."

She jerked at the sound of his voice. It was the first time he'd spoken in the two hours they'd been aboard the helicopter. She'd never heard a voice pitched so low and it rumbled through her like a slow-moving freight train.

"Where are you taking me?" she whispered, hands trembling.

He briefly glanced her way, his narrowed eyes barely resting on her. "It doesn't matter."

Her mouth went dry, fear sucking heat from her limbs. She touched her seat belt, checking the tension in the belt, as though the small firm strap across her

8

lap could somehow protect her from whatever was to come next.

She wanted to say something fierce and defiant, wanted to be brave because that's how Daisy handled problems. But Zoe wasn't a warrior woman and she felt the worst kind of terror imaginable. She'd never even been out of Kentucky before, and now on her first trip anywhere she was...she was...

Kidnapped.

Her heart thudded so fast and hard she thought it might explode. She stared at her captor. He wasn't looking at her, but staring out the window, his gaze fixed on the darkening landscape below. Twilight swathed all in shadows. "What do you want from me?"

Finally she had his attention. He stared at her in the fading light, long dark lashes concealing his eyes, his expression curiously hard. There was nothing remotely gentle in his grim features. "Let's not do this now."

His English was flawless and yet his tone cut razor-sharp. He'd been schooled in the States, she thought blankly, numb from head to toe. "Are you going to...hurt me?"

She heard the wobble in her voice, the break between words that revealed her fear and exhaustion. He heard it, too, and his firm mouth compressed, flatter, harder. "I don't hurt women."

"But you do kidnap them?" she choked, on the verge of hysteria, her imagination beginning to run away with her. She'd been up twenty-four hours without sleep and she was losing control.

"Only if I'm asked to," he answered as the helicopter dipped. He glanced out the window and nodded with satisfaction. "We're landing. Hold on."

The helicopter touched down. While the pilot worked the controls, her abductor flung the door open and stepped out. "Come," he said, extending a hand to her.

Zoe recoiled from his touch. *"No."*

She couldn't see his face in the darkness but felt his impatience. "It's not a choice, Señorita Collingsworth. *¡Vamanos!"*

Slowly, trembling with fear, she climbed from the helicopter. Her legs were numb and stiff, as if cardboard legs instead of tissue and bone.

The night felt warm, far warmer than she'd expected, and yet she convulsively pressed her thin traveling coat closer to her frame.

Lights shone ahead. Heart pounding, she gazed at the illuminated house and outbuildings. But beyond the immediate circle of light there was only darkness. A world of darkness. Where was she? What did he intend to do?

He moved behind her, reached into the helicopter and lifted out her suitcase and another small traveling bag. His, she thought with a shudder.

Bags out, he shut the helicopter door and immediately the helicopter lifted, rising straight from the ground into the dark starry night.

The whirring blades blew her hair into her eyes and Zoe stumbled backward, trying to escape the noise and rush of air, tripping over the suitcases behind her.

She fell backward. Hands reached out to break her fall.

She felt the hard pressure of his body, felt his hands tighten on her as he placed her on her feet.

Immediately, she pulled away, and yet that split second of contact was more than she could bear. In that split second she'd felt his strength and heat penetrate her coat, penetrate her skin, penetrate all the way into her bones. He was hard and unyielding. Just that brief contact left her burned.

Bruised.

God help me, she silently prayed, *get me home safe.*

Hand shaking, she pushed a fistful of hair from her eyes. Her hair clip had fallen out, and the helicopter blades had blown the long heavy mass free. She felt blown to bits.

Physically. Emotionally.

''This way,'' he said roughly, touching her elbow.

This second touch was worse than the first. Zoe jerked, muscles snapping, spring-loaded. The sudden stiffening of her body hurt.

Every time he touched her she shuddered. Every time he touched her she burned.

The noise of the helicopter began to fade. The warm night air wrapped around her. ''What happens now?'' she asked, drawing herself tall, bringing herself to her full five-ten height. It didn't do much good. He was still far taller, larger. He had to be well over six foot three, maybe six-four. He was built strong, too, thickly muscled like an American football star, but in his black coat, black shirt, black trousers he could have been from the Mafia.

"We go inside. We'll have dinner. You'll go to your room for the night."

He made it sound almost civilized. Which should have reassured her, but she wasn't reassured, not by a long shot. She'd heard that some of the most violent men were also the most sophisticated. He could be toying with her before—

Stop it!

You have to stop thinking like this. You can't let your imagination do this to you. You'll just drive yourself crazy.

There were too many unknowns, too many terrifying possibilities. She had to stay calm, had to keep a cool head, as her father used to say. Her father had been a master of cool heads.

She swallowed the lump of panic filling her throat. "Okay. Dinner sounds good." She'd take this step by step, moment by moment. She'd get through this. One way or another.

He picked up her suitcase and his bag and headed toward the house, leaving her to follow. But she couldn't follow, not immediately. How could she just go in there, how could she walk into that house on her own accord?

Zoe stood where he'd left her, turned to face the cement pad, felt the night air surround her. The land was flat and open, with only a cluster of trees in the distance. Nothing loomed on the horizon. No mountains. No lights from a town. Just flat, empty space.

The pampas, she whispered to herself, remembering the postcards Daisy had sent her.

The Galván *estancia* was on the pampas, too. Perhaps she was close to Daisy, closer than either of them knew.

She turned back to face the house with the glow of yellow light. What to do now?

He was waiting for her at the door. She started toward him then stopped. She could feel his impatience and it frightened her. What would happen once she entered the house?

He waited another moment before shrugging and disappearing from view. After a long moment Zoe forced herself to continue.

Climbing the front steps, she arrived at the front door. The dark wood door remained open. The man reappeared.

He'd removed his coat and unbuttoned his dark shirt. A muscle in his jaw jumped as her eyes met his. His eyes were lighter than she'd thought, his eyebrows straight and very black, but it was his nose that dominated his face. His nose was bent, beaked in two places. There was a small scar at the bridge, and another scar at the edge of his square chin. His face looked as though it'd been smashed silly a half dozen times.

A street boxer. A thug.

Zoe's throat constricted. She swallowed hard, terror making her limbs feel like thin splinters of glass.

"You're coming in then?" he said.

Her throat worked and she dug her fists against her ribs to stop her shaking. It nearly killed her to force sound through her throat. "You don't care if I stay outside?"

"You can do whatever you want now that you're here."

"I can?"

"There's no phone line here, no outside communication at all. No visitors, no roads, no disturbances, no interruptions. You're safe."

Hot tears pricked her eyes and she ground her teeth together. "I'm *safe?*"

He reached out to touch the side of her neck, just below her jawbone, his fingers trailing across the soft skin left exposed by her turtleneck. "Perfectly safe."

She quivered and jerked at the hot painful touch. "Is there no one else here?"

"Just an elderly servant, but she doesn't speak English and won't bother you."

He lifted his finger from her neck and she felt as though he'd split her in two. The touch had been light and yet he'd lit a bomb inside her skin, heat exploding in her middle, fire racing through her veins. It was the most shocking touch and she wanted to cry out loud, overwhelmed by the intensity of her response.

"Come inside. You're tired."

"I'm afraid."

His dark head tilted. "Of?"

His deep voice was pitched so low that it throbbed within her, a soft but distinct vibration that left her humming. She hated him, feared him, and yet he was strangely charismatic, too. *Of everything that could happen,* she wanted to answer, but she didn't say it. Wouldn't say it.

He must have read her thoughts because he smiled

faintly. "Think of it as an adventure." Then he moved aside, stepping back to allow her to pass.

An adventure? He must be mad.

Yet his peculiar dark-light eyes held hers, and he waited, neither speaking nor rushing her. He was going to let her choose. He was going to put the next move on her.

What should she do? Stay outside in the darkness, on the endless pampas, or go into the warm yellow glow of the house?

With her heart thudding, she stepped inside.

Lazaro spotted Zoe Collingsworth the moment she stepped from the jet-way at the airport earlier in the afternoon. Young, blond, beautiful, she was the epitome of Argentine beauty. His narrowed gaze had followed her movements as she rummaged in her leather handbag for dark sunglasses.

Her hand had shook as she'd propped the tortoiseshell glasses on her small, straight nose. She could have been a Hollywood starlet. Her sweater's high funnel neck stopped just short of her chin, accenting her smooth, creamy jaw and the long tumble of golden hair.

Lazaro could see that the men in the airport waiting area were already projecting their fantasies onto her. They saw what they wanted to see, the full breasts beneath the thin black sweater and the very feminine hips in wool trousers the color of rich caramel. They were admiring her hair, too, wondering if the glorious color was natural.

It was natural. Her hair was like her sister Daisy's,

only more golden. In fact, the two of them looked remarkably similar.

Only two years after marrying Count Dante Galván, Daisy was already considered a great beauty in Argentina's elite social circles, but Zoe had a different beauty than Daisy's...a softer beauty.

Lazaro shut the door to the ranch house but didn't bother locking it. No point in locks. There was nowhere for Zoe to go.

He watched her now as she took a step into the hall, her blue eyes wide, and apprehensive, the irises more lavender than sapphire. She scanned the interior, as if searching for a hidden door or a secret torture chamber.

"There's nothing sinister here," he said calmly. "No knives, guns, whips, chains. Just a simple ranch house."

Her chin lifted, her full lips trembled, but she pressed them together. "Have you sent a ransom note already?"

"No."

She blinked, long black lashes sweeping down, brushing the high elegant curve of her cheekbone before looking up again. She was so young. Nearly twelve years younger than he. A lifetime between them.

The age difference should have killed his attraction. It didn't.

Ever since she'd stepped from the jet-way this afternoon, his gut had ached, his body throbbing. His response to her stunned him. It was such a primitive reaction, so fiercely and purely physical that he felt raw on the inside. Barely controlled.

The desire was there even now and his body tightened yet again, his black wool slacks growing snug, confining.

He felt hungry. Like a prehistoric creature brought back from the dead. Something about her made him crave her, made him feel ravenous. Ruthless.

He wanted to feel her, taste her, possess her. And in a distant part of his brain he knew he would. Someday.

When he'd crushed the Galváns.

When he'd had his revenge.

But this wasn't the time. Right now she was exhausted and afraid, and she was a guest in his house.

"Let me take your coat," he said, softening the edge to his voice, knowing he had a hard voice, and a brusque manner. He wasn't known for his sensitivity, or civility.

He extended a hand for her coat but she took a frightened step back.

Zoe nearly screamed when his hand reached out. She couldn't let him touch her again. She couldn't let him anywhere near her, feeling trapped, helpless, far too vulnerable. Again she was reminded of his height, his size. There was something about him that exuded strength, not just in terms of muscle, but control…power.

She pressed her thin coat more tightly to her body. "I'd like to keep my coat."

His heavy eyebrows lifted. "You'll get it back."

He was making fun of her. Heat banded across her cheekbones and she lifted her chin. "I'm cold."

"Come closer to the fire then. It should warm you."

He led her from the wide high-ceiling hall into a surprisingly spacious sitting room, the dark-beamed ceiling as rustic as the floor-to-ceiling stone fireplace. Yet the furnishings were luxurious, from the vibrant scarlet and gold rug covering the wood-planked floor to the deep plush sofas and chairs clustered in small groupings. The artwork on the walls were all massive canvases, oversize oil paintings in vivid brush-strokes—electric blue, blood red, hot yellow.

This was no simple ranch house.

Zoe moved past the wrought-iron and leather coffee table with its stacks of books toward the fire. Her legs felt brittle, her muscles taut.

With a fleeting glance at the bookcases behind her, she reached out to the stone hearth, trembling fingers spread wide to capture the fire's heat.

Kidnapped, she repeated silently, she'd been kidnapped. It still hadn't completely sunk in. Would it ever?

She remembered disembarking the plane, remembered filing out of the jet-way with the other passengers and entering the gate area to discover a waiting throng.

She remembered scanning the crowd, looking for Dante, or a driver. Dante had promised someone would be there to meet her. But she didn't see Dante, or anyone holding a sign. There were mothers and young children, businessmen in suits on cell phones, elderly seniors in wheelchairs but no one for her.

Her eyes had suddenly watered as she felt a pang of loss. Normally something like this wouldn't upset her, but it hadn't been a normal month. Her father was getting so much worse. He seemed to have forgotten everything now and it was awful watching him fade before her eyes. He'd been a smart man, and a loving man, always generous with others.

Her eyes continued to well with tears and she dug in her shoulder bag for her sunglasses. She'd cried most of the flight, and the oversize black sunglasses had come in handy then, too. The truth was, she'd cried so much in the last month she should be out of tears, but somehow the tears just kept coming.

Sunglasses in place she felt better. She took a deep breath and tried to focus on the positives. She was here to see Daisy. Soon she'd be reunited with her sister. Things would be better once they were together.

It was at that very moment when he approached her, the man in the black coat and shirt, the unsmiling man with a piercing gaze and a strong beaked nose.

"Miss Collingsworth?" he'd said, his voice impossibly deep, so deep she'd blinked behind her sunglasses as she let his voice sink into her, tangible and real.

Zoe recalled that her travel guide said Argentine men—a blend of Latin passion and European sophistication—were lethally attractive and while she wouldn't call this man classically handsome, he was arresting…no, intriguing, in a primitive sort of way.

"I'm Zoe," she'd answered, her heart doing a strange double beat. She'd been up all night and was overly tired. She'd never traveled out of Kentucky before and had felt ambivalent emotions about the trip to Argentina. She wanted to see Daisy, yet she hated putting her father in a nursing home. True, he wouldn't stay there long, just the two weeks she was in Argentina, but it had been awful driving him there, awful leaving him there.

"Do you have any bags?" the man asked.

"Just one," she answered. "It's a large case so I checked it through."

His dark head inclined, his glossy blue-black hair cut short. "If you give me your tag, I'll get it for you."

His hand stretched toward her, his palm wide, fingers long, well-shaped. He fit his skin somehow. He looked comfortable with himself and she'd given him the tag. They went to baggage claim and he lifted the heavy case off the carousel as though it weighed nothing. A limousine was waiting for them outside baggage claim and they drove straight to the helicopter pad.

It wasn't until they were in midair and she'd begun to ask questions about Daisy and her pregnancy, about the Galván *estancia,* about life on the pampas that he'd told her to stop talking.

Actually, what he'd said was, *Be quiet, do as you're told, and everything will be fine.*

Zoe drew a deep breath and stared at the fire with its red and gold dancing flames.

She was shaking again, more violently now than

earlier, and with each uneven breath she could smell the acrid scent of burning wood and smoke, yet the heat wasn't enough. She couldn't stop shivering. Couldn't control her nerves.

She heard him walk behind her, heard the clink of glass, the slosh of liquid, another clink. He was pouring himself a drink. What kind of kidnapper embraced leather books, modern art and brandy decanters? *What kind of man was he?*

Zoe battled her fear. There had to be a good explanation. People didn't just abduct other people without having a purpose, a plan.

"Drink this."

His cool hard voice sliced into her thoughts, drawing her gaze up, from the fire to his chiseled features, his expression inexplicably grim. "I don't drink."

"It'll warm you."

She glanced at the balloon-shaped brandy glass in his hand, quarter filled with amber liquid, and shrank from him. "I don't like the taste."

"I didn't use to like it much when I was your age, either." He continued to hold the glass out to her. "You're shivering. It'll help. Trust me."

Trust him? He was the last man she'd ever trust. He'd taken her from Daisy, Dante, from the reunion she'd long anticipated. Her throat threatened to seal closed, her temper rising as her anger got the best of her.

She turned on him, arms bundled across her chest. "Who are you, anyway? I don't even know your name."

"Lazaro Herrera."

The name rolled off his tongue, fluid, complex, sensual. The r's trilled, the z was accented, the vowels so rich and smoky they could have been aged whiskey.

Lazaro Herrera.

It was a name that fit him, a name that echoed of strength and muscle and power. "I think I'll take that drink," she whispered.

His fingers brushed hers as he handed her the glass. "Sip it. Slowly."

His skin was warm yet his touch scalded her. She nearly dropped the glass. "Why are you doing this?"

He shrugged, a vague shift of his massive shoulders. "I have reasons."

"But what did I do? You don't even know me."

"This isn't about you."

"Then what is it about?" Her voice had risen.

"Revenge."

CHAPTER TWO

SHE stared at him aghast, the only sound in the house the crackle and pop of the fire.

Zoe shook so badly that brandy came sloshing up and over the rim of her glass. Her mouth felt parched. It tasted ridiculously like cotton. She swallowed roughly, trying to think of something—anything—to say.

Revenge. Revenge against...*whom?*

But she couldn't ask because she knew she wasn't prepared for the truth, wasn't prepared to hear the words he'd say. She knew somehow that his answer would impact Daisy, it had to impact Daisy because Daisy had married here, into the Argentine aristocracy and Daisy had become part of this world, this culture, this other life.

Sick at heart, Zoe lifted the balloon-shaped glass to her lips and took a small sip. The brandy felt cool in her mouth then turned hot as she swallowed. The warmth hit her stomach and finally seeped into her limbs.

Lazaro Herrera was right about one thing. The liquor did help. It bolstered her courage. She wrapped her hands around the glass. ''Does this have to do with the Galváns?''

''You're very perceptive.''

''You want money?''

23

"Doesn't everyone?"

But his answer didn't ring true, nor did his sarcasm. There was something else driving him and she needed to understand, needed to know so she could protect Daisy. "Does Dante know about this yet?"

"He should."

She stared down into her brandy, trying to calm herself. She couldn't help Daisy if she lost her head. "My sister, Dante's wife, is pregnant."

"I know."

"Please don't hurt Daisy." Her voice had thickened. The words came out hoarse. She felt the back of her eyes sting, gritty tears welling. "She's had several miscarriages and it's been devastating for her. She can't lose this baby."

He stared at her, his silver-gray eyes shuttered. "I have no desire to hurt her."

"But you will." Zoe didn't know how she knew, but she knew and it made her furious. Lazaro Herrera would destroy her family and never look back.

"Things happen in life—"

"No," she burst out, gripping the glass tightly. "You're doing this, you're creating this."

"It's complicated, *corazón*. Life has never been easy."

He was sidestepping the issue, turning the argument around, and it infuriated her. She took a step toward him, her slim body rigid with tension. Her family had been through so much in the past couple of years. They'd struggled and suffered and finally, just when Daisy found some happiness, this man threatened to take it away.

''Of course life is difficult. It's full of pain and sorrow and loss, but it's also full of joy and love—'' she broke off, realizing she was dangerously close to tears, and swallowed hard. ''Don't hurt my sister. You can't. I won't let you.''

He wouldn't acknowledge what she'd said. He ignored her fury. ''You're still shivering. You need a hot bath.''

''I don't want a hot bath. I don't want anything from you. Not now, not ever.''

His gaze swept her face. Her face felt hot in places. She knew her cheeks were flushed and her eyes glowed overbright.

''It doesn't exactly work that way,'' he said at last. ''You are my guest here. This is my house. We will be together virtually night and day the next several weeks. I suggest you get used to my company. Quickly.''

He walked out.

Zoe stood there for several moments before her muscles twitched to life. Slowly she placed the half-full brandy glass on the coffee table before wiping her damp palms on the sides of her pale traveling coat.

She remembered when she boarded the flight yesterday evening how chic she'd thought she'd looked in the long thin cream coat and cream-colored cowboy boots. She and Daisy had grown up in boots. Just like they'd grown up in the saddle, working the farm. She might look fragile, but there was nothing fragile about her.

Just her feelings, maybe.

Zoe pushed up her coat sleeve and looked at her wristwatch. Almost seven-thirty. She'd arrived in Buenos Aires over six hours ago. Daisy must be frantic.

Forehead furrowing, Zoe looked about for a phone. He'd said there was no phone but she didn't believe him. Everyone had phones these days. She'd look for a phone jack first. The phone jack would be a dead giveaway that he'd merely unplugged the phone and hidden it away. She'd find the phone and call for help first chance possible.

"Your bath is ready."

Lazaro had returned and he stood in the doorway. He'd changed into dark slacks and a thick dark sweater. The dense weave of the sweater flattered his hard features, softening his long crooked nose and square chin.

He almost looked human.

Almost.

"I'm not going to take a bath. I'm not going to stay here." She left the fire, walked swiftly from the living room to the hall, holding her breath as she moved past him.

She half expected him to stop her as she reached for the door but he didn't move. He didn't even bat an eyelash as she yanked the heavy door open.

"It's a long walk to town," he said mildly. "And very dark. There aren't any streetlights on the pampas."

She gripped the doorknob, hating him, hating his reasonable tone. "I've been in the country before."

"Then you know how confusing it gets to walk

without landmarks, without roads, without any sign of human life.''

''Your ranch can't be that remote.''

His eyebrows merely lifted.

''I'm sure there's *something* out there,'' she insisted.

''Sheep. Cows. Deer—''

''Not very frightening.''

''Jaguars, pumas, cougars.''

Zoe swallowed hard. ''You're lying.''

''I wouldn't lie to you.''

''All you've done is lie to me,'' she flung back at him, turning to face him, hand still tight on the iron doorknob.

''I haven't lied to you yet—''

''At the airport you asked me if I was Zoe Collingsworth—''

''And you said yes.'' A humongous brown moth flit from the front porch light into the hall. Lazaro moved toward Zoe and gently but firmly closed the door. ''I asked you for your baggage tag and you gave it to me. You came with me, Zoe. Happily. Willingly. Immediately.''

Tears of shock and shame filled her eyes. ''You let me think you worked for Dante!''

''And I do.''

Zoe fell back, leaned against the closed door. She pressed her palms to the surface. ''You *what?*''

''I work for your brother-in-law. I work for Dante Galván.''

She couldn't have heard him right. Something had

to be wrong with her head or her ears. "What can you possibly do for him?"

"Everything."

Lazaro's lips had twisted and his cynical smile filled her with fresh horror. She closed her eyes and pressed a fist between her eyebrows, pressing at the throbbing in her head. This was crazy. Worse than crazy. "Please explain what you mean by *everything,*" she choked, unable to look at him. "Are you some kind of Boy Friday?"

"Hardly. I'm the president of Galván Enterprises."

Her head jerked up, eyes opening. "But Dante's the president."

"Dante is the chief executive officer. I run day-to-day operations."

"Since when?"

"Since two years ago."

"But—"

"Enough. I don't want to discuss this anymore, not with you swaying on your feet. You're tired, you need to bathe, eat, relax. Believe me, we'll have plenty of time to talk later."

He turned away but she didn't follow. "How much time?" she called after him.

He stopped walking, slowly faced her. "What?"

"You said we'd have plenty of time to talk later. I want to know how much time it is. How long do you intend to keep me here?"

"Depends. It could be a week, could be two, but if I were you, I'd plan on two."

She opened her mouth to protest but he'd already

turned the corner and disappeared down another hallway into a different part of the house.

Zoe followed much more slowly, passing through
a darkened bedroom into a large luxurious bathroom.
It was the most sumptuous bath she'd ever seen. The
floor, walls, bath—even the shower stall itself—were
covered in a gorgeous red marble. The sink and bath-
tub were made of gold, the tub was oversize, at least
big enough for two people, and already filled with
water.

Lazaro left her to undress, but Zoe couldn't.

She sank to the edge of the tub, sat on the wide
surround and stared at the steamy water. Pools of
scented oil floated on the water surface. He'd put
something in there, something that smelled rich, comforting.

She couldn't reconcile anything he'd told her.

Minutes passed and still she didn't move, couldn't
move.

A knock sounded on the outside of the bathroom
door. She didn't answer and the knob turned, the door
slowly opened.

"Are you all right?" Lazaro's voice came from the
shadows outside the door.

What a question! Was she all right?

No, she wasn't all right, she was anything but all
right. Her father was dying. Her sister was on bedrest
with a difficult pregnancy. She'd been proposed to by
an old family friend who was more old than friend.
All right? No, Zoe concluded silently, savagely, she
was most definitely *not* all right.

Lazaro stepped inside the bath and looked at her.

She hadn't moved, he saw, and he gave his head a small imperceptible shake. He felt sympathy for her and it was the last emotion he wanted to feel.

Moving toward her, he crouched down in front of her. "You're getting yourself all worked up. Nothing bad is going to happen to you. Nothing bad will happen to Daisy, either. I promise."

Her mouth quivered. Her eyes searched his, her lashes damp, matted. "How can I trust you?"

"I don't know." He fought the urge to touch her, fought the desire to reach out and cup her cheek. Her skin looked so soft, so tender. Like her heart, he thought, she was soft. She shouldn't have ever been exposed to a man like him.

This was Dante's doing.

In Dante's determination to protect Daisy, he'd exposed Zoe, rendered her vulnerable.

Lazaro felt a tightness in his chest, anger and revulsion. He'd felt this same anger and revulsion nearly all his life. The dirty, barefoot street kid outside the store window looking in. To want something and be denied, not just once, but your entire life…

He, the outcast, the untouchable, had climbed the social ladder but he hadn't forgotten and he hadn't forgiven. If anything, the rage burned hotter, brighter, and he was more determined than ever to take what was rightfully his. To seize life—opportunity—and shake it by the throat.

Yet looking at young Zoe Collingsworth he realized all over again how ruthless he'd become, how hard and cruel.

He saw her hands balled in her lap. She was pressing her nails into her palms, the bare nails digging deep, breaking the skin.

"Give me your hand," he said quietly.

She shook her head.

"Give me your hand," he repeated.

He could see the fear in her eyes, as well as the uncertainty. She didn't know what to expect, didn't know what he wanted with her. Truthfully, he wasn't entirely sure, either. Sex, maybe. But there was something else, something he couldn't define but powerful, intoxicating. He was drawn to her. Which would only worsen Dante's situation.

He waited for her hand and slowly she slipped her palm onto his. His fingers wrapped around hers, his hand holding hers firmly, securely.

"You are safe with me, Zoe. My fight is not with you. Trust me on this."

Every time he touched her, it happened, she thought wildly. Heat, energy, pleasure. His touch was unlike any touch she'd ever known. There was something in his skin, something warmer, stronger, more real.

Zoe stared at his hand, felt the heat and the ripple of delicious sensation surge through her, hand to heart, heart to belly, belly to legs.

Her heart slowed, her body felt liquid, bones melting, even as her senses became quivery and alert.

"Daisy's everything to me," she said, mesmerized by the back of his hand, with the burnished-gold skin and the wide strong bones of his wrist. "She practically raised me. She gave up college for me—"

Suddenly he leaned forward, his dark head blocking light and she knew he was going to kiss her. It was as though she'd known from the very first moment she'd met him that this would happen, that this kiss was destined to happen.

His mouth brushed hers. It was a fleeting kiss, a kiss so light her heart ached and tears pricked the backs of her eyes all over again. She could feel his breath against her cheek, smell the sweetness and subtle spice of his cologne. He was big and strong and dark, and yet he smelled of light, sunshine, like meadow grass and flowers after an early summer rain.

His lips barely grazed hers a second time. His mouth slid over her lips to the corner of her mouth. "I will try my best to protect your sister from this, too."

It wasn't the same promise he'd made her. She was afraid to ask, but she had to. "What about Dante?"

Lazaro stiffened. "What about Dante?"

His voice had hardened, the tone turning cold. He didn't like Dante. "This is about Dante."

"Yes."

This was about Dante.

Zoe rushed from beneath his arm, fled to the far side of the red marble bathroom.

This was about Dante. He'd kidnapped her to hurt Dante. He'd done this to make Dante suffer.

But she adored Dante. He was the big brother she'd never had. He'd saved their farm, fallen in love with Daisy, had taken care of their father. Dante was the answer to the Collingsworths's prayers.

She felt sick, and cold again, deeply cold, as though fear and pain had settled all the way into the marrow of her bones. Pointing to the door, Zoe ordered Lazaro out. "Go."

He slowly stood, rising to his full height. In the dimmed light his cheekbones looked like angular slashes above his full mouth. His broken nose shadowed his blunt chin. "Someday you will understand."

"I will never understand. Dante is a good man. He's the most generous man I know."

"You don't know the full story."

"Get out." She turned her back on him, wrapped her arms across her chest.

He crossed to the door. "No matter what happens, I will keep my promise to you."

In the bath Zoe soaped and scrubbed, feeling sullied after the trip, the abduction, the kiss. She didn't understand how she could feel so many intensely conflicting emotions. She was afraid of Lazaro Herrera and yet intrigued.

Toweling off, Zoe knew she had to act to get word to Dante and Daisy, knew time was of the essence. She'd look for that phone as soon as she could.

Dry and wrapped in a robe, she faced the open closet in her adjoining bedroom. Someone had unpacked for her. She couldn't imagine it was Lazaro.

Zoe didn't like feeling naked in this strange house and dressed quickly, putting on comfortable jeans and a well-washed yellow sweatshirt. She'd just started to put on socks and sneakers when a knock sounded at the door.

Opening the door, Zoe discovered a tiny old woman, no taller than five feet, with gray-streaked hair and an extremely wrinkled olive-complexioned face. "Hello."

"*¡Vamanos!*" The unsmiling old woman crossed her hands over her stomach. Her voice sounded sharp. "*La cena.*"

Definitely not a warm welcome. "I'm sorry, I don't understand," Zoe answered slowly in English. "I don't speak Spanish."

"*La cena. La comida.*"

"I'm sorry, I don't understand."

The older woman exhaled noisily, tossed up her hands. "*¿Que dice?*"

"I...I don't know what you want me to do. I don't speak Spanish."

"*¿Que?*"

"Señor Herrera. Ask Señor Herrera, *sí?*"

The elderly woman muttered something beneath her breath and stalked off. She made it halfway down the hall before turning around.

With short, curt gestures she motioned to her mouth, and opened and shut her mouth in an exaggerated chewing motion. "*La comida. La cena. La cena.*"

Understanding dawned. "*La cena.*" Food, dinner, Zoe finally got it. But that didn't mean she was going to rush on out and eat. Who wanted to be invited to dinner like that?

Zoe shut her door and it slammed closed far harder than she intended. Wincing, she climbed on her bed, grabbed a pillow and buried her face in the pillow where she let out a muffled scream of frustration.

This was a nightmare.

She couldn't stay here. Nothing made sense. Everything was off kilter, from the brandy to the marble bathroom to the kiss. She felt lost...confused.

Her door banged open less than two minutes after she'd slammed it shut.

"*¡Por Dios!* What happened?" Lazaro demanded from the doorway. "I've never seen Luz so upset."

"Luz?"

"My housekeeper." He braced his hands on his hips, indignation written all over his hard, dark features. "What did you say to her?"

"Nothing."

"Yet clearly you've offended her."

Zoe mashed the pillow between her hands, squeezing the pillow into a ball. "You've got to be joking."

"No. She said you spit in her face and slammed the door. I heard the door slam, too."

Zoe flushed. "I didn't spit. I wouldn't spit. That's rude." She swallowed hard. "And I didn't mean to slam the door. It closed harder than I expected."

He stared at her for a long moment, his jaw tight, his mouth compressed. He seemed to be considering her, the situation, Luz's version of events. "*Que joda,*" he ground out after a moment.

"What did you say?"

"I said, what a nuisance. You don't want dinner, fine. Stay in your room. But I'm not going to send special trays to you. There is a dining room in this house, and a very nice antique table with matching chairs. If you want to go to bed hungry, that's your choice. If you want to eat, you know where I—and the food—will be."

He knew she wouldn't join him for dinner and he didn't have dinner held. It didn't bother him eating alone in the elegant dining room, either. He almost always ate alone, and had ever since his mother died when he was seven.

He used to think it was poverty that killed her. The two of them were always hungry, and despite the fact that she worked every job she could secure, there never seemed to be enough money to get them off the streets.

Luz entered the dining room, reached for his plate, saw that he'd barely made a dent in his dinner. "Not hungry?" she asked sharply, her wrinkled brow doubly lined with concern.

Luz had befriended his mother before she died. Luz had been poorer than his mother, too, and yet she had fire, and a fierce spirit which made her fight back against those who would oppress her. She'd tried to teach his young mother, Sabana, to stand up to the aristocratic Galváns but his mother was terrified of the powerful Galván family.

"I'll have coffee and something light later," he said, leaning back so she could clear his place.

Luz held the plate in her hands. "Who is she, the girl?"

"A friend of a friend."

Luz made a rough clucking sound. "The truth."

"It's half truth, and that's enough for you to know." Lazaro pushed away from the table. "Thank you for dinner."

He walked out, headed for the living room and discovered the fire had burned low. Sitting down on the couch, he put his feet on the massive iron and wood coffee table and stared into the glowing embers.

He'd built this house for his mother. Of course she'd been gone nearly twenty-five years when he had the plans drawn and the house finished, but the attention to detail had been for her, in honor of her. He'd insisted on the best of everything. Crystal chandeliers, silk window hangings, marble bathrooms, French antiques.

She'd been a beautiful girl when Count Tino Galván took her against her will. Just seventeen. Not even out of high school.

But taking her innocence hadn't been enough for Count Galván. After he'd hurt her, Tino Galván had Sabana sent away, exiled to a remote Patagonia village where she delivered her son alone. The Galváns had hoped the baby wouldn't survive.

But Lazaro had.

Since his mother died, he lived for but one thing. Revenge. Revenge on those who hurt his mother, and revenge on those who'd shut their doors on him.

Zoe went to bed hungry and woke up ravenous at three in the morning. Between the time change and the growling of her stomach, she couldn't fall back to sleep. Lying in bed awake, her thoughts quickly turned to Daisy. Daisy would be worried sick and Zoe knew she had to reach her sister as soon as possible and reassure her everything was fine.

She also needed to alert Dante to the danger Lazaro posed, without getting Daisy involved.

Throwing back the bedcovers, Zoe slid out from

between the warm sheets and reached for her thin white cotton robe that matched the pink-sprigged nightgown.

It was a girlish set, something she'd had forever and yet refused to part with despite the cotton wearing thin and the rosebuds fading to peach and cream. The sleep set had been a gift from her dad years ago. Daisy got one like it, only hers had been blue.

Opening her bedroom door, she peered down the darkened hall. She wasn't sure where to begin searching for a phone. She knew there had to be one somewhere, and not just a phone, but a fax, a modem, a cell phone. Lazaro Herrera had to communicate with the outside world somehow.

In the living room, Zoe crept on her hands and knees along the baseboards, searching for a hidden phone jack, running her fingers along the edge of plaster wall and wood base. She worked her way around the living room before moving to the bookcase where she inspected each shelf.

Nothing. At least not yet.

From living room to hall, hall to the cavernous kitchen, around the kitchen islands and huge rough-hewn pillars to the dining room.

She'd just finished circling the circumference of the dark dining room when she heard a cough behind her.

"Lose something, Zoe?"

"No." She rose and brushed off her hands. It was so dark she could hardly see him but she felt him, felt his energy from ten feet away.

A little bit of moonlight fell through the window,

illuminating his profile. "You're not cleaning, are you? Luz wouldn't like it."

"I'm not cleaning."

"Then what are you doing creeping around the house at three-thirty in the morning?"

A long lock of hair fell forward, brushing her cheek, and she tucked it behind her ear. "You know what I'm doing. You know what I want."

"You won't find a phone."

"Not even a computer jack?"

"I've taken precautions. I've been quite thorough."

"Let me go."

"No."

"I'll go back to Kentucky, I'll call Daisy and tell her I changed my mind about coming out—"

"No."

She felt dangerously close to losing it, to screaming and crying and begging. "This isn't fair."

"But we've already discussed this, and we know life isn't always fair. If life was fair your mother wouldn't have died after your birth. If life was fair your father wouldn't have Alzheimer's. If life was fair your only sister wouldn't have moved halfway around the world leaving you to take care of your sick father—"

"How…how…do you know all that?"

"This wasn't a random abduction, Zoe. I made sure I knew what I was doing." He flicked on the dining room light fixture, a large iron and crystal chandelier. "Now go back to bed and get some sleep. You need it. We both need it."

In a white T-shirt and loose black cotton pajama pants with his black hair ruffled, he looked incredibly male. And human. He looked like a man that knew all about women. He looked like a man that knew how to use his hands, his body and his mouth.

Heat seeped through Zoe's limbs, color sweeping her cheeks. She hated that she could find him physically attractive when his character was so appalling. He was awful, cruel, twisted. "I hate you."

She hadn't meant to say it. But the words slipped out anyway.

His dark head merely inclined and his beautiful lips shaped into a small shadow of a smile. "I know."

CHAPTER THREE

THE helicopter that carried Lazaro off just before dawn, leaving Zoe alone with Luz for the next three days, finally returned.

Zoe heard the buzzing of the blades in her sleep, heard the whine grow louder and louder until the helicopter sounded as though it had landed in the middle of Luz's herb garden.

So he was back.

She squeezed her eyes more tightly closed, wishing her heart wasn't flopping around inside her.

She was glad. How could she be glad? She hated him.

I do, she firmly told herself, opening her eyes and staring at the dark-beamed ceiling. She'd grown to like the yellow plaster walls in her bedroom that contrasted with the dark beams. The tapestry cover on her bed was woven in shades of yellow, deep rose and green.

Everything was so different in this house, so different from the way she'd grown up. Four days after arriving here, she still felt completely alien.

Luz didn't help much, either. The housekeeper-cook was less than hospitable, taking every possible opportunity to shut a door in Zoe's face, serve cold food, ignore Zoe's halting questions.

A knock sounded on the door just seconds before

the door opened. Luz entered the bedroom with a tray and her now familiar glare of disapproval. No, Zoe thought, sitting up in bed, relations hadn't exactly warmed up between the two of them.

"*Café,*" Luz announced curtly, setting the tray on the edge of the bed with just enough force to slosh coffee up and over the rim of the cup.

Somehow Zoe knew the coffee would be luke-warm, too. "Thank you," she answered stiffly.

"You might try '*gracias,*'" a voice said from the doorway. "Luz would at least understand your thanks."

And here he was, freshly returned from battle. Or civilization. Or wherever he'd gone. Her temper grew to near bursting point, and she dragged the covers higher against her chest as if she could control her anger. "You're back."

"Happy to see me?"

"No."

His cool silver eyes flashed and she saw a hint of amusement and something else in the pewter depths. He moved to the foot of her bed and stood, arms folded, eyes narrowed in appraisal. "You're still in bed. It's almost noon."

He made her feel difficult, unreasonable. "I didn't know I had social obligations," she answered tersely. But this was his problem, not hers. He was the one who kidnapped her. He was the one who dumped her here and flew away, back to Buenos Aires, because that's where she suspected he'd gone.

Back to work.

With Dante.

"Did you see him?" she asked, fingers tightly stretching the linen.

"See who?"

Lazaro was playing dumb. He knew perfectly well who she meant. Zoe's chest hurt as she drew a deep breath, fighting for patience as well as control. "Dante."

"Oh." Lazaro smiled lazily, and walking around the foot of the bed, approached her side. "Yes. I did see him, but then as I've already told you, I work with him. Closely."

The word *closely* hung there between them, strange, rather sinister. The word implied trust, intimacy, safety.

It still stunned her to think that Dante's confidant, his most senior in command, intended to betray him.

Like Iago and Othello, she thought, and she knew the tragic outcome there. Zoe suppressed a shiver. "Does he know I'm here?"

"Yes."

Lazaro stood so close to the bed that he could touch Zoe with the tips of his fingers if he wanted.

And he wanted to. He wanted her more than he'd ever wanted anyone and he didn't know why, or how. It just was. Something about her made him hungry to touch her. From those brief caresses he knew he liked the feel of her and in the past three days he found himself craving her, craving to know her skin, her smell, her taste.

He'd thought she'd looked beautiful in the black turtleneck and sunglasses, and yet now, virtually stripped bare, long blond hair tousled, her delicate features scrubbed of all makeup, she looked even more astonishing. Beautiful and sweet. Heartbreakingly innocent, too.

He watched her eyes close, her cheeks pale. She took a deep, shuddering breath before opening her eyes again. ''What do you want from him?''

''I've already told you.''

''Revenge,'' she spit back, as if unable to stomach such a word, much less the concept.

''Exactly.''

Her face lifted, her lavender eyes wide, incomprehensible. ''But for what? Revenge against what?''

''The Galváns.''

She drew the sheet higher, tighter, so that it pressed against her breasts, outlining the rise and swell, the delicate ridge of nipple. ''But you work for the Galváns, you are president of their corporation.''

''Yes.''

''You must have spent years working to get where you are.''

''Nearly thirteen.''

''So…why hurt them? Why destroy your career?''

He slid the tray over and sat down on the mattress next to her. She shuddered as he sat down. But she wasn't afraid of him. She was afraid of the attraction.

Good girl. Smart girl. She should be afraid. He'd never felt anything so powerful in his life.

''My career,'' he said carefully, placing a hand on the bed, near her thigh, drawing the cover taut across the tone muscle, ''has but one focus, and one purpose. To destroy the Galváns.''

Zoe had never punched anyone in her life. She'd

never raised a hand, made a fist, used physical violence of any sort. But suddenly she'd closed her fingers, wrapped her thumb over her knuckles and slammed her fist into his chest, in the hollow at his breastbone. It hurt when she struck him and it wasn't even a fierce blow, more pathetic than anything, and he, she noticed through the tears filling her eyes, didn't even flinch.

"How can you be so cruel?" she choked. "How can you care so little about other people?"

He shrugged. "Habit."

"That's a lousy excuse!"

"Blame it on my family then."

"Your family?" Zoe flung her head back, unshed tears glittering in her eyes. "And just who is your family?"

"The Galváns."

Zoe felt sick. She felt physically ill, ill to the point that she actually crouched over the toilet in her red-marble bathroom, hugged the sides of the lavatory seat and heaved and heaved—nothing came up—but the tears didn't stop.

He couldn't be Dante's brother.

Half brother, she corrected, but a brother was a brother was a brother.

My God, they had the same dad. They were practically the same age, born just six months apart.

It had all come out, or most of it had come out, and she'd begged him to stop talking but he hadn't, not until he'd filled her head with words that wouldn't go away.

Lazaro had left her room and she'd run in here, to crouch at the lavatory and gag on the horrible awful things he'd said.

How could a brother destroy a brother?

The bathroom door opened. Luz stood there, dark eyes narrow and unfriendly. *"¿La gripe?"* she asked, freshly laundered towels in her arms.

Zoe sat back, wiped her nose and eyes on a crumpled tissue. *"La gripe?"* she repeated dumbly, hating that she couldn't communicate in the slightest with the housekeeper.

Lazaro appeared behind Luz. "The flu," he translated. "She wants to know if you're sick."

At heart, Zoe thought, swallowing hard. "Tell her I'm fine. Just sad."

His light eyes narrowed. "There's no reason for you to be sad. This isn't your problem."

Zoe rose. "Of course it's my problem." She took a step forward, hands balled at her sides, anger making her head light. "He's my family now, too, and if you think I'll stand by while you do whatever it is you intend to do, you're wrong."

"You don't know him."

She took another step, fury growing by the moment. "Maybe you're the one that doesn't know him. Maybe you're the one that just thinks you do."

He lifted a hand, gestured Luz away before reaching out and clasping Zoe lightly around the wrist. He brought her toward him despite her obvious reluctance. "How well do you know him, Zoe?"

His voice had dropped lower, huskier, and it shivered down her spine even as the heat of his hand burned through the skin at her wrist. The heat was the main thing, the most pressing thing. She felt warm from the inside out, warm just touching him, warm from standing so close to him.

Her mouth went dry. Her heart was pounding inside her chest. She touched the tip of her tongue to her upper lip, trying to ease the dryness. ''Don't you dare insinuate—''

''Insinuate?'' Lazaro softly interrupted, drawing her closer still. ''I'm not insinuating anything. I'm telling you. I'm telling you how this is, how this works. You're here because Dante told me to bring you here. This was his idea, *corazón*. His plan.''

''No.''

''Yes.''

''Dante sent the postcard, Dante arranged the airline ticket, Dante ordered me to meet you. He wanted you here.''

Horror filled her, horror and cold intrigue. This was the most preposterous thing she'd heard in her life. She knew he was lying yet she wanted to hear the rest. ''Why would Dante want me here?''

''To keep you out of trouble.''

''But I'm not in trouble!''

Lazaro smiled faintly, grimly, the smile failing to reach his silver eyes. ''He thinks you are.''

She'd felt as if he'd given her a ferocious one-two blow to the midsection. She hurt badly, hurt all the way through her.

He must have seen her shock because he suddenly clapped his hands on her shoulders. ''You need to get outside, breathe some air, maybe take some exercise. You'll feel better, I'm sure.''

''You're lying.''

His fingers settled into her collarbone, holding her still. ''I wouldn't lie to you.''

''You'd abduct me, hold me prisoner, but you wouldn't lie? Now there are some admirable ethics.''

His expression hardened, the silver glints in his eyes turning silver-white and frosty. His hands fell away from her shoulders but his posture was ramrod straight. ''We're going to go riding. I suggest you change, unless you intend to ride in your little-girl nightie.''

She'd forgotten she still wore her pink-sprigged nightgown and self-consciously reached up to touch the lace at the neck. ''You think I'd go anywhere with you? You're a liar and a kidnapper—''

''Did you think I was asking you?'' His eyebrows lifted. ''My apologies, then. I wasn't asking, I was telling you. We're going riding. We'll leave in a half hour.''

''No.''

''*Sí.*'' He hesitated in the doorway, a strange expression on his rugged face. ''You can ride, can't you?''

''Of course I can ride. My family breeds horses.''

''Yes, but that doesn't indicate any level of…*expertise.*''

She felt rather than heard the innuendo as his narrowed gaze slowly traveled the length of her, resting provocatively on her breasts and the vee between her legs. She felt a blush of mortification that he'd study her so thoroughly, and so thoroughly casually. Yet the slow appreciative scrutiny had coiled the nerves in her tummy and made her legs feel wobbly.

"If I chose to ride with you, I'd outride you, but I'm not riding with you. I don't like you, and I don't trust you, and I know Dante would never ever have me kidnapped. He's not that kind of a person. He's loyal and protective and chivalrous—"

"He's also incredibly self-serving. You're here because you pose a danger to Daisy. It's as simple as that. I'm to keep you out of the way until Daisy has her baby." He glanced at his watch, noted the time. "In a half hour, Zoe. Time's ticking."

She felt a small ripple of fear but something in his eyes and smile thrilled her at the same time. He aroused so many conflicting emotions within her. She didn't understand what it was she felt, but it was intense, more intense than anything she'd ever felt before. "And if I'm not there?" she whispered.

She felt his gaze rest on her mouth, her neck, her breasts. A tingling sensation radiated from her nipples out, the areoles tightening, her body responding.

"I'll come for you," he drawled slowly, "and I won't be as charming as I am now."

He moved forward, dropped a kiss on the top of her head. "I'll see you in half an hour."

She wasn't going to go. She'd rot in hell before she went.

But standing beneath the shower, letting the water stream down on her, she couldn't block out Lazaro's voice, couldn't forget the threat, or the poison of his lies.

What he'd told her had to be lies. Dante would never have her kidnapped, or abducted, or whatever one wanted to call it. He wouldn't send airline tickets behind Daisy's back, he wouldn't ask someone to do dirty work for him. He just wasn't that kind of person.

Zoe grabbed the soap, lathered it up and scrubbed the washcloth up and down her arms as if she could somehow wash away the words and lies and awful things said.

Lazaro was trying to upset her, confuse her, knock her off balance. This was part of his plan for revenge. This was his way of creating strife within the family. He was trying to pit them against each other, sister against sister, wife against husband, Collingsworth against Galván. But she wouldn't let him succeed. She wouldn't buy into his games.

She'd beat him at his game.

"Didn't think you were going to come," Lazaro said as Zoe entered the stable twenty minutes later, dressed in riding pants, a white T-shirt and boots.

"You're right. I could use the exercise," she answered coolly, hating how her heart pounded and her limbs felt weak. She'd felt strong until she'd come face-to-face with him again.

What was it about him that made her feel like this? He turned her inside out, made her into a jellyfish. It was incredible. Painful.

Lazaro's lips twisted. "Why don't I believe you?"

"Because you have a big problem with trust."

Lazaro threw back his head, his loose fleece sweatshirt dipping low enough to reveal the curve of his collarbone and his bronze throat, and laughed.

He laughed.

She'd never heard him laugh before; realized he was a man that didn't laugh often.

"Out of the mouths of babes," he said, choking with husky laughter. "Very good, *corazón.*"

She hadn't expected him to look so virile, so rugged. She'd imagined he'd dress in tight cream jodhpurs, high leather boots, a smart collar shirt. Instead he wore faded denims that clung to his muscular thighs, hugged his hips and sat low on his waist. "What does that mean anyway?"

"It's just an endearment."

"An endearment?" She blushed.

In his boots he towered over her, his immense shoulders even larger in the soft dove-gray sweatshirt, a color that made his eyes look like liquid silver, and she found herself staring into them, thinking he had secrets she could only guess at, and that he'd lived things he'd never share.

He was, she thought, fighting a fit of nerves, frighteningly beautiful, frighteningly amoral, and frighteningly sexual. "What kind of endearment?" she persisted huskily.

"*Corazón* means my heart."

My heart.

The horse shifted behind Lazaro, bumping his shoulder, moving him forward. Zoe felt the wave of heat, and the shimmer of energy as he moved near her. She could feel him everywhere and he wasn't even touching her. His strength was a tangible thing, his chemistry so powerful that blood surged to her cheeks and her belly clenched in helpless knots of feeling.

Of wanting. Of desire.

He was watching her, his lips curving ever so slightly. "Is there anything else you want to know?"

Just how to get out of here, she answered silently, panicked all over again. No man had ever affected her like this.

They rode beneath the thicket of birch, oak and acacia trees protecting the house and grounds, reached open grasslands, and loosened the reins so the horses could run.

Lazaro rode hard, fast, and Zoe had to lean forward in the saddle, knees gripped tight, just to keep up with him. She found it frightening riding so fast. Daisy always liked to fly when riding but Zoe was the careful one, the cautious. She hated losing control, feared falling, getting hurt. Feared lots of things, when she thought about it.

The wind blew her hair free and stung her eyes. She blinked hard and clung harder with her knees. *You don't have to do this. You don't have to go this fast.*

But she didn't stop, and she didn't call out to him. She'd show him she could keep up. She'd show him she was tough.

They rode up a hill, down the hill, and up another slope, this one steeper than the last. The grass was taller, coarser, and now and then her horse would stumble on half-buried rocks and Zoe would feel her heart leap to her throat.

She chased Lazaro along the top of the hill, boots deep in the stirrup, sun shining warmly above. Looking down through the bright glaze of sunlight she realized they were riding along the edge of a ravine. Trying not to give in to fear, she peered over, and the drop went way, way down. Far below she caught a glimpse of white water swirling. A river. And rocks. Lots of them.

My God, one stumble and they'd go all the way over.

Zoe steered her mare from the edge, and caught the look Lazaro shot her way.

"Nervous?" he asked, reining in his horse and waiting for her.

"No," she lied, panting a little. To hide her trembling she leaned over and gave her horse an encouraging pat.

"Good. Because we're going to ride down and have lunch on the river."

Zoe wanted to throw up. "Ride down?"

"To the river." He gestured toward the steep cliff. "You all right with that?"

Say no, say no, say no. "Sure," she choked, trying to sound nonchalant even as her heart pounded at an appalling speed.

His stallion did a little two-step, drifting sideways, eager to be moving again. "Let's do it."

Just don't look down, she told herself as she steered her horse toward the steep slope and deep ravine.

Jaw clamped tight, feet pressed deep in stirrups, Zoe's heart lurched with every stumble and slip as the horse scrambled down the mountain. The horse's hooves thudded against rocks and dust poofed in fine brown clouds as dirt clouds skidded, bounced and fell to the gully below.

Her heart was doing the same free fall and her stomach heaved up, once, twice, with violent measure.

Awful, awful. I hate this. I'll never do this again. Fear screamed through her, razor-hot and razor-fast. This was not her idea of riding. She liked dressage. She liked the ring. She loved jumping pretty white fences. Making her horse high-step. All the elegant, refined activity that earned her blue ribbons in competition but not this...not wild, abandoned dives down steep Argentine mountains.

She'd broken a sweat by the time they reached the river. Her hands shook so badly she gave up all pretense of even holding the reins.

Zoe drew her right leg over the horse and slid nervelessly out of the saddle. Her legs buckled and nearly gave way as she hit the ground.

"*¡Por Dios!* That was amazing." Lazaro's husky laugh reached her where she stood leaning weakly against the mare's warm expanded belly. That was the worst ride of her entire life. Amazing was not the right word by any stretch of the imagination.

She heard him jump from the saddle, his boots hitting the earth with a soft thud. "Hungry?" he asked.

Zoe staggered a step to the rocky outcropping. Her legs gave out. Her bottom slammed down on the warm granite. She was shaking uncontrollably and couldn't even clasp her knees. "*No.*"

She'd never been so scared. She'd been certain

she'd fall, crash, burn. She'd been afraid of pain. Afraid of dying. Afraid of everything.

She was perspiring. Her skin felt cold and clammy. "Why did we come down here?"

"For the fun of it."

CHAPTER FOUR

ZOE shook her head, gasping. "That wasn't fun, that was crazy!"

But Lazaro wasn't offended. He laughed. He seemed *pleased.*

His boots crunched dirt and rock as he walked toward her, his shadow looming large and dark. He held out the plastic bottle. "Water."

She was so angry with him she couldn't answer and she didn't take the bottle.

He nudged her, stepping between her bent legs to tap one of her knees with his own. "Come on, drink."

She moved her legs to break contact with him. Her knee felt hot from his touch and her skin sensitive, almost bruised. But she didn't have the energy to argue with him and knew that even if she did nothing would be accomplished by it.

Zoe took the water bottle and gulped a mouthful. The water tasted cool and it did refresh her, but she was still angry. Very angry.

He stepped aside, taking a seat next to her on the boulder. "You're really mad, aren't you?"

"Yes."

"You didn't enjoy the ride down?"

"Hated it."

"Why?"

"It was terrifying."

"But exciting."

"I didn't find it exciting, I was too worried about sticking in the saddle."

"Then you shouldn't worry so much. You should trust yourself more. You're an excellent horsewoman. One of the best I've seen."

She didn't feel like it. She didn't feel like the best of anything. "I don't need to be flattered."

"It's not flattery, it's the truth. I was watching you closely, Zoe, making sure you were okay, and you were. You handled your horse beautifully. She's not an easy horse. She's one of my most spirited and yet you never lost control, not even for a moment."

His words hummed inside of her, and the sun grazed the top of her head, hot and bright, but it was nothing like the warmth she felt deep inside of her, warmth stirred to life by that one brief brush against her knee, the press of his jeans-clad leg to her own.

She shouldn't respond to such a little touch but she did. She shouldn't listen to the hum of his voice and his words in her head. Instead she was feeling everything, listening to everything, wanting everything.

It was like fire beneath her skin. Fire and lava, smoke and ash. She wanted more from him and she knew that more would burn her alive, scorch her with the intensity.

"Daisy was always the better rider," Zoe said faintly. "Daisy is the definition of tough."

"Until now."

Her brow creased. How right he was. She'd never thought of it that way, but yes, Daisy had always been tough until the miscarriages.

Lazaro suddenly lifted her left hand to inspect the ring on her finger. "So tell me about the lucky guy."

She shifted uncomfortably. She really wasn't engaged, had only worn the ring after Carter insisted she keep it while she consider his proposal. She'd turned him down but he hadn't accepted the rejection. He'd begged her to take some time and think about his marriage offer while she visited her sister in Argentina. Zoe hadn't known what to do with the ring, either, and in the end had slipped it on her finger so she wouldn't lose it. "Carter," she said faintly.

"Who?"

"Carter. Carter Scott."

"Nice guy, I bet."

"Just great." She wasn't about to tell Lazaro that she had no intention of marrying Carter, and that she'd agreed to consider Carter's proposal only because she hadn't wanted to hurt his feelings. Carter and her father had been friends for years and after Daisy moved to Argentina, Carter had begun to befriend her, as well, taking her out for dinner, inviting her to parties and other Lexington society events.

"You must love him a great deal," Lazaro persisted.

She tugged her hand free. "He's a gentleman."

"Unlike me."

"Definitely unlike you."

Lazaro picked up a twig and turned the broken twig in his hands, examining the dove-gray bark, the tiny branches, the two small dried leaves still clinging to the branches. "He wants children?"

She tried not to squirm, unable to imagine making

love to Carter, a man close to her father's age. "He's…family oriented."

"I'd love to meet him."

"Sure." She balled her hands in her lap. "Once you're out of prison, give me a call. We'll see what we can arrange."

Lazaro threw back his head and almost roared with laughter. "Prison?"

"That's where you'll be going for kidnapping."

"Kidnapping?" he repeated, still chuckling.

"Yes, *kidnapping*." She shot him a cutting glance. "Or is there something else you expect to go to prison for?"

He appeared to think it over before shrugging. "No, taking you is probably the worst I've done…so far."

So far. And he didn't even sound repentant. She shot him another scathing side glance and froze.

Suddenly she couldn't tear her gaze from his face. How could anyone with such a hard heart be so beautiful?

With his outrageously long eyelashes, and the sunlight pouring down on his head, she could see the flecks of silver and pewter in his irises, silver and pewter against smoke. Like the Kentucky mist rising from the meadows, or the rich patina on a piece of heirloom sterling.

How could she find him so attractive? How could she feel this kind of desire? What kind of person was she to want a man without morals, scruples, a shred of decency?

Thank God for her fake engagement. If it weren't

for the fact that she had to pretend to care about Carter, she might do something silly...might throw herself at Lazaro and beg for the pleasure and the passion she was sure she'd find in his bed.

Zoe turned her head away, looked toward the splashing river with the swirls of white foam and jagged points of rock. The sun reflected off the water in bright sheets of light and seemed to illuminate even her heart.

If she didn't escape Lazaro soon, she'd do something stupid.

She'd beg Lazaro to touch her, make love to her.

Lazaro tossed down the twig. "We should start back. We've got a long ride home."

They rode along the riverbank, crossing the stream to travel up a grassy hill dotted with oaks and birch trees. The terrain leveled out, turning into more gold grasslands beneath an endless blue sky.

Zoe squinted. A building appeared in the distance. The building became a cluster of buildings. Buildings, fences, cows.

People.

Zoe's heart thudded. People who could help her. People who could call for help.

Swiftly she calculated the distance, measuring the time it'd take to reach them. Even riding hard, she might not be able to outride Lazaro, but perhaps she could attract their attention.

If she did it, she'd have to act quickly. No mistakes. No second thoughts. No exceptions. Could she do it? Hell, yes.

Zoe leaned forward in the saddle, pressed her knees

tight to the mare, and with a tug on the rein steered the horse to a sharp left.

Lazaro's voice rang out. "Wrong way."

She ignored him. Didn't even look back. The wind hummed in her ears and stung her eyes. She blinked and crouched low, holding on even tighter as she focused on her goal. The people in the distance, the people who would help her, the people—

"Zoe!"

His voice crackled with authority. He expected her to stop. He was demanding she stop. Commanding her to stop.

But she wouldn't. She rode on, hair blowing wildly, fingers bloodless around the leather reins.

She heard him riding on her, heard him closing the distance, his stallion's hooves pounding as though the cavalry pursued her.

Just another minute, she told herself, hang on, keep riding. An ear-splitting whistle shattered the air and suddenly the mare drew up short, breaking her stride.

Lazaro whistled a second time and the mare's forelegs left the ground and the horse reared back.

Zoe wasn't prepared for her horse to buck and couldn't keep her feet planted in the stirrups. She knew she was going to get thrown but didn't have time to break her fall. Within seconds she was sailing head over heels, and slammed hard to the ground.

The impact knocked her silly.

For a moment she couldn't move, much less think. She dragged in a breath and staggered to her feet. Dazed and yet unwilling to give up, she began limping toward the house in the distance.

"Zoe, stop."

He could go to hell. She wasn't going to stop for anything.

"Zoe, I'm warning you."

Tears smarted her eyes and she limped on, determined to reach help.

Whomph!

Zoe felt herself slam down a second time, this time leveled by Lazaro's shoulder.

She felt the weight of him on her, felt the hard prickle of the grass beneath her, felt the air sail out of her even as pain washed through her.

He'd tackled her. Like a football, or a calf being roped at a rodeo. He'd tackled her.

In a dim part of her brain she registered that a lady should never be treated this way.

But he didn't think of her as a lady.

She felt his warm breath tickle the back of her neck, heard his muttered oath as he shifted his weight off her and brushed the tangled blond hair from her cheek. "Where does it hurt?" he asked, voice raspy.

She was still lying facedown in the ground where she was eating dirt and clumps of grass, and she pushed herself up on an elbow. "Go to hell!"

"I didn't want to do that."

"Don't talk to me."

"I would never want to hurt you."

She dragged herself to her knees and brushed the dirt from her hands, and then used her forearm to wipe her mouth and face. "Stay away from me."

"I'm not going to let you run away."

"No, you made that pretty clear," she grunted, peeling a stalk of grass from her forearm.

"Promise me you won't try that again."

"I'm not going to promise anything of the sort! You've kidnapped me. This isn't a vacation."

He wiped at the dirt powdering his hair and brow. "At least we agree on that."

"Send me back to Buenos Aires. *Please*."

"Not an option."

"When will it be an option?"

"When the takeover goes public."

She stared at him for a long moment, scrambling to make sense of this last bit of information, and then understanding the big picture better. "You're going after Dante's company."

He stood up. "It's been the goal."

"All these years."

"All these years," he agreed, whistling for his horse.

She stared at him in shock. "How did I get mixed up with the takeover?"

"Timing."

"I don't get it."

"You were never part of the plan. But when Dante approached me I couldn't say no."

Fury swept through her. "Why not?"

He shrugged, reached for his stallion's bridle. "It was too great of an opportunity. I could seize Dante's company even as I framed him with kidnapping. Revenge can't get much sweeter."

She walked away from him, staggering as though drunk. Her head spun. Her stomach thumped. She thought she was going to be sick. "Where's my horse?"

"Gone." Lazaro pointed to the horizon. "Back to my *estancia,* I imagine."

Gritty tears stung the backs of her eyes. She felt ridiculously helpless and painfully reliant on him. This was a disaster on top of disasters.

Sliding one foot in the stirrup, Lazaro swung the other leg over the saddle then leaned down and extended her a hand. "*Por favor,* climb up."

"No, thank you."

"I'm not going to let you run away."

"I'll walk back."

"You'll still try to run away."

"I'm not that stupid. You've knocked me to the ground twice. Do you honestly think I want to do that a third time?"

He had the gall to laugh and his soft laughter goaded her, made her see red.

"I don't know, *corazón,* but somehow I don't think you've given up on running away."

"Go away!"

"Can't do that, *corazón—*"

"I'm not your *corazón!*"

"Yes, you are. Now give me your hand."

He rode up beside her and she glared at him, hating the way the sunshine played his features perfectly, his nose bent, crooked, but still Roman above his sensual lips. No wonder it had been broken so many times. He had to have thousands of enemies.

"Give me your hand," he said softly.

"No way."

"Then we'll do it my way."

Lazaro leaned over, twisted a finger in her belt loop and hauled her onto his lap.

Zoe dropped into the saddle. Her bottom slammed against his hips, throwing her into shockingly intimate contact. She made a desperate wiggle to escape but he clamped an impossibly muscular arm around her waist and held her firm.

"Sit still," he muttered hoarsely, "or you'll knock us both off."

She gave a futile kick, missed his leg entirely. "Put me down!"

"It's not going to happen." His palm pressed flat to her stomach, fingers spread across her belly, creating tension and fire in every nerve. The sensation of his hand on her tummy, the firm insistent pressure against her pelvis, made her feel incredibly conscious of him, of her, of them together.

"Take your hands off me," she gritted from between clenched teeth. "*Please.*"

She felt his chest rise and fall, his ribcage expanding as he drew a short, impatient breath. "I'm not about to let go, *señorita*. I'm tired of hunting you down like a jackrabbit—"

Her elbow found a home in his ribs and he grunted with pain. "If I'm a jackrabbit you're an ass!"

She suddenly felt his hand tug her ponytail, drawing her head back. "You must like to live dangerously," he said, his mouth brushing her ear. One of his hands slid the length of her throat to span the fragile bones in her jaw.

A shudder raced down her spine as she felt a surge

of awareness, a primitive knowledge that they were so very different from each other. He was made differently, shaped bigger, harder, more powerfully. He thought differently, too, and yet something about him, something in him, made her feel strongly. Intensely.

Love, hate…what was the difference? The way she felt now it was all so fierce, all so passionate, she couldn't figure out what she wanted from him, and whether she wanted his touch or wanted to be left alone.

Could opposites really attract like this?

Zoe closed her eyes as his lips traveled across her cheekbone and kissed the corner of her mouth. The kiss sent sharp darts of sensation through her, made her belly clench and her breath catch in her throat.

She felt his hips cradle hers, felt the firmness of his hand against her waist. She could almost imagine him with her, naked, could almost imagine the feel of his skin and the press of his hard body against hers.

It would be both pleasure and pain.

It would be more erotic and more intense than anything she'd ever felt.

He kissed her lower lip and her mouth trembled beneath his. She gripped the pommel on the saddle, fought the desire to touch his leg, cover his thigh with her hand. She wanted to touch him, wanted to draw closer to him but couldn't. Despite her desire, she couldn't let this happen, couldn't give in to the craving for contact, for heat, for skin.

He was dangerous. He was amoral. He'd destroy her if she wasn't careful.

"Stop," she whispered faintly against his mouth,

hoping he wouldn't hear her, and yet needing him to have more control than she did, more discipline than she felt.

He lifted his head. He looked down at her, his light eyes shadowed. "Of course. I can be as much of a gentleman as your Carter."

The ride back seemed to last forever. Every step the horse took jostled her against him, his thighs rubbing hers, his body touching hers, his heat scalding her. Every jostle and touch fueled her imagination. By the time they reached the stable she was tense and wound tight from head to toe. Nerve endings she didn't even know existed tingled, tormenting her with sensation that she didn't want or need.

Reaching the stable, she swung a leg over the saddle and scrambled to the ground, too hot and raw to be touched a second longer.

Lazaro didn't say anything as she fled the stable, but then, he didn't have to, she thought with a shudder. He knew perfectly well the effect he had on her and they both knew it was only a matter of time now before she cracked, and her defenses fell.

Lazaro leaned on the pommel and watched Zoe escape the stable. She wasn't running, but came damn close.

She didn't like him, but she wanted him.

He had a suspicion she didn't want Carter Scott, but felt safe marrying him. Dante was right about one thing. Carter Scott didn't deserve Zoe. At fifty-three, Carter was over twice her age and notoriously lecherous.

Lazaro had looked into Carter Scott, in fact, he

wasn't sure he would have agreed to Dante's scheme if Carter had been a decent man, but Carter wasn't decent. Carter had a weakness for young blondes in distress. He'd proposed to Daisy three years ago, practically knuckling her into marrying him to save the family farm, and now with Daisy out of the picture, he was doing the same to Zoe.

Lazaro's gut tightened. He'd be damned if he let Carter have her. The American didn't have a moral bone in his body.

Suddenly he stopped himself, and grimaced, mouth contorting. Judging Carter Scott felt a little like the pot calling the kettle black. It wasn't his place.

But that was the problem, he thought, unsaddling his stallion. He didn't know his place. Literally.

In thirty years of searching, in thirty years of struggling, he'd never found a place to call home.

He'd never found the place he belonged.

CHAPTER FIVE

Zoe headed for the pool after the ride hoping a swim would work the kink out of her knotted muscles. The twenty laps did help with her knotted muscles but it didn't do much for her tension, or for her craving for Lazaro's skin.

How could she want anyone so much? How could she physically want someone like this?

She'd had a couple of boyfriends, nothing serious, and while they'd made out, they'd never made love. She loved to kiss but she hadn't felt sufficient interest to go all the way...until now.

Somehow she knew she'd find what she wanted with Lazaro, she knew he understood the tension within her, knew he responded with passion.

Already his brief kisses turned her inside out, made her body tremble and ache, but the intensity of her desire frightened her, and more than just a little. Lazaro was the wrong man to want, the wrong man to need. He might represent passion but he also represented chaos. And destruction.

Disgusted with herself, Zoe climbed from the pool, toweled off and was just about to take a seat on one of the lounge chairs when she heard the back door to the house open and close.

Her heart jumped as she spotted Lazaro making his way toward the pool. He was wearing only a pair of black swim trunks and his very broad shoulders emphasized the narrow width of his waist and the length of his muscular legs.

He was all man, she thought, panicking all over again, and she grabbed for her things, dumping the suntan lotion and sunglasses into her straw bag and shoving her feet into flip-flops.

"Nice swim?" he asked as she rushed past.

She couldn't even meet his gaze. "Great, thank you," she said, hurrying on toward the house.

Zoe reached the door, turned the knob, and realized with a stab of horror that her left hand was bare. The engagement ring was missing. That huge, expensive rock was gone.

No! She couldn't lose it, she had to give it back to Carter!

Zoe returned to the pool just in time to see a flash of bronze skin and black swim trunks break the surface of the water. She froze at the gate and watched him swim the length of the pool underwater, rising only once he'd reached the other side.

Lazaro pushed up and out of the water, taking a seat on the pool's tiled edge. Water streamed from his hair, his bronzed skin, the sinewy planes of his body.

With one hand he raked his wet hair back, scraping the glistening ebony waves from his brow. His skin gleamed all over, minute water droplets clinging to his chest.

His head lifted and he caught sight of her standing there, staring at him, absolutely transfixed. He leaned back on his arms, accenting the bulge of his bicep and thickness of the tricep. "Need something?" he drawled.

"Yes," she stammered, sick at heart. "I've lost my ring. The engagement ring."

"The ring from Carter?"

"Yes." Heart racing, she watched as he rose from the side of the pool and walk toward the lounge chairs. "It was his mother's ring. It's an old family heirloom."

He lifted his towel and rubbed it over his chest, down his flat belly and across his wet swim trunks. She couldn't tear her gaze away, fascinated by the ripple of muscle and display of strength.

Lazaro glanced at her and one of his black eyebrows lifted. "*Corazón,* in case you were wondering, I don't have the ring on me."

Mortified, she felt another tide of color surge to her cheeks. She forced herself to move, walking past him to the lounge chair where she'd placed her things earlier. She knelt down, skimmed her hands over the lounge chair cushion, under the cushion and then beneath the chair itself.

"Perhaps you lost it on the ride," Lazaro said, briskly drying his hair before using his fingers to rake the wet crisp hair smooth.

She stood up, shook her head, both frustrated and worried. "I'm pretty sure I had it when I returned to the house." She circled the lounge chair, walked to the edge of the pool, gazed down at the pool bottom. "I shouldn't have worn it. I shouldn't have brought it on this trip. I'll never be able to pay him back."

"I'm sure he won't expect you to pay him back."

"But I'll have to. The diamond was four carats. It's worth a fortune."

"Is that what he told you?"

She stiffened and slowly faced him. "Yes, and why shouldn't he?"

"Because it's not a real diamond."

"What?"

"The stone's fake." He shrugged, immense shoulders shifting as he walked toward her. "It's not even a good imitation."

Zoe staggered back a step, aghast. How dare he! What a revolting thing to say! Just who did he think he was?

Indignant tears burned her eyes and she reached into her straw bag for her sunglasses, but her movements were jerky and instead of landing neatly on her nose the glasses tumbled to the ground.

Lazaro bent over and retrieved the tortoiseshell glasses and, standing, gently placed the frame on the bridge of her nose.

His fingers grazed her ears and he adjusted the bridge piece higher. "Tell me about Carter. Tell me why you love him."

Lazaro's voice wrapped around her heart and she quivered on the inside, hunger, awareness, desire coiling so tight that she felt almost brittle with the intensity of the need. She looked at him through the dark-tinted shades, her pulse racing hard and fast.

How could she keep up this charade? How could she pretend to love Carter when all she wanted was to touch Lazaro, to be in his arms, to feel his mouth against hers? "He's a family friend," she answered faintly. "I've known him forever."

"And that's enough for you?"

"He's good to Dad. He helps with him… sometimes."

Lazaro's brow furrowed, eyes narrowing. "This is your idea of love?"

"I—"

"You what?"

Her lips parted but she couldn't speak. She felt dizzy, light-headed.

His gaze dropped to her mouth and lingered there, as though he could remember the feel of her lips and taste of her mouth.

If only he'd kiss her again…if only he'd touch her now…but he didn't. He just stood there watching, waiting, making her face feel hot, her cheekbones sensitive. She should walk away right now, put some distance between them, but her legs wouldn't move. "Carter's not like that," she defended huskily.

Lazaro pounced. "Like what?"

"Like…bad…evil. He's not that way."

"Maybe he's not evil, but he's not a good person, and he's not a good choice for you."

Zoe flinched at his tone. His voice had cooled and hardened so that the words came out like hail stones, icy, sharp, painful. "How can you say that? You don't even know him."

"I know enough. I know that Carter and I are both con artists. We've made careers out of manipulating the system. I manipulate the Galváns. Carter manipulates pretty young blondes."

"But if that's all—"

Lazaro didn't get it, didn't understand how Zoe could keep defending Carter unless she really and truly loved him.

"It's not all," he interrupted shortly, his temper barely leashed, anger making him see red. "Your Carter Scott is worse than a petty criminal. He's been under investigation for tax evasion, forgery, insurance fraud, including two cases of suspected arson." *Including the fire at your farm three and a half years ago.*

But Zoe didn't believe him, he could see it in the defiant tilt of her chin and the twist of her lips.

"Just because you're amoral, Lazaro, doesn't make every other man amoral, too."

He shook his head, words failing him. He didn't know how to explain to her the circumstances that had brought them together like this. He didn't know where to even begin describing his past, and his mother's disgrace. "I may not be a virtuous man but I'd never take advantage of a woman."

"No, then what do you call holding me here against my will?" Her voice quivered with rage. "I'm your hostage. You're keeping me here, prisoner. Isn't this taking advantage of me? Isn't this denying me my rights?"

He hated the tears in her eyes, hated the loathing on her lovely face. "Yes," he said at last, his voice pitched low, and rough.

She lifted a finger, pointed it at his chest. "Then don't you talk to me about Carter and don't you lecture me about my choices because you are lower than low, you are absolutely completely despicable.''

In his suite of rooms, at his desk in the corner office, Lazaro stared at the pages spitting out of his fax machine.

The takeover had begun. The board members had been notified, the shareholders contacted, the offer made. Now it was a matter of time and patience. And nerves of steel. Because Lazaro could imagine what Dante was going through right now, he could imagine his half brother's shock, anger, and sense of betrayal.

Dante had believed in him.

But Dante had never known him.

The fax machine continued to churn, printing page after page of legal documents. Offer of intent to buy. Price per share. Acquisition of stock.

Dante must be reeling.

The door to his office squeaked open. Zoe stood there in the doorway, a sundress pulled over her pink and white floral bikini.

Her long golden hair had been scraped back and twisted into a severe knot at the back of her head. She wore no makeup and her eyes were enormous, dark lavender shadows in her pale face. "I want proof," she said curtly. "Give me proof that Dante was behind this or let me go. Now."

Lazaro didn't look well, she thought, as she stood in the doorway watching him read through the reams of pages spilling from the fax machine. His color was off, his complexion a mottled gray, and deep lines formed at his eyes and mouth, aging him considerably.

He dropped the papers he'd been holding onto his desk. "Proof?"

"Yes. You must have some documentation somewhere. Something in writing that would incriminate Dante. That's how you'd do it, too. You'd get it in writing so you could torture him later."

She heard herself spit the words at him and each word hurt her and she didn't know why. She was wanting to wound him and yet this only made her ache, her heart mashed to nothing by a situation bigger than any of them.

In her room, she realized she didn't know what to believe anymore. She didn't know who to trust.

Lazaro had done this to her. He'd taken her world and turned it inside out.

How had he done it? How had he knocked her so completely off balance?

Maybe it was because he spoke to her simply, and he spoke directly. He didn't mince words. He didn't try to protect her feelings while Daisy and Dante, her father and even Carter were always trying to shield her from things, and make decisions for her. Her family meant well but it was, she knew now, a disservice.

But Lazaro didn't try to protect her. He'd told her the facts, or his version of the facts, and somehow what he said made sense. She didn't agree with him but she appreciated his honesty. If it was honesty.

Which was why she was here, demanding proof. She didn't know truth from the lies anymore, and refused to let him tie her insides up in knots any longer.

She wanted facts, the cut-and-dried details, and she'd decide for herself what was right, and what was true.

"I know you have paperwork," she added stiffly, her stomach churning, her legs weighted with lead. "I'd like to see whatever it is you have, please."

Lazaro handed her the file and he watched her open the folder and begin to read. She was right, he thought grimly, she knew him well enough to know he'd document everything regarding Zoe's situation, he'd make sure he was covered in case this became a legal situation.

He wouldn't go down without implicating Dante. He wouldn't take the fall without destroying Dante's name and reputation.

Zoe's hands shook as she leafed through the paperwork. He saw her swallow, her pale throat tightening, knotting as she fought for control over her emotions.

The paperwork he'd saved would upset her. There were e-mails from Dante and photos of her at the Collingsworth farm. He saw her study a copy of her passport, examine a printout of her airline itinerary and a transfer of funds between bank accounts.

She closed the folder and slid it across his desk. "He paid you to do this."

Lazaro heard the wobble in her voice. "The funds are actually for you, in case you needed cash while here."

Zoe made a hoarse sound. "Why would I need cash? I'm your guest here. Everything has been so thoughtfully provided for me."

"He didn't mean to hurt you, Zoe."

"Don't defend him. You're his enemy!"

His chest felt tight. "But you're hurt, this hurts, I can see it in your face—"

"Which should make you happy," she interrupted with a brittle laugh. "This is exactly what you wanted, so celebrate."

But he wasn't feeling celebratory. He felt sick inside. Felt awful. Evil. Not like himself at all. "I can't celebrate your unhappiness, Zoe. I care too much about you."

She laughed again and then the laugh turned to a sob and her eyes were filling with tears. "Don't say you care about me, that's the worst insult of all. You don't care about me. You don't care about anyone. You live only for yourself."

"There's so much you don't know."

"I don't think so." Her gaze met his and held. "I think that's the lie you tell yourself, but I think the truth is actually quite simple. You want others to hurt because you hurt. So pour yourself a drink and enjoy your success. You're good. You're good at being cruel. You're really good at what you do."

She walked out of his office, leaving his door open. He stared at the open door, listened to her footsteps echo and then disappear and felt the silence swallow him whole.

This was supposed to have played out differently. He thought he was so smart, thought he knew what he was doing taking Zoe, turning her against Dante, but it wasn't working out the way he'd imagined.

It was one thing to exact revenge on his half

brother. It was another to involve an innocent young woman.

His father was the one who hurt innocent girls, not him. Never him. He'd vowed to protect innocence and yet here he was, holding Zoe hostage, keeping her here against her will.

What kind of man did that to a woman?

A man like his father. But he wasn't his father. He was nothing like his father.

Or was he?

In her yellow bedroom with the dark-stained beams, Zoe dragged her black suitcase from the closet and tossed it on her bed. She blinked away stupid tears as she unzipped the suitcase and flipped the top open.

So it was all true. What Lazaro had said was true. Dante had orchestrated the entire abduction. He'd even deposited money into Lazaro's account.

How could Dante do this to her? What kind of person was he?

Tears blinded her vision and she furiously wiped them away. It was dumb to cry. Crying wouldn't change anything. The only way things would change is if she left, which was exactly what she was going to do.

Blinking, she marched on the dresser and opened the drawers, scooping up shirts and shorts and knit skirts.

"*Corazón,* where do you think you're going?"

Lazaro's voice came from the doorway, his tone surprisingly gentle.

She blinked back scalding tears. "Away."

"Now? At nine o'clock at night?"

Thank God he wasn't lampooning her. He could, she knew, make fun of her. They both knew there was nowhere for her to go, that if she left now she'd be walking in the dark in the middle of nowhere, but he didn't say any of that and she just kept packing.

She shook her head, and returned to the dresser, gathering her panties and bras and dumping them in the suitcase. "I have to go. I can't stay here anymore. I can't be near you anymore."

"Okay."

Okay? She stilled, her hands resting on the edges of her suitcase, and looked up at him. "You agree?"

"Yes."

"So you'll let me go, you'll get your helicopter to come for me?"

"Yes, tomorrow morning. First thing. I promise."

"Why not now?"

"It's late. It was a big day for my business today and my pilot had a long day. He needs his rest, but I'll send for him in the morning."

"How do I know I can believe you?"

"Have I lied to you yet?"

She stared at him for a long, hard minute. She saw him for what he was, and wanted to hate him, but she couldn't. She felt strong things for him, intense things, but hate wasn't one of them.

She moved to her closet, crouched down and grabbed pairs of shoes, drawing them into a pile. And then there, on the bottom of the closet, she saw a glint of white fire against gold.

The ring.

Carter's mother's ring.

Zoe picked up the ring, slid it on her finger and stood. "I found it," she said, turning around and facing Dante. "It was here. On the floor of the closet."

Lazaro leaned against her door frame. "I'm glad you found it."

She frowned. "Why? You think it's fake."

"But you were worried. I don't want you to worry anymore. I want you to be happy. You deserve to be happy."

Suddenly she wished she hadn't slipped the ring onto her finger. She didn't want it there. Didn't like it there. "I don't think Carter's bad," she said softly, balling her fingers into a fist, "but I don't really know him very well and—" she drew a breath, looked up at Lazaro "—and I don't love him, I've never been in love with him. We're not even really engaged."

Lazaro straightened. "What?"

She shook her head, chewed her lower lip, her expression rueful. "You and Dante are both so clever and yet you're so wrong on this one. I was never engaged to Carter, I never promised to marry him. He asked me but I didn't say yes."

CHAPTER SIX

LAZARO moved from the doorway toward her bed. He touched her suitcase. "I don't understand. You have the ring, you've been wearing it the whole time you were here."

Zoe would have laughed if she had the energy. Lazaro's expression was priceless. He looked absolutely stunned. "He insisted I keep it while I consider his proposal, and I was afraid I'd lose it so I wore it." She made a face. "Only I almost lost it wearing it so I don't know how smart that was."

"You don't love Carter."

"No."

"You never even considered marrying him?"

She puzzled over the question, felt the press of the diamond against her skin. "I'm sure I considered it. I'd be a fool not to consider it. I don't have that many options. I should try to keep some open."

It was true. Since Daisy had moved to Argentina, Zoe had been so alone, and so much on her own. She felt no safety or security, no support, either. Daisy had her new life with Dante and Zoe had been left behind to manage their father's care. Zoe didn't mind the responsibility, but it was lonely. In fact, it was downright overwhelming at times.

He sat down on the bed, next to the suitcase. "But Dante really believes you're engaged to Carter. He said he'd talked to Carter, that Carter had phoned him with the news.''

Zoe reached for her cowboy boots and held them against her chest. "Then Dante should have talked to me. I could have set him straight, but why talk to me? I'm just Daisy's kid sister and too silly to make a good decision on my own."

"I don't think that's what Dante meant——"

"Stop defending him!" She tossed the boots into the suitcase so hard they nearly bounced back out. "You're not on the same side. You can't see his point of view, you can't agree with him and you can't try to patch things up, either."

She retreated to the bathroom, gathered her bottles of shampoo, conditioner and bath gel and carried them back to her suitcase. "Are you really going to let me leave here tomorrow?"

"Yes."

She dropped the bottles into the suitcase next to the boots, and leaned on the suitcase. "Good. Because I want to go home." She looked up at him, her eyes meeting his silver gaze. "You'll take me to the airport, get me on a plane?"

"What about Daisy?"

She felt her eyes burn. "What about Daisy?"

"You came to see her."

Her fragile control was beginning to crack. Her hands shook as she pressed the bunched-up clothes flat. "I do want to see her but I don't want to see Dante and there's no way I can see her without him."

"True," he agreed.

She marched away from the suitcase, arms crossed

over her chest. She felt angry and disorganized and utterly beside herself. "How could Dante of all people do this?"

Lazaro's voice followed her. "People make mistakes. Dante made a mistake."

She spun to face him. "I can't believe you keep feeling the need to take his side. You're supposed to be the bad guy. Act like the bad guy, for heaven's sake!"

He rose from the bed, moved toward her. "And what would the bad guy do right now?"

"Smile. Laugh. Savor my torment."

The atmosphere in the bedroom suddenly felt charged and the tension reverberated through Zoe.

Lazaro reached out to smooth a long tangle of hair from her cheek. "I can't savor anything. I'm sorry. I'm sorry I've done this to you."

Her heart squeezed tight within her. "Don't apologize to me. I can't stand the sympathy. It's not like you."

Her rough protest drew a wry smile to his lips. "No, it's not like me. I'm not hero material, am I?"

She couldn't answer him, couldn't speak, not because she was angry with him but because she didn't understand how she could want him now, at a time like this. It didn't make sense to her, this intense desire.

He tucked another tendril behind her ear and the brush of his fingertips against her skin sent darts of feeling from her nipples to her belly and beyond.

She felt him everywhere, felt him in her skin, her muscles, her blood, her bones. He'd only touched her cheek but she felt his warmth and his strength. "I want you," she breathed, her voice strangled. "I need you."

His hands circled her upper arms, fingers firm against her skin. He tried to push her away but she didn't move. His gaze searched hers and she saw his inner struggle, his unwillingness to let this happen. He gave his head a small brief shake. "I can't do this, Zoe."

"Why not? You've done everything else."

"I'd just be taking advantage of you."

"As if that's stopped you before."

"This is different. Sex is different."

She stepped toward him, closing the distance between them. "But this isn't about sex," she whispered. "It's about wanting to be with you, wanting to know you—"

"But you do know me, and we both know what I am." His hands slid down the length of her arms, capturing her wrists. Her pulse leaped at the touch. She felt eagerness, excitement, desire, but absolutely no fear.

"I don't think it's that simple," she answered, her breath catching in her throat. For days she'd wanted to be held by him, touched by him, and it was all she could do not to beg for that which she wanted. "I don't think you're that simple. Yes, there are things about you I don't understand, but there are things about you I do."

He tilted her chin up, stared down into her eyes. "You make me afraid."

It was getting very hard to think clearly, very hard

to be rational. His touch, his warmth, his energy was wrapping her up, binding her to him. She didn't want words, she wanted sensation. Didn't need talk, needed passion.

"What is there to be afraid of?" she whispered.

"Loving you."

She stared at his mouth in fascination. Somehow, even though he was absolutely the wrong man for her, he made the most sense. "Don't be. I'm just Zoe."

"Yes, but I'm not what you need. I'm not an option. I can't be."

"Why not?"

"You know this one, *corazón*. We live in different worlds. Our futures have nothing in common."

He was saying the right thing, the smart thing, and yet she couldn't accept it. She stood up on tiptoe and gently touched her mouth to his. He stiffened and nearly drew back. She wrapped her hands around his neck, cupping his nape, and gently pulled his head back down to hers. "Kiss me."

"This will only make it harder—"

"I don't care." And she meant it. She'd never felt this kind of desire before, never felt so confident of herself as a woman before. She also knew that she and Lazaro had no future together, it would be impossible in the face of such animosity between their families, but for right now, this night, it felt right for them to be together.

Some things came only once in a lifetime, and suddenly she'd felt as though she'd waited her entire life for this. There were so many things she'd missed out on, so many people she'd already lost. Mom, Dad, Daisy. She'd didn't want Lazaro to be another regret.

Slipping her fingers into his crisp hair, she savored the thick silky texture.

She drew her lips across his, felt his breath caress her mouth, felt the contrast of skin and beard and shivered a little at the intensity of her own desire. She wanted him. Wanted to be taken by him, loved by him, possessed by him. "Don't treat me like a little girl. I'm not a kid. I've been through more than most women twice my age and I know what I feel and I know what I need, and I need you. I need to be with you."

His hands clasped her face, cradling her jaw in the span of his fingers. "Have you ever made love before?"

"No. But you should be my first."

Those words did something to him, melted the last of his icy reserve. She could see the protective wall crash down and his expression gentled, his silver gaze warming, his jaw easing.

The hunger he'd fought to contain was suddenly there on the surface and he wanted her, fiercely. She could feel his desire, feel his impatience and as color streaked beneath his cheekbones she placed her hands against his chest, touching the hard plane of muscle with her palms and then her fingertips. "You're gorgeous," she whispered.

He felt amazing, too, and she wanted more. Lightly she slid her hands across the span of his chest following the curve of muscle and shape of ribs before discovering his small hard nipples beneath his linen shirt.

At the caress of her fingers he drew a sharp breath and Zoe looked up into his face, curious, eager, daring. She relished her role as seductress, wanted to know what he enjoyed and if it was similar to her pleasure.

Nails lightly raking, she stroked down his chest, beneath the rib to the taut flat abdomen. She could trace each of the ripples in his abdomen, feel the ridge and dip between muscle and the small indentation of his navel.

Fire surged in her veins, hunger and desire. Her hands hesitated for just a fraction at his belt before she unfastened the buckle and the button on the trousers.

"Have you undressed a man before?"

His question made her feel reckless. "No, but it's pretty much common sense, isn't it?"

He laughed softly, appreciatively, sending fresh trickles of feeling down her spine, trickles of fire in her belly. "Nothing feels common right now, *corazón*."

His husky voice made her breathe deeply, and she felt a thrill of excitement tinged with shyness as she tugged his zipper down, then brushed his hipbones and the soft cotton of his briefs.

He was hard, straining against the cotton and she touched him uncertainly, not entirely sure what to do next and yet enjoying the part of the femme fatale.

Slipping her hand beneath the briefs she covered him with her hand, intrigued by the silky texture of his skin and the hard rigid length of him. He groaned, and grew even larger as she held him.

Suddenly Lazaro's head dipped and his lips covered hers. ''Zoe,'' he muttered thickly, hands stroking from her waist to her shoulders and then down again, making nerve endings dance the whole exquisite length.

It was a sweet relief when he tugged off her sundress. Stripped of everything but her bikini he carried her to the bed.

The mattress gave a little beneath her and Lazaro parted her thighs, moving between them. Hands on her ankles, he lightly circled the fragile bones and slowly caressed up, the shin, the curve of calf, the knee.

In just moments he'd melted the bones in her legs, set her trembling, her belly knotting in unabated need. She felt warm and hot inside and as he slid his hands up her outer thighs, her innermost muscles clenched.

He caressed back down her thighs, over the quadriceps to the knee and when his thumbs moved to the inside of her thighs she nearly jumped out of her skin.

His hands were a delicious torment, stroking lightly, teasingly, maddeningly up the inside of her thighs, fingers brushing at the sensitive hollows near the elastic of her bikini bottoms.

''Please,'' she gritted, reaching up to clasp his shoulders, the muscles bunched beneath her hands, his body hard, sleek, strong. She couldn't bear the bittersweet sensation of wanting another moment longer. She felt as though she'd been waiting forever for this moment. ''Make love to me, Lazaro. Be part of me, now.''

He unclasped her floral swimsuit top and drew it off, the sudden exposure drawing her nipples into aching buds. His warm mouth covered one bud, hot tongue laving the pebbled peak. She gasped, hands moving up his neck, against his scalp to grab fistfuls of silky hair. He felt hard and demanding, sexy and sinful, and she was beyond thinking. Her pelvis tipped, moving of its own accord, wanting to be closer, needing to be closer, her hips slowly grinding, arching, tilting against him.

''You are very much a woman,'' he mouthed against her breast, kissing his way up to find the line of collarbone, the hollow of her neck, the dip beneath her ear. His lips were firm, his tongue felt moist, his breath teased her sensitized skin.

Kissing her mouth, savoring the soft thrust of her lower lip, he stroked her from breast to belly, hand easing beneath her panties to cup her mound before discovering the warm moisture within.

Her breath was caught in his mouth, her gasp stolen by his lips. Nothing had ever felt like this before. Nothing had ever been so beautiful or so pleasurable.

When he stripped her of her bikini bottoms, tugging the flimsy scrap over her hips and curve of her derriere, she instinctively parted her legs, opening her knees for his body.

He made her feel like perfection and with a deep sigh, Zoe wrapped her arms around him and gave herself to him.

He entered her slowly, stopping once when she

tightened, feeling a sudden flicker of fear that he might be too big, too powerful.

Lazaro cupped her face in his hands, kissed her lower lip, sucked on it until she clasped his hands, hung on to him with all her might as her bones were dissolving, muscles melting, senses consuming.

She rose to meet his hips, draw him deeper, hold him completely inside.

"I don't want to hurt you," he whispered, holding back.

"You're not. It's lovely, you make me feel lovely."

He made a rough sound, and sank deeply into her body, filling her so that she could feel nothing but him and the blood pounding in her ears.

"You," he murmured, lips brushing her neck, her jaw, the corner of her lips, "are lovely."

He started to move, thrusting before nearly drawing out. She caught blindly at him, hands catching his ribs, fingers splayed against his warm chest. He moved back inside her and this time she moaned, feeling unbearable pleasure at the intensely erotic sensation of him in her, of them together.

The arch of her hips, the tilt of her pelvis, brought her fully into contact and created rivers of fire in every nerve of her body.

Feeling her respond, Lazaro thrust faster and she clung to him, each stroke arousing more sensation, stirring emotions and cravings she couldn't articulate. All she knew was that he couldn't stop and she couldn't let go.

Her heart pounded and her skin grew damp. The

thrusting became as much a torment as a pleasure. She felt something beyond the moment, felt something out there dancing beyond her, beckoning her forward. Zoe ground her hips, dug her nails into his arms, and pressed her teeth against his satin-covered shoulder.

Take me, take, take me, a silent voice inside her chanted as her muscles tensed, awareness building. She felt as though she'd never be able to hold on to him, never keep him with her, and never contain the building pressure. The desire was bigger than his body or hers, but something they'd created between them, something that had passed safety and reason, intellect and sensation. This was everything, and everything was consuming.

Her focus narrowed; silence filled her head. For a moment she saw nothing but a tiny light far away, but as Lazaro strained against her, his fingers weaving into her hair, holding her close, the tiny light flared up. Filled by him, pushed by him, she exploded, the tiny light becoming a great New Year's firework, white-silver spangles, sparkles, glitter. The intense buildup turned to hot, sweet, blinding bliss.

Bliss.

Oh heavens, it was better than the best, strong and yet seductively sweet. Still shuddering, she felt him arch, his body tensing, driving more deeply into her. Her orgasm pushed him over the edge and for an endless moment they were together in time and space.

At long last, trembling with near exhaustion, Zoe turned her face, kissed his shoulder and the warm spice of his skin. His heart thudded hard beneath her ear. His hair-roughened chest cradled her cheek. She felt like liquid on the inside and honey on the outside. Nothing, and no man, would ever rival this.

Nothing and no man would ever replace this.

Or him.

She didn't know how she knew, but she knew. Everything inside her had shifted, turned, become different and new. Stronger. More certain. Determined.

Lazaro Herrera might be Dante's enemy, but she needed him, might even love him.

Her breath caught in her throat and she opened her eyes to look up at him. He was braced on his elbows staring down at her, silver eyes focused, intense.

"Regrets?" he asked.

She didn't answer for a long moment, searching her heart, searching her conscience. Finally she shook her head. "No."

"Good." He dipped his head, covered her parted lips with his and kissed her deeply.

He was still beautifully warm, his skin damp, and she felt a floating calm. Rolling over, he drew her on top of him. Slowly, he stroked her hair, the dip in her spine, and the curve of her bottom.

"This is dangerous," he murmured.

"I shouldn't get pregnant. You took precautions."

"I'm not talking about that, I'm talking about you, about being with you. I could get very addicted to you, sweet Zoe, very addicted to this."

Her heart turned inside out. They were the right words if he'd been a different man, the right words if he could have been an option. How awful that they both knew that this was doomed from the start. "At least we had tonight," she answered huskily.

He kissed her again. "One night isn't enough."

It was the very thing she'd been thinking. Gritty tears stung the backs of her eyes. She reached out for him, her lips grazing his. "I don't want to think about tomorrow. I don't want tomorrow. Can't we pretend it won't come?"

He laughed but there was no warmth in his voice. Just pain. "I'm not very good at playing pretend."

"I guess you didn't have much of a childhood."

"Probably not enough," he agreed, lifting a strand of her hair, and caressing her flushed cheek. "I thought this would be hard," he added after a moment. "I didn't know it'd be this hard. You make me feel things again, Zoe. You make me want things I didn't think were possible."

She squeezed her eyes shut, pressed her face against his chest. She hurt on the inside, hurt when she thought of the intensity of her feelings and the impossibility of the situation.

He laughed again, curtly, angrily, as though he'd lost all patience with himself. "How am I going to let you go?"

Tears stung her eyes and she kissed his chest, before nestling closer. "Very, very carefully."

CHAPTER SEVEN

THEY'D fallen asleep after midnight, woken at four to make love yet once more. Zoe felt nerveless, her body deliciously relaxed. The lovemaking had completely and thoroughly exhausted her.

"Are you sure you don't want to go to Daisy's tomorrow?" Lazaro asked, his voice deep and rich in the dark, his fingertips lightly stroking her spine. "Your sister doesn't have to know about us. I won't tell and I'm quite sure Dante won't say anything."

"But once I arrive at Daisy's, I won't see you again, will I?"

"No."

She closed her eyes as his fingers trailed across her lower back. She wasn't ready to say goodbye, didn't know if she'd ever be ready to say goodbye, but knew she couldn't do it today. "Where are you going?"

"I've meetings in Buenos Aires."

"Oh." She couldn't hide her soft sigh of disappointment.

"I'd take you to the city with me, and we could spend another day or two together, but we're only avoiding the inevitable."

"Lots of things are inevitable," Zoe quipped, "including death." She suddenly thought of her father and his declining health, thought of the loneliness of

95

the last two years since Daisy married and moved to Argentina. She didn't want to lose Lazaro, wondered if there wasn't some way that she could keep him in her life.

If he didn't persist with the takeover...

If he'd soften his stance against the Galváns...

"What's another day?" she murmured. "How will spending one more day together hurt?"

He was silent for a long moment before answering. "I have meetings late morning and a conference call after lunch, but I should be free before dinner. We could go out tomorrow night in the city. I could take you to my favorite restaurant."

It sounded wonderful. Dinner with Lazaro in the city. Dressing up, going out to his favorite restaurant. Yet he had meetings...business meetings...and she knew what those meant. "Your meetings tomorrow are part of the takeover?"

He caught her hand, carried it to his lips. "This isn't a choice, Zoe. This is something I have to do."

"Even if it's cruel?"

"I didn't start this."

"But you can finish it. You can be bigger than them, you can turn the other cheek—"

"No. I can't. I wish I could, but I can't. I'm not a gentle person. I am not a forgiving person and I can not forget the cruelty against my mother."

Zoe turned her face away, unable to bear hearing him talk this way. She couldn't reconcile herself to the harsh Lazaro, the Lazaro that lived for revenge. It wasn't the man she saw, and it wasn't the man she was falling in love with. "Then take me to Daisy's tomorrow," she choked. "Let's just get this over with."

Morning came and Zoe woke to the sound of a helicopter landing. Stirring she discovered Lazaro gone and for a moment she felt panic, thinking he'd left her here alone again. But then the bedroom door opened and he stood there, showered, shaved, dressed.

"Good morning," he said. "Luz has breakfast waiting."

He looked distant, his mouth tight, his expression shuttered. She tried to muster a smile but couldn't. "I'll shower quickly."

"Take your time. We'll leave when you're ready."

The helicopter ride to Buenos Aires was short in comparison to her memory of the trip out, and reaching the executive airport in Buenos Aires, they left the helicopter pad for the waiting limousine.

As they settled into the back of the car, Zoe's gaze fell on a crisp new newspaper lying on the seat. The huge black headlines were disproportionate to the rest of the headlines and included the word, Galván.

Zoe's heart leaped and fell, like a trout jumping in a stream. "What does that say?" she asked, pointing to the paper.

Lazaro looked at the newspaper lying on the leather seat. "'Rival Upstart Seizes Galván Wireless,'" he read tonelessly.

Lazaro was the rival upstart. He must have his own

company, must have other partners and investors. Dante would be reeling. "Read it all," she whispered.

"Why do you want to do this?"

"I want to know."

"You'll just get upset, and it won't change anything. The offer's made, the news is public, the wheels are already in motion."

The limousine had pulled out of the airport parking lot and was entering traffic. Sunlight glazed the limousine windows, dappling the interior of the car. Zoe gazed out the window. It was a gorgeous day, the sky an endless blue with just a few high, fat clouds scudding high above.

She turned to look at him, her heart mashed inside her chest. "So you might as well tell me just how bad it is."

He read the article, translating it for her, and by the end she felt physically sick. She covered her mouth, closed her eyes, wanting to be anywhere but trapped in the limousine with him.

Last night while they were making love he knew he was destroying Dante and Daisy's world...last night while holding her, loving her, he was annihilating another family's dreams.

"You knew about the takeover," he said flatly, breaking into her thoughts. "This isn't a complete surprise."

"I didn't realize it'd gone so far."

"It's been in the works for over a year."

"Poor Dante," she murmured, shaking her head.

"Poor Dante?" His voice blistered her. "What

about my mother? What about her? When the Galváns sent her away, she was just a schoolgirl, not even seventeen. What did she know about the world? How was she supposed to fend for herself, and a new baby? The Galváns had millions. Couldn't they at least send her away with a few dollars in her pocket?''

''It's been thirty-some years, Lazaro!''

''And that excuses what they did to her?''

''Not they, Lazaro, he, Tino, your father. But the whole family can't be held responsible!''

''Dante's mother was the one who insisted my mother be sent away. She was the one who made it impossible for my mother to return.''

''So why punish Dante? How is any of this his fault?''

''He knows about me. He knows I exist.''

''No—''

''Yes. We met, Zoe, years ago as children. We traveled to Buenos Aires, my mother and me. I was seven and she took me to my father's house. We rode a bus for three days to get there from the mountains, and then we had to walk a long way from the bus station to this big house in a barrio I'd never seen before. The houses there were all so big. They looked like palaces with the big windows and wrought-iron fences.''

He drew a breath, studied the paper in his hands before shaking his head. ''The walk from the bus station made me very tired. I remember how hungry I was, how thirsty, but Mama told me not to complain but to be happy because I was going to my papa's house.''

"She rang the doorbell and I'll never forget what it looked like when the front door opened. There were big bunches of balloons everywhere and a mountain of wrapped gifts on the table. I could hear music in the house and children laughing. I'd been tired but I suddenly was excited. I thought Mama had brought me to play.''

Zoe felt a knot form in her belly. She held her breath for what might come next.

"My father came to the door and he was not happy to see Mama or me. He yelled at her and dragged her out the front door. She tried to push me toward him and he hit her. He hit her very hard but she didn't make a sound. I remember holding on to her legs, trying to keep her from falling and I looked up at my father and saw the devil—''

"Why the devil?''

He shrugged. "Only the devil would hurt a woman that way.'' He shook his head, raked his hand through his black hair, his face lined with silent pain. "Before we could go, a little boy in a red party hat ran to the door. He'd come crying to his papa because it was his birthday and he couldn't have a second piece of cake. He already had blue icing smeared on his mouth and yet he wanted more.''

Tension rolled from Lazaro in great dark waves. "I'd been shivering, holding up Mama, and this spoiled boy cries over not getting more cake.'' He swallowed, fought for control. "I'm glad Tino didn't take me. I'm glad I had to make it on my own. I don't take anything for granted. Not even the time I've had with you.''

Zoe felt a silent sob form within her and yet she couldn't cry, couldn't speak, couldn't reach out to him. She understood he hurt and she hated what he'd been through, but it wasn't all right for him to hurt others. It wasn't acceptable for him to inflict more pain.

The limousine drew before a tall, stately house with three stories and dozens of elegant paned windows.

''This is it,'' he said as the driver stepped around.

She slid to the edge of her seat, glanced out the open door to the house with its formal front door and pair of pruned topiaries. ''I don't know what to say.''

''I guess there's nothing to say.'' He opened his door, stepped out. ''I'll walk you up.''

''I don't think that's a good idea.''

''I'm not afraid.''

But no one answered the door, not even a maid or butler. They waited, too, and tried again every few minutes, but ten minutes passed and no one came.

Zoe's heart lifted. She was glad.

Glad.

She didn't understand this, didn't understand herself, but she knew one thing, and that was that she was thrilled she didn't have to say goodbye…yet.

She turned on the doorstep and faced him. He stood down a step and they were almost eye-to-eye although he still had an inch or two on her. ''I guess you're going to have to take me with you,'' she said.

His eyes met hers. He nearly smiled. "I'm sorry."

"Liar."

His lips twisted. "All right, I'm not sorry. I don't want to say goodbye. I don't know that I'll ever be ready to say goodbye."

Ten minutes after leaving Dante's house, the limousine pulled in front of a tall, very modern hotel. The blue-gray granite gleamed in the sun. The chauffeur opened the back door. Sunlight streamed into the car.

"We're here," Lazaro said, scooping up the newspaper and stepping from the black car. Outside he turned and extended a hand to Zoe. "My meeting is in a half hour. I have just enough time to get you settled."

The hotel was the latest in ultra-sophisticated, ultra-expensive accommodations. Lazaro didn't just have a luxurious room reserved, but the entire top floor of the hotel, a huge, private, four-room suite.

He must visit often, too, Zoe surmised as everyone in the hotel from the doorman to the concierge greeted Lazaro by name, and with obvious respect.

They were whisked to their suite, the rooms decorated in combinations of blues, reds, and dashes of black. It was a bold scheme, very strong, much like Lazaro himself.

It wasn't until the bell captain carried Zoe's suitcase into the master bedroom and Lazaro opened the closet revealing a row of suits and shirts that Zoe realized this was his own suite. *He lived here.*

"You live in a hotel," she said, as the door closed behind the bell captain.

Lazaro shrugged. "I own the hotel. Why not?"

"You own a hotel?"

"Plus three others in Argentina, one in Uruguay, two in Chile, and the new one under construction in Brazil."

She sat down on the edge of the bed, touched the quilted spread, feeling increasingly disoriented. "You don't own these with Dante, do you?"

"No. They're part of my corporation."

"Dante doesn't know you have your own company."

Lazaro smiled but the smile didn't reach his eyes. "He does now."

She felt strangely ambivalent again. It was always like this on her emotions, a constant tug-of-war, her loyalties always pulled. "I would have thought most of your wealth was tied up in Galván Enterprises."

"The opposite is true. I have very little invested in the Galván corporation—" He was interrupted by the distinct ring of a phone. He took the call, finished it moments later after having only uttered a half dozen words. "I have to go, but I'll be back before dinner, in three, maybe four hours."

"Don't worry about me. I'll be fine here. You have a TV, and I have my book. Time will pass quickly."

"I can make arrangements for one of the women from my travel desk to take you out shopping and sight-seeing—"

"Please don't. I'd prefer to stay here, really. I'm not that social. At home I'm alone most of the time."

"All right, if it's what you want." He kissed her, lightly on the lips, but from the warmth in his eyes she knew his feelings were much more intense. "I'll see you in a couple hours."

Lazaro leaned forward in his chair and hung up the phone in his downtown office. A two-and-a-half-hour conference call, a new personal record, he thought, rubbing his jaw and staring blindly at the notepad where he'd scribbled numbers, phrases, names as he, the American investors, and the board members of Galván Wireless hashed out the crucial points in wireless telecom acquisition.

Dante hadn't participated in the call. Dante wasn't taking Lazaro's calls. Dante wasn't going to accept the takeover attempt sitting down.

He was fighting back. He was fighting to save what was left of his corporation.

Lazaro had to admire him for that.

Lazaro lifted the notepad he'd been writing on and stared at the scrawl on the page. Among the numbers, phrases and terms, he saw the name Zoe.

Zoe Collingsworth.

She hadn't been part of the plan. Lazaro hadn't even known she existed when he decided he'd carve up Galván Enterprises, rendering the mammoth corporation helpless, useless, and prove to Dante that he, a nothing and a nobody from a poor part of town, could rise up and challenge one of Argentina's most wealthy and powerful families.

That Lazaro, without financial means, without private elementary schools, without an old family network, could become someone just as smart, just as successful, just as influential as Dante.

That he could match wits with Dante, and win.

Win.

Tomorrow, or the next day, or the one after that, he'd win. He'd own Galváns's assets. He'd control Galván Wireless. He'd dismantle Galván Enterprises. And then what?

Lazaro dragged his finger across Zoe's name, across the black ink on the white, lined paper. Zoe.

He wanted to see her. He wanted to be with her. It was that simple.

Business over, mission accomplished, all he wanted was Zoe.

He took her to dinner that night to a glamorous city supper club. She let him order for her and his menu choices delighted her. He also ordered an exquisite champagne that tickled her nose and filled her with warmth.

She felt Lazaro's gaze. He'd been more silent than usual tonight. "Are you all right?" she asked.

"Yes."

"You're not saying much."

"Words won't help us, though, will they?"

The backs of her eyes burned. The waiter cleared their dessert plates and she struggled to give the waiter a thank-you and a smile.

Lazaro was right, of course. Thank goodness he had a way of bringing her back down to earth. Wouldn't do to let her imagination carry her away. There wasn't going to be a happy ending for them.

"I should call Dante's house. I'd meant to," she said, reaching for the champagne glass and then pushing it away again. Earlier she'd loved the way the cool champagne fizzed its way down, warming her stomach and sending flickers of fire through her veins, but now she couldn't handle the bubbles, the lightness, the sweetness. She couldn't handle anything beautiful at all.

"We can call now," he said.

She pressed her nails to her palms, fighting tears. "Is that what you want to do?"

"It's the right thing."

She felt pulled between her past and her present. She could hardly hold the tears back and they burned her eyes, burned her nose and throat. "You've never done the right thing. Why start now?"

He flinched, a muscle pulling in his jaw. "I'm trying to protect you, Zoe."

The flickering candle accented the hard, lean planes of his face. She reached across the table and touched his mouth, his chin. She loved the feel of him. He was big, hard, strong. Yet he was also dangerous. He still posed a threat to Daisy and she didn't know how to reconcile herself to that. "You're not protecting me if you hurt people I love."

"Zoe—"

She sat back. "Why can't you stop this takeover? Nothing's official. No deal is signed."

"But it is official. The news went public yesterday, it was all over the papers. Dante has been informed. It's happening, Zoe, whether you like it or not."

Her stomach cramped. She felt a rise of nausea. As angry as she was with Dante, she couldn't bear to think of how he must be feeling now. "If your mother were alive—"

"But she's not. And that's the whole point. I won't let her be forgotten, either."

Zoe blinked, reached for her champagne, needing it now. "Isn't there another way to remember her? Can't you do something that would honor her—"

"I am!"

She tipped the glass against her mouth, drank the dry French wine with the wealth of bubbles. *What a mess,* she thought. *This whole thing…*

He reached out, touched her arm, slid his hand around her fingers. "Before me, no one in my mother's family finished high school, much less graduated from college. I not only attended college, I earned a master's degree in the States, from Stanford University, on the West Coast."

"You've achieved so much. Why can't that be enough?"

His hand slipped away from hers. "Maybe my success came too easy."

"Building the business couldn't have been easy."

He shrugged. "It didn't seem hard."

"You must have worked endlessly."

"I made some sacrifices."

He'd made more than some, he'd made many, she thought, understanding that he couldn't admit all that he'd given up in his quest for success. He was thirty-seven and he'd never married, never had children, never settled down. He'd lived alone and fought his way to the top by the skin of his teeth.

Looking at his grim expression now, she knew it must have been a long, lonely battle.

Her heart twisted yet again. She couldn't reject him and yet she couldn't accept him. There was no peace on this one, no peace at all. "Do you like Buenos Aires?" she asked softly.

"I live here."

"But it's not home?"

He looked as though he were about to answer and then he clamped his jaw, swallowed roughly, his cheekbones growing more pronounced. "No."

"Where do you call home?"

His fingers traced the edge his coffee cup, his eyes narrowed in concentration. "I don't."

"I'm sorry."

He lifted his head, his silver gaze meeting hers. "Don't pity me. I don't want it. Not from you."

The horrible sadness was back, sadness for him, sadness for both of them. "I don't pity you. I can't pity you." *I love you.*

"I wish life was different, *corazón*. I wish I was different, then maybe things could have been different for me and you."

She felt as though the air was slowly being

squeezed from her. "I hate talking, I hate all these words."

"Then let's stop talking. Let's dance."

"Tango?" she protested, glancing toward the dance floor.

"I'll teach you."

He led her through the dark, crowded supper club toward the softly lit dance floor. Zoe moved blindly, aware of nothing but the warmth of his hand and the hard strength of his fingers wrapped around hers. She felt possession in his touch, felt something so real and so alive it made her want to weep.

Life with Lazaro would be big, real, consuming. Life with Lazaro would be unlike anything she'd ever lived before.

She wanted to tell him she loved him. She wanted to lose herself in him for just tonight, but looking up into his face, seeing the shadows in his silver gaze, the words died within her.

Words wouldn't help. There was nothing either of them could say.

On the dance floor he half spun her out and then spun her back into his arms, bringing her close to his chest, his hand firm in the dip of her spine.

It felt like he'd lit a fire beneath her skin. Every place he touched, burned. Every nerve ending pulsed. She felt him step between her legs as he turned her, creating an even closer intimacy.

She clung to him as he spun them across the polished wood floor, footsteps fast and intricate in time to the sultry music, yet the guitar played her heart, and the melancholy sound of the accordion was matched by the cry of the violins.

The music captured her emotions perfectly. Love and longing. Hope and fear. Happiness and despair. In his arms, she felt everything.

He kissed the side of her neck, the same spot he'd touched over a week ago when she'd first arrived. "I shall never forget you, *corazón.* I shall never not love you, my heart."

"Ssssh, don't say anything," she whispered, her breath catching, her voice husky. "I can't bear to think. I just want to feel you, be with you."

His fingers played her spine even as the guitarist played the strings on his instrument. "Then tonight I shall try to pretend, too. I shall try to live as though I'm the right man for you."

And he was the right man, she thought, closing her eyes and resting her cheek on his chest, right now no one had ever been more right. No one had ever made her feel more beautiful, more desirable.

She allowed him to move her, lead her, and felt the delicious connection between them grow. She wanted him. He wanted her. The desire grew, becoming larger, fiercer, taking shape as hunger. "Let's go back to the hotel," she whispered, touching her mouth to his cheek. "Let's go to your room."

"And do what?" he answered, drawing her even closer to him so that she felt the ridge of his chest and the hardness of his hips. He wanted her.

Heat shimmered within her. *"Everything."*

In the sweet darkness of their hotel room they made

love fiercely, as though the intensity of their desire for each other would consume them if they didn't love deeply, passionately.

Swept away by the pleasure of being in Lazaro's arms, Zoe didn't hear the phone ring. It wasn't until Lazaro lifted his head and gazed toward the phone that she heard the ring. Then, and only then, was she drawn back to reality. She hadn't been in reality, she'd been on the moon in the most beautiful dance with him.

"It's three-thirty in the morning," Lazaro said, voice raspy with passion. "Who would be calling now?"

Zoe felt a chill. Good phone calls never came in the middle of the night. "I think you better answer."

He slid out from beneath her warm damp body to take the call. He didn't stay on the phone long. He spoke quickly, tersely, and then hung up.

Snapping the cell phone shut, he moved to the bedside table and turned on the lamp. "You better get dressed. Daisy's in labor."

CHAPTER EIGHT

THE hospital was only fifteen blocks away, but reaching the hospital was the easy part. Getting information was next to impossible. With Dante in the delivery room with Daisy, the nurse at the information desk wouldn't, or couldn't, tell them anything.

Zoe paced the blue and cream maternity waiting room chewing her thumbnail, trying not to think the worst but failing miserably. Dread and fear wrestled within her and she felt a gnawing sense of guilt. She felt responsible for this.

If Daisy lost the baby…

"Don't think that way." Lazaro's voice reached her, interrupted her silent stream of worry.

Seething, she stopped pacing and faced him. "How do you know what I'm thinking?"

"It's all over your face. But you didn't do this, you didn't create this—"

"What was I doing? What was I thinking? I should have been with her. I should have been there for her." Turning away, she retreated to the window.

"How could I do this?" But she wasn't speaking to him as much as herself. How could she have let this happen? Daisy had practically raised her. Daisy was always there for her. She should have put her sister first. "I screwed up."

112

"You didn't screw up. We didn't do anything wrong. We were together, that's it."

"I'm sorry, I can't ignore this, or deny my part. I know what I did. I know what I didn't do. I can't pretend I'm innocent. I should have been with her. Period."

In the clear light of morning, in the cool sterile hospital, she saw him, and her, and it made her stomach turn inside out.

What was she thinking? Why hadn't she been thinking?

She gazed out the window into the courtyard below. The sun was just rising, casting fingers of rose and gold across the stone pavers and the delicate statue of a mother and child. But instead of the coral roses blooming in the courtyard, she saw the fat cabbage rose wallpaper in her dining room at home, remembered the framed photos lining the stairs, the pictures of young Daisy and a mother she'd never known.

Daisy's and Zoe's mother had died in childbirth.

Zoe's voice shook. "If she loses this baby I'll never forgive myself."

"You aren't responsible for her—"

"Get out!" She spun around, pointed at the elevator. "You don't belong here—"

"She's right, you don't belong here." It was Dante, standing at the double doors leading to the delivery room. "Leave now."

Zoe rushed toward him. "How's Daisy? And the baby? Tell me she didn't lose the baby."

But Dante didn't answer, his attention focused on

Lazaro, his jaw granite-hard. He drew a short, sharp breath. "I trusted you," he gritted, ice in his voice, rage glittering in his eyes. "I trusted you, embraced you, made you part of the family."

Lazaro barked a laugh. "I was never part of the family."

"I tried—"

"You never treated me as a brother," Lazaro interrupted harshly, upper lip curling. "I was an employee, a hired hand, nothing more than that."

Dante wheeled back a step. "Is that what you wanted? You wanted to be my *brother?*"

"I *am* your brother."

It was Dante's turn to laugh, coldly, unkindly, his voice ringing too loud in the sterile waiting room. "Maybe in blood, but not in spirit."

Zoe couldn't bear this. "Dante, please."

But he ignored her. He marched on Lazaro, his fury tangible. "If you wanted to be family, come to me as family, open your arms in love, and yes, I'll accept you. But you took a knife and you plunged it in my back. What kind of homecoming do you expect?"

Long-buried pain shadowed Lazaro's eyes. His expression turned bleak. "You had a lifetime to welcome me and you never did."

"I don't know what you're talking about."

"You do."

Dante shook his head impatiently, unwilling to listen to this. "What kind of stories have you told yourself? What kind of lies did your mother make up?"

"Bastard!" Lazaro swore, lunging at Dante.

Zoe threw herself between them. "No! Lazaro, no, don't do this!"

But Dante reached around Zoe, his temper raging, too. "No, *you're* the bastard."

Lazaro ducked, pulled Zoe out from between them, pushing her behind him. "You want to fight? Come on—"

"Lazaro, Dante, no!" Zoe saw Lazaro's tight fists, knew his strength. Dante was nearly as big but she had no doubt that Lazaro was the better street fighter.

They weren't listening to her, too embroiled in their own bitter feud. "I was there," Lazaro continued. "I was at your house, I know the life you lived and you can't pretend you didn't know I existed."

"I had a suspicion, yet I never knew it was you."

"Why didn't you look for me? Why didn't you try?"

"I had my own life, and my own problems—"

"That's right, the poor aristocratic Galváns—"

"Stop it!" Zoe screamed, clapping her hands over her ears, hearing more than she'd ever wanted to hear. This was awful, this was impossible. "What about Daisy? We're here for Daisy. How can you do this now?"

Lazaro wheeled away first, ashen, sickened. He wiped his mouth off, drew a ragged breath. "I can't believe I wanted to be part of your family. What was I thinking?"

"Indeed," Dante answered hoarsely, color darkening his hard cheekbones. He stared Lazaro down, disgust written in his eyes and press of his lips.

''You'll never be part of us, and you're not welcome near us.''

''Good, because I don't want you. I don't want any of you.''

Zoe felt cold, all the way to her bones. *''Lazaro.''*

But Dante's rage grew. ''You know, Herrera, you're the worst kind of blood. You're the kind that festers and poisons and kills. Daisy nearly died last night and I'll never forget the hell you've put us through.''

Zoe's legs buckled. ''Stop—''

Lazaro reached for her but she pulled away, too horrified, and trembling.

Her rejection shook him and he stared at her for a long, tense moment. Shadows gathered in his eyes, shadows of confusion and pain. But this time she couldn't reach out to him. She'd had enough. She had to finally take sides.

''You better go, Lazaro.'' Zoe's voice broke. ''Now.''

His silver gaze narrowed. ''So this is how it is.''

She couldn't bear this. She knew he was suffering but he'd chosen his weapons and his weapons hurt. ''Yes.''

He swallowed hard, a muscle pulling at his jaw. ''Fine. I'll go.''

''Do,'' Dante answered fiercely. ''Go quickly, before I call the police.''

Lazaro disappeared into the elevator, and even as the doors shut, other doors opened and a nurse appeared wearing hospital scrubs. Zoe heard a baby wail, the newborn's cry high and thin, piercing in its intensity.

The nurse gestured toward Dante. "*Por favor.* Your wife wants you."

The nurse led them to a private recovery room. The light was dimmed and the room, although spacious, felt stark. Daisy was awake though, and she lifted her head when Zoe entered the room.

"Zo…" she croaked, smiling weakly. She lifted a hand, fingers bending, entreating Zoe closer.

Daisy had purple shadows beneath her eyes and her pale face looked drawn. Carefully Zoe sat down on the edge of the bed, noting the tubes taped to Daisy's hand and the tubes to her arm. "Are you okay?" Zoe asked.

"I'm fine." Daisy glanced toward Dante who stood just off the foot of her bed and mustered another small, weak smile. "Just a little tired, that's all." She reached out to touch Zoe's hand. "How was the flight? When did you get in?"

So Daisy didn't know Zoe had been with Lazaro. Daisy didn't know about the arrangements Dante had made. Daisy knew nothing about Lazaro. What a web of lies…

Zoe swallowed the lump in her throat, still in turmoil over what she'd witnessed in the waiting room. "Not too long ago," she fibbed, hating the position she'd been put in.

"And Dad?"

"Dad's fine. But more importantly, how are you? And what about the baby?"

The door to Daisy's room opened and a nurse

wheeled in a small glass isolete. "Your son," the nurse said, pushing the isolete with the tiny infant toward Daisy's bed.

"A boy?" Zoe choked, turning around to gaze with wonder at the baby. A miniature mask was delicately taped to his face but he looked beautiful. Small but beautiful.

"Oxygen," Daisy explained, fingers outstretched as if she could touch the baby through the glass. "His lungs are still underdeveloped but the doctors don't think there should be any serious problems later. The pediatrician calls him a little miracle."

"Your baby," Zoe repeated softly. "You have a baby. Daddy will be so happy."

Daisy tried to smile but she couldn't quite do it. "Daddy will finally have his boy."

Outside, in the hospital parking lot, Lazaro sat behind the wheel of his Mercedes sedan. The engine was on, the car in drive, but he couldn't accelerate, couldn't move at all.

It was all out in the open now. No more hidden agendas. No more secrets. No more games.

It was what he'd always wanted it to be, brother against brother until the better brother won.

Lazaro knew the moment he moved publicly against Dante that the relationship would end, but he hadn't expected to feel loss.

He did feel loss. Tremendous loss. And shame.

It crossed his mind as he sat with the car idling and the morning sun glazing the hood of his car, that maybe, just maybe, he'd made a terrible mistake.

*   *   *

Daisy needed rest and Zoe joined Dante in the hospital cafeteria for coffee. They both ordered a breakfast roll and Zoe took a couple bites of hers but Dante didn't touch his.

Dante pushed aside his small plate. "I'm sorry, Zoe. I'm sorry for everything."

"Tell me you didn't ask Lazaro—"

"I did. I was wrong."

"Damn straight you were." She swallowed hard, utterly bewildered by all that had happened in the past week and a half. "How could you?"

"Daisy," he answered simply. "I was worried about her."

"You were worried that *I'd* hurt Daisy?"

He shifted, shoulders shrugging. "The engagement to Carter."

"There was no engagement. Just because he asked me didn't mean I said yes."

"He was spending a lot of time at the farmhouse."

"He was kind to Dad."

"Zoe, he's a crook. Lazaro—" Dante broke off, ground his teeth together, struggling to contain his temper. "He wouldn't agree to help me until after he looked into Carter's record." Some of his tension eased. "Carter has quite a record, Zoe. I don't think you're safe there, at the house, with Carter around."

"I'll keep that in mind." She stared at him hard. "But don't try to make decisions for me, and don't think you know what's best for me. I love Daisy, and I love you, but I'm not a kid anymore—"

"You're only twenty-two."

"Twenty-three," she corrected.

"When?"

"Three months ago." Zoe sighed, shook her head, her long fair hair held back with a simple hair band. "I understand how you wanted to protect Daisy, I feel the same way, too, so I won't tell Daisy what you did, but you have to respect my decisions from here on out."

"Agreed."

She looked at him for a long moment, gathering her courage, trying to find the right words without being unnecessarily hurtful. "What's happening with your...business?"

"My business," he repeated softly, mockingly, before lifting his cup and taking a swallow. "What do you think?"

He didn't say more. He didn't have to.

Zoe practically lived at the hospital over the next couple of days. She sat with Daisy as much as possible, even when Daisy did nothing but sleep. Yet her heart wasn't easy. She thought of Lazaro frequently, but just thinking of him made her feel like a traitor.

As she and Dante switched places at the hospital two days later, Zoe asked Dante for news regarding the takeover. "I'm still fighting," he said, lips twisting into a cynical smile.

"Daisy never talks about it. She does know, doesn't she?"

"She knows, but I think she's in denial. She considered Lazaro a friend. I don't think she understands how he could do this to me."

"I'm sorry. I wish I could have stopped him—"

"How?"

If he'd loved her, he wouldn't have done it.

If he loved her.

She blinked, eyes scratchy. Dante noticed her watering eyes. "You should go back to the house, get some rest. You look tired."

"No more tired than you," she answered. But she did take the waiting limousine back to the house, and she did try to nap. Unfortunately, sleep didn't come. Her brain continued to race and her thoughts haunted her.

She couldn't stop thinking about Lazaro. Couldn't stop missing him, either.

Zoe changed into white jeans, a comfortable knit top and laced up her white sneakers for a walk. She enjoyed being outside and liked walking in Dante's elegant neighborhood.

Reaching the corner, she crossed the street and entered a small public garden. Suddenly she was surrounded, or it felt as though she was surrounded, as a reporter thrust a microphone in her face and another man turned a camera and light on.

The man with the microphone rattled off questions in brisk, flawless English. "Can you confirm your relationship with Lazaro Herrera, Miss Collingsworth? And does your family know, or is it a clandestine affair?"

Zoe froze. She lifted a hand to shield her eyes from the bright camera light. "I don't know what you're talking about."

"The pictures ran in this morning's paper. Pictures of you dancing the tango."

She struggled to follow. The reporter's English was impeccable. It was her brain that wouldn't function. Dancing the tango? Why, the only time she'd danced the tango was that night with Lazaro at the supper club, and that was nearly a week ago. "I'm sorry, there must be a mix-up. The pictures must be of someone else."

"You're Zoe Collingsworth, Count Dante Galván's sister-in-law?"

Zoe opened her mouth, closed her mouth, panic setting in. Daisy couldn't find out about this. Daisy couldn't handle this. Daisy didn't need this on top of everything else.

"It's true that you and Lazaro Herrera are involved?" the reporter persisted.

"No, it's not true."

"And the pictures in the paper?"

She had to get out of here. Had to find Dante. "I can't answer that. If you'll excuse me."

She ran home, blindly, breathlessly. Dante was already there. He had a newspaper with him, one of the English versions printed for the ex-patriots living in Buenos Aires. She held her hand out for the paper and he gave it to her without a word.

On the front page was a large color photo of Lazaro and Zoe dancing. Zoe stared at the photo. A lump filled her throat. "This is bad," she whispered.

"Yes."

"How do we keep this from Daisy?"

"She's already seen it. She gave the paper to me."

Zoe paced the hospital corridor that afternoon in despair. Daisy hadn't been unkind to her, nor had she said a single harsh word, but Daisy was shattered, not just by the very public photograph, but by late-breaking news that Galván Enterprises was close to destruction.

The stock had plummeted since word broke about the hostile takeover. Investors were desperately trying to get rid of their shares and Dante, having trusted Lazaro to manage the corporation's holdings, realized now, too late, that Lazaro had deliberately weakened the company just for this.

There was no way the corporation could gracefully recover, no way Dante could wield any effective power.

Zoe's sense of guilt grew. She should have stopped Lazaro. She could have stopped him if she'd only tried harder. But it wasn't too late to do something now.

Shaking, she stood in the hospital corridor and dialed Lazaro's cellular number. She expected to get his voice mail but he answered. "Lazaro, it's Zoe. I have to see you."

He picked her up from the hospital in his large silver-tone Mercedes sedan. Inside the car she stared at him. His face looked fierce, hard. New lines were etched next to his eyes and mouth, accenting the hump in the bridge of his nose.

Pain washed through her in waves. She still felt so many intense and conflicting emotions. "I want to hate you," she said. "I want to hate you for what you've done."

He just stared out the windshield, his expression

shuttered. "Let's go for a drive," he said at last. "Let's get some privacy so we can talk."

He pulled away from the hospital and they wove through city streets until he reached a quieter residential neighborhood.

She watched him as he drove, wondering why she felt so exquisitely alive, so exquisitely sensitive when together with him. She shouldn't feel this way. Shouldn't care.

He pulled over in front of a park, killed the engine. But he didn't speak.

Zoe wanted him to say something. She wanted him to defend himself or apologize or somehow make it better, but he didn't.

Her heart twisted with fresh hurt. "You told me you'd try to protect Daisy, you told me you'd protect me."

"I wanted to protect you—"

"Then why didn't you do it? You promised me you would. I want you to keep the promise you made me. Find a way to fix this."

"I can't undo what's been started—"

"But you can find an end to it. I know you can, Lazaro." She loved him. Still. But she couldn't bear to love a man like him, couldn't bear to be in love with someone who would injure and wound. "They can't lose everything. You must do something. I know you can. I know you. If anyone can fix this, you can."

He sighed, frowned. His dark eyebrows pulled together. "There is a way—"

"Fine. Do it."

"You'd be part of it."

"Anything, as long as you make this nightmare go away."

There was no gentle way to break the news, Zoe realized later as Daisy let out a howl of rage.

"Marry Lazaro Herrera?" Daisy's voice rose, and she staggered up from the chair in her hospital room. "Absolutely not. You can *not* marry him, Zoe. I forbid it."

Zoe knew this would be difficult and tried to stay calm now. "You can't forbid it, Daisy. This is my choice, my life."

Daisy's long silver-blond hair danced as she shook her head. "Don't do it, Zo, don't even think about it."

"It'll save Dante's company."

"Dante would rather go broke."

Zoe didn't believe it, not for a minute. Maybe right now, in the heat of battle, Dante imagined he'd prefer to starve than concede victory to Lazaro, but later, after things calmed down, Dante would realize there were too many people dependent on him to let his pride get in the way. This wasn't just about taking care of Daisy and the new baby, he had his three sisters to think of, as well as an extravagant stepmother in need of frequent cash infusions.

"You don't want Dante to lose everything," Zoe answered softly. She clasped her hands together, trying to hide the fact that she was trembling. Confronting Daisy was the hardest thing she knew how to do. It was impossible standing up to her. Daisy had always been Zoe's heroine.

"Dante won't lose everything. He's fighting the takeover—"

"Making the Galván stock prices fall faster." She got to her feet, approached Daisy with outstretched hands. "I understand the stock has already lost two-thirds of its value. If Dante continues to fight the takeover he'll lose it all."

"He's smarter than that."

"It's not an issue of intelligence, Daisy, it's timing. Lazaro hit Dante when Dante was weak—"

"So how can you even consider marrying him? Lazaro Herrera is evil. Malicious. Manipulative—" Daisy's voice fell away as she drew a strangled breath. "My God, he's destroying us for what? *His father's sins?* Why make Dante suffer for something that isn't his fault? What did Dante ever do to Lazaro but support him…empower him? How could Lazaro betray Dante like this?"

Zoe's stomach hurt. She felt sick all the way through her. "I don't know."

"You can't marry him."

"We've already set the date."

"No!"

Zoe winced at the pain and outrage in her sister's voice. They'd had fights before, disagreements before, but never anything like this. "Daisy, give him a chance to make things right."

"Give him a chance? A chance to do what? Destroy the rest of us?" Daisy's expression turned stricken. "I hate him. I hate what he's doing to Dante. I hate what he's doing to us and I'll never feel differently. Never!"

"We will fix this—"

"You can't fix this one, Zo. And you can't marry him. If you do, you'll have cut yourself off from us."

"*Daisy,*" Zoe pleaded, "please don't say that."

"You marry him, and you're not part of this family."

Tears filled Zoe's eyes and she clasped her hands together to hide the trembling. "Not even if I can help save Dante's company?"

"*No! No, no, no.*" Daisy pounded her fist on the door. "If you marry, you marry for love, and you marry for happiness, but you *don't* marry for money!"

"Maybe I do love him."

"You can't mean it."

"We've already applied for the license and gotten the blood test. The ceremony is Saturday."

Daisy's chin lifted, her blue eyes glacier-cold. "Then this is goodbye."

Desperation swept through Zoe. She'd never felt panic like this. It was as if a frigid wind had blown in and it chilled Zoe's blood. "Tell me you're joking."

"I'm serious. You marry Lazaro Herrera and we're finished." Daisy sounded hard, impossibly harsh, but then her lips quivered as she fought for control. "Don't do it, Zoe, please, Zoe, don't do it. For my sake, if nothing else."

Zoe's heart ached. It felt as though it would burst any minute. "I love you, Daisy."

Daisy ground her teeth together, even as tears welled in her eyes. "Listen to me, Zoe. You marry him, and we're finished. Do you understand?"

CHAPTER NINE

LAZARO looked gorgeous in his tuxedo. With his black hair and hard, chiseled features he looked like pictures of Hollywood leading men. As he stood at the end of the cathedral, just below the altar, Zoe thought of the rugged film star on the red carpet, smiling for the cameras.

He was smiling for the cameras now.

It was their wedding and he was playing it the way they'd agreed. They'd scripted the wedding, scripted their reunion, scripted the merger between Galván Wireless and Argentine Wireless, a merger which still left Lazaro in charge but had stopped the Galván stock from plummeting and protected Dante's personal fortune.

Lazaro had been amused by her insistence on making it a real wedding. She'd told him she was only getting married once, so it might as well be authentic.

Now she knew why he'd laughed at her. Standing in the Buenos Aires cathedral, wearing a twenty-thousand-dollar designer gown, while four hundred guests waited for her to walk down the aisle was not exactly a personal, authentic ceremony.

There was nothing remotely personal, or authentic about this ceremony. Daisy hadn't come. Dante had been coerced into standing with Lazaro at the front of the church, something which made Zoe cry privately with shame.

This wasn't her idea of a white wedding, even though her hand-beaded gown was white, and lavish white lilies and orchids cascaded from the ends of each dark wood pew.

Zoe began to tremble in her new white satin heels. She clutched her bouquet tighter, pressed her elbows to her waist. She could feel the clear sequins and pearls stitched to the fitted white gown, feel the weight of the long silk train and the stiff veil anchored to her jeweled tiara.

She was dressed like a princess but felt like a fraud. This wasn't how it was supposed to go, this wasn't how her wedding was ever going to be. She'd meant it when she and Daisy promised years ago to only marry for love. She'd meant to keep the vow.

Zoe felt a bubble of hysteria rise and it was all she could do to hold it in. She couldn't run away, even if she wanted to. She couldn't disappear...where would she go?

As if sensing her panic, Lazaro turned, and looked down the long carpeted aisle to where she stood at the back of the cathedral. Late afternoon light flooded the massive stained-glass windows, turning the church interior into a living Chagall. The enormous vases of lilies scented the church with an almost overpowering perfume.

His gaze found hers and held. From twenty feet away she felt his confidence and his intensity. He'd never struck her as arrogant, she realized, just determined. He didn't strike her as arrogant now, just more determined.

He was the kind of man who'd move mountains if necessary.

He'd moved those mountains, too.

As his gaze continued to hold hers, she felt a ripple of sensation in her middle followed by a burst of heat. He was the most physical man she'd ever known and she responded to him helplessly, instinctively. Even now she reacted to him as if he were the only man alive. The only man left on earth.

Blinking, she held back gritty tears, forced herself to concentrate on the tall taper candles on the altar and the huge organ pipes on the wall. She'd never seen a church so big before, had never even entered a cathedral before. What was she doing, getting married here? Who did she think she was, marrying like this?

The bouquet in her hands was heavy, the opulent sweetness of the lilies making her head start to ache. She didn't think she could stand here another minute but suddenly the organ swelled, filling the cathedral with rippling sound. The sound was too big, too strong.

Her cue.

It was her turn to move, to walk down the aisle and join Lazaro at the front of the cathedral.

Zoe didn't know how she reached the altar. Her legs were shaking like mad, her pulse racing too fast.

The priest was talking, speaking first in Spanish and then in English, and yet it might as well have been Greek. She understood almost nothing. Time seemed to pass in slow motion.

Lazaro was staring down at her, his expression hard, almost mocking. She wanted to run from the hardness in him, wanted to escape.

"Zoe Elizabeth Collingsworth, do you take this man to be your lawfully wedded husband," the priest's voice pierced her panic, forcing her attention back to the ceremony. "For better or worse, richer or poorer, in sickness and in health…"

Zoe didn't hear the rest, her eyes riveted on Lazaro's face.

He was so angry with her.

He didn't have a right to be angry. He'd started this.

So why was she marrying him?

To save Galván Enterprises. It was the only way to ease the backlash against Dante and his family. The only way to forge a relationship between Dante and Lazaro.

Unity. Family. Commitment.

Zoe pressed down through her white satin heels, locked her knees for courage.

This wasn't a hostile takeover, but a family merger. It wasn't a collapse of Galván Enterprises but a new union of two brothers' fortunes.

"Till death do you part," the priest intoned.

She caught the flicker of Lazaro's eye, caught the tightening of his jaw.

She swallowed. "I do."

And Lazaro smiled without a hint of warmth.

* * *

Ceremony over, they rode in the back of the stretch limousine, heading from the city cathedral to the exclusive country club on the outskirts of Buenos Aires.

"Are you happy?" Lazaro drawled, sitting opposite her.

She didn't even try to smile. She couldn't.

"It's what you wanted," he continued, filling the silence. There was an edge to his voice, anger in his voice. "The wedding was your idea. You insisted on it."

She couldn't look at him. "You were going to ruin their lives."

"It was just money."

"Don't say that," Zoe whispered in the dark, her voice choked. Her chest felt tight, the air strangled in her throat. "You know Dante's whole family depends on him. His sisters, his stepmother, Daisy and now the baby."

"We all make choices."

"Yes, and you chose to wound." Head aching, she closed her eyes, tipped her head against the window's glass, longing to disappear. How was she possibly going to make it through the reception?

Lazaro's voice cut through her thoughts. "You chose to play the sacrificial lamb, Zoe. You came to me."

No, he felt absolutely no remorse.

She opened her eyes, looked at him, watched as the shadows flickered across his face, highlighting the high, carved cheekbones, the long broken nose, the full sensual mouth. His features were so hard, so distinct, they were beautiful.

She was reminded of that first night, in the helicopter, when he'd stolen her from the airport and whisked her to his home on the pampas. Her heart tightened, chest tender. Even at his worst, she was still drawn to him. "I wasn't going to watch Dante and Daisy's world crash down on them."

"But this isn't just about them," he said flatly. "This is as much for you. You didn't want to lose me. You couldn't let go."

Her head snapped up, her lips parted in denial but she couldn't find her voice. He was right, of course. She couldn't hide anything from him, not even her feelings.

Especially her feelings.

"Am I supposed to feel sorry for you?" she choked, nails pressed to the crusted silk skirt. Their limousine was creeping through the city traffic and nearly at a standstill.

"¡Por Dios! Sorry for me? No. I have what I wanted. Everything I've ever wanted."

She flinched inwardly, his words striking her as though they were sharp stones. Turning away, she looked out the tinted window, her gaze scanning the crowded sidewalks. "And what is it you wanted?"

"You."

She shook her head in denial. "You don't want me."

"Don't want you? Zoe, I love you. I've loved you since the first night I met you. I knew then you'd change everything, and you have."

"Words," she whispered. "They're just words."

Outside the car she spotted an elderly man clinging

to a newspaper kiosk, his handsome but weathered face lined with pain.

She drew a small, shallow breath, feeling her emotions dance dangerously on edge. "Why would you love me, Lazaro? What do you love about me?"

He leaned forward, caught her by the upper arms and lifted her off her seat onto his. Her silk skirts swished and whispered as she slid onto the leather next to him and he lifted her face to his, his fingers spanning her cheek and jaw.

"Why would I love you?" he repeated huskily, thumb stroking the curve of her cheekbone, his narrowed gaze studying her closely. "Just look at you."

Her heart ached. "If this is about beauty—"

"Not just beauty, although you're beautiful, but all of you. Your kindness, your sweetness, your spirit, your strength. You are what I'm not. I'm drawn to you, like a moth to a lamp, or darkness to light."

"Don't say it like that."

"But it's true. What am I but shadows and secrets? What do I want but revenge?" He covered her mouth with his, parting her lips with the pressure from his, and drank in air from her lungs.

Zoe felt him draw her breath into his mouth and her head grew light. She placed her hands against his chest to steady herself, and was vividly reminded of his strength. His chest was all warm, hard, taut muscle beneath his white shirt and she flashed back to two weeks ago when they were at the hotel, making love. She flashed to the feel of being in his arms, naked against his flesh.

She loved him, and yet he scared her. She'd never

felt so confused in all her life. Tears seeped beneath her closed eyelids and trickled out.

Lazaro lifted his head, caught a tear with a tip of his finger. "You're crying."

"I don't understand you."

"You don't need to understand me."

Her chest squeezed tight and her throat ached with tears. "How can you say that? I'm going to live with you. I've married you."

"But you're not going to change me. You can't hope to change me. I am what I am, and this, Zoe, is me."

She couldn't answer and she felt his sudden impatience. He lifted her from her knees and returned her to her seat. "Don't cry," he said, "it's your wedding day."

His cool voice and his mocking words made her feel horrifyingly alone. What in God's name had she done?

Averting her head she again spotted the elderly man in the blue blazer. He'd made his way from the newspaper kiosk to the street corner, where he now clung to the streetlight.

The man staggered a step, swayed on his feet, and staggered another. His progress was painfully slow and he'd pause frequently to draw a deep breath and run a trembling hand through his thick white hair.

Zoe felt sick watching him. He reminded her of her own father, reminded her that life was short and time fleeting.

She wanted to help the man outside but didn't know what to do, didn't know how to help.

Suddenly Lazaro opened his door and climbed out. Black tuxedo jacket flapping, he approached the elderly man, and placed a hand on the man's shoulder.

Lazaro's forehead furrowed as he spoke, and Zoe watched, her heart beating hard, and doubly fast. She hadn't realized that Lazaro had seen the man, she hadn't realized that Lazaro would notice someone else's pain.

Her heart turned over yet again.

Lazaro lifted a hand, signaled to a taxi. Placing a hand under the other man's elbow, Lazaro walked the gentleman to the waiting taxi and assisted him in. Lazaro drew bills from his wallet, handed the money to the elderly man and the taxi pulled away.

Lazaro returned to the limousine and the limousine moved forward.

Lazaro didn't look at her and Zoe didn't know what to say. *If he wants to talk, he'll talk,* she told herself, hoping he'd talk, hoping he'd explain.

The limousine made a right at the corner, zigzagged through more traffic before merging onto the expressway. But Lazaro didn't explain.

Dante arrived at the reception late, appearing nearly two hours after the dinner had started. He didn't make any excuses as he took a seat at Zoe and Lazaro's table.

Lazaro said nothing to Dante, but she cast her brother-in-law a worried glance. "Is everything all right?"

Dante lifted the glass of wine sitting untouched until now at his place. "Why shouldn't it be?"

"Well, Daisy—"

"She's not happy."

Zoe chewed on the inside of her lip. "But the baby, he's fine?"

"He's good."

Zoe forced a smile. "Good."

The orchestra had begun to play and photographers approached the table and snapped photos of Dante, Lazaro and Zoe together. Their smiles were tight and uncomfortable, but all were careful to maintain the facade of togetherness for the cameras and guests.

Photographs over with, Zoe danced the first dance with Lazaro but neither spoke. Lazaro was more distant than ever and Zoe was afraid if she tried to talk that she'd end up in tears, and tonight she couldn't, wouldn't, cry. Not for anything.

Dante asked Zoe to join him for the second dance. With the media clustered on the edge of the dance floor, he partnered her in a slow waltz, the elegant Strauss waltz a sharp contrast to Dante's barely concealed hostility.

"Things will get better," she said quietly, "I promise."

Dante's jaw jutted. "Don't make promises you can't keep."

"I do intend to keep them, especially this one. I'll find a way to make it up to you."

"You can't. This is between Lazaro and me. It's always been between him and me."

She heard her name called, turned, and blinked as a flashbulb exploded. "Quite a crowd," she murmured, finding it hard to concentrate on the one-two-three box steps she'd learned back in junior high school when Daisy had insisted Zoe take ballroom lessons as part of her etiquette training. It was a six-week charm school course on Saturdays, and Daisy had driven Zoe to the lessons herself, wanting Zoe to know the things she didn't know, already wanting Zoe to have experiences Daisy wouldn't have.

"Lazaro would put on a show."

"He's happy, and I really do believe he loves me—"

"He can't love you because he doesn't know how to love anyone."

"I don't agree."

Dante's expression turned grim. "I'm not going to let you do this. I won't let you throw your life away. You're going to leave with me. We'll go now—"

"You must be joking!"

"Not at all. We'll walk out together. No one will stop us, not with reporters and photographers here. My car is out front waiting. Don't worry about your things, we'll get you whatever you need tomorrow."

"I can't, Dante, I can't do that to him."

"Why not? He'd do it to you if the price was right."

She saw his lips twist in a hard, cynical smile and suddenly saw Lazaro in him, saw the resemblance between them. It wasn't the eyes, but the mouth. They had the same curve of lip, and the same wide, sensual mouth. Even the way they smiled was the same. Which was probably why no one had noticed the resemblance before. Dante smiled frequently. Lazaro rarely did.

Yet Lazaro was beautiful when he smiled. He was like another man altogether. A man with hopes. A man with dreams.

As they danced, they passed a cluster of photographers. More camera flashes popped, bright blue-white blinding bits of light.

As she blinked, he drew her to the edge of the dance floor. "We're going to walk now," he said flatly. "Once we break through the crowd, just keep going. My driver is in front, waiting. He knows we're coming. Daisy knows we're coming—"

"No." She couldn't do this. Couldn't walk and leave Lazaro here, alone, not tonight, not at their reception.

"Zoe, if you don't leave now you might not get the chance again."

"I know." But she saw from Dante's puzzled expression that he didn't understand.

She couldn't explain it, couldn't justify it, couldn't find any rational explanation, but she loved Lazaro. When she looked at Lazaro she saw someone Dante didn't see. She saw Lazaro the great, Lazaro the tender. She saw a man who needed love and she loved him.

It was that simple. "I'm not walking out on him," she said, eyes burning as she doggedly lifted her chin. She untangled her hand from the crook of his arm. "This is my life. This is my future. I want to be with Lazaro."

The music ended and the orchestra had yet to start a new piece. Dante and Zoe stood at the edge of the dance floor.

''He'll destroy you, Zoe.''

Her chest felt tender and she blinked. ''I don't believe it. He's not like that—''

''That's what I thought, too, until he proved me wrong. I thought I knew him. I thought I knew what kind of man he was. But he isn't like you or me. He isn't like anyone you've ever met. He'll hurt you badly—''

''Bad-mouthing me on my wedding day, brother?'' Lazaro mocked, appearing beside them. He looked relaxed, his expression deceptively friendly, yet Zoe felt his tension and saw the cynicism in his brittle silver gaze.

Dante didn't even flinch. He turned to Zoe, took her hands in his. ''Come with me. I'll get you home, I'll put you on a plane back to Kentucky.''

Zoe's chest felt far too tender and bruised. ''Goodbye, Dante. Thank you for coming tonight.''

Dante's amber gaze turned frosty. ''I'm not leaving without you.''

Her smile hurt. Her heart hurt. This was worse than painful, this was hell. She loved Dante and Daisy but she couldn't live for them, or through them. ''But I'm not going with you,'' she answered as gently as possible. ''I'm not leaving Lazaro. Please, don't do this here, now, not on my wedding day.''

''Zoe—''

''No, Dante. Don't make it worse than it has to be.''

Dante looked exhausted, and spent. ''You'll call, if you change your mind.''

''Yes, but I won't change my mind.''

Dante shrugged. He'd done what he could. "You know where to find me, Zoe, should you need me."

She didn't see Dante leave, didn't see him cross the ballroom or walk out the white-paneled doors, her vision blinded by scalding tears.

Neither she nor Lazaro spoke. The musicians had started up again and the dance floor was filling fast. A peal of laughter sounded from the far side of the room and Zoe glanced that direction, from where the laughter had come.

"You could have left," Lazaro said roughly. "You could have walked just now."

She turned slowly to face him, and met his gaze. "I know."

His expression shifted, suspicion giving way to bewilderment. "Why didn't you?"

"I made you a promise. One's word must mean something. You taught me that."

"He's right, you know. I can't keep you here, I can't make you do this."

"No one is making me do anything."

He lifted a black eyebrow. He didn't understand. She wasn't sure she did, either.

"What am I supposed to think?" he asked, his voice deep, husky with emotion he couldn't express.

He hated this, she realized, he hated not understanding, not knowing, not being able to predict. Far better that she reject him outright than give him hope...

Suddenly she didn't want to argue anymore, didn't want to waste time on bad feelings, or family feuds. This was her wedding. This was her night.

A waiter carrying a tray of champagne flutes passed close by. Zoe lifted two flutes from the oval silver tray and handed one to Lazaro and kept the other glass.

As she handed the flute to Lazaro, her fingers brushed his and she felt a ripple of warmth, expectation, as well as pleasure.

She suddenly felt older. Stronger. More sure of herself. She wanted to be here. She wanted to be with him. "To us," she said quietly, lifting her goblet.

He didn't answer immediately. He gazed down at her, the same puzzled expression that had shadowed his eyes earlier back. "You could have had a great life."

She stared into his silver-gray eyes. "I'm going to have a great life."

"Zoe—"

"You're not the only one that feels deeply. I feel things deeply, too. I feel things deeply for you."

His face could have been an iron mask. There wasn't a twitch of muscle anywhere, not a change of expression. "You're too beautiful. I don't deserve you."

"We all deserve to be loved," she answered gently. "Even you. Especially you."

Lazaro pushed the stiff white veil from her bare shoulder, his fingertips sliding over her collarbone and her smooth satiny skin. His eyes darkened, the silver-gray turning to smoke. "You give me hope, Zoe. You make me believe."

Her head tipped back, her throat revealed, the candles and dim light from the chandelier dazzling her eyes. "You should believe. You must believe in us. I do."

He was beautiful, she thought, and his face with its hard lines and sensual lips made her crave to touch him, to be part of him. Her stomach clenched, belly tightening with need. She wanted to feel him again, to be part of him again, to have him make her his.

His hands on her breasts. His mouth on her lips. His body taking complete possession of hers.

"Then to us," he murmured, drawing her closer to him, nearly crushing the full, beaded skirt. "I will drink to us."

She brought the goblet to her mouth, tasted the crisp barely sweet champagne, the color pale gold, elegant, the stuff weddings were made of.

But she didn't need the champagne fizz to add to the bubbles inside of her. Something else was happening here, something new and strong.

She stood on tiptoe and pressed close to him. Her lips briefly touched his. "I love you, *corazón*."

There was pain in his eyes. "Don't—"

"It's true. I do love you. You're part of my heart now."

He drew her completely against him, held her close, so close she could feel the steady drum of his heart and the heat of his body. "I don't know what to say. I can't find the right words."

Tears smarted her eyes and her throat burned. Zoe felt warmth rise up in her like a hot-air balloon, filling her chest with tenderness, protectiveness. "Then let's not talk. Just dance with me. And if you forget how, I'll show you."

CHAPTER TEN

THE reception was still in full swing when she and Lazaro made their escape. They were driven from the country club back to Lazaro's hotel.

The curtains were open in the living room and they had a magnificent view of the city, lights sparkling under a bright full moon.

Lazaro slid off his tuxedo jacket and dropped it on the back of the white couch. Zoe watched as he unfastened the top buttons on his dress shirt, leaving the collar open and his tanned throat exposed. He rolled up the sleeves of his shirt without either of them saying a word.

Her stomach felt like a bundle of nerves and she pressed her hands to the sides of her skirt. She felt shy all of a sudden, and inexperienced. They were married now. Married.

"Turn around," he said, moving toward her.

She did as he told her, drawing a swift breath as his hands settled on her shoulders. He slid his hands beneath the stiff veil, lifted the starched fabric and kissed her neck.

Just that one touch of his mouth to her neck sent rivulets of feeling through every limb.

He kissed her again and then slowly began plucking the pins from the tiara. "Your head must ache. This crown weighs a couple pounds."

144

"It is a little heavy," she admitted, thinking that it didn't take much for him to waken her senses. She responded so instinctively to him, so attune to his touch, his heat and energy that just being near him made her want so much more.

Carefully he lifted the tiara and veil from the top of her head, before sending it onto the couch along with his tuxedo jacket.

His hands moved to the tiny hooks on the back of her gown. "I want you, *corazón*. I want you, all of you."

He kissed her nape and she dipped her head, her loose hair brushing her cheek. She loved the way he touched her, loved the way he made her feel. When he kissed her like this, and held her tenderly, it felt like it was just the two of them alone, the two of them alone against the world.

Slowly he began to undo the dozens of tiny hooks hidden in the seam of the gown. As he unfastened each hook he kissed her back, kissing each vertebra all the way down until he reached the top of her bustier, and then he touched his tongue to the skin exposed above the delicate satin and silk lingerie.

The feel of his tongue on her bare skin made her shiver. She nearly cried.

"You're so sensitive," he said, sliding his hands down her sides, from her ribs to her small waist, fingers spanning the narrow width.

"Tonight, especially," she agreed, eyes closing as he continued his quest, slipping her wedding gown over her slim hips, down her silk-covered thighs until the expensive jewel-crusted gown lay in a decadent puddle at her feet.

With the gown discarded he slid his hands back up her legs, working from the instep to the ankle, along the inside of her knee.

Zoe sucked in air as his mouth replaced his hands on her thighs, his breath warm against her heated skin, his tongue playing across the fine white silk stocking encasing her thigh.

"I want to kiss you," he said, stroking the inside of her thigh.

She needed kissing, she thought, feeling rather frantic. Her mouth definitely needed attention. "Yes."

And then his mouth touched her at the apex of her thighs, his lips caressing her through silk panty. Her legs trembled, and she grabbed his shoulders.

His breath teased and tickled through the silk, and the sensation of his mouth against her made her half crazy with need. It was amazing to feel so much at one time, from the snug pressure of her boned corset to the tug of her garter strap to the heat of his mouth and hands.

She dug her hands into his hair and savored the feel of his thick, crisp hair, the feel of his mouth against her most tender part of her body. "Lazaro," she choked, voice husky and full of longing.

"What's wrong?"

"I want...I want..." Passion colored her voice. She didn't even sound like herself. "More."

"Like this?" he asked, caressing the back of her thighs, the curve of her bottom.

Exactly like that.

She could hardly breathe, hardly think, mindlessly aware of the heat of his hands against her sensitive skin and the intimacy of his mouth to her sex. It was, this was, the sweetest of pleasures.

He made everything feel good. He made everything right. He could do anything to her, she thought, dizzy with need, and she'd enjoy it. All she wanted was to belong to him, to be made part of him.

Heat burned through her, staining her cheeks. "Let me touch you," she begged.

"No, this is my turn to love you."

She couldn't say another word, or think another coherent thought. He was kissing her through her silk panties again, blowing air against her skin and then tracing the shape of her with his tongue. His breath made her shiver. The tip of his tongue nearly made her scream. She arched helplessly as one of his hands slipped beneath the elastic on the panty leg, pushing aside the tiny scrap of silk to kiss her again.

Zoe dug her hands into his hair, needing him, needing to touch him, needing to hold him as close as possible. They'd made love before but never this, nothing had ever been like this. She couldn't imagine anything ever being more intimate. If she wasn't his before, she was now.

Her body began to tense, the coiling of desire building into growing waves of pleasure. Yet as much as she enjoyed his mouth on her, as much as she liked the feel of his warm mouth on her warm wet body, she wanted to be face-to-face, chest-to-chest.

"I need you in me," she whispered, gently breaking free. "Make love to me, Lazaro, make love to me now. Please."

Lazaro didn't need more encouragement. He'd wanted her all night, had hungered for her for weeks. He'd felt empty without her in his arms, in his bed. But it wasn't sex he wanted as much as love.

Her love.

He needed her love more than he needed air.

Swinging her into his arms, he carried her into the bedroom and together they undressed him before he pushed her back onto the bed, against the mountain of snowy-white pillows. Her hair gleamed in the dark, the lightest shade of gold, and he knelt over her, seeing yet again the beautiful perfection of her face, the straight nose, the wide thickly lashed eyes, the mouth.

The mouth.

He covered her mouth with his own, touched his tongue to hers, and drank her in.

"I love you," he whispered in Spanish. "I will love you forever and ever."

When they finally made love he buried himself deeply in her, filling her, settling into her as though he'd come home for the first time in his life.

He'd never felt so much joy, or peace, and his eyes burned. He was unable to fathom the depth of his emotion. He felt like a man given a second chance, a new life.

He could do anything.

He could be anything.

He could even make her happy.

Lazaro moved in her, deeply, slowly, prolonging the contact, heightening the intensity, allowing the pleasure and sensation to build. He was with her. He was in her. He was giving all of himself to her. They'd never be as close as they were now.

"Lazaro," she whispered, touching his face, bringing him even closer.

"Yes, *corazón?*"

"I love you."

"I know. And I'll never take you, or your love, for granted. I swear."

Later, after they were warm and relaxed, Zoe turned to him, gazed at him in the dark, trying to see his face, wanting to see his eyes. "The man we saw today, downtown..."

"Yes?"

"You put him in the cab."

Lazaro shifted slightly, his arm moving to circle her waist. "He was in pain."

Zoe felt a rush of fierce emotion and suddenly knew she'd done something right by loving him.

They'd come from different places, faced different obstacles, and yet they needed each other. Were meant for each other.

Leaning over, she kissed his mouth, his beard grazing her chin. She cupped his cheek, loving the feel of him. Loved his strength and hard edges. "Thank you for helping him." Her voice came out husky, roughened by emotion, exhaustion and passion.

She could feel his jaw tighten against her palm, his cheekbone growing prominent. "Don't thank me. It was the least I could do."

"I kept thinking it could have been my father."

His jaw tightened yet again. "I'm sure he was someone's father, just as he was someone's son."

Later, after she'd fallen asleep in his arms, Lazaro lay awake for a long time, well over an hour, weighing the past, considering the future.

He'd heard the longing in Zoe's voice when she mentioned her father. She missed him.

For her, the ties to her family were very tight, very binding. He wasn't comfortable with ties like that, had never been connected the way she was connected, yet he was beginning to understand that he and Zoe were different, had different needs.

Had he done the right thing, marrying her? Had he hurt her more than he'd helped?

He didn't know, didn't want to know, in case his motives hadn't been pure.

They spent the first week of their honeymoon doing little besides savoring each other's company. There were dinners out, visits to nightclubs and theater, shopping trips that lasted all day and resulted in bags and boxes of the newest designer fashions.

Lazaro had the means to dress Zoe and he loved to watch her model evening gowns and stylish pantsuits, casual daywear and skimpy swimsuits.

As she slowly twirled in front of the boutique's full-length mirror, Lazaro applauded. He loved her in silver and gold, loved her in white, loved her naked and eager beneath him.

Zoe caught his eye and her cheeks bloomed pink. Shyly she wagged a finger at him. "I know what you're thinking."

"I can't help wanting you. I won't ever stop wanting you."

She placed her hands on her hips, an unconsciously provocative pose in the snug silver-sequin gown. "Are you sure this isn't just about sex?"

His gaze swept her flushed face, taking in her full soft mouth, the bright laughing eyes. He'd never lived until he met her, never felt like a man at all. "If it is, then why does my heart hurt?"

Her smile faded. "It shouldn't hurt your heart to love me."

"It's only because I'm so happy. I'm not used to this kind of happiness."

"Lazaro…"

"I'd lay down my life for you, you know that, Zoe. I'd give up everything for you. You're the best thing I've ever known, the best part of me."

Her eyes filled with tears and she crossed the floor to kneel next to him. Her heart ached with an emotion she couldn't articulate, and barely understood. "I'm not the best part, *we're* the best part," she whispered urgently, hands against his thighs, her heart thumping too hard, as if she'd been running too fast. "It's not you or me, it's us. Us together. Us making a life together."

He reached toward her, stroked her hair, let a long loose blond tendril slip through his fingers. "I think it's too good to be true—"

"No."

"I think sometimes it's wrong to have so much happiness, especially as it has come at the expense of others."

He was talking about Dante, talking about her family and she drew a painful breath. "It will all work out, Lazaro, I am sure of it."

"You must miss Daisy."

Her heart squeezed tight. She did miss Daisy, and she missed Dante and the baby, too. She had a nephew she'd never been allowed to touch or hold and she wanted to sit with him in her arms and stare into his little face and learn all about this new person.

But that wasn't going to happen, not now, not the way things were. "We'll get this resolved one day," she repeated firmly, voice thickening. She didn't want to think about what she'd given up; she had to believe that they'd get through this, find a way to mend the fences. "Things always work out in the end."

He smiled but the smile didn't touch his eyes. The expression in his eyes was sad, troubled. "Sweet Zoe," he said, kissing her forehead. "So innocent."

They returned to the hotel and although Lazaro had made dinner reservations at one of Buenos Aires's most exclusive clubs, Zoe begged to stay in and just lounge at home. "We could rent a movie, or watch TV," she said, "and room service could send up hamburgers and ice cream."

"What about your new dress? I thought you'd want to show it off."

The silver-sequin gown was breathtaking but Zoe didn't want to show off. She just wanted to be alone with Lazaro, wanted to sit close and simply be held. "I'd rather just sit on the bed with you."

They ordered hamburgers and French fries and rented a movie from the hotel cable system. Halfway through the movie, the phone rang. Lazaro glanced at his watch and, muttering something under his breath about the late hour, answered the phone.

He spoke rapidly in Spanish and hung up less than a minute later. "Good thing we stayed in," he said, reaching for his cast-off shirt and pair of trousers. "Dante and Daisy are here, waiting to see us downstairs. They're on their way up now."

Zoe grabbed her jeans from the side of the bed and the fun pink and orange tie-dyed shirt Lazaro had bought her a few days ago. She had just enough time to run a brush through her hair before the doorbell sounded.

Emerging from the bathroom, she looked at Lazaro. His gaze met hers and he must have seen her fear. "It's okay," he said quietly. "We're together, remember?"

Dante and Daisy had come without the baby. Daisy wore a leather coat and Zoe offered to take it but Daisy declined. "I'm fine," Daisy said flatly. "Besides, we're not staying that long."

Zoe felt a pang.

"Dad's missing," Daisy said without preamble, no emotion in her voice. She kept her cool blue gaze fixed on a point just beyond Zoe's shoulder. "I thought you should know."

Zoe turned to ice. She balled her hands with difficulty. "How long has he been gone?"

"Nearly twenty-four hours. He disappeared from the nursing home."

"Why didn't you call me sooner?"

Daisy's head jerked and her hard gaze met her sister's. "I didn't think you cared anymore."

Zoe felt the words sink in and they sliced through her, as though Daisy had cut her with a knife. Zoe's lips parted and yet she couldn't breathe, couldn't speak, the pain too deep. "Of course I care! I love Dad. I love *you*."

Daisy gritted her teeth, her jaw jutting whitely. "Dante's flying out tonight to join the search. He already has Clemente working with the police."

"I'd like to go, too," Lazaro said. He turned toward Zoe. "We both want to go."

Zoe nodded. "Just give us a minute to grab a few things and then we can leave together."

They flew out that evening, less than two hours later, but the drama was over by the time their plane landed in Lexington.

Clemente had found Bill Collingsworth. It seemed that Zoe's father, after leaving the nursing home, walked the twelve miles back to the family farm in his robe and pajamas.

Zoe, hearing the news not long after landing at the Lexington airport, burst into tears. She'd been sick with worry, fearing the worst. "Dad just wants to be at home," she said, wiping away the tears and trying to get some control back. "I don't blame him, either."

"I can't imagine it's an easy adjustment," Lazaro said, taking her hand.

She swallowed hard, around the lump blocking her throat. "He's spent his whole life on the farm. He's used to having plenty of space, lots of fresh air. Of course he'd go home. That's where he belongs.''

As the limousine sailed past the familiar bluegrass meadows and pastures, Zoe felt a bittersweet ache. She loved Kentucky but this wasn't home anymore. Not for her father, and not for her.

On the flight she'd overheard Dante and Lazaro discussing the farm. Lazaro knew Dante was heavily invested in the farm and she sensed it was only a matter of time before Collingsworth Farms was sold.

As the limousine turned down the private road leading to the farm, the white fences and distant farm buildings emerged through the early morning mist. She'd never loved horses the way Daisy loved horses, but Zoe did love the land and old Victorian farmhouse. She loved the history that rooted her here.

The limousine rounded a bend and the old two-story Victorian farmhouse came into view. Zoe leaned on the door to get a better look. She'd been gone a month but it felt like years.

Her gaze swept the house and garden, inspecting everything, wanting to see what had changed and what remained the same. The front steps had been painted. The railing fixed. The climbing rose's tender new canes were tied to the trellis at the side of the house. Clemente had done a good job with upkeep. Thank goodness they'd had his help.

The car parked and Zoe dashed out of the back and up the front stairs before Lazaro or Dante could climb out.

Her father was in his room, sitting in the overstuffed chair that had once been her mom's favorite chair. He looked so small, so lost.

"Dad."

He turned, saw her in the door. His forehead creased. "Is that my baby?"

"Yes, Daddy. It's Zoe."

"Oh, Zoe, where have you been?"

She hugged him until her arms ached, hugged him until the horrible coldness in her middle went away. "I love you," she said, kissing his cheek, and drawing a footstool close to sit next to him. "I missed you."

"Don't leave me anymore."

Her eyes burned and yet she forced a smile. "Let's not worry about anything right now, okay? I'm home, and I'm here and I want to know what you want for dinner."

"Pot roast."

She blinked back the scalding tears, telling herself she couldn't think about tomorrow, couldn't think about anything but today. "Okay. Pot roast it is."

The next few days passed quickly for Zoe. It was wonderful being home. It felt wonderful being back in the old farmhouse. She'd only been gone four weeks but it had felt like forever.

While Lazaro and Dante spent time with Clemente on the farm, going over the farm books and discussing the new stallion barn, Zoe sat with her father and read to him and tried to keep him busy.

Afternoon sunshine poured through the double-hung windows, catching the crystals of the chandelier and throwing tiny rainbows of color on the smooth painted walls. She loved the house, loved the high ceilings, the thick crown moldings and painted casing. She loved the view of the pasture from the front veranda and the twenty-year-old pink climbing rose that would soon begin to bud.

This was home. It'd always be home. Even if she couldn't live here anymore.

They'd been at the house for nearly a week and Zoe knew Dante and Lazaro were both anxious to return to Argentina. Neither had said anything to her but she couldn't help feel their growing restlessness. Soon they'd want to go home, and she'd return with them.

But her father…what about him?

During dinner that evening she knew Lazaro watched her, and knew that he, too, was considering the future.

His corporation and career were in Buenos Aires. She couldn't ask him, or expect him to move to Kentucky, and yet her father's entire life had been lived here, on this land, in this house. Collingsworth Farms was a four-generation horse farm. It'd been started by her father's great-grandfather in the early part of the twentieth century. How to let it all go? How to walk away from a history of love?

Dinner over, she steered her father upstairs to get him ready for bed. Twenty minutes later, as she padded barefoot down the stairs, she heard Dante and Lazaro's voices coming from the kitchen.

"It doesn't make business sense to keep the place, the farm barely breaks even." Dante was speaking, and Zoe hesitated in the hall. "But I'm not in a hurry to sell, either. This is still Daisy and Zoe's home."

"And Bill's," Lazaro added. "He obviously wants to be here. I think he should be allowed to remain here."

"I do, too."

Lazaro attempted a laugh. "Then we agree on something."

There was a moment's silence and then Dante coughed, cleared his throat. "We might agree on Collingsworth Farms, but that's about it. I can't continue with this, Lazaro. I can't maintain this—"

"Continue with what?"

"This. Us. You and me working together. It's a charade and it doesn't sit right with me." Dante sounded tired, his words flat, weary. "It's not the way it was...before."

Zoe pressed her hands to her stomach, knots filling her middle, tension spreading through every limb. She hated this. Hated the sides, the conflict, the discord.

"No, it's not," Lazaro tersely agreed.

"I want out."

"But it's your company."

"*Was.* It's yours now."

She closed her eyes, and leaned against the door frame, assailed by guilt all over again. She'd married Lazaro, loved Lazaro, but it hadn't changed anything. The marriage might have saved Dante's wealth, but it hadn't saved his pride. It hadn't fixed the hurt, or healed any of the deep wounds.

She felt the weight of the problems, felt worn out

by the problems. Her father. The farm. The rift between families.

She'd spoken to Daisy only once in the past five weeks, and it'd been the night she and Dante came to the hotel with news that their father was missing. What had happened to her family? What had happened to all of them?

Lazaro abruptly appeared, turning the kitchen corner, a platter in his hands, a dish towel across his shoulder. He nearly tripped over her in the dark. "Zoe!"

She blushed, realizing he knew she'd been standing there, eavesdropping. "Dad's in bed," she said in a breathless rush. "Hopefully he'll have a quiet night."

She felt Lazaro's gaze search her face, felt the strained silence between them.

But he didn't speak. His mood changed, shifting into something quiet, and distant.

"Let me take that," she said, reaching for the platter. "I know where it goes."

"So do I."

She took the platter anyway, needing the task to give her something to do. Anything would be better than standing there, feeling helpless, feeling hopeless.

She and Lazaro didn't need words. They could read each other's thoughts, read each other's emotions without saying a word. And right now they both knew they hadn't escaped the past, or the pain. Instead of starting a new life together, they realized at that very moment that they'd only succeeded in dragging heartbreak into the future with them.

Later that night, after they'd gone to bed, Zoe

reached for her husband in the dark. Wordlessly they made love, slowly, passionately, straining against each other for greater intimacy. The intensity of Zoe's orgasm shattered her and she clung to Lazaro afterward, her body quivering, her heart tender, tears in her eyes.

She loved Lazaro desperately but felt a dark cloud moving over them. Something was going to happen, something was going to change but she didn't know what, and she didn't know when.

She tried to hide the tears from Lazaro but she couldn't. He rolled her onto her back, and lifted her hair from her damp face. "You feel it, too," he said softly.

She shook her head. "No."

"You do. We both do. I think we both know this is impossible."

She wasn't sure what he meant, but she heard the sorrow in his voice. She pressed her mouth to his bare shoulder, fear growing, rising, threatening to consume them. "Nothing's impossible," she answered fiercely. "Nothing is ever impossible if we believe."

CHAPTER ELEVEN

NOTHING is ever impossible if we believe.

Zoe's words rang in his head and Lazaro wanted to believe her. He wanted to cling to her optimism, find some peace in the future but he didn't have that kind of faith. Especially not in himself.

He held her closely, drew the blanket over them as if the blanket could protect her. Deep down he knew better. The person she needed protection from was himself. "I will never make you happy."

"You already have."

Lightly he stroked her satin shoulder, the smooth expanse of back. He wanted to remember this, wanted to remember the softness of her skin, the sweetness of her nature. He'd never loved anyone this way before and knew he'd never love anyone so intensely again. "But I've driven a wedge between you and your family. You and Daisy were once so close, now you can hardly be in the same room together."

She didn't immediately answer, kissing his chest and pressing her cheek to the curve of muscle above his heart. "One can't have everything in life."

He swallowed hard. The weary wisdom in her voice hurt him. She was only twenty-three. She shouldn't have to feel this way now. Shouldn't have to know so much at such a young age. "You deserve better, *corazón*.'' He cupped the back of her head, the long silky hair cool and slippery beneath his fingers.

He'd never loved anyone so much.

He'd never needed anyone so much.

She shouldn't have had to choose between her family and him. He'd forced her to choose, too. He'd wanted to isolate her from those that knew her, from those who loved her. He wanted her to be like him.

Alone.

Lazaro swallowed again. Felt the huge lump return, blocking his throat.

He'd ruin her life, had already come frighteningly close to ruining the lives of those she loved.

"Lazaro." Zoe shifted in his arms, lifting her head to look at him.

He felt her concern. It felt gentle, soft, a velvet throw and for a man who'd never felt plush-velvet fabric until nineteen, velvet was a dream.

Her palm touched his cheek, moved tenderly across his face to brush his mouth. "What's wrong? Tell me."

Air squeezed into his lungs. His chest ached. He'd never not love her. Never not want her. He kissed her fingertips. "Tonight I couldn't stop looking at you. You're the most beautiful woman I've ever known—"

"I was wearing jeans and a purple T-shirt!"

"Yes, and you had your hair pinned up on top of your head and you were humming while you mashed potatoes. I loved it. I loved watching you. I've never seen you laugh so much before. You don't need jewelry and designer gowns. You just need your family around you.''

She shifted and slid across him, covering him, her long hair spilling like a silver-gold curtain around them. ''I need you,'' she answered, dipping her head, touching her mouth to his. ''I love you.''

His heart twisted. ''And I love you, my Zoe.'' But this time love might not be enough.

It was time to return to Buenos Aires and despite Zoe's efforts, and Dante's pleading, Bill Collingsworth refused to even consider leaving the house again. He wouldn't discuss returning to the nursing home and outright rejected the suggestion of moving to Argentina.

''I live here,'' he said flatly, ''I'm staying here. In my house.''

Zoe knew he couldn't care for himself but Lazaro suggested having Clemente move into the house until they could find a suitable live-in nurse. It wasn't a perfect solution but it was better than forcing Bill into returning to the convalescent home.

It was the last morning of their visit to the farm and Zoe had finally finished packing. The suitcases were loaded into the limousine's trunk and all that remained were the goodbyes.

But Zoe didn't know how she was supposed to say goodbye to her father this time. She didn't even know when she'd return next. Lazaro said she could visit as often as she liked, but things could happen, things did happen and she worried about the changes that would take place between visits.

Her father met her at the front door, dressed in a chambray work shirt and khakis. With his shoulders thrown back, and his silver-streaked hair combed, he looked amazingly like his former self, as though the Alzheimer's hadn't eaten away his memory and cognitive powers.

His piercing blue eyes focused on her small travel bag she clutched in one hand. "Where are you going, Daisy?"

"I'm Zoe, Daddy."

"That's right. Zoe, my baby. Where are you going?"

She couldn't do this. She couldn't leave him now. He might not even remember her when she came back. "On a trip," she answered brokenly.

"Will you be gone long?"

"Not too long, I hope." Her voice cracked again, and she dug deep for strength. She couldn't fall apart now, it would only worry him, make him uneasy.

She pressed down into the heel of her boots, locked her knees, squared her shoulders. She had to go, her future was with Lazaro, but it nearly killed her to walk away from her past. "Clemente has the phone number where I'm staying. If you need anything…"

"I won't need anything."

"But if you do—" and she couldn't continue, couldn't get around the lump filling her throat. "Call me, Dad, please?"

"All right, baby."

She was in his arms, holding him tight. He patted her back, slowly, firmly, as though she were a child again. This is how it'd always been with them. Before his illness. Before the problems. Her heart ached, wanting the impossible, wanting things simple again.

But they'd never be simple again. She'd grown up.

As he released her she stepped back, and she smiled through her tears. "You raised me right, Dad. You did a good job. I hope you know that."

He smiled back. "That's good. That's my girl. I'll see you tonight at dinner."

But there was no seeing him tonight at dinner and she knew it.

Back in Buenos Aires, Zoe and Lazaro tried to settle into a routine but Lazaro wasn't easy, and couldn't seem to relax.

At first Zoe thought it was the time change and jet lag when Lazaro left their bed in the middle of the night to go work in the sitting room, but as one week turned to two, she worried about the new distance between them.

They made love less, far less, and when Lazaro did reach for her she felt his tension, felt an anger and despair he refused to acknowledge, much less discuss.

Three weeks after their return Lazaro stopped coming to bed with her altogether. He slept in the small guest bedroom that adjoined the suite and didn't explain his decision, or defend it. He just moved away from her.

Zoe couldn't pretend that the distance between them was a figment of her imagination anymore. There was a problem. A big problem and she didn't know how to solve it.

Zoe desperately wanted to talk to Lazaro about

what was happening between them but each of her attempts to talk was rebuffed. He still took her out to dinner every evening, he still wanted her to dress up and play the glamorous bride, but he didn't want her. He didn't reach for her. Didn't express tenderness anymore.

Zoe didn't know what to do, didn't know where to turn. Three weeks turned to a month and she felt painfully alone, worse than alone. Felt alienated. This was his country, his world, and she didn't belong.

She climbed from bed and slid her arms into her light cotton robe. It was close to three in the morning and she hadn't been able to sleep, worry and fear going 'round and 'round in her mind.

Lazaro sat at the desk in the living room. He was working on his laptop computer, typing away and looked up when she entered the room. "What's wrong?"

She stared at him, numb, tired, too tired to play this game. "What do you think's wrong? You don't come to bed with me anymore. You don't touch me anymore. You tell me. What's wrong, Lazaro? What's happened?"

"It's work, that's all. I'm just under the gun."

"It's more than that," she answered quietly. "Your feelings have changed."

"They haven't changed."

"Then why have you pulled away? Why are you so distant?"

"It's nothing personal—"

"Not personal? Lazaro, I'm your wife!"

"And wasn't that a mistake."

Tears filled her eyes and Zoe's lips parted in silent protest but in the end she couldn't speak. She shook her head, tears clinging to her lashes and returned to the bedroom.

Lazaro stared at the bedroom door which she'd gently closed behind her and knew he should get up, go to her, try to comfort her, but maybe this was better, he told himself flatly, maybe this was the best way.

It would never work long term. He felt too guilty, felt too destructive, and he hated dragging Zoe into his world of anger and revenge and pain. From the beginning he'd wanted to protect her and yet all he'd done was hurt her.

Over and over again.

Lazaro sat for long tense minutes fighting himself, fighting his desire to go to her, fighting his need to hold her and love her. It was a terrible battle, a battle that made his heart burn, but he kept himself there, motionless in the chair, until the fire began to burn out and the desperate craving subsided.

He didn't deserve her love. How could he? He was nothing if not pathetic and low.

Zoe dressed slowly in the morning, her fingers trembling as she buttoned the lime-green silk blouse, and tucked the blouse into the waistband of her cream, linen trousers.

Morning sunshine poured through the bedroom blinds, burning her eyes. She'd cried herself to sleep last night and had cried nonstop since stepping from her morning shower.

How could Lazaro stop caring for her? How could

his feelings change so quickly? He'd managed to shut himself down completely. It was as if he'd forgotten her, pushed her from his heart, and his mind.

She didn't understand. She couldn't understand. She loved him.

Suppressing a cry of anguish, Zoe grabbed her wallet and took the elevator downstairs. Outside the doorman hailed a cab for her and Zoe gave the driver Daisy and Dante's fashionable Recoleta address.

The maid showed Zoe into the formal living room with the high ceilings and beautiful old plaster walls. The fireplace was enormous with the most beautiful pink marble surround.

Daisy entered the living room moments later, wearing faded jeans and a soft buttercup-yellow T-shirt. She was carrying the baby high against her shoulder as though she'd been burping him when informed of Zoe's arrival.

"Am I interrupting?" Zoe asked, rising from the chair she'd taken, self-conscious again.

"He's almost asleep," Daisy answered, standing in the doorway, gently patting the tiny infant's back. She looked thin. She'd already lost all the baby weight and more.

Zoe reached for her wallet. "I can come back—"

"No," Daisy cut her short. "This is fine." But she didn't draw closer and her expression didn't change.

Daisy was so guarded, Zoe thought, feeling an almost unbearable sadness that their relationship had become so strained. That they had come to this.

She and Daisy were strangers.

Just like she and Lazaro were now strangers.

Her stomach in knots, Zoe gripped her wallet tightly. Now that she was here, she didn't know what to say, didn't know how to start talking. Daisy didn't even like Lazaro, why did Zoe think she could possibly come to Daisy with her problems?

Because Daisy had always been there for her before.

Because Daisy was her sister and Zoe loved her with all her heart.

Tears filled her eyes and she realized it was a mistake to come. Zoe rose a second time. "This wasn't a good idea. I should go. I'm sorry I bothered you."

She walked quickly toward the door, passed Daisy and hurried down the black and white marble hall, anxious to reach the front door.

"Do you want to hold him?"

Daisy's question drew Zoe short. She stopped in the hall, facing the door, pressed her wallet to her stomach. *Did she want to hold him?*

Slowly she turned, gazed longingly at the baby. "Yes. Please."

In the living room, Daisy handed Stefan over. The baby had dozed off and his little hands lay folded across each other, as though he were the most angelic child ever born.

Zoe silently marveled that he weighed nothing at all. As she settled him more firmly in her arms, he stretched and sighed, and her heart turned over. "He's beautiful," she whispered, in awe over his miniature perfection. Black hair, nub of a nose, sweet lips.

She couldn't resist kissing his cheek and she breathed in his baby-powder smell.

"You'll be a great mom someday," Daisy said, taking a seat opposite her, her long legs tucked beneath her.

"I hope we have kids."

"Why wouldn't you?"

Zoe couldn't answer. At the moment she didn't see how her marriage would last another month, much less a year. If she didn't reach Lazaro soon, they wouldn't be together long enough to have a baby.

Zoe felt her throat start to thicken. She couldn't tear her gaze from her nephew's face. To sleep so peacefully, to feel so safe…

She glanced up, met Daisy's eyes. "I'm glad you have Stefan. He's so lovely. He's perfect."

Daisy smiled but the smile didn't reach her eyes. "What's wrong, Zo? What's happened?"

Zoe blinked, fought the tears, fought for her control. Tears wouldn't help. Swallowing hard, she found her voice. "It's Lazaro."

Zoe didn't return to the hotel until nearly six, a half hour before Lazaro usually returned from work. But tonight he was already back when she opened the door, sitting on the living room sofa reading the newspaper.

"Hello," she said, closing the door behind her. She felt an odd prickle seeing him home already, seeing him here, waiting for her. It wasn't as if she'd done anything wrong but she felt anxious, strangely defensive. "How long have you been home?"

"An hour or so." He folded the newspaper, set it on the sofa next to him. "I'm sorry about last night."

The sweetest relief surged through her, relief so strong she felt dizzy. "I am, too."

"I want you to be happy, Zoe."

"I am. With you."

He gave his head a slight shake, his jaw tight and she dropped her wallet and keys on the dining room table and moved toward the couch. Leaning over the back of the couch she kissed him. "I'm so glad to see you," she whispered, her heart impossibly tender. "I've felt just terrible."

"I'm sorry." He reached up, cupped her cheek. "Where have you been? I've been phoning the apartment every half hour. I was worried about you."

"Is that why you're home so early?"

"I thought perhaps..." but he didn't finish the thought. He shrugged, shoulders lifting. "At least you're home now."

She took a seat on the couch next to him. "I...I saw Daisy." Zoe tucked a strand of hair behind her ear. "I've just come from her house. I got to hold the baby. He's really beautiful—" she broke off, hearing her babble. At least she felt as though she were babbling. "Do you mind?"

"Mind what? That you saw your sister? *¡Por Dios, Zoe!* I'm glad. I hate what's happened to you two. I hate what I've done—"

She reached over, covered his mouth with her palm. "Let's not talk about it now. Let's just go to dinner, relax, and enjoy each other, okay?"

She was glad she suggested going out. Dinner at Hermes was magical. Lazaro acted like his old self. Charming, warm, attentive. He ordered champagne, toasted her, saying he was the luckiest man alive. She told him about the day she'd spent with Daisy, more about Stefan and how much he'd grown since his birth.

Lazaro listened to everything, half smiling, his silver gaze focused. "It was good to see her, wasn't it?"

She couldn't hide her happiness. "It was wonderful. I've missed her so much." She told him then about the dinner invitation for the next night. "Would you please go with me?"

He looked at her for a long moment, his thick lashes lowering to conceal his expression and then he looked up at her again. "They are not my family, *corazón*."

"They could be."

Lazaro's expression gentled even more. "I humiliated Dante before all of Argentina. I have nearly bankrupted him. I do not think we will ever be family."

"But we can try. We can start somewhere."

His lips twisted, a small crooked smile, and Zoe saw a weariness in his eyes she'd never seen before. He looked less like Lazaro the warrior and more like Lazaro the defeated. Her heart ached for him, ached for both of them. Her gaze searched his. "Lazaro, we have to start somewhere."

"Maybe."

"Come to dinner with me tomorrow."

He gave his head a rueful shake. "All right, for you, I'll do anything."

After their late dinner they returned to the hotel and made love for the first time in over a week. Lazaro slowly undressed her before loving every inch of her skin, touching, kissing, licking. He made her quiver and melt, prolonging her pleasure to make it more intense. When she finally came, it was with him buried deep inside of her. The orgasm was so powerful she felt as though he'd shattered her and she clung to him during and after, needing his comfort and strength.

''I love you,'' he whispered, kissing her damp neck, her chin, her still sensitive mouth.

He hadn't said the words in so long that she felt both joy and pain. Zoe nestled closer. ''You're sure?''

''Yes. It's the only thing I know for certain anymore.''

Lazaro left early for work the next morning. He skipped lunch, not having time between meetings and discussions, and worked straight until four when he poured a glass of mineral water and took a break to stand at the window.

As he stood there, watching the busy street traffic below, he couldn't help marveling at his success. He'd done it. He'd done exactly what he'd intended.

He'd been completely successful, completely ruthless, and he was completely wrong.

Instead of peace he felt only anguish. Instead of pleasure he felt remorse.

He'd done what he'd wanted and it had alienated him from those he wanted—needed—most.

For a brief point in time he almost had the life he wanted. He had Zoe. He had the closest thing to family he'd ever known. For a brief point in time he was in heaven.

He returned to his desk, sat and clicked on his computer. Jaw gritted, he began deleting his personal files from the hard drive, one file after the other.

As he deleted files he swallowed hard against the wretched taste of self-disgust. He'd earned two university degrees, learned complex management theories, built a career, become accomplished in arts and developed an ear for music—for what?

To be alone.

To live alone.

To die alone?

Impossible. Unfathomable. Who the hell was he kidding? This wasn't ever the kind of life he wanted for himself, this wasn't the kind of person he wanted to be. As a kid he worked harder than anyone to succeed, to be accepted, to be liked. As a kid he wanted nothing more than to be...*loved.*

How had hurt and anger twisted him into this? How had loneliness become such a vendetta?

Lazaro paused, pressed two fingers against his brow, the tension in his head nearly unbearable. He wasn't sleeping anymore. Wasn't able to eat. Couldn't rest.

He stared at the last file on his computer, a file marked DG. Dante Galván. Swiftly he deleted this last file, dragging it to the trash and then removing it from his drive. Gone. Done.

There was a knock on the office door. The door opened, and Gabriel Garcia, a thick-set lawyer with an equally thick black moustache, entered Lazaro's spacious office, followed by a young paralegal and Lazaro's executive secretary.

Lazaro's secretary shut the door gently behind her, her expression composed and yet there was sadness in her eyes.

"We're ready," Señor Garcia said, opening his briefcase. Lazaro nodded and they all wordlessly moved to the conference-style table in the corner. Each took a chair, the mood tangibly oppressive, deafeningly silent.

Lazaro's secretary, dressed today in an unusually severe black suit with a cream silk blouse, placed stacks of binder-clipped papers on the table. Lazaro wanted to say something to Imelda, reassure her somehow, but the words stuck in his throat.

As Imelda passed out the paperwork and the paralegal passed out pens, Lazaro felt Gabriel's gaze, the lawyer's expression brooding.

Lazaro was grateful Gabriel didn't attempt conversation. Lazaro couldn't handle conversation. He could barely go through the motions right now.

Zoe glanced at her watch for the umpteenth time in the past hour. Where was Lazaro? He was supposed to be here ages ago. Daisy had delayed dinner twice now. What was holding him up?

Zoe glanced at her watch yet again. Dante had gone to phone the office and Zoe glanced at Daisy where she sat on the couch with the baby. Daisy looked tired. It was growing very late, even for a fashionable Argentine dinner.

Chewing on the inside of her cheek, she tried to hide her growing anxiety. Something urgent must have come up at the office for him to be delayed so long. She didn't want to think what urgent could mean.

The door to the living room opened and Dante appeared with a stranger, a dark-suited stranger with thick black hair and a thick black moustache.

"Zoe," Dante said quietly. "Come with me."

Something was wrong, terribly wrong. Zoe's nerves screamed on edge. She glanced at Daisy then Dante. "What's happened?"

"We'll talk in the library."

She shot Daisy another glance. Daisy looked as baffled as she did. "No, let's stay here. I want Daisy here."

Dante and Gabriel Garcia stepped into the living room and Dante closed the doors. Zoe watched as the man with the black moustache opened his briefcase and pulled out a sheath of papers and a pair of reading glasses. He slipped the glasses onto the bridge of his nose.

"I am Gabriel Garcia. I am your husband's attorney."

Her stomach cramped hard. She slid into a chair. "Why isn't he here? Where is he?"

Dante gazed at her steadily. "He's not coming tonight."

"Why not?"

"He's going away, Zoe, and he's asked Señor Garcia to handle the paperwork for him."

"The paperwork? Paperwork for what? I don't understand—"

"Lazaro has given everything away."

"Given what away?" She'd begun to shake, hands, arms, legs.

"Everything. His corporation, his shares of stock, his hotels. Everything. He's given it back to the Galván family, to be divided between the baby and me."

Her eyes hurt. She blinked, as if she could get the gritty feeling out. "And Lazaro?"

"He leaves Argentina tonight."

CHAPTER TWELVE

THANK GOD, Lazaro's attorney knew where Lazaro was going, and knew the time Lazaro was leaving. Señor Garcia hadn't wanted to break Lazaro's confidence but Dante wouldn't let Gabriel leave the house without telling them what Lazaro intended.

Dante immediately called for his driver and instructed the chauffeur to drive Zoe to the harbor as quickly as possible. Lazaro was scheduled to leave by boat, chartering a friend's one-hundred-and-twenty-foot yacht for an extended trip along the South American coast. Dante knew the yacht Lazaro would be sailing and described its location to Zoe.

It was dark when she reached the dock. Lights glowed from the tethered yachts, strands of white lights strung from some ship masts, music coming from others.

She found the massive yacht exactly where Dante said it would be anchored. The boat swayed on the water. The engine already hummed. Yellow light shone from within.

Zoe hesitated and then before she could take a step, she heard Lazaro's voice from the deck. He was speaking Spanish, sounded as though he were giving instructions. She was just about to shout his name when he jumped down a ladder and appeared before her.

"¡Dios! Zoe!"

She backed up a step, felt a tremor of anguish. He was really going to leave. He was going to pull anchor and sail away, leave her behind, just like that. "Where are you going?"

He didn't say anything. He shook his head.

The activity continued on the yacht's upper deck. She heard the sound of boxes being stacked and a scrape of metal.

She stared past him to the yacht, where moonlight glinted off the glossy white finish. Her heart seemed to fill her throat. He hadn't even planned on saying goodbye. He was just going to go. Just going to get on that damn white yacht and leave her behind.

"I don't understand." Her voice came out strangled. Good Lord, she was close to tears. Not just a couple tears, but horrible wrenching sobs.

How could he do this?

How could he do this *to her?*

Fury overrode her shock. "Am I that easy to let go?" she choked, heat surging through her.

"Zoe—"

"Am I just someone you throw away?"

"It's for you I do this."

"Bull." She jerked straight, shoulders squared, nails digging into her clenched fists.

She stared him up and down. He wore jeans and white canvas deck shoes. Sailing shoes. He really had intended to go.

"What about me?" she demanded huskily, fighting to keep the pain contained, fighting to keep some vestige of control.

His face was expressionless. "You don't need me."

"But I want you."

"You'll get over me."

She was shivering on the inside, shivering with alternating waves of hot and cold, rage and grief. "And not saying goodbye would help?"

His brow furrowed. "You're young, Zoe. You can have anything you want in life—"

"Fine. I want you."

"No."

"You said I could have anything I want, well, I want you." Although right now she didn't know why. He was awful, hateful, cruel. He was going to leave her. Leave her. Just like her father, and her mother, and Daisy... "Damn you, Lazaro."

His shoulders lifted, a careless Latin shrug. "It's better this way. I'm not the right man for you."

"Too bad. Too late. I love you." And she did, even if she was furious. Even if she was scared out of her mind. All she knew was that she couldn't, wouldn't, let him go without a fight.

"Zoe, I've given it away. I'm not destitute, but I'm not the man with twenty million in the bank, either."

She trembled with anger. "When did I ever want you for your money? When did I ever need you for *things?*"

"Money is important."

"Money pays the bills, but money doesn't buy happiness. Trust me on this one."

"My mother died because she didn't have enough money."

"Your mother died because she didn't have enough love." Zoe's anger deflated and her heart suddenly felt tender. She saw him as he must have been as a child. He would have been gentle. He would have adored his mother, and he would have desperately wanted to protect her. "But, Lazaro, I'm not your mom, and I'm not Daisy. I'm Zoe. I'm a simple person and I have simple needs. I need you. That's all."

"Easy to say now—"

"No, it's not easy to say now. I'm stunned at everything that's happened, and hurt that you'd actually leave me without saying goodbye, that you'd send a lawyer to deliver the news."

"I didn't mean it that way. I only wanted to make it easier."

"Easier? For whom? If you go now, my life will never be the same. Part of me will shrivel up and die."

"Zoe—"

"It's true," she continued urgently. "I feel alive when I'm with you, I feel like me when I'm with you, I feel like the Zoe I was always meant to be."

"But I want to protect you. I need to protect you."

"From who, Lazaro, from what?"

He didn't answer and she suddenly understood. He was trying to protect her from himself. She moved forward, moved to touch him, but he took an unsteady step back.

"You're not protecting me if you break my heart," she added softly. "You're not helping me at all."

"I want you to be happy, Zoe."

"And I am, with you, happier than I've ever been,

happier than I've ever dreamed. Like you, I've lost people I've loved, and felt great pain, and yet when I'm with you I only feel hope. I only see possibility." She reached out to him again and this time he didn't move away. She placed a hand against his chest, just above his heart. "Don't take the hope away. Please, *corazón*."

He closed his eyes, passed a hand over his face. "Zoe, I can't stay here. I can't live here anymore."

She understood. Too well. The memories here would always be hard, the past would always be with them, the failures as well as the mistakes. "Then we go somewhere else. We start a new life in a new place."

He didn't answer and yet she felt his heart thudding beneath her palm. Leaning forward, Zoe kissed his chest, kissed the place where she felt his heart. "Just take me with you. Keep me with you."

"I want to." His voice broke, the words almost strangled in his throat. "God knows I want to."

"Then do it."

He stood very still. He opened his eyes and stared at a point beyond her shoulder, a place on the water where the moon reflected high and white and full. A small yacht motored out and the inky water churned white and foamy in the wake.

Slowly he shook his head. He looked defeated. "I don't want to be cold anymore."

"You aren't that man, Lazaro. You haven't been that man for a long, long time."

"I need to start fresh somewhere else."

"Yes."

"But I don't know where to go. I've never belonged any place—" He broke off, looked down at
her, and reached out to touch her cheek. "I've never
felt accepted until I found you."

She moved into his arms, felt him draw her close
and she let out a quivery breath.

He held her even tighter. "Have you thought about
Kentucky?"

Zoe squeezed her eyes shut as a wave of longing
swept through her, the longing so intense that tears
burned the back of her eyes. *Kentucky. Her father.
The farm.*

But she held the emotion in, and fought for control.

"You wouldn't want to go home?" he persisted
gently.

Zoe gazed up into his face. "You'd go to Kentucky
for me?"

"I'd go to the moon if that's what you wanted."

"I don't want to go to the moon."

"Then how about Kentucky?

"You'd really do that for me?"

"Of course. I'd do anything for you." Moonlight
drenched his profile, easing the hard grim lines of his
face, gentling the length of his nose and the curve of
his mouth. He traced the shape of her lips with the
tip of his finger. "I love you."

Her heart contracted, a sharp swift knotting that
made her ache. "Then don't you dare leave me."

"I won't."

"And yes, I'd love to go home, back to Kentucky.
I miss my dad so much, but not if you don't
want to."

"I want for you to be with your family again. I want us to be a family. I've never had a family...until I found you."

Her eyes burned and she blinked, unwilling to cry. He clasped her face, fingers spanning her jaw, and gazed into her eyes for the longest time, saying nothing and yet she knew what he was thinking, knew what he was feeling. They'd always had this bond, always had a special connection.

Lazaro's voice sounded rough. "I don't know that I'd make a very good horse breeder, but I'd try."

"You don't have to breed horses, you could do business, start a new business—"

"It'd be difficult."

"Which you should like. You love challenges. You're thrilled by that which is impossible."

He suddenly laughed, his voice warm and husky in the night, and with the water sloshing behind them and the boats creaking at the dock, the world felt full of beauty, and opportunity. "You know me too well."

She grimaced ruefully. "And I still love you."

The laughter faded from his eyes. "I am the luckiest man alive."

"We're both lucky."

He caressed her cheek. "I wish I hadn't put you through so much—"

"Things happen. Life happens."

He kissed her, his lips covering hers, drinking her breath, drawing her into him. A shiver of pleasure raced beneath her skin and her body warmed, wanting him, needing him, craving him, but she couldn't forget that he'd nearly left without her, that if she hadn't rushed to the wharf he might have gone.

Zoe's fingers curled into a fist and she pounded once on his chest. "How could you even think about going without me? How could you do that?"

A tugboat horn sounded in the distance, a low distinct cry that echoed off the tethered boats and slap of waves against the wooden pier.

"I don't know," he answered at length. "I just wanted what was best for you."

Gritty tears filled her eyes. "You're what's best for me."

He reached up to wipe the tears from her lower lashes. "I don't deserve you, Zoe, but if you're willing to give me another chance, if you're willing to try to make this work, I will be yours, and only yours, for the rest of my life."

"Yes."

He continued to wipe the tears from beneath her eyes, his touch infinitely gentle, and loving. "I'm glad my mother never knew the harsh things I've said and done, but I do wish she could have known you. I wish she would have seen what a beautiful woman I married, and I'm not talking about the outside, Zoe, I'm talking about your heart."

A sob formed inside of her. She was about to lose the last of her self-control and he brought her against him, wrapped his arms around her.

"I love you," she whispered, remembering their vows, remembering the commitment she'd made to him, a commitment she fully intended to keep. "For richer or poorer, in sickness or in health—"

"Till death do us part."

"Amen."

He laughed softly, and it was the sweetest, warmest sound she'd ever heard. The darkness that once haunted his eyes was gone, and only light remained— the whitewash of moonlight, the warmth of his heart, the flicker of hope.

"Over time, after we settle into life in Lexington, maybe I can build my business again," he said. "I did it once, I don't see why I can't do it again."

"You can do anything you set your mind to."

He blinked, a sheen in his silver-gray eyes, tenderness in the curve of his lips. "Life's good, isn't it?"

Smiling through her tears, she nodded and drew his head back down to hers. "Life's great."

MILLS & BOON®   1105/01b

Live the emotion

Modern
romance™

THE ITALIAN'S CONVENIENT WIFE
by Catherine Spencer

When Paolo Rainero's niece and nephew are orphaned
he must protect them. A marriage of convenience to
Caroline Leighton, their aunt, is his solution. But he must
show Callie that he's changed since their fling nine years
ago. Their mutual desire is rekindled – but Paolo feels
that Caroline has a secret…

THE ANTONAKOS MARRIAGE *by Kate Walker*

An ageing tycoon is blackmailing Skye Marston into
marriage – but she'll have one night of passion first…
Theo Antonakos is furious when she slips away from him
– and still furious when he goes to meet his stepmother-
to-be. Only to find that they already know each other
– in the most intimate way…

MISTRESS TO A RICH MAN *by Kathryn Ross*

Celebrity agent Marc Clayton knows a gold-digger when
he sees one. And when gorgeous Libby Sheridan shows
up, to cause a scandal for his top client, he knows he
needs to keep her close – *very* close… Libby won't be
bought off – but as their power struggle turns to passion
Marc takes her out of the limelight…and into his bed!

TAMED BY HER HUSBAND *by Elizabeth Power*

Everyone thinks they know Shannon Bouvier – heiress,
wild child, scandalous man-eater. And she's happy to let
the world believe the lies. Kane Falconer thinks he knows
her too. It's his job to tame Shannon – and this ruthless
millionaire knows just how…

On sale 2nd December 2005

*Available at most branches of WHSmith, Tesco, ASDA,
Borders, Eason, Sainsbury's and most bookshops*

Visit www.millsandboon.co.uk

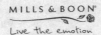

GIFT OF A FAMILY by *Sarah Morgan*

A&E consultant Josh Sullivan is happily single – and despite many women's attempts he intends to stay that way! Single mum Kat O'Brien would usually be strictly off-limits – except he can't get the stunning doctor off his mind. But will Kat ever believe he can offer them a future?

The Cornish Consultants: Dedicated doctors by day... playboy lovers by night!

CHRISTMAS ON THE CHILDREN'S WARD by *Carol Marinelli*

Nurse Eden Hadley hopes for two things this Christmas: that the little orphaned boy on the children's ward can have one real family Christmas, and that consultant Nick Watson will notice her again – and remember what they once had. It's up to Nick to make both her wishes come true...

THE LIFE SAVER by *Lilian Darcy*

Gorgeous Dr Ripley Taylor is a life saver – not just a doctor! He saved fellow GP Jo Middleton by helping her out of a king-size rut and revitalising her love-life! Now that Rip is single their attraction is snowballing into a passionate affair. Until Rip's ex-wife appears on the scene...!

On sale 2nd December 2005

1105/03a

MILLS & BOON®

Live the emotion

Tender romance™

A MOST SUITABLE WIFE *by Jessica Steele*

Taye Trafford needs someone to share her flat – and the bills
– fast! So, when Magnus Ashthorpe turns up, Taye offers him
the room, not knowing he actually has an entirely different
reason for living there: because he believes Taye is the mistress
who has caused his sister's heartbreak!

IN THE ARMS OF THE SHEIKH *by Sophie Weston*

Natasha Lambert is horrified by what she must wear as her
best friend's bridesmaid! Worse, the best man is Kazim al
Saraq – an infuriatingly charming sheikh with a dazzling wit
and an old-fashioned take on romance. He's determined to win
Natasha's heart – and she's terrified he might succeed…!

THE MARRIAGE MIRACLE *by Liz Fielding*

An accident three years ago has left Matilda Lang in a
wheelchair, and hotshot New York banker Sebastian Wolseley
is the man who can make – or break – her heart. It would
take a miracle for Matty to risk her heart after what she's been
through, but Sebastian knows he can help her…

ORDINARY GIRL, SOCIETY GROOM
by Natasha Oakley

Eloise Lawson has finally found the family she's never known.
But, cast adrift in their high society world, she can only depend
on one person: broodingly handsome Jeremy Norland. But
if she falls in love with him she could lose everything. Will
Eloise have the courage to risk all?

On sale 2nd December 2005

*Available at most branches of WHSmith, Tesco, ASDA,
Borders, Eason, Sainsbury's and most bookshops*

Visit www.millsandboon.co.uk

Experience the magic of Christmas, past and present...

Christmas Brides

Don't miss this special holiday volume – two captivating love stories set in very different times.

THE GREEK'S CHRISTMAS BRIDE
by Lucy Monroe
Modern Romance

Aristide Kouros has no memory of life with his beautiful wife Eden. Though she's heartbroken he does not remember their passion for each other, Eden still loves her husband. But what secret is she hiding that might bind Aristide to her forever – whether he remembers her or not?

MOONLIGHT AND MISTLETOE
by Louise Allen
Historical Romance – Regency

From her first night in her new home in a charming English village, Hester is plagued by intrusive "hauntings." With the help of her handsome neighbour, the Earl of Buckland, she sets out to discover the mystery behind the frightful encounters – while fighting her own fear of falling in love with the earl.

On sale 4th November 2005

Make your Christmas wish list – and check it twice!

Watch out for these very special holiday stories – all featuring the incomparable charm and romance of the Christmas season.

By Jasmine Cresswell, Tara Taylor
Quinn and Kate Hoffmann
On sale 21st October 2005

By Lynnette Kent and
Sherry Lewis
On sale 21st October 2005

By Lucy Monroe and
Louise Allen
On sale 4th November 2005

By Heather Graham,
Lindsay McKenna, Marilyn
Pappano and Annette Broadrick
On sale 18th November 2005

By Marion Lennox, Josie Metcalfe
and Kate Hardy
On sale 2nd December 2005

By Margaret Moore, Terri Brisbin
and Gail Ranstrom
On sale 2nd December 2005

By Lisa Jackson, Barbara Boswell
and Linda Turner
On sale 18th November 2005

ght thinking," she said in a very
never sent me. I am at all," He was
r heard their

e. "It should... hurt your heart